POLYCARP
a destroyer of our gods

A novel by

RICK LAMBERT

Grow in Grace Series

Printed in the United States of America

Second Printing, 2015

ISBN-13: 978-0-9909299-0-1
Library of Congress Control Number 2014918711

Landbright Publishing LLC
9378 Mason-Montgomery Road, Suite 413
Mason, OH 45040

Cover layout, interior design by Gavin Anderson, Sterling Studios
Cover illustration by Charles Forrester

Dedicated to
My dad and mom – my first heroes of faith

Acknowledgments

I am profoundly grateful for the help, encouragement and advice I received from Geoff and Patricia Davis, Rob and Melissa Robbins, Tim and Vanessa Collins, John and Esther Greenewald, David Lambert and Trish Somers.

Special thanks to Gavin Anderson for his help in formatting the novel; Charles Forrester for his outstanding artwork; Sarah Lambert for her content review, and my editor, Garry Breland.

Without their support, I would never have published this novel. *Bear one another's burdens, and so fulfill the law of Christ (Galatians 6:2 - ESV).*

Introduction

Polycarp, a destroyer of our gods, is not a typical novel as it illustrates through the life of a pastor named Polycarp how God forms and fashions his message in our lives. It is a story built on the four cornerstones of discipleship: faith, obedience, spiritual desire, and godly virtue. God establishes our faith and guides us into and through the struggles of obedience. Obedience awakens joyous, spiritual desires in our heart that mature us into godly and virtuous people.

Polycarp was a prominent second-century Church Father. He was born into slavery, purchased as a young boy, and raised by a godly woman in Ephesus. He, along with several others, became leaders in the church after the death of the Apostles. According to tradition, Polycarp was a disciple of the Apostle John. Little is known of Polycarp's life and ministry except for a few reverent thoughts shared by his disciple, Irenaeus, and other church historians. His letter to the Philippian church has survived to this day and has been included in this novel, along with the accounts of his death.

The story unfolds during the period when the New Testament scriptures were being penned. The passages cited have been paraphrased as accurately as possible to imply that the characters did not have access to the Bible as we know it and use it today. The references provided in the footnotes are offered for personal study.

May the name of the Lord be glorified, and I pray you will be blessed as you read this novel.

RL

Table of Contents

PROLOGUE

*...These are the men who have turned
the world upside down...
For they have done the opposite of Caesar's
decrees by saying their king is Jesus.
(Acts 17:6-7)*

IN the year Marcus Aurelius published his most famous philosophy, a lesser-known, but in my mind a far more worthy and eminent writer invited me to carry on the task of preserving the account of his life. Therefore, I, Irenaeus, bear witness of the extraordinary life of my friend and mentor, Polycarp, Pastor of the Church at Smyrna, faithful martyr of Jesus Christ—his and my Lord. What follows is the account in his own hand, up until that time when, at the age of 86, as he was losing the dexterity required to apply quill and ink to parchment, he commissioned me to continue chronicling his life, which task I humbly accepted.

Little did I know that one of the darkest days of my life was looming near, the day I would witness the martyrdom of Polycarp. He not only refused all offers to bend the knee to Caesar, but persisted to the very end to press the claims of Christ on the very Roman Proconsul who condemned him to death by fire in the arena at Smyrna. His faithful service to the One True God earned him the reputation of the destroyer of the gods. This is his story.

1

SURROUNDED BY THE
SORROWS OF DEATH

The sorrows of death surrounded me, and
the stress of hell sought me out;
I found only trouble and anguish.
(Psalm 116:3)

EPHESUS, the great Roman City of Asia, appeared lifeless. A place that always teemed with life was shrouded in a disturbing stillness like a hushed crowd in disbelief as they watch their champion fall in the arena. The sound of laughter was replaced with sorrow and hope was overcome with despair. The shadows of death hovered over the homes of the rich and poor alike; the gods were merciless, as a plague had slithered through the city dragging grief along its path.

The sights that poured into my mind left me with inescapable memories. The stench of decaying bodies was only intensified by the hopeless cries of the bereaved. Some were interred in caves or marble crypts, but most were stacked and cremated. "What a terrible way to die," I thought to myself. "What if they were to awaken in the flames?" The despair I observed haunted me.

I was only eight years old when this dreadful reality of death found my home. I felt the full brunt of sorrow as it crept in and stole the life of my mother and father. There were no relatives to claim me, for I had none; neither did I find any close friends to take me in, for I belonged to someone else. I was born a slave in the year 58, during the reign of Nero.

A few months before my birth, my parents were seized in a rebellion in northern Macedonia. It was the practice in Roman conquests to take captured prisoners and sell them into slavery in order to fund the defense and expansion of the Empire. Some slaves were fortunate enough to be purchased by wealthy families who treated them with respect and kindness, perhaps even being better off in some ways than when they were free. However, this was not a reality for most slaves, nor was it for my parents. My father spent his days either mining for silver, or working around a hot furnace melting it down. Mother busied herself feeding the workers on the meager provisions provided for her.

Our rustic quarters consisted of flat stones placed irregularly across the floor, and like the walls, they had weeds growing out of some of the cracks. I recall that the furnishings were sparse and poorly lit with only one window covered by wooden shutters and a poorly hung door. Our house was terraced in a hill with dwellings for other slaves above and on both sides. While I can recall some occasional frivolity, our little slave village was cruel and harsh.

My parents despised the place, but I didn't mind it, so long as they were nearby. We lived high enough in the hills so that you could see the harbor about two miles away, as well as much of the city—the Great Arena and lower agora where merchants sold their wares, and the Temple of Diana being the most prominent structure. The temple was a very important part of our lives, for my master and his brother, Demetrius were business partners, silversmiths who made shrines for the worship of the goddess Diana, or as the Greeks called her—Artemis.

I never knew freedom, and when I would see Roman children at play it seemed as if I were looking into another world. The life that defined my existence was brutal, unforgiving, and void of hope. It incensed my father to see Crixus, our owner, or his foreman striking me or the other children. I lived on the emotion of hate from fellow slaves and anger from Crixus, but my emotional state never grew beyond fear. Crixus may have owned me, but it was fear that enslaved me. I hated Crixus and was praised for it.

When he was drunk, which was often, he would shoot off his mouth and gloat over his patriotic duty to punish us, or make our lives harder since we were the enemies of Rome. Escaping seemed to be the most common conversation in our home, but the risks always outweighed the courage.

Crixus was a wicked man, hated by all. He was driven by his obsession for wealth and angered at its elusiveness. Exploitation was his talent, and he used me and the other children to peddle his shrines, idols, and religious trinkets. Whenever he wasn't counting his silver, he was worshipping at the Temple of Diana where he had to hire the religious harlots as his nightly companions, for no one else would have him. As for his appearance, it was revolting, and if I weren't afraid of him, I would be prone to laugh at him. His hair was clumped together, uncombed and greasy as if plastered to his head. I observed that even in the strongest breeze, his hair never seemed to move. What few teeth he had were rotten, making his breath smell horrible, and when he spoke, spittle spewed everywhere. I always tried to turn my head when he talked to me. I can recall that even when he wasn't angry, his eyes seemed to bulge out of their sockets. He was an unseemly man in every sense of the word. This was the man and the life I was about to confront alone.

◇

The effects of the plague were diminishing; thousands had perished. My tears expressed the hopelessness of my soul as I gazed upon the lifeless bodies of my parents. The memory is frozen in my mind as I cried aloud, "Wake up! Who will take care of me?" and then sobbing when there was no response. Can there be anything worse than calling out for help, and hearing only silence as the echo? At that moment, terror seized my soul extinguishing any hope of security and draping me in darkness.

Other slaves came in to check on me but before they could offer any comfort, Crixus walked in to inspect his losses. With pitiless eyes, he glared down at me and said, "You have lost little compared to me. I have lost ten slaves these past few weeks, and who will repay me for those losses? They were valuable. You are worthless." His words filled my soul with bitterness, and I began to believe him.

As he surveyed the room, he peered over at the growing number of slaves that had entered. "The gods have dealt harshly with us, and I know why. You!" he shouted as he pointed to a group of slaves in the corner. "You Christians are the reason for the gods' displeasure. I will not put up with your atheism. Perhaps the gods will smile on us more favorably if we honor them during the Festival of Artemis." He was speaking of the day set aside for the worship of Diana, or Artemis. It was nothing more than a day for him to get richer, and for us to work harder to make that happen. "I expect you all to give due honor to the gods. I need good fortune. Bless them so that they will bless me. Curse them, and I will be a curse to you," he growled.

He glared over at one slave in particular, Murcia, and said; "Don't think that I haven't noticed you either. You are one of those miserable Christians, and severe punishment awaits any of you caught associating with them. Are you listening to me," he screamed. His anger frightened us all, but Murcia stood motionless at his stern warning.

He turned to look at the bodies of mother and father as if he were looking at dead cows or horses, and after letting out a groan of exasperation, said, "Take these bodies down to the burning pit. Make sure they are thoroughly reduced to ashes. I don't want the dogs dragging legs, arms or anything else back up to my door." He stormed out grumbling about how much it was going to cost him to replace them.

My ears felt like they were on fire, and my heart was pounding. I was frantic as I realized what was about to happen to my parents. I tried to stop the men from carrying them away, but Murcia and some of the others restrained me. I hated death, yet I wished I would die; the pain overwhelmed me. The true dread of eternal separation consumed me as I saw the smoke and ashes rise from behind the hill and disappear into the sky. Now I was abandoned, lost with no hope of being found, for no one was looking for me.

You would think that there might be enough humanity in Crixus to let me grieve, but I don't think the thought ever crossed his mind. The city was about to be inundated for the celebration of the goddess. Ephesus had endured the grief of death, and the city seemed revived as it prepared for the holy day.

To the Christians, this would be a dreaded, month-long celebration of drunkenness and immoral debauchery, and Crixus was especially drawn into the festivities that usually made his demeanor even more repugnant. He filled me with hatred, and I desired to kill him and while I was at it, Diana too. The heartless gods had created a heartless boy.

Over the next few days, work was forced upon me as if nothing had changed, and for some strange reason, I had hoped that maybe life might return to some degree of normalcy, but what a senseless thought that turned ought to be. The surprises that were awaiting me would take my grief to even greater depths. While I can scarcely recall those grievous days, I do recall my first introduction to the Lord Jesus Christ. It hurt Crixus, and if for no other reason, that impressed me.

A famous leader among the followers of Christ had arrived in Ephesus; his name was Paul, an Apostle of the Lord Jesus Christ. The first time we met I tried to sell him an idol of Diana. Crixus had placed me at the harbor to sell the silver shrines to those entering the city to celebrate Artemision. It was not a chance encounter, though it may have appeared so at the time. God, in his faithfulness, used the great Apostle to plant the seed of his Word in my heart, and over time it would bring forth much fruit to the praise of God.

Paul was walking right towards me as he disembarked the boat and made his way toward the Harbor Way and the lower agora. As he approached, I nervously asked if he would like to make a purchase.

"Sir, would you like to purchase a shrine in honor of the great Artemis?"

He didn't even look at the idol, but rather knelt down and patted me on the head. "Young man, what is your name?" he asked.

"I am Polycarp," I answered, thinking it strange that he would take an interest in me, for no one else seemed to care. "Are you here for the celebration," I asked.

"Diana," he replied, "No, lad, not for her. I come with better news than a goddess of hopelessness can bring." Those words gave me a jolt. "I am here to present the only way to salvation from the wrath of God, and I am searching out those whose hearts God has opened to hear and receive this salvation, and I am compelled to share with everyone I meet, including little boys like you."

"Where are your parents," he asked.

"They died a couple weeks ago," I responded.

He appeared genuinely sad at my plight and said, "My dear boy, I grieve for you. Are you a slave?"

"Yes, that is my master over there," as I pointed to Crixus standing at the entrance of the agora.

He appeared a bit perplexed as if wondering what to say. He looked into my eyes, and I could see tears welling up in his eyes as he stated, "There is only One True God, Polycarp, and while he is angry at sin, he came to save sinners and give his life as a ransom to pay the penalty for those whom he would save."

Before he could utter another word, Crixus yelled out, "If you are going to make a purchase, then get on with it, otherwise, leave the boy alone. He's working, if you hadn't noticed."

Paul stood up, patted me on the head and prayed, "Holy Father and Almighty God, lay claim to little Polycarp, and by the power of your Holy Spirit give him your gift of salvation through Jesus Christ, my Lord." He smiled at me, and then walked away toward Crixus, who made it very clear he was not interested in anything Paul had to say.

About a week later I saw Paul again. Crixus and his brother Demetrius were alarmed at the scores of people that were abandoning the worship of Artemis for what was being referred to as "The Way," which was being heralded by Paul throughout the city, to both citizens of Ephesus and visitors alike. Crixus was distressed as the sale of his wares dropped off significantly. Many of the tradesmen who made their living from selling idols met at The Odeon, a small auditorium next to the upper agora, or political center.

Demetrius, with Crixus standing next to him, was the first to speak, "Men, this business has made us wealthy men, and this man, Paul, has had a negative impact on our prosperity here in Ephesus, and throughout the province of Asia. Now many are saying that our gods are made by man, and therefore cannot be gods. They will very soon undoubtedly say that we run a dishonest business and our great goddess, Artemis, will be viewed as nothing, and people will carelessly lay aside her magnificence—she, whom Asia and the whole world adore."

As soon as he said this, the crowd became enraged and began shouting, "Great is Artemis of the Ephesians!"

The people were so stirred and threatened, that word spread like a flood through the streets, and throngs of people began to crowd into the room and adjacent hallways to see what the commotion was all about. Within minutes, two of Paul's companions, Gaius and Aristarchus, were forced into The Odeon. Paul, however, was detained from entering by other followers of Christ, including some of the Asiarchs,[1] who were his friends. I was quite

1. *Town leaders*

frightened by the frenzy and was nearly crushed by the weight of people crowding in the room. Confusion was everywhere as people sought direction. Some of the Jews that had gathered in the room put forward a prominent spokesman named Alexander, who did what he could to bring order. He had a small degree of success until it was pointed out that he was a Jew, and had no vested interest in the preservation of the sacred goddess. Then, as if under the influence of an invisible force, the people began to chant over and over, for two hours, "Great is Artemis of the Ephesians."

Right next to The Odeon was the office of the town clerk, who at first didn't rush in to see what the commotion was all about, but hearing the escalating chant of the people, and being compelled by concerned citizens, decided to intervene. The crowd recognized who he was and made way for him to reach the stage at the foot of the seats where he shouted with all his might, "Men of Ephesus!" After repeating this a couple times, he was able to quiet the crowd, and then began to speak in a more normal tone. "Men of Ephesus, is there anyone who doesn't know that the great city of the Ephesians is the caretaker for the temple of the great goddess, Artemis, and of the sacred stone that fell from the sky? These facts are undeniable, for this reason I urge you to be peaceful in your demonstration, and don't do anything rash. What these men have been saying has neither been sacrilegious nor have they blasphemed our goddess."

He stopped for a moment to pan the crowd and looked over at Demetrius and said, "If you and your fellow craftsmen have a complaint against these men, or anyone for that matter, our courts are open, and the Proconsul is available to hear you. If these men have harmed you, then press charges against them, which is our proper way. Hear me on this unless you all wish to be charged with rioting, for I see no justifiable reason to stir up such a commotion. Now, enough of this; I order that this assembly be adjourned. Go to your homes in a peaceful manner."

◇◇

A few weeks had passed since the celebration, and according to Crixus, there was very little to celebrate since his sales were much lower than expected. Though hardly over the death of my parents, I was again confronted with more devastating news as I heard Crixus' dreadful voice yelling out my name from the barn;

"Polycarp! Polycarp, get in here; now!" "You're wasting my time you impudent clod! If you keep me waiting another moment, my strap will rip your back open."

I ran as hard as I could, panic growing with each step. Breathlessly I entered the barn, "Yes, master, I am here."

"Get in here you worthless dumb ox," he blasted.

"Y-y-yes master," I replied, hoping that by being agreeable, he might deal more gently with me. He reached into a pouch attached to his belt and dug out a few silver coins, and then holding them in front of my face said, "My time is measured by these, and you're spending it by making me stand here and wait for you. I've got more important things to do than to parade around here waiting for you to get your worthless carcass in motion. I would wager that it makes you happy to see me upset. You're no different than all the other unprofitable scum I have to buy to run this place," he shouted while throwing tools and kicking some buckets towards me.

I didn't move a muscle but stood perfectly still bracing for his slap across my face. He got down into my face, his own face blood-red with impatient rage. "I swear; it seems as if I must always get someone else to do your chores. How could your parents endure your laziness, for I sure can't? Look at these stalls! Why haven't they been cleaned out? How can I bring my goats into such a filthy barn? Why did your pathetic parents have to die and not you?" Then in unleashed rage he struck me in the face, hurling me down to the ground.

I was unable to hold back my tears, and my face stung from his blow. I couldn't imagine why he would hit me. I stood up, feeling dizzy and frightened. Other slaves were nearby, but they knew that worse punishment awaited them if they dared to interfere. I looked up at Crixus, who appeared unmoved by the tears on my face, and for a few moments he just stared at me, and then shattered the silence with, "Are you brainless? Why are you waiting? Get to work before I decide to beat you again."

I hastily picked up a shovel and began working as hard as I could; at least for an eight year old. Crixus watched for a while, not saying anything. I threw out the old hay, brought in new, and replenished the water trough. When it appeared that my job was complete, I looked up at him and innocently asked, "Master, where can I sleep tonight? Other people have moved into my house." As I said it, I could hear another slave in the adjacent stall telling me, "No, no; don't ask him that," but it was too late.

"Your house," he grunted sarcastically. "That is my house, and those slaves are hard workers who deserve a house. They make me money, and you don't. Sleep out here in the barn, and perhaps it will motivate you to clean it better."

As he started to walk out of the barn, he halted for a moment and turned around so fast he lost his balance for a moment and nearly fell. As he regained his footing, he stared at me as if he just encountered some great surprise, and a grin began to grow across his ugly face. "Hmm, perhaps there is some value to you yet," he mused stroking his unshaven chin. Shaking his head as if approving he added, "Yes, I may be able to make some money off you after all. Tomorrow is the slave auction," as he clasped his hands together. He grabbed my head and turned ever so slightly, "I wonder what I could get for you? Maybe some poor fool will buy you and turn you into a fighter in the arena. You sure wouldn't last long in a fight would you? Now that's one fight I would pay money to see," he said with an irritating cackle. Armed with a new scheme, he walked away chuckling and congratulating himself for coming up with such a good idea.

Fear paralyzed me! I just stood there unable to move a muscle. As bad as it was living there, this life was all I had ever known. It didn't bother me to have to sleep in the barn. Nervous energy finally broke me free, and I ran towards Crixus and grabbed the back of his cloak, fell to my knees and begged him not to sell me.

"Please master, please let me stay. I will work harder, I promise, and I will be happy to sleep in the barn."

"Get off me, you dog," he said as he threw me down to the ground.

"When I look at you, I see pieces of silver. The question is; how many pieces of silver are you worth? I guess we're going to find out tomorrow," he said through his grin.

———◇◇———

The anxiety of it all came crashing in on me as he walked away. I could not stop the torrent of tears that followed. "What will happen to me," I thought to myself. "Is there anyone who can help me?" All I wanted was a home and to have my mother and father back, but even I knew that was impossible. Dread filled my soul, and I could not overcome the gnawing sensation that was growing in the pit of my stomach. As I recall, I could not stop crying for the rest of the day. Never in my entire life have I felt more alone. It's as if something evil was taking delight in destroying me, and I was defenseless to stop it.

As night fell, I made my bed in the barn. I was cold, hungry, and tormented by fear and the depravity of my circumstances. As God would have it, Murcia, another slave and friend of my mother was searching the farm calling out for me that night. As she came close to the barn, she heard me whimpering, and with only a small lantern to guide her, she entered into the dark shadows, "Is that you Polycarp?" she tenderly asked. Though I knew her voice, I did not reply, but to tell you the truth, I was desperate for her to find me and comfort me.

She searched and soon found me curled up in a ball in the hay, and she sat down next to me and wrapped her shawl around me. I got chills from the warmth of it touching my skin. Though she was a slave, I remember that she was a pious woman and desired to help me through this dreadful time. She held me close and whispered out a tune about trusting God.

"What are you singing," I asked.

"Do you like it?" she asked. "I'm not a very good singer."

"It's pretty. I've never heard anything like it before," I answered.

"It is called a psalm; I learned it in the fellowship of other Christians, we call the church," she replied.

"The fellowship of the church; what is that?" I asked.

She thought for a moment, then replied; "The church is a group of people the One True God has claimed out of the world to belong exclusively to him. They no longer belong to the world. We meet as often as we can to encourage and help each other, and to set aside time to learn about the One who saved us, and to worship him."

I sat up surprised by what she had said, and inquired; "Don't you worship Diana, Zeus, or your ancestors?"

"No. Those are false gods, gods men have made up to fit their lifestyle or excuse their evil deeds. The true God commands us to destroy these false gods." This thought troubled me.

"But we're not strong enough to destroy the gods," I responded.

Her eyebrows rose as she said, "It's easy to destroy something that's not there. My God, the Creator of all things wasn't created by man, but as the Creator of man, he has used his creation here on Earth, and in the heavens above to declare his existence and his glory. His existence is undeniable, and history is filled with the proofs of his claims."

"But Crixus believes in the gods. Aren't you afraid of him? Aren't you afraid to die?" I asked.

"Oh, I suppose that there is some fear, but not the controlling kind. It's in times of distress that my faithful God hears my prayers, protects me, and above all makes me stronger. Like you, Polycarp, when I have found myself surrounded by the sorrows of death, I cry out to the only true God to hear my plea for help. And it's like he bends down his ear close to my mouth to listen, and this he does for as long as I live."

"But what do you pray?" I quizzed; for such a thought was too lofty for me to comprehend.

"A simple little prayer, like; Deliver me, my God. Help me to escape this."[2]

"But you're still a slave, Murcia. You haven't escaped yet," I said.

"This is what separates the true followers of God from those who follow false gods," she said. "I live in the reality of joy and happiness that comes from trusting God to place me where I can learn the most about him. If I can see and learn more about God as a slave, then I want to be a slave, and if I can learn more of him free, then I trust he will make me a free woman. My God is gracious in that while he may not change my circumstances; he changes me to rise above those circumstances. So long as I live in this world, Polycarp, I will conduct my life before the watchful eyes of my true Lord. Even if I were to die by the cruel hands of Crixus, my death would be precious in the eyes of my Lord. Do you know why I can say that?"

I just shrugged my shoulders for I had no idea. Gesturing toward the darkened barn door, she said, "Because death is not some dark, foreboding shadow to dread, but to the ones who belong to God, it is like a doorway into the palace of our God and King. I am the bondslave of God. He's a master not anything like

---

2. *Psalm 116*

Crixus or any other master. Polycarp, the deeper God takes your trust in him, the greater your spiritual growth and joy. Trusting in him will make you fearless."

She looked warmly into my face and continued, "I know you are afraid of what will happen tomorrow. Will the person who purchases you be ill-tempered, or kind? Trust my God; He will take of care of you wherever you end up."

As odd as all this sounded, my heart felt warm, and her words were a comfort to me, though I could not explain why. I liked her God but had no concept of how to reach him. Murcia described him like someone close, but he seemed so far away from me. At least with the goddess Diana, I could go to her Temple, and see what she looked like though I often thought she looked rather odd.

As we sat in silence, she began to hum another tune until I interrupted her and said, "Murcia, have you ever been sold before?"

She smiled and replied, "Yes, Polycarp, this is my third home. I was a teenager when I became a slave. I don't even know what happened to my parents or family. I just know that I belong to the True God, and he has placed me where I can do the most good in His name. Do not fear, little one, God will draw you to himself, and he will guide you all the way, and take care of you better than any other person could ever do."

Then leaning her head down, she kissed my brow, and rested her head on mine, and while wiping the tears off my face, she prayed: "My gracious and kind Father, take care of little Polycarp. Give him to a new master who will love him and direct him to discover how you alone are his God."

Her singing and praying calmed me enough to sleep, and I dozed off into a restful sleep right there in her arms. The next morning, however, I awoke with that same sense of dread pounding in my heart. It all seemed like a bad dream to me, and I just wanted to wake up and find my mother and father again, and for a passing moment, I thought I had for I was immediately overcome by the smell of hot food.

"Ah, you are finally awake," Murcia said. "Don't tell Crixus, but I figured since this was your last day here I would give you a good breakfast. All our friends dropped off some food for you. I have eggs, cheese, fruit, bread, honey, butter, fish, and nuts for us to enjoy together."

For a few minutes, I forgot my problems and dug into the feast set before me. I couldn't believe my eyes, for I have never had so much delicious food. Though still anxious about the day, I felt now that I had some renewed strength to endure the trial that lay ahead of me. Shortly after enjoying my last morsel of food, the breakfast was ruined when I heard the annoyed voice of Crixus echoing across the barnyard.

———————◇◇———————

"Polycarp, get out of here. You're going to help me make some money today, so don't make me late," He stated rather gleefully.

I took my time emerging from the barn. I figured he wouldn't beat me, for that could damage my value. For the first time in my life, I felt valuable to Crixus in a queer sort of way. As I entered into the sunlight of the yard, there he sat, waiting impatiently in the wagon. When I climbed up into the back, he turned to look at me, and with a devilish grin informed me; "I spoke with the auctioneer last night, and he has arranged for me to sell you to a man who was going to make a fighter out you. You think I'm tough, just wait till he whips you a few times. Yes Polycarp, by the end of today I'm going to look at the silver coins in my hand and say, look what Polycarp has finally done for me."

As we rode out, I saw Murcia standing near the barn and waving to me. Her words of trusting the only true God gripped my soul. Though I didn't know him, I hoped and prayed he wanted to know me.

Crixus drove his team faster than normal along the country roads, and I tried to pray to the One True God. Would he even hear me? "God, Murcia, your bond slave told me that you would take care of me. I can't see you, but if you made these trees, mountains and animals I see; then maybe I was made to talk to you. Help me, for I am afraid. Please have someone who is kind purchase me, but if you want me to be a fighter in the arena, then make me a good fighter, but I don't really want to be a fighter."

Crixus stopped the cart and turned to look at me. "What are you mumbling?" he demanded.

"I was praying," I said, though I didn't say to whom.

"Praying," he shouted. "There's no god that is interested in an imbecile like you. Just shut up and think about how happy you're going to make ole Crixus today. Besides, your gibberish is making me nervous. People shouldn't talk to themselves," as he drove on talking to himself about what a great idea he had conceived.

⸺⸺⸺◇◇⸺⸺⸺

Panic set in as we arrived at the auction yard. I saw hundreds of men and women who were to up for sale and, like the rest, I was taken behind the platform, stripped of all my clothes, and a cord tied around my neck. When they were ready to start the bidding some man came to me and pulled me up the stairs so hard that I fell and was choked by his tugging. After I had regained my footing, he cursed me for my clumsiness. On the platform, he tugged all the more on the cord to move me to the front of the stage.

When I finally looked up, I was horrified by the sea of faces peering back at me. I felt ashamed and tried to cover myself; I was shaking and trying hard to hold back my tears. Standing in the front was Crixus. "Does Murcia know what she was talking about?" I thought to myself. "How can I trust her God in this? Does anyone out there even care for me? Maybe Crixus was right."

2

A FUTURE AND A HOPE

I am intimately involved in the purposes
I have prepared for you,
proclaims the Lord, plans that bring you into perfect peace
and not destruction, to give you hope for the future.
(Jeremiah 29:11)

ON the very same night that Crixus decided to sell me, an unmarried woman named Callisto, was abruptly awakened by a very odd, disturbing dream, unlike any dream she ever had before. In this dream, she did not see a person but heard only a voice—the voice of an auctioneer taking bids for a little slave boy, and she was bidding for the child. When she awoke, she realized that it was just a dream, but the scene felt real and left her with a heavy burden as if she had been there. The problem was that she had never even been to a slave auction; she had no idea how slaves were sold. It was still a few hours before dawn, and she couldn't go back to sleep. She was troubled and felt foolish that she would even be considering going to a slave auction. How could she possibly put any stock in a dream? She needed counsel, but who would listen to her without bursting out in laughter or worse, writing her off as deranged?

Callisto was a godly woman who sought the Lord with all her heart in all matters. Was this a prompting from God, and if so, what did it mean? She sought assurance that if this was the way for the Lord to direct her, then the desire would get heavier, and if it wasn't, then his peace would return to her if she sought for it. This decision had to be a spiritual one first, for her emotions could not be trusted to guide her in such an unusual decision. The Word of God would, on the scales of her heart, tip the weight to one side or the other. She took what parchments were available to her, and began reading the Psalms of David and pouring out her heart to the Lord as she prayed and sang them back to God. From here, she was moved to read from a copy of the Apostle John's letters to the churches; "Divine-like love is understood through the example of Jesus Christ, who laid down his life for us. For this same reason, when we have the opportunity, we should be willing to lay down our lives for others. If you have the means, and you see someone in need, and close your heart against helping them, how does God's love live in you? My children, stop limiting your love to just words and talk, but let your love be in action and truth."[3] While she heard no voice confirming or deterring her, this passage did fill her with peace; enough to seek further counsel.

The next choice for help and guidance was a logical one; her closest neighbor and brother, Decimus and his godly wife Beatrice could be trusted to give her a safe opinion. Decimus was her only living sibling, a godly man who served as a deacon in the local congregation. After reviewing how she would share her dream, she went next door and found the two sitting at the table finishing their breakfast.

"Greetings Callisto, beautiful day, wouldn't you say? It is wonderful to see you this morning," Decimus greeted her with a warm smile.

"Welcome my dear," added Beatrice with a hug. "Won't you sit down and join us?"

"Well, yes; I think I will. I do need to talk to you both," Callisto replied. Both Decimus and his wife sensed that there was something weighing on her heart, for she was normally clear-minded and had an effervescent personality. She looked at them for a moment and chuckled, "First, let me say that what I am about to share with you is going to sound irrational, but I am serious, and in need your wise counsel. Try not to laugh at me."

"Has someone proposed marriage," he jested as Beatrice slapped him on the arm, and told him to be serious.

The humor helped Callisto feel more comfortable. "No, Decimus; no one has proposed to me, and if they did, you would likely be the last to know. Truly, I think this decision, is in its own way, as large a decision as marriage."

"All right, all right, you've got my attention; let me see if I can lighten your load. What's on your mind?" he finally asked.

She took in a deep breath and said, "Here we go. Last night I awoke from a very odd dream. In this dream, I was at a slave auction, and there was a little boy being sold. Though I could not

_____
3. I John 3:16-18

16

see him, I was bidding for him." She stopped and looked at them. An awkward silence followed as Decimus and his wife looked at each other and then at her waiting to hear the rest of her dream.

"Okay, then what," he said.

"Well, that's it," Callisto replied. "I believe that I'm to go to the slave auction and find this little boy and purchase him out of slavery. I know this sounds bizarre, but the impression this has made on my soul is beyond description. Never have I been more moved in heart."

Beatrice placed her hand on Callisto's and said, "Are you sure that this is not simply a woman's yearning for children? Both of us are childless, and I know how precious one would be to me."

"I have considered that, and have searched the depths of my heart, and the only answer is yes and no," Callisto replied. "Of course I want children! Yes; I can't deny it. But no, also, since I don't want just a child; I would only want a child God would give me. Why would I dream this dream, and find my heart so entangled by it? Oh, please help me," as she placed her face in her hands and began to weep.

Decimus looked startled, and it was obvious he didn't know what to say in response. Beatrice got up from her chair and knelt down, placing her arm around Callisto.

"Now, now, dear," Decimus said, "hold on. Don't trouble yourself like this. Let's go together and seek counsel from the Wonderful Counselor. We can't even begin to navigate a course of action until we do this." So he prayed; "Our holy God, who peers into the depths of our hearts, who knows all things, and directs our paths by the power of your great might, we plead for your wisdom. You have blessed the servitude of my sister, and have used her to bless the lives of thousands, many of whom are slaves. In ways that we cannot explain or pretend to understand you have put a burden on her heart unlike anything I have ever seen. As your prophet Isaiah has so beautifully penned, so we pray that you will see to the needs of your flock like a caring shepherd, and gather your lambs into your arms; carrying and holding us close as you walk, and gently lead the young ones along.[4] Bring us to the decision that magnifies the glory of our Savior, the Lord Jesus Christ. Amen!"

---

4. Isaiah 40:11

Decimus still looked worried and asked Callisto, "Have you ever been to a slave auction?"

"No! Never! The sight would be too heavy to bear," she replied.

"It is a rather pathetic sight," he continued. "They are all brought to the front of the platform, completely naked and bid upon until the highest price is reached. They are not cheap either. Do you have enough money to make such a purchase?"

"I have a little over fifty denarii,"[5] she replied.

"Well, for a small boy that may be sufficient, not that I'm an expert," he added.

Beatrice was worried about her sister-in-law and asked, "Callisto, you are a very capable woman; I do not doubt your abilities. But you have never raised a child. Can you do this? What if the boy has never been properly taught? What if he is crude, disrespectful, and harmful to you or others? Slaves are unpredictable you know. How can you possibly know? Of course, my dear, you know that I will support you in your decision, but this is no light decision."

"I know," admitted Callisto. "This is why I covet your advice. I don't know what abilities I lack or what I will need. I am confident, however, that if this is truly from God, then he will give me wisdom and grace to fulfill my mission."

Before she could continue her thought, Decimus suddenly interrupted her and said; "Well, I don't want to be a pessimist at all in this, but it was a dream, and you may get to the auction at the Koressos Gate, and find no little boys for sale."

Callisto just looked at Decimus for a moment, then laughing a little said; "That has crossed my mind, and that's why I have been reluctant to tell anyone."

"Well, dear, what are you going to do?" Beatrice asked.

Callisto thought for a moment as she gazed off towards the lush, green hills as if looking for one more sign. After a moment, she said with resolve, "It won't hurt to go and see; so I guess I'm going!"

"That's fine, but would you want us to go with you," Decimus asked? "We would be happy to join you."

---

5. In the Roman currency system, the denarius was a small silver coin that has been estimated as equivalent to $21.00 US.

"No, I will do this alone, but thank you for asking," Callisto replied with a smile. For the moment, her determination outweighed her doubts, and she returned to her home, and taking all the money she had saved, departed on the twenty-minute walk to the Koressos Gate.

––––––––––◇◇––––––––––

Callisto abhorred slavery and did all she could to encourage slaves and lighten their loads, both believers and non-believers. She was motivated by a love to meet the needs of others, and if she had the ability and means, she would work tirelessly to serve them in the name of the Lord. Her love and good works were known and respected throughout the community. As she walked around the outskirts of the city wall, she sought wisdom from God.

"My dearest Father and my comfort, this task is too great for me; fear and uncertainty assault my soul. Give me faith to obey you and to follow you in unfamiliar places. Bless the work you have called me to do, and make me a living expression of the glory of your Son, my Savior, the Lord Jesus Christ, regardless of the outcome."

She refused to worry as she neared the gate, by reflecting on the challenge she received from her pastor, Timothy, on the previous Lord's Day. As God told the prophet, Jeremiah; "I am intimately involved in the purposes I have prepared for you, proclaims the Lord, plans that bring you into perfect peace and not destruction, to give you hope for the future."[6]

"My heart has devised this plan, but it is the Lord that will ordain my steps,"[7] she whispered to herself. "I trust his plan, even if it wasn't what I thought it was going to be. I trust his plan!" She believed that God was to change the direction for her life that day, and if it was his plan; she would purchase the life of a slave boy.

She was stunned as she arrived at the gate, and intimidated by the immense crowd that had gathered. It wasn't like anything she had imagined; it was much worse! As she stood waiting to enter the courtyard, she glanced at another woman standing next to her and said, "There seems to be more people here to purchase than there are to sell." Being new to this and nervous, she didn't know

6. *Jeremiah 29:11*

7. *Proverbs 16:9*

what to say. She had never been to the slave market, and knew nothing of the procedures or how much money was necessary. She came armed only with trust in God, and a desire to see if he were truly leading her through an odd dream.

Next to the gate was a courtyard that most of the crowd was pouring into, so she followed them in, but before taking more than a couple of steps into the yard she felt someone tap her shoulder. It was a gate attendant who asked, "You can't go in there without paying a bidder's fee. Didn't you read the sign? You're not trying to sneak in here without paying are you?"

A little offended and anxious she answered; "No, certainly not. I'm just not accustomed to the procedures or aware of your requirements."

"I take it that you have never been to a slave auction?" he asked.

"No, and I'm quite startled I must admit. Can you share with me anything else I should know?"

Amused by her naivety, he said, "The process is simple; when the bidding begins, the auctioneer will start the bidding with a price, simply shout out that price if that is what you're willing to pay. If no one bids against you, you made the purchase. When the auctioneer proclaims 'sold,' well, you just bought yourself a slave. At this point, you can't back out, and there are no returns, of course."

The attendant leaned in closer to her, moved by curiosity, and in almost a whisper asked; "What exactly are you looking for, a maid perhaps?"

Reluctant to answer too specifically, she simply stated, "I'm looking for a young boy to free from slavery."

The attendant was stunned and stood straight up; "I've never heard anyone say that before. Are you sure you know what you're getting into?" he warned. "Let me speak plainly. You are begging for trouble. You have heard of Virius, haven't you?" he asked.

"No," said Callisto, "should I know him?"

Incredulous at her answer, he replied, "He just happens to be one of the most brutal slave owners in the city, and he usually bids for boys and young men to fight in the games. He is a vulgar man who uses sadistic tactics. His uncivilized manner makes him an imposing force in the auction, and if you are bidding against him, he won't take in consideration that you are a woman as he hurls his insults at you. Get in his way, and he's liable to eat you alive."

Callisto just silently stood there, unsure of what to say. "Consider yourself warned," as he held out his hand to receive the bidding fee.

Paying and thanking the attendant for his advice, she proceeded into the courtyard to see the slaves being sold that day. Her heart melted as she observed the mass of humiliated men and women being paraded around for potential buyers to inspect. "How heartless and cruel," she muttered under her breath. She felt both a rush of sympathy for them, and a torrent of anger at the obvious abuse. Her modesty made it difficult to look at them, and she held her hand up to shield her view from their nudity. As her eyes wandered over the horde of slaves, she saw a little boy standing off to the side of the platform. He appeared so disheartened that Callisto found it difficult to contain her tears. "Truly, if God is leading me," she whispered, "This is the boy I am to purchase."

———————————◇◇———————————

"Silence! I said silence!" bellowed the auctioneer as he waited for the crowd to grow quiet. "The bidding is about to begin. Before we get to more valuable merchandise today, I offer for your consideration this fine little man," as he pulled the cord wrapped around the child's neck forcing him to the front of the platform. "He is eight years old; almost nine. He's a hard worker, looks healthy and holds a lot of potential for the future. He's a little young for gladiator school right now, but a few more years and you will have yourself a very fine fighter."

With the confident inflection of an experienced auctioneer, he began what he hoped to be a small bidding war, for his reputation hinged on how much money he could make for the various sellers. "Since you are going to have to invest a little more money in him, the owner wishes to give you a bargain you can't refuse. The bidding for this future warrior or whatever you wish him to be will begin at fifteen denarii."

———————————◇◇———————————

I could not comprehend how I had arrived at this place in my life. A week ago my parents were alive, though unwell, but I was with them. Now I was standing in front of hundreds of people, totally exposed and humiliated, and being sold. Tears streamed down my face, and my composure was shattered by the roar of the crowd and by the terrifying sight of seeing Crixus next to the man who was bidding for me.

"Fifteen," echoed from the front of the crowd. It is Virius, that crude, heartless man who made his fortune in the Roman Circus training slaves to be gladiators to fight, and in most cases die for the amusement of the crowds.

Seeking to ignite greater enthusiasm with potential buyers, the auctioneer continued; "Do I hear twenty? Come now, don't be so reserved. He looks scrawny, I know, but that's easy enough to change."

Another voice in the crowd shouted out "Twenty," then another "Twenty-five." There was a momentary pause, and then the auctioneer yelled out, "Will someone pay thirty denarii for this fine lad?"

Virius shouted angrily, "Thirty, though I don't think he's worth it." A chuckle rippled through the crowd for most knew that Virius despised others bidding against him. The auctioneer, knowing this about Virius, and realizing that he was a customer who could be counted upon to buy up any leftover slaves, attempted to end the bidding. Before he could complete the sale a woman's voice was heard from the back of the crowd; "I'll pay thirty-five denarii for the child," she yelled with a quivering voice. It was Callisto.

Irritated, but not to be outdone by this newcomer, Virius growled out "Forty," and then turned and glared at her as if daring her to continue. But Callisto did not hesitate when she declared "Fifty" in response with far more confidence than her first bid. Her resoluteness was about to be truly tested, for even though anyone could bid, there were unspoken rules in place, and not bidding higher against Virius had become one of those traditions. Only the very rich or very powerful felt the confidence bidding against him.

"Come, Virius," pleaded the auctioneer; "Will you pay fifty-five?" Virius impatiently bellowed, "My cows don't cost this much." In a fit of rage, he turned and threw people out of the way as he made his way back to Callisto. As he approached her, he moved in close to her face and shouted, "Listen to me you sow,

I don't know who you are or what attempts your worthless good works hope to accomplish around here, but that boy is mine. I am going to make a fighter out of that worthless slave. If you know who I am, then you would be wise to leave me alone."

Though flustered, her virtue guided her response. "Sir, I know who you are. I am on an errand of godliness and kindness, and the True God, the Creator of all mankind is leading me. Indeed, sir, while you may refuse to acknowledge it, any success you feel you have garnered for yourself, even the ability to enjoy it has been granted by my God. If you continue in the evil direction you are currently heading, you will discover that your destiny is not one of success, but of the judgment of God against you."

Silence filled the air for a moment, and then an eruption of laughter; some hysterical over such a foolish notion and others happy to see Virius put in his place.

Being incensed, his voice swelled over the noise of the crowd, "No one possesses that power over me. I control my destiny; in fact, I control the destinies of others too. Stay out of my way, or you may discover that I control yours as well, you hag. My advice to you is to leave now!" With that Virius stormed away growing more irate by the moment.

Observing all this, the auctioneer needed to protect his reputation, and realizing that he was about to lose control of the crowd interrupted the commotion by yelling over the crowd; "Do I hear any more offers?" hoping to end the tension and get on with the other auctions.

He looked over at Virius, who was fuming.

"I hate that wretch," he said, "but I'll pay fifty-five."

Seeing Virius distracted by the woman, a competitor decided to add to the tension and was hoping to make his rival pay more than the boy was worth and gamble with the price. "I'll pay sixty-five."

Now Virius had a war on two fronts. People were looking at Virius and then over to Callisto, who by this time was frantic. "God, what are you doing?" she thought. "I have no more money to bid. How can I let these evil people take that little boy?" At this point, it became obvious to all that Callisto had reached the limits of her buying power, and having no more available funds or credit was forced to stop. Poor Callisto could not have been more broken-hearted. It was like waves of hopelessness were crashing in on her. She knew that God had not forsaken her, but was quite distressed over how easily she could misunderstand his will, and be led by a simple dream.

Virius now saw that his last opponent was his arch rival and fellow competitor in the arena. So with a smug look as if having just conquered his first challenger, he grandly declares, "I'll pay seventy-five." Now you must understand that this amount of money was what one would spend on a young, strong, healthy adult. Such an amount was unheard of for a male child.

"Do I hear eighty?" declared the hopeful auctioneer. Just as Virius' rival was about to raise his hand, a deep, booming voice was heard from the back of the crowd; "I'll pay one hundred denarii for the lad, and more if necessary." A gasp rolled over the crowd at this unprecedented sum of money. Who in their right mind would pay so much for someone who could do so little? After a momentary pause, Virius finally speaks up and laughing states, "He can have him. Is he made of gold or something?" as others joined in his laughter.

Much to the great glee of Crixus, the auctioneer ended the bidding at one hundred denarii. I suppose I found out how much I was worth. Then the auctioneer said to the purchaser, "You may pick up your merchandise behind the platform."

Shaking his head in disgust, the auctioneer turned and looked down at me and said, "Slave, the gods must be smiling down on you. I've only seen that type of money being spent on potential winners in the arena, and never an ordinary slave, much less a child. Get back there and let the man have a look at you."

―――――◇◇―――――

Callisto just stood there, numb by what she had witnessed; she was bewildered. She had entered the bidding with such resolve and commitment, and now she had lost, and that poor boy would no doubt end up dying in the arena. Despair began to pour into her heart. She knew that this must not be allowed, for God was directing her and the events of this day. She must trust God even in this tragedy. As she watched me through eyes blurred with tears being escorted off the platform, she heard a familiar voice behind her—it was Decimus and Beatrice. Both stood there just beaming with delight.

Decimus clasped Callisto's hands and with overflowing, joyous sincerity declared; "I figured that the amount of money you had would not be enough to get you through, so we both knew that God would have us come down here and guarantee you won the boy."

"He was quite prepared to go higher if he needed to," Beatrice was exuberant to add.

"Come on, let's meet this little miracle," Decimus said.

Callisto could not believe her ears. Was this possible? Here it was. The little boy was hers, and God guaranteed it by bringing in his special reinforcements.

As they began to walk away, Callisto stopped, and with a loud voice and arms raised toward heaven, she exclaimed loudly; "I will bless my Lord from this moment forward and forever. Praise the Lord!"[8]

As the three of them rushed behind the auction platform, Decimus handed the money to my elated master who could not believe his eyes. Callisto received the documents of ownership, as well as the end of the cord that hung about my neck. As Crixus turned to walk away, Callisto asked him, "How did you come to acquire him? Are his parents still alive?"

Stammering a bit, he replied; "I purchased his parents while his mother was still pregnant. They were spoils of war you know, and I bought them to help pay for the war effort," he said rather defensively. "A while back his parents died in the plague. I found that he required too much care, and I don't want to lose any of my other slaves to care for him. With a diminished workforce I was forced to recover what I lost, so here we are. I had to sell the boy."

Then he looked at me, winked, and said, "If I had known I would get this much for you, I would have sold you a long time ago. The gods have honored me!"

Tears were streaming down Callisto's face as she looked down at me while Decimus took off his cloak and wrapped me in it. She knelt next to me, removed the cord from around my neck and threw it to the ground, and with a sweet softness said to me, "My dear little child; you have nothing to fear. The One True God has sent me to take care of you. What is your name?"

---

8. *Psalm 115:18*

In almost a whisper, I replied, "Polycarp." Though I said nothing at that moment, the name of the One True God startled me. "Did he actually deliver me," I wondered.

Still holding my shoulders, she leaned back to have a look at me and with a beaming countenance and said; "Polycarp; what a wonderful name. It means one who is rich in fruit; a fruitful man. What a promising life I believe you will have. I am confident that God desires to give you a future and a hope, my child. Let's begin this adventure and see why God brought us here together on this day. Are you up for this adventure Polycarp?" Of course, I was! I loved her the moment I saw her walk towards me behind the platform.

"Well then, my dear boy, you shall be free, and I shall raise you and love you like my son."

With the local magistrate present to authenticate all sales and a group of witnesses, Decimus declared me a free man, and now a Roman citizen with all the rights, privileges, and responsibilities associated with the new liberty. You should have seen the look on Crixus' face. It seemed strange to me, but we were now equals.

Some present applauded, but most of the crowd observing this simple ceremony thought it was a waste of money and resources. Callisto hugged me, kissed me on the cheek and held me closely to her. I resisted for a moment, but soon I melted into her arms. I felt loved and protected. The adventure was just beginning.

3

IMITATE WHAT YOU HAVE HEARD AND SEEN IN ME

Imitate what you have heard and seen in me,
regarding faith and love which is in Jesus Christ.
(II Timothy 1:13)

I WALKED out of the slave auction a free boy, where just an hour ago I entered as a bondslave. The same sun was still shining, and the same shops were open; everything seemed the same, yet I was different. I was nervous and uncertain, but relieved and happy. I knew I was no longer a slave, but I felt insecure in my freedom. I didn't know if I was allowed to run ahead of everyone, or stop at a shop and just look around. "What do free boys do?" I thought to myself. Though only eight years old, slavery was all I had known. Now here I was walking as a free Roman citizen where a few hours ago I walked as a worthless slave to Crixus.

Callisto didn't say much as we walked, although I noticed that she couldn't stop smiling. Now and then she would glance down at me, grin and laugh. Decimus and Beatrice did most of the talking, and they enjoyed introducing me to several of those whom they knew along the route. Many times Decimus would rub his hand through my hair and exclaim what a fine young man I was.

The next morning I awoke, and to my relief it wasn't a dream. I didn't wake up in a barn, but in my own room, with a bed, a table, and chair—even some toys and clothes that had been given to Callisto for me the night before. All this was difficult to comprehend; so much had happened within the last week. I was free but still thought like a slave. I wondered how was I to show Callisto affection when it made me feel disloyal to my parents. It's strange to describe what my feelings were, for, on the one hand, I was happy, but on the other, I was still frightened and felt out of place without my mother and father.

As I made my way down the wooden steps to the main room of my new home, no one was there to greet me except Timo, Callisto's dog. He took an instant liking to me and became my constant companion. As I walked out into the courtyard, I heard voices on the other side of the hedge, and as I rounded it, I found Callisto, Beatrice, and Decimus sitting at the table eating breakfast.

"Good morning, little man," Decimus said. Callisto stood up and putting her arm around my shoulders escorted me to an empty chair at the table.

"I thought that with all the stress of yesterday, it would do you good to get plenty of sleep. I hope you rested well, dear," Callisto said. I just nodded my head. Set before me was a nice array of food, and I wasted no time filling my plate and eating.

The first few days in my new home were filled meeting Callisto's friends, especially those with children my age. Some thought it strange that she would adopt a slave for her own child, but most were not surprised. Indeed, many were amazed she didn't purchase more, to which she was quick to reply, "Who says I won't? I don't know the outcome of Polycarp's life, but one thing is sure, joy fills my heart for being able to deliver him from bondage."

———◇◇———

One event I remember from those early days was a discussion Decimus had with me. It filled me with curiosity and helped me begin to develop a sense of family-honor and the responsibility of protecting it.

"Polycarp, let's go for a walk together. There is something I wish to show you," he suggested. We stopped at several places around the town where he introduced me to others, and asked general questions about my parents. We soon arrived at a rather odd place; we came to a cave filled with tombs. I had never been in one before; it seemed like an eerie place to be. We made our way over to a small, carved-out room off the main corridor, and in it were sealed tombs and a few still open. Decimus smiled at me as he noticed my awkwardness.

"I suppose you are wondering why I have brought you here. This cave is where my family is buried. There are my grandparents, my brother, mother, and my father. You see the name inscribed on the stone? It's Trophimus. That's our family name. I am Decimus of the house of Trophimus, or more formally Decimus Albinus Trophimus; Albinus is the particular line of the Trophimus family. You will be known, if it pleases you, as Polycarp of the house of Trophimus, or Polycarp Albinus Trophimus. Sometimes you will be referred to by your praenomen, your personal name; Polycarp. Rarely will you be called by your *nomen* or your particular family line which is Albinus, though some like the prestige if it is a great family. In formal settings it is appropriate to be referred to by your cognomen; your official family name, which is Trophimus." All of this was fascinating to me. My parents never told me of my lineage, or if I had a family name. As far as I knew, Crixus named me.

Decimus continued to share the family's history, which at the time did not seem significant to me, but later it was a precious gift. "My father—and Callisto's, of course—was one of the first saints of the church in Ephesus. The Apostle Paul, during one of his visits through Ephesus, preached to a pagan crowd, and my father was part of that gathering. Through the power of the Gospel, God changed his heart and that of my entire family, and they were spiritually reborn by God. I remember the change that took place in my father like it was yesterday."

"He grew spiritually and became a leader in the young congregation. Paul took a keen interest in my father, first for his piety, but also for his ability to manufacture parchment, and to write. He was parchmenter,[9] which is our family trade as you'll soon see. He journeyed with Paul all over the empire writing for the Apostle. My father was a godly man, and the spiritual fruit we observed from his transformed life was what the Spirit of the One True God used to change my entire family, even my grandparents who worshipped Diana. Polycarp, this is the name you will bear if you will have it. God has blessed our family, and it is our most sincere hope that he will continue to bless it through you."

It's interesting to look back and see the importance they placed on the family name. It wasn't due to their place or reputation in society, nor for the name of the family business. The importance

---

9. *Parchment maker*

of the name was for the glory of God and their reputation as one of his followers. Even at that age, the importance was driven deep in my heart. There was something special about getting a new name.

◇◇

The next several days were like living in a dream, and I was soaking in all the attention. Callisto and I had no idea what was to confront us next. I thought Crixus was awful, but the enemy I was to face next knew exactly where to hit me. Even though I was young and unfamiliar with the ways of sin, from the depths of my wicked heart emerged the ravenous two-headed dragon of guilt and fear. Both separate in their attacks, and yet both feeding off the other. I was unprepared for the invasion of guilt, and it attacked me where I was most vulnerable.

Callisto asked me to join her as she went about town ministering to the poor and picking up a few items at the market. We also stopped in to visit a very elderly and frail woman, one whom I would like to have known better, but I was too young to appreciate her significance, but her name was Mary, the earthly mother of the Lord Jesus. She had lived with John for a short time, but eventually some of her children came to Ephesus to assist in her care. I do recall her great humility and love for God. She did not seek any self-glory, and seemed to enjoy ministering in secret, in fact, it was Callisto who often carried out her ministry of love to others in need. I admired her godly zeal, love for people, and for refusing exaltation above others in any fashion.

◇◇

As Callisto continued with the morning errands, I saw the Temple of Diana at a distance, and it pierced my heart with guilt. Just a short time ago I had walked hand-in-hand with my mother as she offered incense on the altar and prayed for Diana's blessing with me kneeling right beside her. Without warning, I was overcome with guilt holding Callisto's hand, and for not honoring my mother by praying to Diana. In my mind, I imagined seeing my mother kneeling at the shrine, and looking at me with shock and sadness in her face. I felt ill and torn in my soul as I pulled my hand out of her hand.

"Do I not love my mother anymore?" I thought to myself. Her presence seemed so real to me that I struggled to hide the tears welling up in my eyes. I wanted to run away and hide. Callisto observed my struggle, but had no clue as to the agony that troubled me.

"Polycarp, you seem distressed. What troubles you?" She asked.

I looked off toward the Temple, and feeling uncertain, simply asked, "Shouldn't we stop and put incense on the altar over there?" as I pointed back towards the shrine at the steps of the great temple.

Callisto stopped and was staring at the grand structure, probably uncertain how to respond. Should she rebuke me with a stern "No," or perhaps just ignore the innocent question. Instead of these, she walked with me over to a bench under some trees between the harbor and the temple where she shared with me a story.

"There once was a great king of long ago, who greatly honored the One True God. In fact, God referred to this man as 'a man after my own heart.' He was a great hero among God's servants, and he wrote a song about the greatness of the True God, a song whose words can only really be understood by those who know God. Those alien to Him would never understand this, but I believe that He wants to teach it to you. It is called faith. Faith is what we believe, and how we act upon those beliefs." I remember the drama in her voice, but it was deeper than trying to entertain an eight-year-old boy. She quoted the story as if it were her own words.

"This King in the song commands all nations to recount the splendor-filled ways of God. The words of the song are: 'All people, marvel at his great feats, for God is the greatest of all; indeed, our every word, thought and deed should extol His greatness, for this is a praiseworthy practice. We are to stand in awe and reverence of His greatness over all the so-called gods of this world; for the gods of this world are worthless. Look up into the sky and behold the heavens; he did all that for us. That is just a small reflection of His true glory. He made all that can be seen for us to enjoy because we know who made it.'"[10]

---

10. Psalm 96:3-5

With a smile born out of confidence, she continued; "Diana, nor Zeus nor any other gods of man could have accomplished that and greater things we have yet to discover about him. This is my God, the One True God you have heard about, the God who saves his people from eternal punishment for their willful disobedience and transgressions, and guides them through the relationship of his grace instead." She pulled me close to her and said, "He is the same God that gave you to me."

"Aren't you afraid that the gods will be angry with you?" I asked.

"No! No! Never! How can I fear what does not exist? These are the gods men have conjured up from their imaginations. They are human-like gods, made in a fashion of the One True God. Men have created gods to fit their lifestyles and to control other men for political purposes, evil or immoral intentions, or as a way to amass more wealth for themselves."

"The struggle between mankind and God took place before man was even formed, and before the earth was even created. Among God's most beautiful and powerful creations was a mighty angel named Lucifer. An angel is a servant of God in His heavenly palace. The problem with Lucifer was that he wasn't happy with the way God had made him, and even though he was the most powerful of God's angels, he lusted for more power, and in his wicked heart, proudly desired to be above God himself. Lucifer wanted to be a god. Well, as best as I can understand, a war broke out in Heaven, a war that Lucifer could never win, but a war all the same. In this heavenly conflict, God cast Lucifer and all those who wanted to make him their god out of the heavenly palace. Ever since then, Lucifer, who we call Satan, the devil or the evil one has sought to put this same corrupt desire into all mankind. The devil is behind the gods of man, and he has birthed their conception in the minds of men."

"Mankind creates gods they can control. The gods of men must have vulnerabilities that the other gods of men can exploit. The One True God, however, is different from any man-made god. His love is selfless and proves it by redeeming us from the bondage of evil, much like I redeemed you from slavery the other day. In fact, as you mature to understand this, you will see that God desires to use his children to be the destroyer of man-made gods. History is filled with examples of his servants whom he has used to tear down the gods of this world."

That night I tossed in bed. The words of Callisto sounded right, but they were new to me and seemed impossible. As I turned about in the bed, the next head of the dragon began to eat away at my soul, for guilt gave way to fear. I thought guilt was bad, but fear was worse; especially in the dark. Turmoil corrupted my thoughts and panic caused my heart to pound. "What if Callisto and Murcia were wrong, and there wasn't One True God? Wouldn't the other gods be angry at me? To compound my fear, I remembered how my father used to pray for help and protection from our ancestors. Were they in the room with me, and angry at my reluctance to request their help? Images of my weeping mother and grieved father tormented my soul all night. Even when I did fall asleep, my dreams fled, leaving me with nightmares. I awoke the next morning exhausted and heavy hearted.

I approached the breakfast table dispirited and unwilling to make eye contact.

"It would appear that someone didn't sleep well," Decimus said.

"Is that true," asked Callisto as she walked over to caress my hair, and kiss me on the head. "What's troubling my boy? It hurts me to see you sad."

"Nothing," I mumbled. I tried to eat, but choked as I attempted to hold back my tears. I felt alone with no one to turn to for help. I was convinced that my affections toward Callisto would hurt my mother. I couldn't resist any longer, and began to weep. Out of panic, I got up from the table and darted out of the house.

Decimus pursued me, "Polycarp, please stop. Let me help you," he yelled out.

It was silly to think I could outrun him. What startled me was the sudden reality that I was actually running back towards my old slave home; to Crixus. It didn't take too long for Decimus to catch up with me, and probably could have sooner, but it looked odd for a grown man to be chasing a crying boy. He grabbed me by the shoulders and turned me around to face him. I didn't see anger in his eyes, though he did appear worried.

"Polycarp, what weighs heavy on your heart?" He asked.

"Nothing," I whispered.

"That can't be, or else you wouldn't have fled from the house. There is something bothering you. I assure you that it is not too great a matter that I cannot help you. Please trust me. Share with me what troubles you," he requested.

I wept more as the reality of my mother's absence had finally awakened within me. "I fear making the gods angry, and hurting my mother and father," I finally blurted out.

"How could you possibly hurt your mother and father now?" he asked.

"They are with me; all my ancestors are watching me and are displeased with me," I said.

"No, no, you misunderstand and have not been told the truth about life," he responded. "Your parents can't see you, or any of your ancestors, but if they could, I'm sure they would be proud of your courage. They would desire your happiness, as does your new family. You have fallen prey to fear and to guilt, and you don't need to. Fear isolates us and leaves us with a sense of dread and loneliness as if there was no one to help us and as if there was no way out of the troubles we have encountered. You must not believe the lie of fear, Polycarp. Cast that horrible creature out of your thinking. Fear will take you back to slavery and will be brutal with you; and guilt too, for it exists only to punish your joy. It is guilt and fear that wearies you. Fear gets stronger as it eats away at our courage. It drains the well of happiness, steals the treasures of what gives us peace, and stands in triumph on the neck of our freedom."

"I know only one way to conquer this type of fear, and that is with genuine love; being loved, and accepting that love first of all, and then learning to love in return. Only with this weapon can fear be defeated. Polycarp, Callisto loves you; Beatrice loves you, and I love you too," as he gave me a gentle shake. "The more convinced you become of this, the weaker your fear and guilt. Our responsibility is to lead you into an understanding of God's love. Here you will find that there are no gods made by man; no gods that have ever, or could ever exist that love as our One True God loves. 'In genuine love there is no fear, but the completeness of God's love throws fear out of our lives.'[11] Come back home

---

11. 1 John 4:18

with me, and let us teach you about the love of God. Will you come back with me?" He asked. I wiped the tears from my face, and stood up, taking his waiting hand, and we walked back to our home.

———— ◇◇ ————

There was an influx of visitors in Callisto's home that first week. Most were curious to meet the little slave boy she purchased. One visitor in particular was to become a great and wonderful friend, though a great trial was soon to separate us for a time.

"Polycarp, I would like you to meet the Apostle John," Callisto said. His smile and his personality set me at ease. He sat down at the table and invited me to sit with him.

"So you are the infamous Polycarp," he remarked. "Your adoptive mother sure made quite a stir at the auction. I never knew that she possessed such courage and resolve. I understand that your previous owner was Crixus. Is that correct?"

I nodded my head.

"I know Crixus and his brother Demetrius.[12] They had quite the conflict with one of my colleagues not too long ago. They are villains disguised as merchants. Tell me, did he ever beat you?"

"No, but he slapped me across the face," I replied.

"Hmm, in some ways you are fortunate, for he is a brutal master, I hear. Some of his slaves are my fellow believers, and they must worship in secret."

"Do you know Murcia?" I quizzed.

John's countenance brightened, and he said, "Murcia! Yes, I know her. She is a godly young woman. You know her too?" He inquired.

"Yes," I replied. "She is very kind."

"Indeed," John agreed.

"Tell me, do you have any heroes?" he asked. I thought about it for a moment and said, "Hercules."

"Ah, so is it his great strength you admire?" he suggested.

"Yes, I liked it when he killed Hydra," I said.

"I'm not familiar with all the stories associated with him but wasn't Hydra a snake with eight heads," he asked.

"Nine heads" I replied.

———————————
12. Acts 19

"Oh, of course," John said. "But why did he kill Hydra?"

"He did this and other feats in order to be free," I said. I paused for a moment and then asked him, "Who is your hero?"

Smiling, as if hoping I would ask, "The King of Kings and Lord of Lords is my hero. I knew him as Jesus Christ. Though I have many heroes, he is undoubtedly the greatest of them all. Indeed, I believe it safe to say that for all my other heroes, he was their hero too. I would suppose that would make him the Hero of Heroes."

"What did he do?" I asked.

John laughed a little and said, "Now that would require a very long answer. My entire life has been, and will continue to be telling the story of what my hero accomplished. To begin with, he's the God of the universe, creating it all in six days, but powerful enough to have created it in a moment by just a mere thought if he desired. He directs the hearts of kings and emperors; in fact, no person can even ascend any throne unless he puts them there, including our own Caesar. He even controls the weather. I can remember being with him during a great storm on the sea, and the other men on the boat with me feared for our lives. My master was asleep in the bow of the ship. We awoke him just before we thought we would perish under the waves, and you know what he did? He rebuked the wind and the waves and commanded them, as one with authority, to stop and be calm, and scarcely before he finished stating those words, all was calm. There was not a wave; not even a ripple."

As he leaned in closer to me, he continued, "It's important that you understand that he describes in detail his own attributes, and does not leave it up to men to make him up, adding and deleting from his accomplishments as men do with their own gods. He is fierce with his enemies, both in the invisible, spiritual realms, but also among the children of men. He hates sin; that is, those who transgress his written will. There is eternal judgment for those who disregard him and don't obey him. He is to be feared; feared out of terror from those who do not know him, and feared out of reverence and awe for those who belong to him."

"He's the God of his children, Polycarp. He came down to earth born in the body of a man, yet still the Supreme God of all. On behalf of his children, he lived a perfect life, obeying his Law to perfection without the slightest transgression from it. But that

36

was not enough, for the Law requires death because of the violations against it, both by man's actions and also his very nature. What distinguishes my hero from any others is that he died as a replacement for sinners. He died to save his children. Now tell me, when have Hercules, Zeus, Diana or any other god or goddess ever given their life as a sacrifice for their own people?"

"I don't know," I responded. "I don't think they ever did?"

He then added, "Furthermore, when he died; while his body was still in the grave for three days, he conquered the greatest enemies of mankind: death, sin and hell. Now how's that for a hero?"

I was impressed but didn't know how to respond.

"Young man," John continued, "we have a book called the Holy Scriptures; the words of our ever-living God. It consists of all His great feats, and other heroes through whom he worked to accomplish great and mighty wonders. It's important that we look to these heroes and model those qualities and traits that made them mighty in the power of God. You too can be a hero God uses in the lives of others; your children someday, or perhaps others in the family of God. God knows! I shall talk to Him about you; thank him for you, and ask him to claim you as his personal possession; as one of his children."

My thoughts were beginning to connect with conversations I had with others.

"Is he the one True God as Murcia, Callisto and Decimus have told me?" I asked.

John's eyes brightened as he said, "Yes, child, he is the one True God as Murcia, Callisto and Decimus have told you."

John stood up to talk to Callisto as I listened. "He needs examples and role models; it's important to have examples to follow: spiritual heroes. However, it is vital to understand the role of those whom we admire; our role models and heroes are to be the ones who introduce us to the Savior and deepen our relationship with him. I would hope that you, Decimus and Beatrice are the first role models he will follow. Make sure your words back up your life. Remember what our brother Paul wrote in his letter to the church, 'Don't exasperate your children' through hypocrisy and shallow commitment in following Christ, our Lord. They are to be nurtured through discipleship and daily exhortation.'"[13]

---

13. *Ephesians 6:4*

"Your responsibility Callisto—indeed the responsibility of every parent—is to disciple their children in following Christ. Jesus set the example when he called me in saying, 'Follow me, and I will make you a fisher of men.'[14] We introduce them to what we know about Christ, and for that reason, we had better not stop learning about him and passing it on. Even to this day, I must make it my joyful duty to discover his glories, or else I will render myself ineffective as one of his ministers. I am moved by the example of King David when he was passing on the crown and rule of God's people to his son, Solomon. He lays out for us a true picture of discipleship when he states, 'Solomon, my son, discover in every way the God of your father. Set your heart to be contentedly enslaved to him. For he treads in the hearts of men knowing who seeks him, and who doesn't seek him for he reads the thoughts of men. If you set your heart to make him your pursuit you will find him, but if you loosen yourself from him in pursuit of other things, he will cast you away as if he had never known you.'[15] Discovering the glory of God is true discipleship; this is what the Lord did with his disciples, what pastors are to do with the sheep of his flock, what Christian brethren are to do one for another, and what parents are to do for their children. Train Polycarp to be a follower of Jesus. As you yourself learn of Jesus, so teach your son. Let him see you pursuing the Lord, and growing in love for the Lord with all your heart. Don't limit your instruction to telling how he ought to live; show him! Being an example is the primary role of a parent."

"Oh John, I'm so afraid he'll see my imperfections and sins, and become discouraged," Callisto replied.

"Well of course he will, but that's not what I'm talking about. How do you approach the One who has covered your sins, and has exchanged your sins for his righteousness? Polycarp must see you running the race! He must see you fall and getup again. It is vital that he see you struggle and grow and struggle again, not as one discouraged, but as one being sanctified, being made holy by the Spirit of God as Jesus is holy. Children will see perfection as they look to our Heavenly Father, and they will see His mercy,

---

14. Matthew 4:19

15. I Chronicles 28:9

loving-kindness, forgiveness, and justification when they look at us," John explained.

"I believe many children rebel against the Lord because they do not see this pursuit of godliness in the home. The wife needs to see her husband in pursuit of God, and the husband is encouraged and helped in the race as he sees his wife running the same race at his side. When children see their parents are growing spiritually, it will become a powerful tool in the hands of the Spirit of God to motivate the children to follow in their steps. And this goes beyond even one's parents, for the children should see their uncles, aunts, grandparents, and close friends living a life of worshipful obedience. 'Follow me as I follow Christ,' Paul exhorted Timothy. Remember, Paul was not one who had reached the goal, but anyone could clearly see he was in the race. Others must see us in this race."

"So when I teach him of the heroes in God's word, I'm to tell him about who they are, why they are heroes, and how their lives introduce us to the secrets of God?" Callisto asked.

"Yes," John responded, "and above all, you show him out of your life. Hypocrisy in us first makes self-righteous critics of others, then turns us into godless cynics, and before you know it, a fool emerges from that ruined life. Hypocrisy is scandalous! Trust God like the heroes you place before Polycarp, and you'll develop that desire in the lad. Genuineness born out of love is the only way to train a child properly; the only true way to make disciples. Take him to the Scriptures, and introduce him to the great heroes of the faith. Let's see if we can't give him some new heroes to capture his imagination and inspire his life."

Before departing, he turned to look at me and stated, "Real heroes tear down the gods of men leaving only the truth of the One True God. I am delighted to have met you, Polycarp."

———— ◇◇ ————

On Sunday, I had no idea what to expect. We walked with Decimus and Beatrice to a large hall between the hippodrome and the agora. I had been past this building as a slave many times but was never aware of its use. From what I understand, it was once a storage house for goods brought in from the harbor, but now it served as a meeting hall, and this group of Christians, also called the church held their meetings in this place. I met many of my new friends there, and also met the overseer, Timothy, but one surprise was yet to come.

After the meeting, I heard a shriek come from behind me, and as I turned there was Murcia running towards me with her arms wide open.

"Polycarp, my dear child," she exclaimed as she threw her arms around me, picked me up and twirled me around. "I could not believe my ears when I heard you had been purchased and freed by my friend, Callisto. When I prayed that God would deliver you, I could not have imagined that he would he use her to do it. Praise God for his everlasting kindness!"

By this time a crowd was forming around us and many were sharing in her enthusiasm with laughter, tears, and praises to God. I even cried, for Murcia was a very kind person to me. The reunion was short, for she had to make sure Crixus didn't discover that she had been in attendance that morning. Fortunately for her, Crixus was usually at the Temple of Artemis on Saturday nights and slept late on Sundays. As long as Murcia was back before he awoke, she was safe.

◇◇

Life was wonderful for me over the next couple of years, but I began to feel a pressure unknown to me before, and that was fear for my mother and family. It had been four years since the great fire destroyed most of Rome. It was Nero's tenth year as Caesar, and rumors as to how the fire was started spread as fast as the fire itself. Some said that Nero set the city ablaze being moved by a sinister desire to rebuild from the ashes a city reflecting the splendor of his glory. Others claimed that some enemy from the North was responsible for this act arson. But another tale was circulating; it was subtle, below the surface at first, but over the next few weeks seemed to gain momentum; the blame was to fall on the new religious sect called the Christians.

While the rumor spread like wildfire, its destruction was slow, much like a smoldering flame that slowly grows to combustion. At first, blaming the Christians seemed idiotic, but we began to hear of it more and more. Christianity was growing enough, but still too insignificant to leverage any opposition. Over the following years, no proof was ever presented that could indict the church, nor any trial ever conducted. Reports circulated that Nero had gone mad, and was bent on justifying himself by ultimately blaming the Christians for the arson. As his power grew, so did his accusations. Soon a plan was concocted to take the suspicion off Nero and on to the Christians. He ordered that Christians be arrested and executed for crimes against the Emperor and his glorious city, Rome. Like the wind that spread the flames through the city, so the intensity of his edict rushed throughout every corner of the Empire. In some Provinces, little was done, but in others where the church was thriving, the enemies of Jesus Christ fanned the flame of hatred. In Rome, arrests began, and executions soon followed. News poured in that the Emperor had many church leaders crucified, some covered in wax and used as human torches in his gardens, and others killed in the stadium. In cities further away from Rome, churches were simply forbidden to assemble. Even as a young boy who had yet to discover the life-changing power of redemption, I too came face-to-face with the treacherous intentions of evil.

I had accompanied Decimus down to the docks where he was overseeing a shipment of parchment to Athens. I was doing what little boys do, simply playing as I imagined myself as a captain of a large vessel I observed sailing into the harbor. I listened as I heard orders yelled out as they approached the dock, and repeated them as if I were standing on the bridge of the ship. I wandered a little way from Decimus, occasionally picking up a stone and seeing how far I could throw it out into the water when all of the sudden I was grabbed by my arm and yanked into the alley and thrown against a wall. It all happened so fast that I didn't even have time to get frightened until I looked up and saw a man emerge from the shadow. It was Crixus.

He walked around me. He wasn't smiling, and the bitterness he wore on his face caused a surge of terrible memories. He finally spewed out; "Look at you, you scrawny worm. Have you missed me?"

Like a flash of lightening, I was filled with fear, and angrily cried out, "What do you want?"

"What do I want, you ask? Well, I'll just tell. At last, Caesar has discovered the type of people you Christians truly are. Your kind has ruined this town and have brought dishonor upon us from the gods. Now it looks like we're finally going to get you. The Emperor has demanded the execution of the Christians, and I just want you to know that I'm eager to obey his edict."

Of course, I could have claimed that I wasn't a Christian, but I was so afraid, I couldn't think. I hardly believe it would have made a difference.

With a sick grin, he slowly drew a knife from its sheath and then glared at me with contempt I could never forget as he said, "Perhaps I will just start right here with you. I will cut you open and gut you like a fish." I tried to get up and run away, but he quickly grabbed me and threw me down again. He then moved to put the knife up to my throat when I heard Decimus shout from the other end of the alley.

"Get away from that boy!" I had never heard Decimus angry before, and I am glad because he sounded terrifying.

Crixus stood up stiff as a board; obviously frightened by the command of the order. He slowly turned to face Decimus, who had run down the alley toward us, but stopped as Crixus extended his knife towards my uncle. "You Christians are going to burn," Crixus declared as the knife trembled in his hand.

"Our burning, as you say it, has nothing to do with you threatening this child. What kind of man are you to threaten a little boy, and stand there shaking like a leaf before a man? This boy is no longer your property. He is a Roman citizen, and I plan to report this to the authorities at once," Decimus declared.

"The authorities," Crixus laughed. "I've just come from the garrison, and they're talking about how to round up all of you, and execute you. Go, run to the authorities and spare them the time to search and arrest you."

"You are a devilish man, Crixus. Does your bitterness know no limits?" Decimus asked as if trying to stir the conscience of the man.

"My hatred is my strength. It gives me the will to get up each morning," Crixus said rather boastfully. He then sheathed his blade and walked past Decimus. As he walked away he said, "I'll see you all killed, and you'll live only long enough to see how hate always wins the day."

Decimus reached down to help me up, hugged me, and said, "Are you injured?"

"No, but glad you saved me," I replied.

"Let's return home at once," he said. "I need to see what is happening around here."

As we entered the agora, a group of men came running towards us. I soon saw that they were church leaders who came to inform Decimus that John had been summoned to the garrison.

---◇◇---

Decimus told me to stay close to him as we made our way through the crowded streets. A great uneasiness hung over the abnormal commotion in the city. The Christians had a strong and caring reputation which made the Emperor's edict very difficult to carry out. It created a great deal of awkwardness, for people who would normally greet Decimus shunned him. Their behavior didn't seem to bother him as he warmly smiled at those who walked by him as if assuring them that he understood their predicament.

When we arrived at The Odeon in the upper agora, we found John and all the overseers from area congregations, elders and deacons of each congregation in and around Ephesus. Decimus was the last one to arrive. When John saw us, he smiled at me, and then turned to gain the attention of the group before him.

"Men of God, we must redeem the time," John emphasized. "Even as I speak, soldiers are being dispersed to stifle what they believe will be an uprising by our brethren. However, I have assured both the city leaders and the Proconsul that such an act is not necessary. We will not take up arms against them. There has obviously been a great misunderstanding in Rome, and I'm sure, if the Lord wills it, that Paul will sort this out. I received correspondence from him this morning that he sent a few weeks ago. He is in communication with several in Caesar's household, as well as a couple of Senators who are followers of Christ. I will not deceive you, for while the situation is grave, Paul has been guaranteed an audience with the Emperor. Peter has also communicated with me from Antioch, where the situation appears to be more fragile. Apparently, the Romans believe that this could precipitate another Jewish uprising with the Christians joining in on the revolt. The city has been locked down, and Peter has been placed under arrest for the time being. He wrote me from prison, and it appears will be moved to Cæsarea for trial."

Before John could utter another word, one of the city leaders entered the auditorium. Though he was not a believer, he was sympathetic toward the church. "I beg your pardon for interrupting you, but I have urgent news for you, John," he said.

"Please, share with us the news," John requested.

"Nero seems determined to carry out his edict. Your leader in Rome, Paul was executed two weeks ago after a brief meeting with the Emperor." Silence covered the room. All I could hear was my own heart pounding out of fear.

"Paul is with the Lord; he is dead," John said as if he couldn't believe it.

"Yes," the town leader repeated. "He was beheaded. However, that is not all. Soldiers are on their way to arrest you. They have also decided that since there are so many Christians in Ephesus, that you will be taken away from the city to face execution." Now all the men were on their feet, and for a moment, I thought they would take up arms and fight.

"John turned to look at each of them and said, "Do not fear little children, and gird yourselves with the armor of the Lord, praying at all times. We must not rise to our feet, but to our knees we must fall." Then looking back to the town leader he asked, "What of the church, the people?"

With a lowered voice as if not to be overheard, the replied, "The Proconsul is reluctant to carry out the edict. Those in Rome or with close connections with the Emperor fear his wrath and are moved to action, but the Proconsul seems to be holding out for something else beyond my knowledge. He has issued an order for the Christians to be contained in the Hippodrome until he determines the course to take."

John looked at the floor as he contemplated the instructions. He looked up and around the room at each of the men before him, and said, "Do not wait arrest. Collect those for whom you are responsible, and conduct them peacefully to the Hippodrome. Sing, fellowship, challenge and praise God together. If you have those in your congregations that feel led to leave the city, do not detain them, but send them on their way with your blessing. We will trust God in this. If the Proconsul meant violence, he would be poised for the mass executions the law of Nero requires. But he doesn't do this. Pray that our God moves his heart to compassion."

John looked over at Timothy and said, "Go now, my friend, communicate my instructions to the Proconsul, and then meet the people there. Comfort and lead them."

It was at this moment that Timothy felt the weight of grief in his heart upon hearing the news of his mentor, Paul. John smiled as tears began slowly moving down his face, and he walked over to Timothy and embraced him. He held Timothy by the shoulders and simply stated, "Our dear brother Paul was faithful unto death. He knew that he was to suffer in this fashion. Take up his mantle my dear son, and run your race with perseverance." Timothy nodded and wiped the tears from his face.

As John was about to address the church leaders and pray with them, the Roman soldiers entered the building. The centurion approached John and said, "The Emperor has ordered your arrest along with others called apostles. You are to be taken from Ephesus. Will you come peacefully?"

John looked over at the church leaders, and then patted the hand of the centurion who was gripping the handle of his sheaved sword. "Yes, I will accompany you peacefully," John replied.

They did not chain or tie him, but slowly they walked him out, and I figured I was never to see him again. I glanced up at Decimus, who could not hold back his tears of sorrow and perhaps anger as well. I cried seeing him cry.

———————◇◇———————

It seemed strange to me as we made our way to our home, and together with my mother, Beatrice and several of our friends, we made our way solemnly to the Hippodrome. As we arrived, the place was quite full, and I was surprised by the joy of everyone. It was like a great reunion of long-lost friends. I forgot my fears when I saw many of my friends and was off exploring the great stadium where so many adventures, races and fights had taken place.

To the surprise of all of us being detained, there appeared to be a great outflow of sympathy from the community. Yes, there were some like Crixus who hated the Christians, and they did what they could to make us miserable. They were incredulous by the Proconsul's reluctance to carry out Nero's edict. Indeed, no one knew why he hesitated.

It was inconvenient to sleep, eat and see to personal needs in such a crowd, but we managed. Food was abundant, and the authorities did allow certain representatives to leave to gather needed supplies, they even permitted the infirm to return to their own homes.

Two days later, news came that astonished everyone in the town, and perhaps gave some insight as to what the Proconsul knew, but could not share. Nero was dead! For the church, it was a reprieve, but for the Empire, it would mark a two-year, internal struggle for power.

As I recall, Nero committed suicide after the Senate turned against him and declared him a public enemy. The Proconsul's father was a Senator, and it would appear that he shared the plot with his son. It seemed odd to me that a city noted for its love of the emperors became euphoric at the news, and flocked into the streets to celebrate his demise. We were released to return to our homes and lives as if nothing had ever happened. But our celebration was not without its losses either. Paul was dead. Reports had arrived of Peter's execution. While we received no word on John, all assumed that he had been taken a short distance from Ephesus and also killed. Several began an immediate search for him, or any news about him, but it was as if he had vanished from the earth. While the church rejoiced in the salvation the Lord provided, we also grieved over the loss of one so deeply loved.

While I knew only peace in the aftermath of Nero's death, the Roman Empire knew only strife and civil war. Over the next year, Rome would see three emperors rise and fall, and after much bloodshed a forth would bring stability. Upon Nero's death, Galba, with the support of the Spanish Legions, seized power. But he served seven months as Caesar and was assassinated by the Praetorian Guard, who made Otho the new Emperor, but he reigned for only three months. There was a third man seeking power, and that was Vitellius whose friendship with the commanding generals of the German Legions placed him in power after they defeated Otho at the battle of Bedriacum. Otho committed suicide after his defeat. There was one more man who seemed to have support in the right places, however, and that was General Vespasian. His troops assassinated Vitellius after eight months as Emperor, and thus established Emperor Vespasian, who had the military might to hold off any other contenders. He would reign for ten years.

4

I FOUND MY LOST SHEEP

My sheep hear my voice,
and I know everything about them, and they follow me.
(John 10:27)

MY memories as a slave seemed like a lifetime ago. I was fourteen and had fully grown to appreciate my new life. I could even call Callisto "Mother" without feeling disloyal to my birth mother. I felt that she would have been happy that I was living free as a Roman citizen, with a mother who loved me as if I were her child. I had also grown quite accustomed to the daily routines of life, and joined Callisto and my uncle in the parchment business.

As I understand it, the word *parchment* was derived from its city of origin, Pergamum. It's not too far from Ephesus, and is where Decimus and Callisto grew up working with their father, who had learned the craft of making parchment from his father. It's a noble occupation, for mostly scholars and government officials desire parchment and are willing to pay for it. It's more expensive than papyrus, and can last for hundreds of years, plus it was better for binding than the scrolls of papyrus. The manufacturing process was complicated, tedious and very smelly. It began with Decimus going to local slaughterhouses in order to inspect the hides of sheep, cows, goats, and other animals. Unlike a bag or coat, it was going to be written on, and for this reason it had to be as blemish and disease-free as possible. After he had made his purchase, the hides were brought into the cleaning area where they had cold water constantly poured over them for a day and night to loosen the hair. When they are clean, they were either hung up until the hair started to fall off, or we soaked them in lime and water for several days, stirring the pot with a large stick throughout the day. The next step, we would take them out and lay them hair-side up to dry. At this point, a worker would use a long blade with wooden handles on each side to scrape away the remaining fur. This process took several days of more rinsing, drying, stretching, and more scraping until we reached the desired thickness of the parchment. It's a delicate job, for it is easy to pierce the hide and render it useless. You can guess what my job was? I was the one who got to stir the large kettles of water and lime. I lost many good meals as I tried to endure the horrible stench. My uncle would just laugh at me, and tell me he's making a man out of me.

The work was very important to my uncle, for church scribes, elders, and even some of the Apostles would order his parchment. Many referred to it as vellum as well, and it was used for writing letters, or to copy the letters from the Apostles and church leaders for the churches. Many wealthy families would also order it for additions to their private libraries. He seemed emphatic that since the words of the Lord were being recorded on them, the work be the highest quality.

When I wasn't working, I was being educated by Callisto, and she was hoping to earn enough money to hire a tutor in order to educate me in more advanced areas. Secretly, I knew that my mother desired that I would become a pastor in the Church. However, there remained one problem with this; I had yet to discover the Savior, the Lord Jesus Christ. It wasn't that I was resistant, perhaps I didn't fully understand the work of redemption, or maybe my heart was still hardened by the power of sin. One thing was for sure: the enemy of God had blinded my eyes from seeing the light of his glorious gospel, and that didn't seem to bother me. When blindness is normal, who craves the light?

I had stopped praying to the gods and my ancestors years ago, and felt a sense of personal righteousness in that. I was happy and loved, and though surrounded by godly examples, my spiritual need lay dormant. I did have times of conviction; especially when John or Timothy preached. Since my uncle made parchments, he also sought out older parchments and papyrus of the ancient texts for his personal enjoyment. As you can imagine, I was encouraged to read the Psalms and Proverbs, the books of Moses and the prophets. I liked the Scriptures, but I must confess I didn't understand their significance.

In the second year of Vespasian's rule, in the year 72, an event took place that would be life-changing for me, and would be used by God to ignite the church with a freshly rekindled fire of strength and confidence.

The Ephesian church was prospering in this city of over two-hundred and fifty thousand people, but as we would find out, we were prospering in the wrong direction. The Christians of Ephesus were busy in spiritual matters. From one standpoint, they were accomplishing spiritual feats that caused their reputation to flourish abroad. Overseers and other church leaders came from all parts of the world to examine the "Ephesian Way" as it was being called. The church was flourishing far beyond one man's ability to oversee properly, evidenced by the influx of erroneous teaching and abominable heresies that were dividing and damaging the flock. Timothy was providing oversight as best he could, and while he was highly esteemed, he didn't appear to have the authority John held in the church. Overseers were being trained and commissioned to provide spiritual service to the growing number of congregations sprouting throughout the city and countryside.

Everyone who visited seemed impressed with the churches and those people who were part of their fellowship. They were socially active, politically involved, financially influential, and were overall considered good people and upstanding Romans. I do recall, however that Timothy and other church leaders seemed alarmed that while the church looked active in right areas, something was missing. They worked frantically to steer the churches toward the work of grace rather than works without grace.

One Lord's Day in particular was a day I would never forget for as long as I live. It probably was the closest I would ever get to what it must have been like when our Lord raised Lazarus from the dead. The church assembly had scarcely begun when a hush fell over the entire congregation. You would have thought that perhaps a dignitary had just walked in, but as I glanced toward the rear of the meeting hall, I saw what had startled everyone. It was an elderly gentleman walking with the aid of a crooked staff, but he was no ordinary man. He was extremely scarred to the point of being grotesque. It was like his skin had melted and was reshaped in a very deformed manner. His eyes and countenance gave no indication of grief or the slightest embarrassment. He limped into the room not as an invalid beggar, but with the confidence and poise of a commander who returned from a violent battle as the victor. I felt I knew the man, but I would never forget meeting someone so mangled and scarred.

Surely he must have felt some humiliation at the silence his presence had created. He had barely taken a few steps into the room when Timothy stood up and made his way through the assembly towards the man. When he was only a few feet away, he abruptly stopped. He began to struggle to hold back his tears when he broke the silence, "Forgive me, but is that you, John?" The question stirred the congregation to a higher level of attentiveness as all awaited the reply. With a sob of emotion and a bowed head, the stranger replied, "Yes, I am John." Gasps, wails of joy and some of grief at the sight of him erupted throughout the hall. Timothy embraced the great Apostle, and the congregation overflowed with awe and praise to God.

After much time had elapsed, John finally made it to the front of the room, and when the commotion had calmed down, he began to explain the works of God that brought him joyfully, though scarred, to this very moment. "The only place I would rather be at this time than with you would be kneeling before the throne of my loving, Almighty God. To see you, is like being healed from a dread disease, or to have run a long and wearisome race and to have crossed into the relief of the finish line."

"Four years ago, by decree of our late emperor, Nero, I was arrested for my alleged part in the burning of Rome. As I have since heard, several of the Lord's apostles also lost their lives, including Paul, who was beheaded in Rome, but you already know this, don't you? Because of my so-called popularity in Ephesus, the Proconsul thought it wise to remove me from the city for my execution. I was taken to a nearby deserted island of Patmos, only sixty, perhaps seventy miles from where I stand. When we arrived, I was taken ashore and was told that I would be drowned in a cauldron of boiling oil as my form of execution. To this news I was determined to endure for the glory of Christ, by the grace of God. I never had a trial, nor was given even the slightest opportunity to declare my innocence. There was a small brick building with a courtyard a few yards away where I was escorted. I observed an area where similar executions had taken place. I was tied to a post for the remainder of the day and the night as the cauldron was being heated. The next morning, it was boiling."

"With the resolve of my Savior, the Lord Jesus Christ, I prayed as he prayed in the Garden of Gethsemane, 'My Father, if it is possible, remove this cup from me, but if you will not, it is not my will I seek, but your will be done.' [16]His grace was upon me, and I knew that I could endure until death, and would be freed from this body of corruption and ushered into the presence of my Lord forever. I did not fear death, though I would be lying if I said I didn't feel some fear as to how I was to die. I was encouraged to see how his grace would sustain me through the dreadful pain of it all. Little did I know at that moment, that my time had not yet come and that I would be called upon to endure much more pain than I could have ever imagined."

"The Captain of the Guard walked up to me that first morning and said, 'It is time. It has been my experience that it takes two to three submerges to bring on death. The first will be the most painful. You will be lifted out, and submerged as many times as it takes to bring on death. I am not a Christian, and I am truly sorry you must suffer in this way. Beheading is far more civilized. Pray to your God you die right away. Indeed, if I felt I could get away with it, I would simply thrust my sword into you and make your death swift. Prepare yourself.'

"As I prayed and sought the peace of God, I noticed in the horizon another Roman ship docking next to the ship that brought me to this place. I assumed it brought others facing execution along with me."

"A guard untied me from the post and escorted me up the ramp where I was girded about with chains, and then hoisted up over the boiling vat. Some of the soldiers didn't appear fazed by what they were about to see, but a few I could tell had never witnessed an execution like this one. Slowly I was let down towards the oil and I could begin to feel its bubbling splashes burn my feet and lower legs. Link by link they lowered me towards the oil to intensify the torture. Finally, I was let down into the boiling pot of pain and death until at last I was baptized into the oil. The pain was immediate and intense; indescribable to be honest. It was the Roman way to elongate suffering. I imagine that to suffer crucifixion would have been worse."

---

16. Matthew 26:39

The report moved the congregation. Some fell ill and quickly fled the room while others remained and sobbed, but everyone was grieved by what he suffered. I was angry, but not for the reasons you may think. Yes, I was angry about Rome's cruelty, but I had always been angry for that. What angered me the most was that God would permit this gruesome torture against one of his choice servants. What I had yet to realize was that this was a sin expressing its intense hatred towards God through the cruelty of man. In time, I would see this dark billowing cloud as the backdrop to God's brilliant mercy that shines through the gloom.

John continued with his experience. "Once submerged, I was swiftly lifted out in order to be dropped in again. Much of my body was wracked in pain, with some burns so severe that I lost all feeling. I did not cry out, much to my amazement, and to the surprise of my executioners. Just as they were slowly lowering me into the oil again, a courier from the other ship arrived and seemed quite ill after beholding me. The captain read the message, and then communicated its contents: 'A couple of weeks ago, Emperor Nero committed suicide. Servius Galba is the new Emperor and has ordered a stay of execution on the sect called the Christians pending further investigation.'"

"Was this cruel injustice, or did God have some other service for me to fulfill?" That question stirred in my mind as I hung over the oil before I fell into unconsciousness."

"I awoke many days later in a bed next to a window overlooking the Aegean Sea. There was a slight breeze filtering in, but I did not find it necessarily refreshing, for even the slightest movement caused great pain on the parts of my body that had been covered with my clothing. My caretakers wrapped me in white linen strips, and what appeared to be a concoction of honey paste. A family that lived on the island and farmed a small parcel nursed me back to health."

"They cared for me, which was a long and painful process. I would have contacted you all sooner, but very few boats came, and most that did were trying to avoid Ephesus due to their illegal cargo. However, I could not speak for months, and then only in a whisper. It took a couple of years to learn to walk again, and to command the use of my arms and fingers. My muscles rebelled against my will, and my skin had hardened into inflexible scars that you can see before you."

"Last year, I found myself able to get around the island, and began to set my mind on returning to you all. But it was during that time I discovered the real reason I was on Patmos. It was on the first day of the week, the Lord's Day that I was taken up in the Spirit to behold things and events almost beyond human description. I found myself in the presence of God sitting enthroned before the hosts of Heaven. In that holy place, I saw my friend and Savior the Son of God, Jesus Christ, unlike I had ever seen him before. His appearance was so terrifyingly magnificent that I dropped at his feet as if I had just died. But he laid his right hand upon me and told me not to fear. I was there to write one more revelation of God's reality and his plan for the ages culminating in the final and eternal establishment of his Kingdom and His Church. It would be his final revelation to which a curse would be added to any who felt a careless liberty in adding to it."

I recall how he reached into his shoulder satchel and pulled out a book of parchments tied in between two heavier pieces of leather. He then lifted it up above his head with both of his hands and stated, "This is the written record of the Revelation of Jesus Christ. This document is His Apocalypse; the great disclosure of what remains of God's plan for the ages."

The recent events were powerful tools used by God to change my heart. The true heart-wrestling with God began on a Sunday as a result of Timothy's message from the letter to the Colossian Christians. Timothy's voice rang out with authority and with great emphasis. "And you, who at one time were estranged and hateful, committing evil acts, he (Jesus Christ) has now reconciled in his fleshly body through his death, for the sole purpose of presenting you before God as holy and without blame, if you work out faith by being established and immovable, not carried away from the joyful expectation of the great news you have heard, which has been heralded throughout all creation under heaven, of which I, Paul, was appointed a steward."[17]

These words were like a spear in my soul, for I was the estranged one from God. Though I had the appearance of an innocent lad, I was a hateful man who seemed to have hellfire

17. Colossians 1:21-23

53

fueling desires to do evil. You must understand that I wasn't committing heinous crimes; I just simply enjoyed living life without having to think too much about God.

"Could there be any greater evil than that, I wondered? How is it that Jesus would even want to reconcile me to himself, much less present me before God as holy and without blame?" That thought moved beyond my comprehension.

The problem was confounded by great fear that was welling up in my heart as a result of those words. By faith, I was to be established and immovable resulting from that work of reconciliation, and to be resistant to not being lured away from the reality of the gospel.

"But what was faith?" I pondered.

"How could I not be carried away since I seemed to enjoy the ultimate of evil acts—living as if I was a god?" I suddenly realized that I had become my own form of Zeus or Baal. What surprised me was that instead of repentance, I put up resistance. I resented God's expectations of me; my heart was hardened.

I lived in misery for the next several days. My family was aware that something was bothering me, and I suppose they knew the source of my struggle. A life and death conflict is hard to hide.

The grip of sin on the soul is violent; it is predisposed to consume the deadness of a man's soul much like a tomb holds a rotting corpse. If I had wished to rid my soul of this affliction, I could not, for I was fighting against myself. I had a spiritual enemy that made me an enemy to myself. As the days passed, the pressure of conviction built up in my soul. The days seemed longer and my chores harder. Finally, I could take no more and fled to my favorite spot on a hill overlooking the sea. I would like to say I found the time peaceful, reflective and relaxing, but it was hardly any of those.

"Why are you tormenting me?" I asked God aloud as I heard the subtle echo of my voice carry over the water. "Leave me alone, I don't know what to do!"

The conviction agitating my heart grieved me, and it seemed like my soul was sick and could find no relief. Finally, as if a volcano was erupting inside of me I yelled up to the heavens in exasperation; "Why do you keep troubling me? What am I supposed to do? I feel like I'm going to die!"

At that very moment, I just about jumped out of my skin when I heard a voice behind loudly exclaim; "I heard my Lord Jesus Christ say, 'I am the resurrection and the life. Anyone who believes in me, though he dies, I tell you he actually lives, and everyone who lives and has faith in me surely will never die. Do you believe this?'"18

As I turned around to see who had intruded on my privacy, I saw John walking up and taking a seat on a boulder next to me. "What an inspiring prospect you have here, Polycarp," he remarked as he surveyed the landscape. "Do you come here often?"

"Yes," I replied, "especially when I need to think."

"What's consuming your thoughts now, for it seems to all who know you that you are thinking on something weighty? I don't recall ever seeing you struggle so much," he remarked.

As I spoke, a waterfall of emotion erupted out of my soul. "I feel God is against me! He won't leave me alone."

John didn't seem to panic; in fact, he looked a bit relieved. "He is very persistent I will grant you that, but He is not against you. If he was, you would know it. God doesn't simply pressure his enemies; he destroys them. No, my boy, God is for you, and the pressure you feel is God finding you. You are like a lost sheep, and the shepherd has found you. You are like Adam and Eve in the Garden of Eden after they had sinned. For in the cool of the day God came to fellowship with them, and they hid themselves not wanting God to find them. They had missed the mark of God's desires for them and willfully transgressed. Both of them knew it and hoped they would not have to face their Creator."

"Like all of us, they were created with the understanding that He is perfectly holy; the righteous standard by which all things are measured, and for this reason they could not escape the troubling reality that they could not measure up to His requirements. You see, they knew that while He was a God of love, His holiness and righteousness demanded that He hate sin more. I guess in some way they were smart in their attempt to hide, for that's what any human would do in the presence of such righteous perfection. What they didn't know, and were soon to discover, is that you can't hide from God, and you can't even resist Him finding you. He knows all things, sees all things, and can be everywhere all the

_____

18. John 11:25-26

time. Not only can he peer down from heaven and see you on this hillside, but he can go deeper and see without obstruction the thoughts and intentions of your soul."

I had to ask, "But why do I feel as if God is against me?"

John was animated in his response and said; "Because God is against your sin! What you are feeling is the Spirit of God exposing your sin to you in the light of his perfection; your pride, lust, and like Adam and Eve, that subtle desire to be a little god; that's what he's going after. It's those very sins that produce the guilt that make you want to die instead of face the all-exposing light of God's righteousness. The life that we can have in Christ not only delivers us from the bondage of sin, but gives us grace so that we no longer feel obligated to obey sin. In the truest sense, Jesus has exchanged his righteousness for our sin, those egregious offenses and willful transgressions, and this becomes our standing before this perfect and holy God. Find yourself outside of Christ, and all you have is God's wrath."

"So God is not angry with me for praying to false gods?" I nervously asked.

John, with equal caution, responded; "Yes, and no. God is indescribably angry with your sinful actions, so much so that the penalty for such offences, indeed any sin no matter how seemingly minor places man forever under the furor of His wrath. But this is where Jesus Christ, God's Son saves us. Jesus, though a man with all the fleshly weaknesses and frailties, lived the perfect life that God's Law required both of us to live, and I tell you as an eyewitness, he was perfect in every way; of that you can be certain! While it is true that the devil came to tempt him, his best and most aggressive attempts were futile, for Jesus was the living reality of righteousness."

"The prophet, Isaiah, gave a vivid description of God's wrath toward sin. It was a prophecy I witnessed firsthand in the death of my master, the Lord Jesus Christ. Come, Polycarp. Walk with me. Let me tell you what I saw," John said as he stood up.

We walked along the shore in silence for a few minutes, when he uttered the words, "It was God's will to shatter and crush him. It was for our stubborn determination to sin that God crushed the Lord. It was on account of us, Polycarp; you, me and all who need redemption. It was that harsh chastening that made peace possible between the Holy, One True God, and the rebellion of man.

Truly, he took upon himself our sin-diseased soul, and has borne the burden of the pain due to sin; yet mankind looked at him ruined by sin, punished by God, and put down. That was God placing on him our iniquities.[19] As I stood at the foot of the cross with the Lord's mother, Mary, I saw the agony of sin. His flesh was torn from his body to such a degree that you could not tell his identity unless you had witnessed the torture as I had. His clothes had been removed to humiliate him in front of his enemies. He was covered from head to toe in blood, and the ground beneath the cross was saturated. But that was only one side of it, for he was tormented spiritually when all the sins of people from generations past to those yet to come were laid on him, and I thought I would die when in anguish he cried out, 'My God, my God, why have you forsaken me?' Tears gushed from my eyes, and I bent over in grief at the reality that my sins were on him."

I looked up at John and saw tears streaming down his face too. I was confused, for though I was sad, it didn't seem to bother me to any great degree. "May I ask you a question?" I said to him.

He wiped the tears from his face and said, "Of course. What do you wish to ask?"

"If the other disciples abandoned him, why were you and Mary still present? Didn't you fear for your life?" He seemed a bit surprised by the question as if frustrated that I was changing the direction of the conversation.

"Well, yes, of course, we felt threatened. I'm sad to say that it wasn't courage that brought us to the foot of that cross. My family was close friends with a prominent family who knew the High Priest's family. When I fled from the Garden of Gethsemane, I ran to tell Mary what had transpired. We cautiously made our way to the home of Caiaphas, where my friend saw me and ushered us in with him. When word reached the authorities that we were present, we were ordered to accompany the Lord to Golgotha. The Jewish leaders wanted me to witness their power over the one who claimed to be their Messiah, and they wished to shame Mary for giving birth to him. It was when watching him suffer that the impact of Isaiah's prophecy hit me so hard, for everyone was treating Jesus as he was a leprous man; unclean and to be avoided at all costs. But my dear child, that's what makes the Lord's sacrifice

19. *Excerpts from Isaiah 53*

so profound. While we were being ruled by our sinfulness, God expressed his love towards us through the atoning work of his beloved Son. We love him, because he has always loved us first."[20]

"Polycarp, Everything he did was absolutely perfect; he could not sin. It was impossible! That's what makes our salvation so invincible. Jesus gave himself up to die the death you and I deserved. He gave up his life as the final and perfect requirement God's Law demanded. So then, when you have been birthed from above, your old nature has been killed and a new, perfect nature has replaced it. God has forgiven you of the sin of idolatry, and all other sins that you have, or still may commit in the remaining years of your life. Now permit me to clarify that such a reality never gives God's children the opportunity to keep willfully sinning; on the contrary, he has given us a new nature that grows within us so that we obey him in our actions. Our outer man, our fleshly body, will struggle and be tempted, but the new, inner man is trained by God's Spirit to resist the compulsions of the flesh."

"It is the work of the Holy Spirit of God to train, guide, and equip us for obedience. This is the great work of sanctification, whereby we are made holy as Jesus Christ is holy. What do you think of a God like that?" John continued. "Can you think of any gods of men who can change their followers to meet their standards of perfect acceptance? Perhaps I have said too much, but how could I ever stop? Have you understood what I am saying to you?" John asked.

I was moved by what John was describing. "What an uncommon trait among the gods. Is there such a magnanimous, kind, loving, and gracious God?" I said.

We sat down, and I thought on what he had been saying, and then asked; "Why do people resent and resist His kindness? Why do I resist him?"

John smiled and chuckled a bit, and said as he pointed his finger into my chest, "Yes, why do you? Can you see how dreadfully sin has blinded the hearts of the unbeliever, including you? It's like this, just as your mother purchased you out of slavery, so God through the life and death of Jesus Christ seeks to redeem you from the bondage of sin. Man cannot create such a god, nor

---

20. I John 4:19

can man make himself be a god like this. The man-made gods of men are as blotted and botched as their creators."

John stood up and stretched, and invited me to join him as we continued our walk along the rocky shoreline. "Polycarp, I wrote a book on Jesus as great news sent from God. In this Gospel, I pointed out near the beginning of the book why people resent and resist this wonderful work of God. He was declared to be 'Light of the world.' His nature and presence on the earth exposed the true heart-wickedness of those lost in trespasses and sins. 'Everyone who commits any evil does so because he despises the light of God, and refuses to enter the light for the light will expose the evil.'[21] For this reason, they hate the exposure of that light; in fact, they flee it if they can. These people are convicted by their sins, and dislike that discomfort and guilt it brings into their lives. Their contempt is displayed not only in their determination to sin, but also in how they profane the name of a loving Savior, and belittle his followers."

"I suppose that explains why I have been resisting this message. I'm trying to flee the light," I said.

"That's not all," John interjected. "I can't tell you how it fills me with joy to see how miserable God has made you regarding your sin."

"You're joyful over my misery," I quickly retorted.

"Only because it's a good type of misery," he replied. "What's happening to you right now is the inner work of the Holy Spirit of God. I think of it as a spiritual birthing process. The Holy Scriptures describe this work as the washing of renewal or spiritual birth. The old nature is being washed away, and a new, God-honoring nature is being instilled in you so that you can truly, with a sincere heart call on the name of the Lord and be saved, or as my Lord described it to a man named Nicodemus, you are being birthed from above."

"This is the grace of God saving your soul through the gift of faith in Him; he's giving you the ability to believe in him. Your struggle is one of attempted self-justification; your feeble faith is out of your desires and out of what little strength your will can muster. True belief is the first proof of God's gift of salvation. It is necessary to destroy the old nature. A man is not capable of will-

---

21. John 3:20

fully rejecting God one moment, and—out of that same depraved will—the next moment willfully accepting God out of deep love. How can a man hate and flee the light of God one moment, and out of that same godless nature suddenly love that Divine Light and run to it?[22] The old nature is not capable of producing the faith required to destroy itself. God gives grace, which is evidenced in the faith He gives that regenerates a new nature in us, and instantaneously reveals a newly born desire to call on the name of the Lord as proof of redemption."

I was comforted realizing that God was truly working in my heart, and hadn't abandoned me to my sinful destruction. John then added another dimension that I wasn't aware of, but it helped me understand why I struggled so.

"In my first letter to the churches, I explained that one of the reasons that Jesus, the Son of God came was to 'break up and destroy the works of the devil,'[23] and the most vital place we discover that great work is in our hearts. He destroys the many gods we have tucked away in our hearts. The agony you are experiencing is the devil's work being destroyed in you. Now you don't expect Satan to give up without a fight do you; even if he is destined to lose?"

"I suppose not," I whispered. I looked up into John's face and could see he was truly a man filled with delight in Jesus Christ. "John," I asked, "What was he like? What was it like to walk with Jesus and be taught by him?"

John paused for a moment as if to consider where he wanted to take his answer, and then continued. "Though he often spoke in parables and prophesied in words beyond my comprehension, he would spend countless hours teaching me, the other disciples and any willing to listen. He taught all the time, as we walked along the countryside up around the Sea of Galilee, the Mount of Olives, at the Temple in Jerusalem, or in synagogues. The size of the group didn't matter either. He declared the truth with power to thousands or to individuals like a Samaritan woman preparing to draw water from a well." As he shared, I could sense his growing enthusiasm with each word.

---

22. John 3:16-21

23. I John 3:8

"For those who believed in him, Polycarp, his words were life-changing. You could not help being changed for he was life itself, and it is like his words breathed life into those who followed him. What impressed me the most about his life was his constant patience, for his disciples were quite a vain and proud group. I can remember a rather embarrassing time when my own mother approached the Lord and requested that in his kingdom, my brother James be permitted to sit on his one side of his throne, and me on the other, of course."

He covered his face and shook his head, and said, "Oh, how I shudder to recall that thought today." He stopped speaking long enough to look at me with a sense of joy-producing tears and said, "He never lost sight of his mission due to our sin, and in his death we grew to understand that it was for those sins he died. Can you imagine how every day that he lived, he was confronted by the grotesque evil of mankind? He knew that it was that display of evil, for which he would have to suffer, and not only those living in his time, but for the sins of all generations past, from Adam and Eve, to you, to the thousands of generations yet to be born? It's a sobering illustration of the creation treating its Creator with hatred."

He surprised me when he turned and grabbed me by my shoulders and with no small measure of exuberance declared, "Even after his death, we all found ourselves unable to battle the doubts in our hearts. Some hid it better than others, but we all struggled. But did our doubts stop his plan? Never! He appeared glorified in our presence on many occasions after having arisen from the dead and that same resurrection power was soon to be poured out into our lives."

He slapped both of my shoulders and boasted, "There are no other god's of men that can make that claim. That's our savior, young man, and the One True God! I cannot contain my voice in exclaiming Jude's thoughts. 'Now to the One True God who has the power to keep you from stumbling, and with joy places you before his glorious presence as perfectly unblameable. To the only God, our Savior, through Jesus Christ our Lord, be exaltation, unparalleled majesty, unlimited power and mastery over all things before time began, now and for everlasting. Amen!'"[24]

---

24. Jude 24-25

To say I was a little stunned would be misleading. The depth of experience John had with Jesus was too deep a well for me to comprehend. John was greatly moved, and his understanding of the Lord was a giant to my feeble understanding. Feeling a bit perplexed, I asked John, "What am I supposed to do next?"

"The answer is not complex," John declared. "If God has opened up your heart and is breaking up the hardness; if you are experiencing the life-changing power of regeneration, then do what is natural; call on the name of the Lord and be saved. If God has given you the faith to believe in the Son of God for salvation, then you must act upon it."

At that very moment, I felt as if my heart had been set free. Tears of sadness, on the one hand, and tears of joy on the other flowed down my face as I became overwhelmed with God's loving-kindness and forgiveness of me. With a changed heart, I was free, and no longer felt the heavy hand of God's judgment on me. I looked over at John and smiled like I had never smiled before, and right there with the disciple whom Jesus loved, we talked to God together in prayer.

I lifted up my voice to God as one newly born, and said; "God, thank you for claiming me as one of your children, for I have resisted you, and I have tried to hide from your presence, but you found me and have changed me. As my mother bought me out of slavery and gave me her name, so you, in a greater way, have bought me and given me your name. You have spared me from your wrath and have destroyed the devil's work and claim on my life; thank-you for saving me. I am yours."

And with that John simply added, "Amen."

———◇◇———

Well, quite honestly, I was as excited as a disturbed beehive, and I could hardly wait to sprint home and tell Callisto, Decimus, and everyone else for that matter. John laughed with me and suggested I get on my way.

So off I went, like a runner eyeing the finish line. I don't know if my feet were even hitting the ground. It all seemed strange to me; I was the same, yet indescribably different. No longer a slave to sin, but now a slave to righteousness; what a happy condition! Powerful, godly passions and pure desires had awakening in me, and my heart wanted to drink in all of it. When I was purchased out of slavery, I was quite frightened by my new life, but now being purchased out of the bondage of sin, I was not afraid at all; quite the opposite.

As I ran through the front gate of my home, my family was already eating supper, but they could tell by my countenance that I had experienced a great change. I stopped at the table and told them that Jesus had saved me, and made me his own. Callisto stood up and hugged me as tears of happiness flowed down her cheeks. Decimus and Beatrice were also thrilled. As I sat down to eat, I hardly touched my food, and what I did try to eat, I'm not sure I even chewed as I attempted to describe to them my conversation with John, and how God overcame my blindness.

That evening, before going to bed, God brought to mind some Scriptures I had recently heard; the first was from John's Gospel. "Anyone who receives power to believe in the Son of God has eternal life. Anyone who does not obey the Son of God, can never receive the power of life, but rather finds himself trying to survive under God's wrath."[25] Next was Paul's exhortation to the Christians in Thessalonica: "God has not placed us aside for his wrath, but has preserved us like one safe-guarding his property, for salvation is only through our Lord Jesus Christ."[26] Those thoughts alone filled me with confidence, but my God added to it with one more thought before drifting off into sleep. I glanced up to the wall where I saw the moon casting its soft light on a piece of parchment Callisto had hung on my wall. "I am the light of the cosmos, those who walk with me will never walk in darkness, but will have the life-giving life."[27]

---

25. *John 3:36*

26. *I Thessalonians 5:9*

27. *John 8:12*

5

DON'T BE SEDUCED
BY THE WORLD

*If you belonged to this world, then the world would love
you as its own, but because you do not belong to the world,
for I have plucked you out of it, the world hates you.*
(John 15:19)

EVERYONE wanted to be friends with the popular Cæso
Erebus Drusilla, who we all called Erebus. He was a fifteen-
year-old boy and the son of a wealthy aristocrat. I liked him
because he was an audacious, fun-loving, and outgoing friend. But
it would be our friendship that would put my beliefs and love of
God to the test. Normally, a boy from such an upstanding family
would have little to do with a middle-class boy, especially one who
had been born a slave, but Erebus' father prided himself on being
open-minded and encouraged his family to do the same, with
restraint, of course. We met a few years ago when his father purchased parchment from Decimus for official government work.

Erebus was a year older than I, stocky and quite athletic. He
had a great personality and was very popular. If anyone ever
struck me as having it all—looks, intellect, charm, wealth and
popularity, it was undoubtedly Erebus. I had always envied him
and wished I could have been wealthy like him. He had everything a boy could wish for and more. He traveled to exotic places
throughout the Roman Empire, and had servants and slaves that
saw to all his needs. He even had a guard for the sole purpose of
protecting him. For the most part, however, the guard was used
by Erebus to hide his unruly activities from his Father. I would
like to think I was a better judge of character in choosing good
friends, but envy and jealousy have a way of stifling the voice of
common sense and reason.

I was well-warned about my friendship with Erebus and felt
the need to keep my friendship with him a secret. Everyone

who cared for me warned me about the negative influence he would have on my life because he was the dominant friend, and that whether or not I realized it, I wanted to be like him. I recall Decimus instructing me while at work that wrong friends will make my heart yearn for sin more than it normally does. Compromises will be easier, and folly will replace wisdom. I just figured that they didn't know him, and therefore were judging him. Plus, I told them that Erebus was interested in becoming a Christian, and that was the basis of our friendship. My biggest mistake in this debate was when I told John that Jesus spent time with sinners far worse than Erebus.

"Oh foolishness, you forget I was with Jesus when he was in the homes and company of sinners," John chided. "Jesus did not come to make friends, but to call sinners to repent. Do that long enough and let's see how many friends you pick up. Jesus came to minister, not to benefit from the lives of others, but to be that benefit, and to give his life as a price for the ransom of many sinners.[28] His visits were hardly a social call. They were soul-sick and needed a physician; he was that physician. When Jesus entered the house of the infamous, cheating Zacchaeus, he wasn't there to join the festivities. He went into that den of thieves to rescue Zacchaeus. Even Matthew, one of my fellow disciples was a hated tax-collector for Rome; he too was rescued by Jesus. He did not save any lost soul by living like that lost soul. He came as light intruding into their darkness and rescued them from eternal death even before they were aware of their need. I shall pray fervently for you, Polycarp. I will pray that the Lord opens your eyes to what is truly at risk in this friendship. Until Erebus sees Christ in you, you are as guilty of leading him astray as I'm afraid he is leading you astray."

I could see sadness and frustration in John's eyes. Before he left me, he turned and said, "Let me remind you of the warning given to us by the Apostle James; 'You adulterous people! Aren't you aware that to be friends with this world's godlessness puts you in opposition to God? If it is your wish to be a companion of this mindset, it makes you an enemy of God.'"[29]

---

28. *Matthew 20:28*

29. *James 4:4*

My face felt red hot, and I squirmed a bit due to my anger, and the shame of being rebuked. John had never spoken in a harsh manner to me. The problem was that while I had no reason not to believe him, I didn't want to believe him, and so chose to ignore his warning for the time being. At least, those were my intentions. But as I was to discover, there are some thoughts God won't let you forget.

Needless to say, I laid low for the next few days and tried to avoid talking at length with my mother, Decimus, or anyone else, and especially John. As you can guess, there was one person I did talk to, who fully sympathized with me and the harsh treatment I had received from others. Erebus agreed that I should be able to choose my own friends. He assured me that he would never get me into trouble, for his father would never tolerate any behavior that could in some way embarrass the family.

———— ◇◇ ————

Over the next several days, I would create excuses to leave the house and meet up with Erebus and his other friends. Being accepted in his circle of friends made me feel special, and I enjoyed the identity of being popular and well-liked. Furthermore, I didn't feel ungodly, nor for that matter did I encounter much guilt over my disobedience; Callisto and the rest just didn't understand. My intentions weren't evil; I just wanted friends. What I didn't realize was that if you aren't leading a friendship, then you're being led, which is not bad unless you're being led in the wrong direction.

I came to the crossroads of my Christianity and faced decisions that would affect my life-direction forever. The first problem was that I had chosen the wrong friends, who at the moment seemed like right friends. Add that to the fact that Erebus and his little gang were all bored, and the ingredients for disaster were in play. I observed that their conversation became reckless as the fellows spoke of their sinful acts as conquests, and I knew enough to realize the truth that they were being conquered by sin. But did such insight spare me? I wish it had. But like a fool walking toward the stocks, I played along and laughed on the outside while I groaned inside.

"I've got a secret," Erebus said. "We can't do it all together because it will draw attention."

"What's the secret?" asked one of the guys, then another, and soon all of us were begging Erebus to tell us his secret. His smile said it all; he controlled us.

"Be quiet you idiots, and I will tell you," he said. Then in a whisper, as if forcing us to lean in and listen he said, "Yesterday I was walking past the ceremonial baths outside the Temple of Diana. I saw a man sneak out from behind some bushes, so I waited for him to leave, and then I went in behind them and discovered his little secret. There's a gap in the wall, and you can see into the ladies' bath."

Wicked laughter ensued chained by wanton lust. I pretended to laugh, but the reality was that a monster had awakened within my soul for which I was unprepared to confront. While I understood that lust was a natural struggle in the flesh, left unchecked, it would become a bonfire in my soul and spread into a raging forest fire consuming my virtue. The boys begged to be first, but the enemy of my soul had his plan at work, and Erebus was the tool.

"You all will get your chance; I promise. But Polycarp gets to be first," he said. All eyes were on me, and I blushed, which, of course, prompted an outburst of laughter and teasing.

"What do you think of that, Polycarp?" Erebus suggested with a mischievous grin.

"Um, well, sure," I stammered. An inferno raged within me unlike anything I had ever experienced before; a strange blending of guilt and pleasure. You would think that the guilt would have stifled the pleasure, but I found the opposite to be true; guilt made the pleasure stronger. I knew it was wrong, but an inner instinct sounded an alarm as a city about to be overtaken by the enemy. I quickly mastered the skill of trying to look normal as war was unleashed in my soul. I wanted to see what Erebus had discovered, but I desired to flee it as well. It felt like my eyes were on fire and could only be quenched by looking.

They teased and taunted me like they knew something about me I didn't know. They wouldn't have teased each other this way. Why would they jest at my expense? Angry at the embarrassment they were causing, I scolded them; "Why are you guys mocking me; what's it to you?"

"Leave him alone," Erebus interrupted. "Just because he's a Christian doesn't mean he can't have a little, innocent fun."

That statement jolted me. I was a Christian, but at that moment in my life I wished I weren't, I must shamefully admit. Now I was being attacked on two fronts: lust was raging and hypocrisy was advancing. Erebus added, "You Christians are strange. I worship many gods who are powerful, who can destroy other gods, and become even greater gods, but you worship a God, who was a criminal and crucified as he deserved to be by the great and powerful Romans. Who would want to be part of a little group like that? What did your God ever do for you?"

I stood there speechless. I felt betrayed by my friends, seduced, unfulfilled and rejected by God. "I wish I had never been born; I wish I were dead!" I thought to myself.

Erebus continued to break me down. One sinister plot led to another when Erebus picked up a stone and started to etch a drawing on a secluded section of the city wall.

"What are you drawing?" asked one the boys.

"I'm going to draw a picture that will help Polycarp see how stupid his God really is. Come on, all of you join me.

"Someone start drawing the head of an ass up here," he demanded. "I'm going to draw a man's body under the head, and someone draw a man kneeling with his arm raised as if hailing his God. Polycarp, you draw a criminal's cross below the ass's head."

As I picked up a stone to join them in their engraving, it suddenly hit me what they were drawing. The ass represented Jesus, and the man kneeling was the Christian demonstrating his allegiance. But did I stop? No, I'm ashamed to admit. While I did not find satisfaction in this shameful act, the power of my peers over me was greater than my commitment to Jesus Christ. My heart filled with grief for God had never done anything harmful to me, yet here I was mocking him with my friends. Never in my life have I felt so devastated and stunned by my actions.

Finally, the drawing was complete, and we all stepped back to look at the graffiti. The guys laughed and jeered, and even bowed down to add to their hysteria. Erebus looked over at me and with an inquisitive look and raised eyebrows pointed to the drawing and said, "Behold your God, Polycarp; the crucified criminal!"

My heart sank within me. Never before had I ever experienced such grief in my heart. Sin ambushed me and now was making me face Jesus Christ, whom I had discovered as precious, but now relegated to profanity and mockery. And there I stood, offering no defense or rebuke.

The thought that I was under a spiritual attack had not occurred to me. However, God gave grace even though I didn't realize it at that time. You see, I was experiencing deep conviction, which in its own way is a wonderful gift of God when understood in the light of his grace. My conscience was under assault, and my new spiritual nature was resisting. My soul was a battlefield where the prize was my affections, loyalty, and virtue.

Erebus threw the stone in his hand at the graffiti we had drawn, and turned toward us all and said, "Can you all see, this is the God of the Christians; a criminal and a Jew. I will never worship such a ridiculous deity. I believe in me, in my abilities, and my dreams. Someday I may even run for the Senate, be elevated to Caesar and become a god myself." Some of the boys declared; "Hail Erebus, Sovereign Caesar." And then they of course, mockingly bowed as if to pay him homage.

"Polycarp, is Jesus, whom you call the Christ, your sovereign Lord or is Caesar?" asked Erebus with no little degree of arrogance. All of this seemed surreal. I just wanted friends, but here I was with my friends denying and mocking Jesus Christ.

"Was I truly one of God's elect, a follower of Christ?" I thought to myself. I crossed the line in my sin which now opened the door for other, more dreadful iniquities to invade with the assignment of taking me deeper into evil and trapping me in worse transgressions.

"Hey, Erebus," yelled out one of our companions, "When are you going to take us down to the baths?"

Erebus' demeanor changed as he looked at me for he was still awaiting my answer. He glared into my eyes as if to see if he would be able to drag me a little lower, and obviously seeing vulnerability in my countenance replied that now would be a good time.

At that moment, it would seem out of nowhere; a thought popped into my head. It was a passage from Pastor Timothy's exhortation from the previous Sunday. "Everyone who professes me before men by their words or actions that they belong to me, I will, in the same way, declare them before my Father. Whoever denies me before men by words or actions, that they don't belong to me, I will in the same way deny them before my Father. Don't permit yourself to assume that I came to bring peace. I did not come to bring peace, but rather a sword."[30]

"This is a real war," I whispered.

"What did you say," inquired Erebus. "I couldn't hear you. Do you want to go or not?"

Then, as if a surge of strength came over me; strength I had neither asked for or was looking for gave me the ability to decline. Immediately sin lost its grip in my soul, and strength replaced weakness. I asked God for help, and all I heard in my mind was "run!" So, like Joseph, before Potiphar's wife, I ran away from their scorn and laughter. When I had run far enough where I could no longer hear their jeering, I stopped and slumped on a nearby log. I didn't weep, though I probably should have; I just sat there telling myself how stupid I was, and that I could not possibly be a follower of Christ. I felt like I needed to talk to someone, and of course my friend, John came to mind. However, I questioned in my soul how I was going to explain what I had done to one who took the sufferings of Jesus so deeply? I stood up and said out loud, "he'll probably hate you too."

I found the elderly Apostle where I figured he would be; in a side room of the home he rented. I just walked in and slouched down in a chair near his table, and just sighed hard with a sense of dread.

"You look like a man with a lot on his shoulders," he observed.

I wasn't quite ready to confess, so I adjusted the facts of my story a bit in order to gauge John's reaction. "I am stunned at what my friends drew on the city wall," I said.

"Oh, what did they draw," he asked.

"They drew a picture of an ass hanging on a cross with a Christian worshipping in front of it," I declared with an air of judgment in my voice.

To my surprise the expression on John's face didn't change. He stared at me with gentle eyes at first and then said, "No sinner will be held guiltless. I am not surprised to hear it, but is that all you wanted to tell me?"

---

30. Matthew 10:32-34

By now I could not look him in his eyes, so I stared aimlessly into the floor, and ever so cautiously as not to arouse his suspicion I added, "Well, there was someone who says they were a Christian. He also drew part of the graffiti."

"Then I would imagine his heart is truly broken right now, wouldn't you agree?" He suggested.

"Here was my chance," I thought; John seemed compassionate, and I felt a great need to bear my soul. Then in almost a whisper I said, "He is;" and then with what seemed like an eternal pause I added, "I am."

"I would be lying if I said I wasn't disappointed, Polycarp," he replied. "However, I have seen worse. You must come to understand that the godless world, which is under the control of the devil, truly desires to reclaim you, and all Christians for that matter. Satan doesn't want to lose any of his children. He is ambitious in his attempts to claim all creation as his own. We observed this through this godless world with all its vain delights, sinful pleasures and excessive self-love, which resents all those it has lost to Jesus Christ. The godless world lives to seduce simple Christians and persecute the dedicated ones."

As he got up from his chair at his study table, he walked over and took a seat on a bench closer to me and inquired, "Your friend is Erebus, am I correct?"

"Yes" is all I said, still looking at the cracks in the well-worn marble floor.

"He needs the Savior too, and so does his father and mother, whom I have had the opportunity to share Christ with on a few occasions, though they are quite resistant to the gospel. They are a very wealthy family, and it can be difficult for the rich to see their true spiritual need and desperate condition. Did you and your friends do anything else?"

Finally, I was able to look up at him and filled him in on their plans to spy on bathers at the bath house.

With a little more urgency he pressed further, "Did you go with them?" I shook my head no.

John leaned back in his chair and let out a big sigh of relief. "I imagine you don't know how closely you came to being ensnared today, lad. The Proverbs of the great King Solomon tell us that it is a fool who goes about being led by his lusts after immoral pleasures. 'He is like an ox going into the slaughter house, or a silly man who takes his punishment with no regard until he experiences the true pain of his decisions. He is like a bird that is ensnared, but since it has the bait it coveted, it has no regard for that fact that it will soon lose its life.'[31] Your determination in having a friend like Erebus may cost you your soul; is this what you want?"

The crossroads of my life became clearer at the moment, and it would do no good to say what I thought John wanted to hear. I can't hide my intentions from him; it seemed like he could peer into my soul anyway. "I like Erebus, but he isn't worth losing my soul," I replied.

"What is it that makes this friendship so appealing to you? Your desire for his friendship puzzles me," John entreated.

To be honest, I wasn't exactly sure why I wanted his friendship either, but I attempted an answer. "I suppose I like the feeling of being accepted by him and by those who see me with him."

John leaned forward and placed his hand on my arm. "I understand how acceptance and rejection makes us feel, but God's Word is clear in its warning. 'What possible advantage is it for a man to gain the affection of the whole world but destroy his own soul in the process?'[32] No friendship outside the Lord Jesus Christ is worth that cost. As I see it, friendships are grown where you all are going in the same direction, and can help, encourage, and protect all involved. Friendships are not to be reckless, but constructive and purposeful where you are building each other up and improving each other's character. If this isn't that inner, guiding principle of all the friends you hold, then what direction is it actually going, and what good will be derived from it? If friends are not making each other better, then they're fulfilling the role of our spiritual enemy by tearing down what is good and ruining what had potential. You may be sincere in your desires to be the friend of Erebus, but I have heard nothing that indicates he is interested in being a friend to you."

"While I am hardly a follower of the Greek philosophers, I am familiar with how Aristotle described friendship; it is one soul dwelling in two bodies. Polycarp, our friends reveal our true heart desires. If sin, worldly-seduction and inflated pride is what you seek, it will be displayed in the friends you choose. If impurity

31. Proverbs 7:22-23

32. Mark 8:36

is your heart-desire, you'll choose friends that will help accommodate that desire. If you love lukewarmness, even though God despises such a condition, then you'll choose friends that, while never aggressively pursuing the pleasures of sin, will certainly have no real interest in God either. Such people only want heaven, but do not seek after Christ. If Jesus himself were not going to be in heaven, that wouldn't bother them at all so long as they can go to heaven. Lukewarm Christians want the pleasures of eternal life without Jesus Christ. God would have us either hot or cold, but he is repulsed by lukewarmness, as you should be too."

What John was saying made sense to me, but I didn't know how to change, for a change in friends wouldn't necessarily change my heart; though it wouldn't hurt, either. After thinking for a moment, I looked over at John, whom I would come to discover as the truest expression of a friend, and asked him, "How can I change my heart in order to change my friends?"

"Oh, that's easier than you think," John exclaimed. "I'm sure you've heard from your spiritual friends that we obey by faith, and then understanding follows. Many erroneous ones wait for God to change them first in order to obey. You, however, must put down the old fleshy desires which have been dictating your direction, and by faith determine to obey Callisto and the other spiritual-investors in your life. You'll see that within your new, spiritual nature are those discerning desires you seem to be missing. They've been there all the time, but their voice has been muffled by your fleshly desires. Let me explain it this way; God is pouring out his grace into your life, but instead of building virtue towards godly growth, it constantly has to spend its power withstanding the corruptions of your lusts. Many Christians never excel in spiritual maturity, nor fall into great sins as we would see them, but instead never change in either direction. This mindset produces spiritual decay."

"So this is conducting my life by faith and not just by what I perceive with my eyes?" I asked.

"You are quite right," John rejoined. "It's by faith that God preserves our souls, and by the neglect of faith we introduce spiritual decay in its place. Let me pray with you and ask our faithful God to protect you and give you wisdom."

Together, we bowed our heads, and resting his hand on my shoulder he talked to God about me. "Lord of all Creation, out of the splendor of your holiness and through your perfect sacrificial Lamb, you have declared us to be holy, exclusively yours, belonging to no other. You have called us your friends and have made us your family. As you are fully aware, we live in a godless world that thrives on seducing your servants and seeks to marginalize our calling and our faith through the snares of sinful desires, godless friends, and evil actions. I never cease to be amazed at how you protect your servants, and I would ask of you to protect Polycarp from worldly enticements. If he has your love in him, which I believe he does, then this will be a natural response he has yet to discover. Persuade him to discover your strength-building desires alive in him so that instead of being swayed by friends, he would wield your power in the lives of all he encounters and walk in the strength of your joy. As my Lord Jesus prayed on the night of his betrayal, I pray for my dear young friend: 'I have imparted to him your word, and he has discovered that the world hates him because of it and because he is not part of this godless world system, just as I am not. I'm not asking that you would take him out of the world but that you would protect him from the wicked one. Help him to know that he is not part of the godless world, just as your Son Jesus was not of the godless system. Set him apart from the world by your truth, for your word is truth. As your servant Jesus was sent into the world, and as he sent me into the world, so I send Polycarp into this world.'[33] To you, my Lord Jesus Christ, my God, be the glory throughout our lives and all of your servants in every succeeding generation. Amen!"

33. John 17:14-18

6

TRAIN YOURSELF
FOR GODLINESS

*Godliness is of value in every way, as it holds promise
for the present life and also for the life to come.
(I Timothy 4:8)*

GOD revealed an inner work taking place in my life, and though I did not fully understand it, I observed that changes were being made in my heart revealing itself in the awakening of new spiritual desires. Among these new desires was an unexplainable longing to be a minister of the Lord. I had always assumed that I would follow Decimus as a parchmenter, but as each day passed my passion for preaching and teaching the Word of God grew greater. My heart's desires were being rearranged by God, old desires moved into insignificant places, and new desires brought into prominence. Though I was only fifteen, John set out to discern whether or not the Holy Spirit had imparted to me the spiritual gifts to be a pastor and teacher. He planned to oversee my discipleship with the assistance of godly leaders in the church who would aid in my preparation, spiritual growth, and my development in godliness. The church was to sponsor my training, but in return I had to fulfill work obligations, and eventually ministry services to the Lord's people.

On the next Lord's Day, as the congregation assembled, I found myself eager to listen and learn as Timothy declared the Truth of the Word. As he spoke, I found myself stirred by his testimony of perseverance and faithfulness, for it had never occurred to me that he had ever struggled over anything. What he shared on that Sunday clarified my understanding of God's work in my life.

"I remember as if it were yesterday," Timothy reminisced. "I was new here in Ephesus, when I received a letter; an alarming letter from my dear friend and mentor, the Apostle Paul. It was his second and final letter to me, for he was under house arrest in Rome. This letter was sent to me just days before his execution by Emperor Nero. By the time I received it, he was no longer a resident of earth, but as a citizen of Heaven, he had taken up his eternal residency in the presence of our Lord and Savior Jesus Christ."

Sadness stirred in his voice, and he stopped speaking for a moment to allow the welling up of emotion to subside. After a short period of silence, he cleared his throat and proceeded.

"You can imagine the impact this letter has had on my soul these past several years. Even to this day, these words still fill me with spiritual power, and give me grace and joy to obey and do God's will. What you may not know is that he wrote the letter because I wavered in my faith. I was on the verge of defecting from the Gospel of Jesus Christ. Don't misunderstand me; I was not abandoning the Lord for this godless world-system. My challenge is that I struggled under the pressure from other church leaders, false leaders I might add, to abandon the New Covenant established by my Lord Jesus Christ in exchange for the Law; the works of personal righteousness."

With added intensity, Timothy continued: "Men were abandoning the gospel that Paul and the Apostles taught; the Gospel of justification by faith alone in Jesus Christ. Many churches were defecting from the security of Christ for what they felt was greater security in self-righteous works without the empowerment of the Holy Spirit, and I was strongly tempted to join with them. They pressured me since I was one of Paul's apprentices, and my inner weakness stirred additional doubts as to the effectiveness of Christ's work on my behalf; this nearly led to my ruin. These false leaders still live today; perhaps you know some of them. They establish congregations not built on the justifying work of Christ, but seek to build on a foundation of self-righteousness too, and they insist on being lords over the flock of God where they are the interpreters of Scripture and not the laymen. Nicolaitans!" he shouted. "These are the devoted followers of the apostate and former Deacon, Nicolaus. They control the people by making their misguided followers dependent on them. Let us not forget how Peter exhorted pastors; 'that we are not to be lords over the flock, but examples to them.'"[34]

---

34. I Peter 5:3

"Paul was aware of my struggle, and that is why he wrote this second epistle to me. As God has used it in my life, I desire that it benefit your spiritual growth, and edify all who read it. I have faithfully exhorted you these past weeks from the text given to Paul by the Holy Spirit, I now long to bring you into what I believe was the primary principle of his letter to me. My thoughts to you this day are these: 'For these reasons my son, find your power in the grace that is in Christ Jesus alone. And the teachings you have heard me deliver to others, those same lessons you should commit to faithful men who will carry the work on. For these reasons then, endure the hardships of spiritual growth like a resolved soldier facing battle. No man contending for victory allows himself to be distracted by anything not associated with victory and the strategy of his superior officer.'"[35]

"Many of you may see this illustrated this week as Ephesus hosts the Roman Games. You will see highly skilled athletes determined to win; famous heroes of Rome are competing for the prize. Don't be captivated by their fame, for they strive after a temporal crown. We, however, are to strive for a permanent and eternal crown. Does our commitment to the pursuit of godliness, for example, compare to their pursuit of fleeting glory?"

That question was like a spear being shoved into my heart. "If I were skilled at anything, it was the art of vacillation," I thought to myself. My spiritual nature longed to be victorious in the fight of faith, but my flesh pulled for the pleasure and ease of being nothing more than an ordinary cosmopolite. Today was different though; I felt as if God was growing me, building up determination, a renewed sincerity, and godly desire. It seemed like a sleeping giant was being awakened in my soul. As Timothy led the congregation in his closing benediction, I prayed that God would make me a warrior of the cross. I wanted to be a soldier of Christ who lived to deliver the souls of those deceived by man's gods, and who are choked lifeless by the cares of this world.

Later that day, I asked my uncle if I could read his copy of Paul's second letter to Timothy. Being a parchmenter, Decimus had set out to add the works of the Apostles and church leaders to his collection of sacred writings. As I read the parchments, I found the spot where Timothy had preached earlier that day, and

---

35. *II Timothy 2:1-4*

I read further. The visualization of the soldier, athlete and farmer captured my imagination; all in the context of faithful Christians and zealous overseers of God's people. I felt an excitement welling up in my soul as I saw the analogy between the vigilant soldier and my need for spiritual training and alertness. I saw the striving athlete who wins without cheating and my need to contend in this race of faith. I observed the patient farmer and how laboring against what he cannot control, patiently endures until the harvest. I was being grown and developed by God for the harvest of the fruit of his Spirit. The longer my eyes pored over those words, the greater my spiritual hunger and thirst. I wanted these things. I wanted to be that soldier, that athlete, that farmer. I wanted to be a faithful man. I wanted to be a shepherd in God's flock!

I went to bed that evening, barely able to sleep due to this new spiritual awakening. I felt like the shepherd-boy David ready to go out and defeat the mighty Goliath.

In the morning, I awoke to the refreshing discovery that I still desired to grow in my spiritual walk with God. My first thoughts fell on the first Psalm of King David. I can't explain it, but it's like the Holy Spirit put it in my mind, and said; "Think on this!" I was impressed with the thought of the blessed man and how everything he did grew and prospered. Everything pressed upward to God, even in the face of opposition. He was a truly prosperous man, for his life was one of forward movement, growth, and fruitfulness. I realized that this was the fruit of endurance, and I wanted it to be the priority of my life. I took the time to recall the promises of God to grow me, and I prayed for courage to stand for Him.

No one could have conjured up a more beautiful day. I saw a real and living spiritual nature at work in me. As I stepped outside, it was still early and the sun was just rising over the mountain. There was a song in my heart, and a cool northwestern breeze was blowing off the Aegean Sea that made the temperature just right. It was about to get crowded around our town with all visiting guests and athletes. As the capital of the Roman Province, Ionia, and as one of the favorite ports of entry for the affluent and aristocrats, the honor fell to the citizens to prepare for what always proved to be a great spectacle. So I wanted to walk and talk with the Lord before the hustle and bustle of the day.

As I walked near the Roman fortress at the entrance to the town, I observed the soldiers already drilling and preparing for a surge of people coming into the city. My mind was drawn to Timothy's words as I observed the focus of a warring soldier being trained not to be distracted by trivial concerns of the ordinary man. As I stood there, observing from a distance, I saw a shadow moving up from behind me. As I turned, I was startled by the towering figure standing over me. His presence intimidated me, and I gulped out of nervousness.

"You must admit; they are a very impressive sight," he suggested as he surveyed the training men.

"They are impressive. I certainly would never want to fight against them," I stammered.

The Centurion smiled for a moment and replied, "That's the idea now, isn't it?" What you see before you are the First Cohort, of the Fifth Maniple, which is attached to the Sixth Legion, stationed in Judæa, and serves under the command of the great General, Gaius Licinius Mucianus."

"Do you command these men," I inquired.

"Indeed, I am the Primus Pilus,"[36] he clarified. "The First Cohort is the largest of the ten that make up the Legion, and I am the senior Centurion."

"How many men do you command," I replied.

"What you see are four hundred and eighty of Rome's most fierce warriors on that field, and that's excluding the officers" he claimed.

"My officers and I drill them to ingrain right discipline, right practices, and correct wrong actions. These drills are not for punishment but are necessary to prepare the soldier for success, though some of my men may disagree. The goal is to have a proud, alert and obedient soldier. The better my men perform in their drills, the more predictable they'll be in the crucible of battle. We want our enemies to think twice before engaging us in battle; wouldn't you agree?"

---

36. *The senior centurion of the legion and commander of the first cohort*

"Yes," I said as he walked down the embankment from where we were standing, and in Latin he began shouting out orders, and the soldiers responded without hesitation or any sign of confusion.

"Ad signum" he shouted, and the soldiers immediately gathered behind their standard and stood in perfect formation.

"Mandata captate," was ordered, and the soldiers snapped to attention awaiting their orders and objectives for the day.

The next order was given: *"Ad gladium, clina,"* and all the soldiers in one fluid motion turned smartly to the right. *"Ovete,"* and they marched straight and in perfection formation to the pulse of the drum until the next command, *"Ad scutum, clina,"* and they unhesitatingly turned to the left.

The drills went on for some time with other commands, like *"Accelero,"* and they all sped up, or *"Tarda"* and they all slowed down.

What got my attention was when the Centurion called out, *"Ad aciem,"* and like an impregnable wall, the soldiers formed a battle line.

With unfailing confidence, they stood awaiting the next command: *"Gladium stringate!"* Every soldier simultaneously drew his sword. I waited with baited breath at what they would be commanded to do next, and I wasn't disappointed.

"Parati, percute!" And with that four hundred and eighty, fully armored, shield-carrying, sword-wielding soldiers charged without even breaking formation. It was an overwhelming display of the discipline of controlled power.

"What enemy could stand in front of such discipline, strength, and fearlessness?" I whispered to myself. The only way I could think of describing it was a fast moving wall of death against the enemy. For a moment, it made me proud to be a Roman.

On the one hand, their discipline and skill made them enviable. Who wouldn't want to be a soldier? I could just picture myself decked out in all that shining armor. But, on the other hand, I was a fully armored soldier of Jesus Christ. I had the breastplate of righteousness, and the helmet of salvation, and I attacked hell with the sword of the Spirit. Such a thought defies human reason, but with growing faith, I was exhilarated with a real desire to wage a strong and disciplined warfare against the devil, the fake gods he created, and the power they possessed over mankind. I didn't want to destroy men, but like my Lord Jesus

Christ, be used to destroy the works of the devil that for centuries have ruined the lives of so many. Hell has claimed many thoughtless souls, and I wanted to invade the territory of the enemy and snatch as many as I could from the gates of Hell.

This sight truly inspired me. I didn't have to be afraid of Erebus or anyone for that matter. They were captive and needed to be set free. My job was to be a trained soldier of the cross; to learn the commands and to develop the discipline of immediate obedience. Such skill is necessary for overcoming fear, intimidation, and the feelings of inadequacy. The splendid reality was I didn't have to sign up; as a child of the King, I was already in training. I had the strength, armor, and a host of spiritual weapons. However, I didn't know what I had, or how to use it. That's when my thoughts turned to the attitude I need in my training. I need patient endurance like a soldier being properly trained. But this thought, while inspiring, left me overwhelmed; for I was truly ignorant of being a soldier. In my imagination, it's easy to be fierce, but in my imagination, I never lost a battle, either. I needed something to grow my understanding for effective spiritual warfare.

Later that week, after completing some work for Decimus, I went to see John. God was using him to shape my daily walk as a follower of Christ.

"Polycarp, you're here," John remarked as I entered his study chamber. "You will find today's training a bit strange, I'm afraid, but I promise that it will be quite illustrative. Perhaps you know Ezra, an elderly gentleman who is part of our congregation. About my age, I believe."

"Yes," I replied. "Isn't he a farmer?"

"Indeed, and he needs help with the harvest," John said, "and I volunteered us. I hope you don't mind."

We rode for a while in the cart out to the farm where we met up with Ezra and other workers. John seemed rather amused as he picked up a basket and said to me, "Follow me; we have to gather up the rewards of the harvest." We walked through the tall stalks of wheat, and John took the opportunity to make this my classroom.

"Polycarp, there are many illustrations given in the Word that describe the great responsibility of being an overseer in the Lord's church. Being in this garden reminds me of one of the greatest lessons. We're here picking vegetables and fruit because a farmer practiced patient endurance. As a farmer, the pastor plants and waters the seed of the Word in the hearts of man, and like all growing things, it is God who supplies the growth, not the farmer. A good farmer must plow the ground, plant and water, weed and cultivate. He must protect the tender plants from damaging insects or disease. He cannot control the weather or the success of the crop; all he can do is endure the elements and grow the plants. Over time, after dedicated work, he can begin to see the rewards of his labor. It may have been a bad year, yet if he has the potential for harvest, he is rewarded. It's tough work, for circumstances beyond his control, like a drought, may destroy his entire garden, but he must go back again planting, watering, and cultivating with the hope of a future harvest. He cannot quit. Weak men quit. Strong men find the strength and persevere. Too many people are relying on that farmer for the rewards of the harvest. Just as a farmer is rewarded by the yield, so he can make it available to others for their benefit."

We had reached the end of a long row next to an unplowed knoll which John said beckoned him to climb in order to survey the farm. From the top, we could view the entire farm toward the fence that divided the pasture from the wheat, the barns, and the vineyards.

Something captured John's attention, and he told me to follow him to the vineyard. "Look at this vineyard," he said. So I looked.

"It seems like a normal vineyard to me," I replied.

"No, you're not looking. Look at the clusters of grapes. How numerous and plump. Notice the trellises upon which they rest.

"John, I don't understand what you want me to see," I replied.

He smiled and said, "That's obvious. The farmer doesn't spend his time on the fence or trellises. He builds the necessary structures, but his attention is on the cultivation of the plant. No true farmer is famous for the structures, the barns, fences, or trellis, but on the produce of the harvest. However, it's easy to get focused on these. A great barn doesn't equal a great harvest, nor does a beautiful trellis produce delicious grapes. Structures are easy, and can appear more impressive than the fruit. Focus on the fruit, Polycarp, and don't get distracted by the structures."

We continued walking along the path around the vineyard. "Understand what I am saying," John instructed. "A farmer must plow the ground, and that is not easy, for rocks, stumps, and other impediments make the work hard. After the seed is planted, then the farmer watches as growth takes place. It's a joy to see the growth, but even growth doesn't mean immediate harvest. It takes great patience to plan, plow, plant, cultivate, protect, and prepare the crop for harvest. Working with people and their spiritual growth is very much the same idea. It takes time and patience. You can't rush growth or enjoy premature fruit. Keeping people busy is not fruit. Keeping them in the Word is what you must do. They must see the living word. They must taste and see that the Lord is good. They must grow in grace and in the knowledge of the Lord Jesus Christ. In addition to this, you must be an example of that growth. Your preaching must prepare the listener to go and receive from the Word of God the nutrients necessary for growth. And yes, you will experience disappointments as you see people grow in some measure, but fail to grow fruit. These are people who neglect the Word; who neglect the growth of the Gospel and the work of grace in their hearts. These are the ones that you must watch for and devote much of your effort. In the latter part of Isaiah's prophecy, the Lord declared that he wants to call His people 'Oaks of righteousness; that which the Lord has planted, in order that He may be glorified.'[37] So you see, even at the harvest, the farmer cannot technically take the credit, nor does he wish to. The harvest is his reward; the blessings of God on his behalf."

The week was full of spiritual lessons. Among them was how the Lord uses the sermons presented on the Lord's Day and the various studies throughout the week. I realized that these spiritual messages were divine agenda-setters. The application of these exhortations wasn't hinged to my ability to apply them, but served as an insight into how God would be applying them in my life over the following days. Attention to his work and the joy of participation in sanctification was to be my focus. Every week thereafter, I set my heart to discover how God would make me a living illustration of what I was being taught from the Word of

---

37. Isaiah 61:3

God; both in the struggle and the victory of growth. John called such a focus expositional listening; living out the meaning of the text. It's listening to be directed by the Word and not be content with just knowing what it says.

———————◇◇———————

As I walked back home, I thought how God had taught me about the soldier and the farmer. "How would he teach me about the athlete?" I wondered. I didn't have to wonder too long, just two days.

From the back of the shop, I heard Decimus warmly greeting a customer. There seemed to be some commotion, so I went in to investigate. As I walked in, I saw Tychicus, one of the original seven deacons from Jerusalem, and now an itinerant preacher working closely with John here in Ephesus. He traveled all over Asia and Greece to help small congregations and pastors needing assistance. I didn't know him well, but he was good friends with my uncle. I also noticed that he was not alone.

As I entered the front of the shop, Decimus had just instructed one of his employees to bring out the parchments set aside for Tychicus, when I caught his attention. "Ah, Polycarp, I was just about to send for you, come on in, son," he said.

I walked over toward him and smiled at Tychicus, who reached out and putting his hand on my shoulder said, "Good to see you again, young man. John tells me you desire to join the ranks of the Lord's shepherds."

"Yes," I replied. "I think so."

Then stepping aside, Tychicus extended his hand behind him to invite the other man who was with him. "Well, Polycarp, let me introduce you to a young man who is seeking the same."

Stepping out in front of me was a man I would guess in his twenties. "This is Galeo Malleolus Atilia," Tychicus declared, "maybe you have heard of him. He has raced in the Roman games, but he has discovered the saving grace of our Lord and had astounded the world by his decision to leave the sport and to devote himself to another kind of race."

"Have you run in the great circus in Rome?" I eagerly inquired.

"I have many times. I ran in front of Caesar and members of the Imperial Senate," Galeo answered.

"Did you get to meet the Emperor?" I persisted. He chuckled a little and replied, "Yes, and it wasn't what you might expect. He was accommodating, but also condescending. We were nothing more than the entertainment. I think it's the gladiators and charioteers who capture his true interests."

"Have you stopped racing, or will you be running in the Ephesus games?" I continued.

"No, I don't race professionally any longer," he replied.

His answer puzzled me. "Why did you quit?" I asked.

"I don't expect many will understand, but the reasons were simple. I suppose the best way to describe it is that I have a sincere desire to serve my Lord with all my energies directed to Him, not to mention that the immorality and idolatry associated with the Roman Games are beyond what my conscience will allow. God has changed my interests. I can't explain it, nor do I want to change it. It was Tychicus here, who introduced me to the work of redemption by Jesus when we met during the Athens games about a year ago. From my perspective, our meeting was an accident, but as I understand it, God had it planned before the foundations of the world were established. I can only imagine what my life would have become without being found by the One True God of all."

"How does your family feel about your decision," Decimus asked.

"I come from a wealthy Roman family, and they still will not speak to me. They feel as if I have blemished their name. My father told me that the involvement in religion is a good thing if it elevates you in society; it's a tool, but not a lifestyle. They know little of Christianity except that Emperor Nero accused them of setting Rome ablaze years ago, and that some of their slaves are followers of Christ. My father says that it's a poor man's religion. I pray for my family and hope that someday they will discover the glories of Christ and that my life will serve as a witness of his grace to them. I run a new race now."

"That seems like a great sacrifice," Decimus said.

"Not really," Galeo replied. "How could being saved from God's wrath be a sacrifice?"

As he was talking, I realized that I had never looked at that way. In the scope of eternity, we never give up anything when we claim Christ.

The next day held a surprise. Decimus greeted me at breakfast and informed me that Galeo wished to take me to see some of the games today if I was interested.

"Yes, of course; yes!" I replied.

A couple hours later, I found myself entering the stadium with Galeo. It was exciting to be with him, for he had access to areas not normally open to spectators. We walked all around and talked to many athletes who knew him. Some tried to understand why he left the sport, but others weren't as understanding, and ridiculed him. I was impressed with how he responded to his critics. He didn't seem threatened or even offended, but was understanding and even sympathetic towards them, not in a demeaning or haughty way, but as one concerned as if he knew that they were the one's suffering.

The day was spectacular. It was impressive seeing the strength, agility, speed, and skill of these athletes. I appreciated, however, the godly perspective Galeo shared with me throughout the day.

One thought in particular stood out to me. After we had watched the race that was his event, I asked if he missed participating.

He replied, "Yes, to some degree. But it's a fleshly impulse, and not spiritually driven. I have a new drive, and it's captured in the Words of the Apostle Paul: 'Train yourself for godliness. While there is some benefit in training your body, training yourself for godliness is advantageous in all things.'[38] These men you have seen on this sports field today stretch every bodily effort for their sport, but what do they get? They obtain fading applause and a crown that withers. While that reward is fulfilling for the moment, it soon fades away. I want that incorruptible crown and the eternal glory of knowing Jesus Christ. Understand Polycarp, these are not normal human desires, but they must be new, normal spiritual desires. To desire anything less as a Christian, is to be deceived."

"Callisto has often told me that we must practice righteousness like people would develop a skill or build a structure," I said.

"She is right," Galeo replied. "It's not drudgery, but a joy for the follower of Christ. It is done in what I call my gymnasium of

---

38. I Timothy 4:7-8

life. Your friends, chores, responsibilities, even your enemies and trials of life are part of teaching us to build righteousness in our responses, worldview and friendships."

That night as I was lying in bed, I couldn't sleep. The excitement of the day kept turning over in my heart. The more I learned, the greater my spiritual desires grew. My thoughts finally settled on the words of my teacher, John: "I am writing to you, young men, for you have won against the evil one."[39] My zeal for the Lord grew from the lessons of these past few days. Watching the discipline of the soldiers, the patient endurance of the farmer, and the training and goal of the athletes made me realize that the Holy Spirit was training me. I was being trained to live as an overcomer of the evil one and the gods of men.

---

39. I John 2:13

7

THE WORLD DOES NOT LOVE YOU

*If the world hates you, know that it has hated
me before it hated you.
(John 15:18)*

TIMOTHY'S preaching moved me as I listened. "Stir up the gift that is in you. Fan that flame started by God in your soul. It is vital for you to do so, for difficult times, and resentful people will confront your fears. However, God has not given you a spirit of fearfulness. No! On the contrary, God has given you a spirit of dynamic ability, divine love and disciplined conduct."[40]

"These words were embedded into the depths of my soul by my mentor, the Apostle Paul," Timothy exclaimed. "It is the gift of God's Spirit within you that makes you strong and effective."

I was eighteen, and Callisto, seeing the proofs of God's work in my life released me for further training as a future shepherd in the Church. For many years since arriving in Ephesus, John had worked with Timothy and others in Western provinces of Anatolia[41] to train and mentor future church leaders—along with Peter in Antioch, Mark in Alexandria, and Thomas in the Far East. The Church was multiplying everywhere, both inside and outside the Roman Empire, and all of the Apostles trained their disciples the same way our Lord had taught them. John was my mentor, and since my childhood, he has always taken a special interest in me. His wife died not long after they arrived in Ephesus. They never had any children, and I suppose that I filled that part of his life to some degree. There were many pastors who

---

40. *II Timothy 1:6-7*

41. *Modern day Turkey*

had been trained by John, and by God's design, I was to be his last pupil.

Being in his nineties, I would not only be mentored by him but would also be called upon to assist him as a secretary and personal helper. I couldn't think of a greater privilege. Don't be deceived by his age either, for he was as busy as if he was in his prime. God empowered his zeal and love by the joy through submission to his will. So while we were very busy from early morning to late at night, he always made the work a pleasure to fulfill.

"Polycarp, Polycarp, what's outside that window that has you so captivated," John inquired, breaking me as it were out of a dead stare.

Startled, I turned and smiled, "Nothing important; I was just deep in thought."

"It must have been a powerful thought," John replied.

"If you must know, I long for that day when the elders of the Church would lay their hands on me and commission me as a pastor for the Lord's people," I said.

"Surely you must realize that it isn't some course to fulfill, but more an act of being proven over time. It is a gift given by God that is both stirred up by opportunity and the needs of others," John reminded me.

"Yes, that's what I desire. I want God to give me a spiritual gift that He will use for His glory. I find my heart filled with that desire," I explained.

"That in itself is the reality of a gift given and being developed," John added. "As Paul instructed Timothy; 'stir up the gift that is in you.' Fan the flames as it were. And when the flame is full and bright, then we will send you out. But until then, you must dedicate yourself to the One who teaches us all, and that is the Holy Spirit of our living God. Everything we encounter today is used by God to prepare us for tomorrow. He wastes no trials, withholds no blessings, nor does he hold back on the discipline of his soldiers. All he does prepares us for future usefulness as vessels of honor."

After a few hours of instruction, I met up with Samuel, a disciple of Timothy. John desired that we would learn to bear one another's burdens, and so we would every few months be paired with a brother in order to pray and encourage one another as we trained. We had met before but never had the time to develop a friendship.

I sat on a bench in the park adjacent to the amphitheater. It was part of the agora, the market area, and just a few steps from the parchment shop.

I saw him walking nearby, and yelled out and waved; "Samuel; I'm over here."

He waved back at me and waded through the crowd until he arrived at the bench. "I'm glad I found you. The area seems more crowded than normal," He said.

"Do you live here in Ephesus," I asked.

"No, but close. I live with my family in Miletus. Aristarchus is our overseer," he replied. "My parents left Jerusalem shortly after the murder of Stephen. Jerusalem had become a hostile place for the followers of our Lord, and was especially dangerous for my father who was a priest in the Temple. After hearing the Gospel of Jesus Christ preached by the Apostles, the Spirit of God moved in the heart of my parents to realize that Jesus was the Christ; the true Lamb of God who would take away their sin. On many occasions, my father has said that he joyfully gave up his priestly robes for the Lord's robe of perfect righteousness."

I shared how God had worked in my life; bringing me out of slavery, how he saved me and placed me under the ministry of John. Samuel also shared that when his parents fled Jerusalem, they resided for a few months in Cæsarea where Peter shepherded the church.

"How did you come to live in Miletus?" I asked.

"Due to growing political pressures, the Apostles thought it best to leave Israel, and many in the congregation journeyed with them to their various destinations. John stayed and assisted the church in Cæsarea for a while. Peter went to Antioch and the Apostle Matthew, along with Phillip the Evangelist, sailed to Asia in order to minister to a small and struggling congregation in Hierapolis near Laodicea. My parents left with them but stopped in Miletus in order for my mother to give birth to me. A few months after my birth, they decided to stay and help Aristarchus as part of the church in that little town," he said.

As we fellowshipped together, what I dreaded was now about to confront us. Walking right towards us was Erebus and his crew, and I could tell by the mischievous grin on his face, he was coming with some new concocted idea to torment me.

"Samuel, brace yourself; you are about to meet an old friend of mine who finds our faith in Jesus Christ to be offensive. He will not be polite; I can assure you," I warned.

My mind began to race for thoughts to confront his sarcasm. I had no idea what I was going to say or how I would respond.

"Hey fellows, look what we have here—fishers of men," Erebus scorned. "How many of you feel like getting caught today?" He said as they all laughed. "Maybe Polycarp can deliver us from hell. Isn't that where you say we are going?" He seethed. "You Christians are all the same. You think you are perfect for helping people and living with all those rules, but you are all frauds."

"If we do good things and live righteously, why should that bother you? And is imperfection fraudulent?" I asked. "Followers of Christ strive to be sincere and genuine in all we do."

Almost in derision Erebus replied, "Your God is a criminal, Polycarp. He was crucified by the gods of Rome. In their displeasure, they led Pontius Pilate to put him to death with two other thieves. You are a fool! Look over there," he said, pointing his finger down the road. "Right there is a beautiful temple to Diana. She is the daughter of Jupiter, the chief god, and the goddess of fertility, and you know what that means," he lewdly suggested. "Your religion says to abstain from fornication, but my religion says enjoy it for the glory of Diana."

"I am very familiar with the perversion and corruption of what takes place in that house of Satan you call the Temple of Diana," I rebuked. "My former master made idols and other worship trappings for that corrupt religion. It is a false religion that spreads its net to catch people and drag them into hell. It too fishes for the souls of men; not to save them, but to destroy them in this lifetime, and for all eternity."

There was silence for a moment, and then they all broke out in hysterical laughter. "That's right," Erebus replied in between his laughter. "I forgot that you were once a slave. Don't tell me, but I think your previous master was ole Crixus. Yes, that is the man isn't it?"

He stood erect as if to add some form of dignity to his next gimmick and insisted on the attention of anyone within earshot of his voice. "All the peoples of Ephesus give ear; this foolish man,

Polycarp serves a criminal God who was crucified by the might of Rome, and he himself was once a pathetic slave. Who here wants to follow his religion? A religion of criminals and slaves mind you?"

Some stopped and laughed; others gave obvious signs of their disapproval, but most just went on with their business. There were a few that spoke up in the name of the Lord and their support for Samuel and me. Erebus simply shouted back at them, "Just another cluster of idiots that are part of what they call 'The Church;' they think of themselves as sacred, called-out ones."

"Erebus," I replied, "thank-you!"

"For what, you fool?" He asked.

"For heaping upon me rewards from the One True God; for my God says 'How very happy you will be when men reproach you and pursue to cause you hurt for my sake. Thrive on this, and let your joy know no limits, for in heaven there awaits for you a large reward.'[42] So again I say thanks for increasing my reward in Heaven," I replied.

Like a heavy rain spoiling an outdoor meal, so their countenance fell. "You are worthless, Polycarp," Erebus hissed with anger and bitterness. "I hate you, and I hate Christians. You are a blight on society, and a scourge to our city. Come on, let's find Crixus and buy an idol, and then go the temple and have some worshipful fun."

We watched them walk away, and then Samuel said, "That went well."

I just looked over at him and laughing said, "Oh, now you finally decided to chime in."

Thinking he may have offended me he said, "I'm sorry; I really didn't know what to say. Why does Erebus hate you?"

"I'm not sure; I do know that when we have been part of this godless world, and God redeems us and makes us His own, the world hates losing us. They want us back living the way they live. They hate the light of God in Jesus Christ, and Jesus Christ in us. I suppose we are a reminder that God exists, and they detest the reminder. To be honest, I was surprised by my response. Just a short time ago, I would have been frightened out of my wits to engage Erebus. But I felt courage and confidence. I truly was

---

42. Matthew 5:10-12

desirous to help him. What surprised me the most is that I felt no shame or embarrassment. I like this change taking place in my heart," I said.

<hr />

Our studies intensified over the next several weeks, and much time was set aside for studying the Scriptures. A limited number of parchments and papyrus documents were available, so when you had a copy of any book or epistle you took advantage of the opportunity. I was more fortunate than most seeing that my uncle Decimus had copies of the great writings of the Old Testament, and the letters of the Apostles reproduced on his parchments. It was a painstaking process and carefully supervised so that there were no discrepancies from one transcription to another.

Even still, people traveled great distances to work in his library as the parchments were available. While scholarship was stressed and required, a living, fruit-producing relationship with the Lord Jesus Christ was paramount. In this world of intolerance towards Jesus Christ, we were taught that no amount of learning could sustain us without a firm faith in Jesus Christ. We were to be shepherds of the Lord's flock, his church, and were responsible for carrying out the orders of the Great Shepherd himself, and following his example in doing so. "What a great God," I would often think to myself, "who not only commands obedience, but gives enabling grace for the obedience required."

Our lives and words must draw the focus of the observer to our great Savior and his gracious work in us. Being a proud and vain man like all mankind, I found this not only a difficult task, indeed, an impossible one without the power of God's Spirit working in me.

During one of my talks with John, I inquired, "It seems that the greatest enemy I face is me. I know my battle is truly against the invisible forces of the devil, but I seem to be the one inflicting the greatest wounds upon myself. I feel like Satan has nothing to do, but sit back and watch me ruin my life."

John replied with a different angle for me to consider. "I fully understand your perplexity, Polycarp. However, it is the core of those seemingly good intentions of yours that reveals the true culprit of your anxiety and the very presence of the devil's chief weapon. What you are seeing is one of the many sides to pride."

"Pride," I questioned with eyebrows raised; "I thought I was expressing humility."

John smiled and nodded his head. "Do you think you can do anything out of any power you feel you possess? Do you believe that God has given you direction, and now just sits back awaiting you to do it?"

"No, I suppose not," I answered.

Seeing my cautious answer, he said, "You are right! God gives us the tools, abilities and gifts in order to obey him. He isn't seeking our self-effort any more than he depends on our self-righteousness. He looks for yieldedness, placing upon an altar of sacrifice, like Isaac, for God's purposes alone. From putting to death sinful impulses of our flesh, to performing unexplainable miracles and everything in between, are all wrought by the power and presence of God in us and through us by the Holy Spirit. Having just an intellectual comprehension of Scriptural teachings is important, but not the most important part of your training. God's work in you is to be the primary focus; this is called sanctification. You are being grown to be holy as Jesus is holy."

He smiled at me and added; "You are being developed for obedience one wobbly step at a time."

"Come with me," John said as he started for the door. "Let's go outside and take a stroll through the garden." We walked in silence for a few minutes. The sun was setting, and a cool evening breeze was blowing through the trees. "I love times like this," John said. "It reminds me of walking in the Garden of Gethsemane with the Lord. The heat of the day was being blown away and being replaced by the calm coolness of the night."

He headed for a bench that provided a wonderful prospect of the valley. "Let's sit here," and patting me on my forearm said, "Let me describe what I mean; our personal strengths, how we view our abilities, or what we feel must be done—all of these reveal one great and overlooked aspect of what weakens spiritual virtue. My old friend Peter, on the very night Jesus would be arrested, boldly, with undiminished determination swore he would never allow the Lord to be taken. We all knew Peter to be a strong-willed man, and figured he meant what he said. Furthermore, he was armed with a sword just in case. Despite being furnished with admirable affection and a weapon, in a moment of simple questioning in the courtyard outside the home of Caiaphas, the High Priest, his courage evaporated, and his great resolution vanished. I saw this; I was an eyewitness to his defeat. He was shattered by what he had done, and honestly, I could hardly fathom what I had just observed. Seeing his fear ignited in me a new level of fright I had never experienced.

Eleven of our Lord's most dedicated followers fled into the shadows. It's a humbling recollection. I hope you can gather the intensity of what I'm trying to explain, Polycarp. We saw his miracles in the past. I even spoke to Lazarus after he had been resurrected from the dead. But in this grave hour of the Lord's trial, we all discovered we had no inner-strength to depend on. It wasn't until Pentecost, just a short time after the Lord ascended into heaven following his resurrection that we discovered the secret. We needed not only the power of the Holy Spirit, but his constant counsel and training; his work of sanctification. Even to this day, now as an old man, I dare not grasp for any confidence in my flesh. I have none."

"You must understand this young man. All your effectiveness, your purpose, and yes even your happiness depends on this vital role of the Spirit's work in you. Those spiritual desires that stir in you; desires to serve God whole-heartedly; desires to live by faith; to be powerfully used by God, and to love Him with every part of your being were given to you by our gracious Heavenly Father. We can't even take credit for those noble, godly desires. When our Lord awakens those desires in us, He is the only one that can bring them to fruition. He's the source of your good days, and your truest comforter in the bad ones. Even a man's ability to obtain power or influence in the world or to accumulate wealth is a gift from God. Indeed, even the ability to enjoy one's wealth is a God-given gift. Our world is full of people burdened with the weight of wealth but lack the ability to be satisfied by it. Riches are like drinking salty water in that they create a thirst, but can never satisfy that thirst."

———— ◇◇ ————

Over the next couple of years, I focused on the study of the Scriptures and ministering to people. It wasn't the collection of knowledge that drove me, but more a daily discovery of truth and the blessings that accompany it. It didn't occur to me then, but later in the ministry this approach to study would keep me focused, encouraged, and refreshed through many troubling times.

John and Timothy were the motivators behind my studies, and their example incited in me the desire to see and live like they did. They were cautious that I learn by observation and application and that simply knowing the answer wasn't enough. John was adamant when he began mentoring me that as he was taught by Jesus, so I would be taught, and must commit to teaching others in the same fashion. He shared on many occasions that when he was exiled to Patmos by the Romans, he had no parchments or scrolls, nor did he have anyone with whom to fellowship over the Word. His communion was with the Lord. He told me how he had learned more over the months of exile than any other time in his life.

◇◇

On my twenty-second birthday, I was to enter a whole new stage in my training. It began as I sat with my family for our morning meal.

They appeared oddly excited, but strangely quiet. Each looking at the other with glancing eyes and repressed grins. "What's wrong with you all? Why are you all smiling at me," I quizzed.

"We're not smiling at you," my mother replied.

"It's just a lovely day, sweetheart," Beatrice nonchalantly added.

"Certainly is," Decimus said, "is there anything wrong with smiling on a lovely day?" They all just sat there as if they knew something I didn't know and they were reveling in that fact.

"You know something, don't you?" I asked.

"I know many things," Decimus was quick to remind me.

"I don't mean you don't know anything. You know that. Something is about to happen, but you are keeping it from me. That is it, isn't it? Had any of you even remembered that it was my birthday?" I said.

"Oh, is it?" Callisto chuckled. "Well, happy birthday, dear."

"I can see I'm not going to get any answers out of this group, am I?" I said with sarcastic exasperation.

Finally, Beatrice, the weakest in the group broke first, and started laughing with Decimus and Callisto soon joining her. "I'm sorry," my mother finally said as she wiped the tears from her eyes.

"Finish your breakfast, and then go see John. He has the answer you seek."

"You still are not going to tell me, are you?" I asked.

"John will tell you, besides, it may affect your appetite, and we wouldn't want that, would we?" Callisto said.

"Right, as if the suspense won't," I added. After a few large mouthfuls of food I don't recall ever tasting, I was up and ran to John's home.

As I rushed into the courtyard, I heard the old familiar voice of my teacher behind me. I turned to find him sitting under a date palm, enjoying its fruit. "Polycarp, I'm over here. Come sit with me," he requested. "This is a special day is it not?"

"You're not going to tease me too," I thought to myself. "Yes, my mother told me you have news for me."

"News? You don't say," John said with twinkle in his eye. "I thought today was your birthday. You're twenty-two are you not?"

What was I to think, I wondered? Was John in on this joke as well?

"Yes, today is my birthday. Is that what you wanted to tell me?" I asked, trying to hide my anticipation.

"Of course not," John said, "nevertheless, it is true, and I am happy to be with you on this day. What a joy it has been watching you grow up over the years, and become a godly young man. Your countenance, your zeal for Christ, your courage in sharing the Gospel, your love for others edifies me every time I hear your voice or see you minister. Did you know that my twenty-second birthday was an extraordinary day for me?"

"No, I don't recall you ever saying," I replied.

"It seems strange I would have left out that detail over the numerous times I have recounted this life-changing event," he said as he extended his hand inviting me to enjoy some of his dates.

"When I was twenty-two, I lived in Galilee where I worked as part of my father's fishing fleet. On that remarkable day, while my father, brother James, and I were fishing near the shore, a lone figure was walking along the shoreline, and yelled out to us and said, 'follow me, and I will make you fishers of men.' Strangely enough, James and I felt powerfully compelled to leave our nets, our father, the other servants, and jump out into the shallow water and follow this man. What normally would have seemed unnatural, felt normal as if a close friend had called us to shore. Oh, the glory of how God empowers us by faith, for at that moment what would ordinarily appear as an absurd decision was every bit pleasant and remarkable in our souls. What's even odder is that our father didn't seem to be particularly alarmed either. Of course, you probably have already figured that the man was our Lord Jesus Christ, and on that day, my twenty-second birthday, I started following him and have never stopped."

"That is why I have called you here," he continued. "I'm afraid that my age is beginning to take its toll on this old body of mine, and while I have some energy left I feel it prudent to take one more journey and visit several of the churches, for I long to lay my eyes on what the Lord has wrought in the harvest of souls. My hope is that you would be willing to join me and assist me in the work of the ministry. So what do you think? Would you like to join me?"

While all I said was "yes, I would be honored to join you," I felt that deeper, more powerful words were appropriate, but I could not find any.

"Where will we be going?" I blurted out.

"Well, the itinerary, as best as I can foretell will take us from Ephesus to Cyprus. From there, we will journey to Israel. I desire to visit the saints in Cæsarea and afterwards go up to Jerusalem. As I understand it, the city still lies in ruins, and the possibility of another Jewish uprising is not out of the question. It will not be a safe trip, for Christ is still not welcome in that great city, not to mention that I too am a Jew entering what the Romans could still consider a hotbed of trouble."

"If we can visit David's City, then we will stay only a short time and head north, stopping in Tiberius, near my childhood home, then on to Antioch, where I long to see our brother Ignatius, and to check on his welfare. When our work is complete in Asia, if the Lord wills, we will sail to Greece, where the western churches have requested I visit with them. I anticipate ministering in Philippi, Corinth and finally Athens. From there, my friend, I anticipate our return to Ephesus. I expect that we will be gone one, maybe two years. It all depends upon how I find the Churches."

John stood up and placed his hand around the back of my neck, and said "You are an example of the believer, dear one, and I trust our gracious God will use you to edify his church."

He was thrilled at the prospect of visiting the churches, and I shared in his enthusiasm though perhaps for different motives. This trip was going to be an adventure since I had never travelled outside of Ephesus.

As John started to walk away, he stopped and turning back towards me said, "I am the last living Apostle of Jesus Christ. I want to see and be seen. It's important to me that what I have observed and learned be passed on to you, and in turn you pass it on, so that each succeeding generation can know that Jesus was a man, but no ordinary man, but God who came in the flesh. He was the incarnate God, and I am a witness to this, and you must pass it on. These are not just the stories men tell that become legend, for Jesus is alive today and sits at the right hand of the Throne of his Heavenly Father. He is alive in me and is alive in you and all those are called to be saints. His Holy Word and the lives of his people authenticate the message and validate the truth about him. I believe this journey will have a dynamic impact on your life, not to mention that I shall certainly be delighted to have you with me."

"John," I inquired, "when is our departure?"

"Oh yes, I suppose that would be helpful to know. We sail out of the harbor on Friday morning. Don't be late."

My feet felt light as feathers as I made my way back home. Joy was overflowing in my heart at the realization that God would deal so kindly with me and permit me this opportunity to travel with John and minister in the churches. My imagination was adrift with the dreams of what I would encounter on this adventure. I let out an audible chuckle as I was ushered back to reality by a familiar, but an unwelcome voice behind me. As I turned, I was right, it was Erebus standing there in his brilliant white tunic with the prominent purple strip exposed from under his toga advertising his high rank in society.

"Well, if it isn't Saint Polycarp," he sneered. "Still trying to save the world?"

"No, but I would settle for you," I said. Though I wished I had said that differently with less sarcasm in my voice. He laughed and assured me that my odds were better with the world.

"I haven't seen you around for a while," I said.

"I've been at our villa in Rome being tutored by the great Suetonius, perhaps you have heard of him," he replied.

"Suetonius! Who hasn't heard of him?" I replied. "Doesn't he also tutor Caesar's children?"

"Indeed. You seemed well informed," he said as if surprised. However, he also appeared a bit disappointed at my visible lack of envy, and so not having achieved his apparent goal, he pressed the issue further. "You should be honored, Polycarp, for I spoke of you to my great teacher."

"Honored? I'm sure you said only the nicest things," I said.

"I would not put it that way," he responded. "It is honorable that I spoke your name, but that's all. He scoffed at your aged mentor, and confessed that you have no education upon which to build your life. He says your life is at best an apologue. I have watched you Christians, and you are a weird sort. Your kind doesn't fit in. Suetonius agrees, and we have had many jovial occasions as we have discussed your strange religious sect. He says it's a religion that can't be accepted into Judaism and doesn't appreciate the superiority of being Roman. He is incredulous at the thought that the anomalous Christians think themselves citizens of heaven, with a crucified criminal as their king."

"Tell me, Erebus, name his crime," I requested.

"Subversive to Rome, he and his band of followers," he retorted.

"I would have imagined you of all people to be more acquainted with the historical facts, for the public record states that Pontius Pilate announced that he could find no guilt in Jesus of Nazareth." I replied.

"That's a moot point, since he was still crucified," he countered.

"That is true, but while I don't expect you to understand, it was the fulfillment of prophecy, that Jesus, the Christ had come to be the final atoning sacrifice for sin. He was the Lamb of God," I responded.

Erebus laughed and said, "If you could only take a step back and see how absurd that statement is, you would flee such nonsense and embrace a more enlightened path. But I suppose that it is the type of teaching you receive when your tutor is an uneducated fisherman from a conquered country."

I had to hold my tongue for a moment to suppress my anger of the insults he directed towards John. "The One true God delights in confounding the worldly wise with what they call foolishness. What I am telling you are spiritually discerned principles of life. The impact of their meaning cannot be experienced through mere intellect alone. It requires a new nature, made pure and perfect by the indwelling power of the presence of God in our lives. I don't expect you to understand; it's beyond human comprehension," I said.

"Wait! Don't say another word," Erebus ordered. "Are you now telling me that God dwells in you?"

Now I had to laugh, for I could imagine how this must sound to him. "You are insane, and the old man you follow. You all huddle around a gross and pathetic cross. It's a God-forsaken means of death, Polycarp," He scolded.

"It was God-forsaken; that is true," I replied. "It also was God-uniting. The substitutionary atonement of Jesus Christ broke down the barrier and bridged a great chasm of impossibility necessary for God to reach fallen mankind. This is the One True God appeasing his own wrath, unlike your gods, which seem beyond satisfying. This is the glory we find in the cross of Jesus. What god of the Romans or any other religious deity would humble themselves to die for their followers, and then go as far as to adopt them and make them part of their own family? Erebus, there are none, save the One true God."

He stepped up close to me and blurted out, "Curse your God and curse the gods of Rome! I serve the gods as they serve me. I am my own god."

Again, I had to suppress my laughter as I replied, "How splendorous."

"Don't mock me, you fool," he warned. "I follow my own roads and determine my own destiny. I know the plans for my life."

"How can a man truly believe this?" I thought to myself.

"Your passion is no different than the rest of mankind," I said. "You are chained to covetous thinking. You are in the pursuit of what you desire not realizing it is your master, dragging you around through life, and leaving you with a never-ending, insatiable desire for more. Your eyes drink in salacious pleasures, but can never be filled, and you seek self-exaltation like a dog chases its tail. Once you catch it, what have you got? These are the actions of a man seeking to be a god."

"You have such a narrow view of life. You want to give glory, and I want to receive it," Erebus replied.

"If that is your view of life, then I suppose it is narrow," I said. "But better to follow a narrow, even difficult path that leads to eternal protection and life with God, than to parade down a broad way that leads to eternal judgment." I could tell he was growing irritated with my words, but what he said next startled me.

"Man is glorious in this ability to live independently from the gods. They have their place, and if we give them due honor, they leave us alone. Caesar wins battles because of their favor; our crops grow because they bless us, and we grow rich because some of us are their favored ones. As my teacher has told me, your religion is the product of oppressed thinking and one man's attempts to control the behavior of others. I defy your God, Polycarp." He then lifted his arms to the heavens and declared, "God of Polycarp, strike me dead if you dare." After a moment of silence, he dropped his arms and laughed. "I'm still here," he jested.

Feeling deep grief over his foolish blindness, I said, "Erebus, you still have a part to play in this life. If it weren't so, I would be looking down at your dead body. Everything has been created by God to fulfill its purpose, even wicked men for the Day of Judgment.[43] Someday you will be required to give an account for your life. On that day, you'll hate this day, for God will appear before you in regal splendor, and at that moment the reality of your foolishness will haunt you. I will pray for you with all hope that God will take away your blindness to the truth of life."

"Pray all you want. We'll see who has the fulfilled life at death's door," he scorned.

But I replied, "The door you face is one of doom, but the door I face will be as welcoming as the door of my home. Erebus, why do you detest me? Did I do something in the past that built this wall of animosity?" I bemoaned.

"If you are too moronic to figure it out, why should I waste my time trying to correct you?" he contested. "There is no reason to become a Christian. There is no heaven or hell; no proof of an

---

43. *Proverbs 16:4*

afterlife. Don't you see that I'm happy, and I don't see your Jesus able to make me happier? Life is fun without him."

He turned away in anger and stormed off, and I stood there discouraged over his stubbornness and my inability to crack it. As I watched him disappear around the corner, I whispered a prayer, "My gracious Father, I have planted. Send someone to water the seed of the Word in the heart of Erebus, and out of your mercy, be pleased to make it grow and save that man. Help me to live to see your purpose for him in my life." I headed home, glad to have shared, but heavy-hearted too.

That evening, as I sat at the table stirring my food around the plate, I asked my mother why Jesus would say that the world hates us because it hates him.

She pondered the answer and then said, "The world is fickle. They can be your friend one moment, and then it's like they receive orders to turn against us. Remember that when Jesus entered into Jerusalem, he was hailed by the crowds as a triumphant King, and the next week they became a mob and had him crucified. They hated him without cause."[44]

"They are unchanged in nature," I heard my Uncle Decimus say behind me. "And therein we find our problem," as he walked over and pulled up a chair. "The Lord calls us the light of the world like he is, but the godless world hates that reality because darkness is forced to flee the light. Evil feels free under the cover of darkness, but when the Lord, his Word or his people enter into that realm, the light naturally overcomes the darkness. As the Proverbs reveal, 'The actions of a wicked man are disgusting to the obedient, and the one who is righteous is disgusting to the wicked.'[45] That is what concerns me about those who choose ungodly companions. I'm not saying they cannot be our friends, I just find it suspicious when they find our friendship so comfortable. If they don't mind the light, then it should shine through us in its fullness. But alas, many put a basket over that godly light in them, and while the world suspects something different, the truth never channels its way through us to them."

---

44. *John 15:25*

45. *Proverbs 29:27*

"John said something similar to me recently," I replied. "'If you were part of this world, they would love you as their own, but because you are not part of this world, but have been chosen out of this world by God, the world hates you for it.'"[46]

Callisto framed this in light of all that transpired today when she quoted from Matthew's Gospel, "I am sending you off as sheep surrounded by wolves, so be cautious like a serpent, and innocent like a dove."[47]

46. *John 15:19*

47. *Matthew 10:16*

8

A DOOR OF OPPORTUNITY

...a large door for active work has opened to me,
and there is much opposition.
(I Corinthians 16:9)

IT seemed as if Friday would never come, but here it was. As I boarded the vessel, I already was sick—homesick that is. But as we set sail, seeing Ephesus and my family fade away on the horizon impressed upon me the joyful reality that I was actually going on this trip. I felt a sense of courage and adventure, but my ego was put in its place as our ship was gently tossed about in the Aegean Sea, and the next several hours were spent throwing up the contents of my stomach over the side. John and others assured me that I would eventually become comfortable with the motion of the vessel, but at the time, the word motion was the last thing I wanted to hear.

The next morning I was feeling better, but ate only a small portion. As I picked at my food, I couldn't help observing John staring at a distant island.

"What is that island?" I asked to a passing crewman.

"Patmos, a desolate place if you ask me," He answered.

"The Island of Patmos," I spoke under my breath. I walked over to stand next to John.

"Does seeing that island bring back unpleasant memories?" I asked, hoping to be a comfort to him.

He looked at me as if he had been jostled out of a deep thought, and after clearing his throat, replied, "No, nothing unpleasant."

I observed the tears welling up in his eyes as he extended his arm and pointed to a craggy slope, "It was up there, above that ledge God changed my life forever. Never have I felt closer to my Heavenly Father. Never have I been so powerfully moved by his grace. The Romans sent me there to chastise me, but God sent me there to meet with me. To me, that island is holy ground."

The depth of passion I heard in his voice moved me, and it gave me an idea. I rushed away down into the hull of the vessel, into the cargo hold, where I found a crate holding the parchments John brought with him. Some were his personal copies, and others were for the churches we would visit in the east. As I searched the box, I came across John's copy of The Revelation of Jesus Christ. I took a copy, found a secluded spot on the deck and read The Revelation as we sailed past this special island.

"The revelation of Jesus Christ, which God gave to him, to give to those who belong to him and reveal what must soon take place. He made this known to his bond slave, John, by sending an angel who was a witness to the word of God and to the testimony of Jesus Christ, even to all the things that he saw. How very fortunate is the one who reads the words contained in this prophecy, and to guard what is written therein, for the time is near. John to the seven churches which are in Asia: God's intense pleasure be upon you, and Divine safety from him who is, and who was and who is to come, and from the seven Spirits who are in the presence of his throne, and from Jesus Christ the most faithful witness, the firstborn of the dead, and the ruler of the kings of the earth. From him who with everlasting love, has cleansed us from our sins in his own blood, and has fashioned us as kings and priests to his God and Father – to him belong the highest and best of thoughts and great dominating power forever and ever. Amen."[48]

As I read those words, and imagined John receiving them on that island in front of me, my heart swelled with gratitude that God, who rightfully and justly could condemn us all to eternal hell, has chosen to deal kindly with us, treating his church as his special creation. How is it possible that we could ever hold anything back from him, or render any less than whole-hearted devotion to him? After the island had faded into the horizon, I was still reading, and didn't stop even to eat until I had read it all.

———————— ◇◇ ————————

After a few weeks at sea, with a short stop in Cyprus, where John greeted the church that gathered on the dock, we finally

---

48. *Revelation 1:1-6*

arrived in Cæsarea. The harbor was magnificent, and the palace built by Herod at the sea's edge was a marvel to me. While I soaked in the sights as we entered the busy harbor, John seemed far more subdued. I moved closer to hear him speak with our travel companion, Tychicus.

"This is a blood soaked city," John exclaimed. "Many of our brothers and sisters in Christ, not to mention many of our countrymen were executed here in this town."

"If I recall, close to three thousand met their deaths in that arena over there," Tychicus added pointing to the amphitheater nearby.

"One very special brother," John said softly as Tychicus nodded. "To whom are you referring," I carefully inquired.

"Peter. My friend Peter died by crucifixion here in Cæsarea. As Nero killed Paul in Rome, he had the Jewish rebels and the Christians rounded up out of Jerusalem, Damascus and Antioch, and brought them here to face execution."

As we disembarked, a crowd approached us being led by two aged men; Cornelius, one of Peter's first converts in Cæsarea, and Apollo, the overseer. After a tearful greeting and introductions, we were escorted to the home of Cornelius where we would stay as his guests. I was given Peter's old room as he had been a guest in that home many times. The next morning, John laid out the details of his hopes for this trip, but immediate cautions were raised.

"I greatly desire to go up to Jerusalem first, and then to Galilee to visit with family members still living near Tiberius," John said.

"Jerusalem!" Cornelius repeated. "This is a dangerous itinerary. Just to move around the rubble of the city is treacherous, not to mention that Jews are prohibited in the area."

"I don't wish to enter the city, but draw near, perhaps from the Mount of Olives and reminisce," John replied. "Besides, I have spoken with others who journeyed to the city, and they have informed me that the Roman officials have loosened some of their regulations and are not as strict with people passing by the ruins."

"That may be true for some, but you are the last living disciple of Jesus Christ, and that alone could make you a target," Apollo interjected.

"An old man like me will hardly be a target. I shall be like Nehemiah of old and move closer to the city and pass by the guards at night. Then from the safety of higher elevation, perhaps I could gaze upon that special city one more time," John said.

"I can appreciate your passion, but I think it's a bad idea. There is nothing to see. A shrine to Jupiter stands on the site of the Temple. John, you don't know what you are requesting. There is a Roman Garrison on the western edge of the ruins, but other than that, the city is a pile of stones. Please reconsider," Cornelius pled.

John smiled but said nothing. Everyone knew he was determined to go. Cornelius glanced around the room for support, and realizing no one was going to stop John, gave in to his request. "If you are determined to go, which I caution you not to, I will send an armed escort with you. His name is Icarus, a former Roman soldier and devoted brother in Christ. If you should encounter a problem with the local authorities, I trust him to keep you safe."

———◇◇———

After several days of fellowship, preaching, and discipleship, we began our journey up to the ancient City of David. I was full of anticipation, and even though we would not be able to enter what was left of the city, walking around it and seeing it would be good enough for me. The journey was not difficult, though it was hot. Icarus thought it best to approach the city from the east, atop of the Mount of Olives in order to avoid any Roman patrols.

As we walked through a grove of olive trees, I heard John gasp as we laid our eyes on the ancient city. I know the city had been destroyed a few years back, but I could scarcely comprehend what I was seeing. With the exception of the foundation where the great Temple stood, and a small fortification off in the distance on the west side of the city, I saw nothing but total desolation. There were heaps of stones, boulders and broken brick which could hardly be traversed. I saw a few lanes that ran from one end of the ruins to the other, but from what I could observe, the city was uninhabitable.

I had seen John weep before, but not like this. His cry was one of deep sorrow; however, I didn't perceive that it was as much over the destruction as much as it was the rejection of the Messiah that so deeply grieved him. In between the sobs I heard him mutter, "Oh Jerusalem, Jerusalem, the city that kills the prophets and stones those sent into it. How I would have loved to have pulled your children close to me as a hen gathers her bridling's under her wings, but you did not desire this. Look now, for your house is left desolate."[49]

Icarus broke the long silence, "I was here at the siege."

John looked up at him and requested that he inform him regarding the event.

"I was new to the army, and had been assigned to the Fifth Macedonian Legion, which had been dispatched to assist the great general, Titus, in conquering the Jewish rebellion. It was in its third year, and the entire north had been conquered. All that remained was Jerusalem and some fortifications in the Negev. One of my first assignments was to serve in a team of bodyguards charged with protecting the life of one of the rebellion's leaders, Josephus. To spare his life, he agreed to the terms of being a historian and was appointed as an aid to Titus. The bond became so strong between the two that he took the name of his captor, and became known as Titus Flavius Josephus. He served as a scribe noting the events of this tragic war and was also a powerful negotiator in subduing other Jewish rebels. However, as you can imagine, he was also greatly hated and considered a traitor by his countrymen."

"I knew Josephus and his family," John interjected much to our surprise. "Our fathers were friends and our properties bordered each other in Galilee. His father was a priest, and that is what allowed me access into the home of Caiaphas during the trial of my Lord. While I did not support the rebellion, I too was shocked to hear of his defection. Please continue, Icarus; I want to hear what transpired in that battle," John said.

"The three legions approached the city from the north and the west converging on the plains outside the walls. In reality, I suppose that's the only place an effective attack could be made seeing the cliffs and steep grades that protect the other parts of the city; however, there were a few skirmishes in the Kidron Valley. At first, Titus seemed magnanimous to the inhabitants; almost as if he were willing to negotiate. Since it was the Jewish Passover, he permitted pilgrims to enter the city from any gate, and when the city was full and overcrowded, he surrounded the city and barred any from leaving. At first it caused little alarm, but after a couple

---

49. Matthew 23:37-38

of weeks everyone on both sides realized what he was doing, for the city was not capable of sustaining the immense crowds for a long period of time."

"I had family in that city," John said.

"Weren't you imprisoned on Patmos when this took place," I asked.

"Yes, I was. It was about a year before I received the news of the destruction and massacre," he said. "Please Icarus; continue."

"After it was obvious the people were starving and thirsting to death, Josephus was sent to the gates of the city to negotiate. I was one of the guards who accompanied him. He and Titus approached close to the wall, and then Josephus and his guards moved towards the gate with the anticipation that it would open up, and the delegation would emerge to discuss the terms of surrender. To our surprise, the Jews inside the city launched a full-scale attack. Josephus was wounded; several of his guards were killed, and even Titus barely escaped the barrage. Once he was safe, he ordered a counter attack at another gate in order to distract the throng of angry rebels. I narrowly escaped with my life as I helped Josephus to safety. It was upon our return to the encampment that Titus ordered an all-out assault on the city."

"Archers launched firebrands into the air over the city walls; thousands upon thousands and massive siege towers were strategically placed. The volume of arrows shot at the same time appeared as a dark rain cloud that masked the sun. Within minutes, you could hear the panic and mayhem. As the gates were ablaze, battering rams were brought forward and began to bash against them. Archers overwhelmed the defenders on the walls. After a few scorching hours, the outer gates were breached, then Fortress Antonia, and finally, parts of the city began to fall, being overrun with angry, fierce, out-of-control Roman soldiers who showed no mercy. John, it was an all-out slaughter; no one was spared, not even the children. Buildings toppled over as the large boulders and bricks showered down on the people. The Temple was the hardest to penetrate, but once we retook Fortress Antonia, it was just a matter of time. Everything was set aflame, and what couldn't be burned was torn down. Even the magnificent Temple was stripped, burned, and toppled. The valleys were filling with blood as the dead bodies heaped upon one another. At one point in the battle, Titus tried to subdue his soldiers, but to little avail. It was a heartless bloodbath. Close to a million people died in the city, with another ninety-seven thousand taken prisoner."

We all sat silently for a few moments. I could see the impact of this account weighed heavy on John.

"Did you engage in the fighting," John finally asked.

"No. I confess that I was angry that I had to stay with Josephus, who sat in horror over what he was forced to behold. Now that I am a follower of Jesus Christ, I believe God was protecting me from participating in those horrors."

John stood up and said, "I cannot stay a moment longer. Cornelius was wise. I should not have come. Let's leave at once and head down to the Jordan River."

The walk in the wilderness down the mountain range into the Jordan valley was a solemn one. What we had seen and heard was moving and sobering. As a Roman citizen, I felt shame, and yet I knew that Rome had been a weapon in the hands of God. As Paul describes God's work through Pharaoh so he had worked through Rome, "For this cause I released you to fulfill your plans in order that I might demonstrate my power in you, and that as a result my name would be declared throughout the entire world. So God will have mercy on whomever he wills, and he will harden whomever he wills."[50]

--------◇◇--------

The next few days we traveled slowly up the Jordon valley along the edge of the river. John suppressed his lingering sorrow by telling us stories and of encounters with the Lord Jesus along the way. I remember at one point as we rested by the River, he said, "Polycarp, being here refreshes me and reminds me of what a wonderful Savior we serve. Even in the deepest of sorrows, or under the load of daily pressures, our faithful God never ceases to find ways to make our hearts glad."

As we approached the base of Mount Tabor, we were met with a wonderful surprise, and one that did much to lift the spirit of John. Along the road we were greeted by some of his relatives, mostly a few nephews, nieces and cousins. It was quite a reunion and brought a lot of joy to us all. We continued our journey together around Tiberius to a small fishing community south of

---

50. Romans 9:17-18

Capernaum. Here I found John's childhood home and the location on the shore where he and his brother James left their father and his servants as they fished, and where they followed Jesus as fishers of men. We spent several weeks here with John preaching to groups of Christians still living in the area. We even went fishing in one of Zebedee's old boats.

After a couple of months in Galilee, we had a surprise visitor, Ignatius, the pastor in Antioch, was helping resolve a dispute in the Damascus church and decided to head south to meet us and escort us to Antioch himself. He ministered along with us for a few days, and then pressed us to begin the journey to Antioch. However, there was going to be a change in plans.

"Ignatius, I feel too weak to make the journey with you at this time, and feel that I should stay a bit longer," John expressed.

"Oh, I had so longed to spend the time fellowshipping with you. Could you possibly reconsider?" asked Ignatius. Personally, I was a bit concerned about how direct Ignatius was, and how he seemed to take charge of everything. It some ways I found his forwardness irritating.

"No, my friend," John replied. "I'm not the spry, energetic man I used to be. Just look at me," he said with a smile. "I've come to a point in my life where my fastest speed is slow. You must go on without me, but take Polycarp with you. If I regain my strength, I'll catch up with you later. Truly my dear brother, I believe this will be the last time I see my kinsmen here on earth, and I didn't realize how much I missed them until seeing them here again. No, you must go on without me."

Ignatius agreed and instructed me to be ready to depart in the morning. Not having John at my side made me anxious, and I desired to stay with him.

When he left the room to make his preparations, I approached John with my apprehensions. "He seems so forceful and direct like he's driven to control," I said.

John seemed amused by my assessment and replied, "He's a great deal like his first mentor, Peter. He is very assertive I'll grant you that, but he's just what Antioch needs. After the Jews and Christians were forced to leave Jerusalem, most of the Apostles headed north to Antioch, which in many ways became the cradle of Christianity."

"Many congregations were established, and for the most part Peter was overseeing the work. The other Apostles appointed me to Ephesus, Mark to Egypt, Thomas to Persia, and Paul to Greece. Peter and the others ministered from Antioch. When on a trip to Cæsarea, Peter was captured and killed for his faith during Nero's persecution; Ignatius was given oversight of Peter's congregation in Antioch. With the Apostles being hunted and killed, the church needed strength and decisive direction. They needed an example to follow; someone who loved them and would keep them obedient to the truth. I agree that he appears rather controlling at times, but the truth is, he loves people and is deeply loved by all who know him. He'll give out orders, but I have found that he also demonstrates great meekness with that authority. He is a joyful bondslave of the Lord first and foremost, and beloved friend. I truly believe you two will become great friends. He'll learn from your steadiness, and you'll learn from his boldness. I see it as a true picture of iron sharpening iron, my child." I felt a little better, but was determined to be cautious.[51]

<hr>

The next morning we gave our farewells and boarded the horse-drawn cart. We were to ride back up to Damascus, where Ignatius wished to check in on the struggling congregations, and then proceed on to Antioch. He said the journey would likely take about three weeks. To my surprise, the trip turned out to be enjoyable, and John was right, Ignatius and I developed a great friendship that would last until his death. He was wise, and was also the type of person that took charge, perhaps a bit more quickly than he should, but his motivation was always for the good of those around him. While pushy, he was not impatient. He loved serving people with all his energy. Truly, a man zealous of doing what is good for the glory of God.

Antioch was a large and thriving city, much like Ephesus, though there was a substantially larger Jewish population. There were as many synagogues as there were church meeting houses. As we rode over the hilltop looking down into Antioch, Ignatius asked, "So Polycarp, what do you think of our fair city?"

---

51. *Proverbs 27:17*

"It's impressive and considerably different from Ephesus, which as you know, is defined by its proximity to the coastline."

"True," replied Ignatius, "but we too are defined by water. That is the Orontes River that runs around and through the town. A vital element to our economy"

"What is the greatest challenge you face here in Antioch," I asked.

"You might think it was combating paganism, but you would be wrong," Ignatius replied. "Lies, false truths, wolves in sheep's clothing; those are my daily challenges and shall be undoubtedly yours as well. Teachers of false doctrine slither into the hearts of men and distort the true gospel and seek to make Jesus out to be a good man, but simply a man. Their words rob him of his deity."

"How do you confront such heresy," I asked. Then smiling as if he hoped I would ask that question responded, "You shall discover that soon enough my friend."

A wave of nervousness came over me since I had no idea what he was talking about, or what he was going to compel me to do. "I guess this is a good thing," I thought to myself. "I've always had John or Timothy to lean on, but now I guess it's time to lean on my Lord." I reflected on the great exhortation from the Proverbs of Solomon; "Be confident in the LORD with all your heart, and never rely on your limited discernment of life. Instead, in all your ways seek to discover his ways, and you will find his direction lying straight before you."[52] I must confess that while I loved that text, I didn't fully understand it. I guess that is what makes faith, true faith. Faith begins where my ability cannot take me, or my sight guide me.

After a day to recover from a long journey, I joined several other pastors in the city for a time of prayer and mutual edification led by Ignatius. The fellowship was stirring and brought a greater sense of reality to me regarding the ministry and the challenges that accompany it. I admit that I had been perhaps a bit shielded by my mentor. The work a pastor must put forth in new congregations, and the challenges faced by normal pastors with no claim to fame gave me insight into the reality of ministry and the need to see one's self as a faithful steward of God. What pleased me was the focus of these men of God. They didn't have

---

52. *Proverbs 3:5-6*

John, Timothy or even Ignatius standing by their side. They were soldiers of the cross—daring the field and faithfully fighting the good fight of faith, right where the head of the Church, the Lord Jesus Christ, had placed them. I longed for that same passion and contentment.

As we worshipped together, and enjoyed each other's friendship, Ignatius requested our attention. "There is a matter that demands our consideration. As defenders of the gospel, we must be ready when false doctrine enters our fold like a wolf in sheep's clothing. Let's not forget Paul's strident warning to the Romans; 'Fix your eyes on those who produce divisions and impediments contrary to the teachings we were taught to practice. Shun their company. These people are not in subjection to our Lord Jesus Christ, but out of their gluttonous appetites, and by persuasive and polished language they seduce the hearts of simple ones.'"[53]

The way he said those words captured the attention of everyone in the room.

"False doctrine is growing out of a faction in Rome that has begun to spread into the churches and lead many astray from the faith," Ignatius warned. "In a corrupted passion for helping others turn from the worship of the goddess Diana, they have placed the mother of our Lord on a dangerously high pedestal and were making her an object of their worship, referring to her as the Queen of Heaven."

He stopped and singled me out to ask, "Mary lived in Ephesus with John. Did you ever meet her?"

"Yes, though I was a young boy at the time," I replied.

"As you know, at John's invitation she relocated to Ephesus with some of her family, Ignatius added.

"She died not long after I met her, but my memory of her and her reputation was one of kindness and devotion to our Lord," I said.

"I'm glad you knew her. She was a godly lady and devoted to the gospel of her Savior. I knew her well, and I tell you, she adored the Lord as her redeemer more than she loved him as a son," Ignatius continued.

"When I was being mentored by Peter and John in Cæsarea, she and some of our Lord's brothers were part of the congregation.

---

53. *Romans 16:17-18*

She was truly an exemplary follower of Christ, but I guarantee she would be mortified to see how others are attempting to exalt her above measure and steal the glory belonging to the champion of our souls. Sure, they teach the truth that salvation is found in Jesus Christ, but they pervert his work of redemption with the teaching that redemption can be found through his mother, too. This error is one of the doctrines you must oppose with great determination, men of God," he declared as he pounded the table in front of him.

"As shepherds of the Lord's flock, we must not tolerate the preaching of another gospel. The best news God can give to the lost is found in Jesus Christ, alone! They are too quick to overlook the fact that Mary was a sinner and needed redemption as much as Paul, the chief of sinners. Like Noah, who found grace in the eyes of the Lord and was given a special mission to be used by God in saving humanity, so Mary found grace in God's eyes and was also chosen to participate in the redemption of the Lords' elect. She is not a redeemer, but as a mother to a human male child who, by miraculous design, was also the Divine child. Now we don't attribute greater glory to Noah, nor should we Mary. She was the mother of the Son of Man; blessed among women, but not above or even equal to her son. He was God in the flesh, and that is where her motherhood ended! I am gravely concerned that so many find her more compassionate or approachable than God, our most gracious heavenly Father. There are only two who intercede on our behalf, and the only two one could ever wish: The Lord Jesus Christ, and the Holy Spirit. We can expect no more from Mary or other great servants of the Lord than we could expect praying to our ancestors for intercession before God's throne of grace."

I felt the ardor and exasperation of Ignatius. I was aware that this false teaching was becoming more popular in Ephesus, where the worship of Diana was so strong.

"Beware of this smooth, but deceitful teaching, men of God. They declare that since she is the mother of the king that she becomes the queen. She saw her situation correctly in her response to the angel when she said, "Behold, the bondslave of the Lord.""[54] Mary was blessed among women, but that doesn't mean she was

---

54. Luke 1:38

given a throne in heaven. God's Spirit has worked in the lives of God's choice servants throughout all history. We have all been ruined by the fall of man in the Garden of Eden. Mary too was ruined by the fall. She realized that she had no special advantage to justification before God. We must be faithful to teach that 'no one holds a righteous stance before God. There is no one! No one can bring the mind of God and the mind of man together in harmony. No one follows after God. Every human being has deviated from the truth. United, they have become worthless. They are incapable of doing what is right, not even one. All humanity loses when it stands on its own righteous in the face of the glory of God.'[55] The universal church must be pure in its devotion to Jesus Christ, by the power of his Holy Spirit, for the Glory of God the Father. No one else can be permitted to share in HIS Divine glory. No one!" he proclaimed.

There was a question stirring in my mind, so I raised my hand to catch the attention of Ignatius. "Polycarp; do you have a question or comment," he asked.

"Yes; I am concerned at how easily false teaching intrudes in the church. What is the cause?"

"It is rather simple," Ignatius replied. "I can sum it up in one word: superstition. Many have been delivered from pagan religions that are built upon superstitions, rites, and other erroneous practices and beliefs. Many people are enamored with statues and angels, for example. They worship artifacts associated with our history. They are interesting finds, and many have a fascinating history, but they are relegated to history and should not find their way into the worship of God. People are alarmed to terror at the thought of the wrath of God, and out of weak faith that can't seem to trust the work of Christ, they must add to their religion with vain practices they hope will appease the God we already know to be appeased. Did he not appease his wrath with our Lord on the cross? Beware, Polycarp, and take note. When the faith of a Christian grows weak, superstition and vain works replace it. It's a mixture of Judaism and paganism that creates a false Christianity. That will be a constant danger for generations to come in the universal church. Mark my words!"

---

55. Romans 3:10-12, 23

The days were busy with ministry, discipling, and being discipled. People were curious about this group called "Christians." That's interesting when you remember that it was here in Antioch the saints were first called Christians. They meant it as a point of derision, but the Church claimed it and made it a name of honor. The pagan referred to themselves as followers of Caesar, thinking that they were insulting us by calling the saints followers of Christ, who was conquered and killed by Caesar. They never considered what took place on the third day after the crucifixion of Jesus, especially since there are eyewitnesses to this event living in Antioch to this day; Ignatius being one of them. The power of the Church isn't limited to the eyewitnesses of Jesus death and resurrection. The power is in the supernatural change that takes place in the nature of one who becomes a Christian. Truly, Paul captured this in his second letter to the Corinthian Church when he described conversion as being an "entirely new creation with the old, antiquated nature banished, and being instilled with a brand new nature."[56]

A couple of months after my arrival, I had received word that John returned to Ephesus due to his poor health. There was great concern that he would die, and I felt especially pressured to leave and be with him, but he left clear instructions that I was to remain in Antioch for a few more months. Ignatius kept me busy, and I was able to begin ministering the Word of God to small groups around the town. After a few weeks of consistent ministry work, Ignatius desired a report on my work.

"Tell me Polycarp, you have been faithfully ministering these past several weeks, what have you discovered?" he inquired.

I hesitated before answering for there were many things I was discovering. "I believe the greatest discovery is that I love ministering the Word of God to others. I enjoyed the planting and watering of the Good News to those who were dead in trespasses and sins, and learning to tend the flock of our Lord with his saints. I love the work with all its pressures, disappointments and joys," I replied.

"I noticed as much," said Ignatius, "God has truly imparted to you the spiritual gift of pastor and teacher. While people have

---

56. II Corinthians 5:17

noticed your knowledge of the Word, it's your love for the Word that stands out. When a pastor loves the Word, it's because the Word is alive in him, and gives him the ability to love others as Jesus loves them. You speak as a man with authority, not as a lord over the people, but as a youth experienced and persuaded by its power. You are my friend, an example of the believer."

I didn't know how to respond to his praise. I didn't want to appear proud, but, on the other hand, I didn't realize people were watching so closely. So I said the only logical thing, "I can't possibly take credit for what people see, but only give the praise to God for his great grace."

"Amen," Ignatius replied. "The gods of the nations are idols," he went on to say. "They must force and frighten people into following them. But Christ wants others to see his servants as living epistles, whose lives are read like the obvious words on parchment. Our lives should be a public testament, born out of private devotion to God's greatness," he admonished. "Why, even his law, which is impossible for a human to fulfill to perfection, was given to serve as a teacher to bring us to Christ. What will be a harsh, even ruthless headmaster for some, is the best and favorite teacher for those who have spiritually been born from above. God will destroy the gods of man, and he will use his church, and men like you to be his hammer."

9

FOR WE DON'T WRESTLE AGAINST FLESH AND BLOOD

Be endued with strength from the Lord and in the
power of his might. Be always adorned with the
armor of God, in order that you may be able to hold
your place against the cunning arts of the devil.
For our fight is not against flesh and blood, but towards the
spiritual instigators of evil, and their command to do evil,
against the evil use of power over the darkness and against
the powers ordered from the prince of this age.
(Ephesians 6:10-12)

IGNATIUS had established several congregations throughout the city because the size was too much for one man to shepherd. This particular Lord's Day I was to preach to a small rural congregation on the northern edge of town. I was requested to minister in his place and tend to the needs of the church. I preached from my current studies in Peter's first epistle along with some corresponding thoughts in Isaiah.

"He alone placed upon himself our sins on an accursed tree, so that we, being dead to our sins should live as ones made acceptable to God. By his wounds, we have been made whole."[57] I emphasized that this was the heart of the Gospel and best news possible for the redeemed in Christ.

Following our time in the Word and fellowship, I was overjoyed to leave the folks with some of the apostolic letters, including Luke's work on The Acts of the Apostles. Decimus had instructed me to pass them on to a needy congregation. They had only a couple worn and tattered manuscripts. They had no small

---

57. *Isaiah 53 & I Peter 2:24*

amount of joy in receiving this gift, though I do believe that mine surpassed theirs in being able to give it. My short time with them was a great honor, and while I already knew I was to preach the Word, this experience solidified my desires.

During the week, Ignatius called me into his study chamber with another assignment. "I heard from the congregation up north, and they informed me that you gave them a great deal to work with and meditate on for the week, and that pleases me. Did you enjoy the opportunity," he asked?

"Yes, more than I can describe," I responded. "I think I experienced Paul's heart-cry, 'Woe is me if I don't preach the Gospel.'[58] My reward is preaching the Word of God and helping others in their spiritual walk."

"It is an indescribable delight isn't it," Ignatius added. "But remember, to preach it rightly, we must live it. We must study; that is for certain, but many will study and share only what they have learned and not what they have lived. We are not lecturers who declare facts; we are persuaders urging people to 'taste and see that the Lord is good.'[59] We teach people how the Holy Spirit is growing them to live, and how that life is made possible by grace and the love of God shed throughout the hearts of his people. If we persuade people with the Word of God, the result is faith; the ability to believe and act on that belief."

"I agree. In good conscience, if it's not growing in my heart, I'm not sure I could adequately preach," I responded. "I greatly desire to minister again wherever I may be useful."

"Splendid!" exclaimed Ignatius, "I have another assignment for you, and I must warn you, it will likely reveal the harder side of ministry. Return to me praising God in this, and I'll be assured of your true calling. I desire for you to head up to Hierapolis. I'm not speaking of the one in Phrygia,[60] but north of Antioch; about a three day journey from here. You will be traveling alone, for I have no one to spare to join you. The road, while well-traveled, is still fraught with dangers. A man ruled by fear or controlled by hidden lusts will find this journey rather treacherous. A man with the love of God in his heart and controlled by the Spirit will find

58. I Corinthians 9:16

59. Psalm 34:8

60. Near Ephesus

it an adventure. I hope for your sake it's an adventure. I would be grieved to be sending you into the cruel snare of temptation."

"The congregation to whom you will be ministering was formed years ago under the ministry of Barnabas, Paul's companion you may remember, but it has been neglected. It breaks my heart to say it, but immorality is decimating the congregation, and they err in misunderstanding the grace of God. It seems that they find conquering or enduring the struggle of sin impossible, and they compensate by misinterpreting grace as a license to sin. They do not understand that grace is not an excuse to sin, but a pattern for growth out of sin's bondage. The overseer I have in mind for them is in Corinth, and John has sent word to him to come to me and take oversight of this flock. The challenge I face is that he won't be here for several more weeks. Come see me here again tomorrow morning. I'll have the funds to sustain you, food for the journey and a donkey for your transportation. I'll also give you final instructions."

The next morning I found out what he meant by "final instructions." Apparently a rogue group of rebels was terrorizing Roman citizens throughout parts of Syria. After sharing what little he knew of the situation, he smiled at me, told me to be careful and then slapped the donkey on its haunches sending me swiftly on my journey. My mind began to get the best of me as I made my way alongside the river. Every little sound startled me, and I could picture bandits charging out after me from the darkness of the nearby woods. Ignatius advised me to travel with others I found going in the same direction, so you can imagine my relief when the first group I encountered going in my direction was a Roman patrol. I soon figured that if the rebels were to attack someone, wouldn't they start with a Roman patrol? My fear disgusted me, and I rebuked myself. "If God plans for me to die today," I thought, "then it doesn't matter if I am at home in bed, or riding on the back of this donkey."

I started humming some psalms of assurance and found it abated my fear. After the patrol headed in a different direction, I joined up with an Arab family who were making their way up to Mesopotamia through Hierapolis. As we got closer to the city, the larger the knot in the pit of my stomach grew. I had no idea how I could help this congregation. My only hope was that God wanted me here, and would use me for his glory. Indeed, if anything good comes out of me that can help others, it would be glorious.

———————◇◇———————

Hierapolis, also known as Hierapolis Euphratensis, was about thirteen miles west of the Euphrates River, and was the first major city to receive water from the large aqueducts that transported fresh water from the river to the arid, southern regions. As I entered the gates of the old city, I was immediately struck by the grotesque paganism that dominated the city. It was an immoral scene I was not completely prepared to encounter. I was familiar with immoral pagan practices in Ephesus, but what was happening in Hierapolis was more flagrant. As I navigated my way through the crowds, I wondered what Ignatius was getting me into; "This mission would be better suited for a blind man," I muttered to myself. I rode straight on trying not to look to right or left.

I was embarrassed and tried to ignore the gross comments and solicitations that both immoral women and men were making towards me. It was profoundly evil, and what is even odder is that I never felt as if they were talking to me, but rather were searching my soul, fishing for any sign or manifestation of secret lust. The fact I could even be tempted discomfited me. For a moment, I thought I had missed my town and ended up in Sodom and Gomorrah. A wave of apprehension came over me, and I felt intimidated by the dominion of evil before me. As I tried to ascertain the power that was stirring up my fear, I concluded that it wasn't over the temptations I was currently facing, but was more how the evil one would use those temptations later when I may not be as alarmed. "Be sober and watchful," I thought to myself. "I can hear the roaring lion as he prowls looking for a simpleton to devour." I didn't want that to be me.

Being already fatigued from my journey, and having been forced, as it were, to walk the gauntlet of temptation, I finally arrived at the home of my hosts, Theocritus and his wife Jana, who, observing my approach from the rooftop, came down to greet me in their courtyard, which immediately set me at ease. I first observed that they were dark skinned, and I assumed that they were not from this area. With outstretched arms, Theocritus greeted me. "It is obvious you were not instructed to proceed around the wall to the North Gate. The west gate, the one you entered, is known locally as the Gate of Atargatis. Its official name is the Mabog Gate. You were undoubtedly introduced to, shall I say, the unrighteous part of our city. I am truly sorry you had to see that young man."

"It did take me by surprise," I confessed, "but I rode through without being defiled I think. It must have been an amusing sight to others as they observed me trying to navigate the streets with my eyes closed."

As I slid off my donkey, Jana said, "You must be Polycarp. The letter from Ignatius described you quite well. Welcome to our home."

As we sat around the table that evening, I asked Theocritus about the unbridled immorality that has a godless hold on the city. "As I understand, you are from Ephesus, and they worship the goddess Diana don't they?" He inquired.

"Yes, in fact, the Temple of Diana is in Ephesus. Pilgrims come from all over the empire to visit and offer sacrifices to her, even the Emperor," I replied.

"Does the worship of the goddess involve immoral practices?" he continued.

"It does, but not to the extent I have seen here, at least not in public. My knowledge of immoral practices in the Temple is limited to what John or my family have told me. I'm ignorant of the evil, and prefer to stay that way if I can help it," I responded.

"You are wise to follow that commitment," Jana said.

"What can I say except that the grace of God has spared me from that kind of life? He gave me a pious mother and family, not to mention a godly mentor in the Apostle John, and Timothy as my pastor," I replied.

"Strong and godly families are vital," Theocritus added. Many of the young people in our congregation struggle against the great sins of the city, and have yielded and shipwrecked their faith. As a result, they have thrown themselves into a pit of destruction. Some have tried to maintain a form of piety, but I see it as an attempt to gain our acceptance of their sin, and not seek the power of God to repent and pursue righteousness."

"Polycarp," he continued, "the goddess Atargatis was the same Greek goddess Aphrodite, the origins of which can be traced back to the false god, Baal. Perhaps now you can understand the rampant immorality. Their form of worship is immoral and an excuse to pursue whatever sexual sin they desire. There are no restraints. Many try to resist the flood of immoral temptations with their fleshly strength, and of course, the result is what they thought to be their strength turns out to be their greatest weakness. They try to flee the sins of the flesh, but have never learned the importance of following after righteousness and godliness."

"That's exactly it," Jana said, "they run in circles fleeing the lust of their flesh only to run right into it again. What a hopeless cycle of life."

"John has often told me that our joy is not defined by the absence of sin, for we will never experience that in our earthly lives," I replied. "True joy is finding a growing love for Christ, whereby we see him sharpening our spiritual desires to obey. Perhaps I can illustrate it for you with an anecdote that my uncle, Decimus used to share with me. Let's say that my uncle was going into town for supplies. While running his errands, I was instructed to clean out the stalls, make sure that fresh feed and water had been provided for the animals, and when that was done, some fences needed mending. After assigning the chores, he climbed up into the wagon, and then looked back at me to remind me that there was a nest of vipers in the rocks at the edge of the field, and he warned me to stay away from it. But as I watched him ride off, I immediately ran toward the rock pile to watch for vipers. I didn't disturb them, but stopped just short of the nest, and there I stood. I wanted to get closer and see them for myself, but I knew that it's not only wrong, but was also dangerous. I even rebuked myself for having such stupid curiosity. After several hours of resisting my urge, I noticed my uncle riding back towards the barn, and I ran to greet him. As I arrived, I noticed him looking rather perplexed as he walked out of the barn. As I happily approached him, he asked, 'Why haven't you fulfilled your chores? Why haven't you obeyed me?' Instead of answering him, I proudly exclaim, 'Decimus, why are you disappointed with me? I didn't get into the viper's nest.' My point is this; I defined a good day based upon what I didn't do, when the opportunity to do right had been laid out before me. It is the work of the Holy Spirit, through the instruction of God's word, to show what we should be doing. He guides us into what grows, protects and helps us in the Way of Truth. He makes us doers of the Word."

"It sounds like you are describing sanctification," Theocritus asked.

"Exactly!" I responded. "It is how God uses the power of His Word in us, wielded by the Spirit's work, to make us holy as Jesus is holy. John speaks of this in his illustration of the vine and branches. Jesus told his disciples, 'you are now clean or pruned by the Word.'[61] But we will never live in that reality unless we abide in Christ. He is the vine, and his Father is the vine-dresser, the growth and fruit production comes from the vine, and the care and cultivation come from the farmer. I suppose one way that gives us understanding of this is that we are, as branches, being prepared to produce the fruits or proofs of God's Spirit in us."

"I was thinking on that passage just the other day," Theocritus added, "and was struck by the words, 'I have said all this so that you would see my joy in you and that it would cause your joy to overflow.'"[62]

Already feeling the pressure of my circumstances, I asked why they were without a pastor. Their silence exposed an uneasy answer. Finally, Theocritus said, "It is complicated and disconcerting. Let me say first that I'm surprised Ignatius would send such a young and inexperienced person. Please don't misunderstand me either, Polycarp."

Jana interrupted her husband and said, "We do like you. You seem like a virtuous and godly young man."

"Very true," Theocritus added. "My comment is not meant to insult you, but I think you may be in over your head. The church is trapped in legalism; the city is overrun with immorality; war is about to consume the province; and, to answer your question, our last pastor was murdered."

"Murdered! Why? Was it for his faith in Christ?" I cautiously asked.

Theocritus nervously exhaled and replied, "Yes, but not as you might expect. The entire Syrian countryside is being terrorized by a large Jewish sect under the leadership of a man named Lukuas. Their fight is against Rome, but not necessarily Christians. They

---

61. John 15:3

62. John 15:11

are a remnant of zealots that survived the Roman destruction of Israel, and they raid small towns, farmers, and travelers—killing anyone who is a Roman citizen. Our previous pastor, Agapetus, a man like you, trained by the Apostles and appointed to this congregation by Barnabas, was killed for being a Roman. They ambushed him while why he was traveling to a local farm owned by a family in this congregation. He knew the danger but felt the need of that family was worth the risk. He was beaten and stoned to death."

"Aren't you in danger?" I inquired.

"No, no we are not Romans. Both of us were born as slaves in Cyrene, in North Africa near the Great Sea. After the war ravaged our homeland, we escaped and fled. By God's design, we ended up here. This city is where we first heard and responded to the Gospel, and we decided to make it our home. Most of the congregation are converted Jews who were forced to leave Israel, or Gentiles, whose homelands were conquered, and they fled here and to other parts of the region to escape the bloodshed. The Roman population here is declining, but most are native to this land or from Persia. You'll find the congregation is poor, but hard-working, and they are not the object of Lukuas' hatred. You, on the other hand—you are a Roman, and you'll need to be cautious."

"A Roman general, Lucius Quietus has been dispatched from Rome to come here with a legion and capture or kill the zealots. He suppressed an uprising in Parthia, just east of here," Jana added.

"Lukuas has sworn he will slit the throat of every Roman citizen in the town," Theocritus said as he leaned back in his chair and gave me a slight smile and added, "So you see, you are in a hotbed of trouble. Welcome to Hierapolis. We'll do what we can to protect you, but you must be sensible where and when you travel about the city. Our first rule for you is that you do not travel alone. Will you give me your word that you'll honor my rule?"

The last time I felt my life at risk was as a slave of Crixus. The sensation was surreal. "Yes, of course," I replied.

That evening as I went into my bed chamber, I knew that I had to run to God's Word for comfort, strength and direction. It was true; I was in over my head, but not over the head of God. I needed him to lift me up over my worries and fear. Naturally, my mind and heart embraced the psalm:

> *God is my place of safety and my might,*
> *always present help in times of deep distress.*
> *For this reason, I will not give way to fear, though the*
> *whole earth is moved, though the mountains are shaken*
> *into the depths of the sea, though the tumult of the waters*
> *overflow, though the mountains quake at the swelling seas.*
>
> *There is a calm river; the channels of that river*
> *encourage me for their source is the city of God,*
> *the sacred habitation of the Most High God.*
> *God is there, unshaken and unmovable.*
>
> *The nations were in an uproar, and the kingdoms are*
> *toppled, and by the sound of His voice, even the earth melts.*
> *The Lord of hosts is with us, the God*
> *of Jacob is our stronghold.*
>
> *Walk with me and gaze upon the works of the*
> *LORD, and how he deals harshly with the earth.*
> *He stops wars from one end of the earth to*
> *the other; he snaps the bow and smashes the*
> *spear; he destroys the chariots with fire.*
>
> *For these reasons, be still, and find out that I am God.*
> *I will be held high among all the nations;*
> *I will be held high throughout the world.*
> *The LORD of hosts is with us, the God of*
> *Jacob is our secure place of refuge.*[63]

I thought it a strange irony that Lukuas could likely be thinking on the same passage, but being a rejecter of the Messiah robbed him of true insight into that Psalm.

◇◇

---

63. Psalm 46

For the first couple of weeks I devoted myself to the study of the Word and much prayer. There were some beautiful fields just outside the North Gate that provided me a wondrous prayer closet where I walked and talked with God to give me the grace necessary to fulfill his plan, and ability to strengthen His church. The rest of the time I followed John and Timothy's example, meeting with families and individuals within the congregation seeking to discover their understanding of Scripture and grace in particular. I simply wanted to know to what extent they had been discipled to be imitators of Jesus. John preferred this method to just preaching alone. He was always reminding me that tending the flock of our Lord was more than just preaching. Part of a pastor's preparation is to till the ground of the heart, to remove distractions from people's thinking, or to determine their needs. I found this increased my burden for the people and aided me in presenting the passages in a way that would make it a true feast for those seeking spiritual nourishment. And true to my word, I always had a travel companion with me.

One evening in particular stood out to me when I visited with a group of men of various ages. I was a bit intimidated at first, for what could I teach these people? But once again, I discovered God's grace at work in me giving me courage and wisdom, and working through me providing me with answers to their questions. In fact, I found it quite remarkable and exhilarating. After sharing some things I had been taught regarding the principle of fleeing worldly lusts and pursuing righteousness, faith, love and peace,[64] I asked if they understood or had questions. The flood of questions flustered me, for I thought I had done a good job at addressing the issue at hand.

Jonah, a newly married man, was the first to respond. "Polycarp, I'm not sure you have had to face temptations like we do here in Hierapolis, but what do you think we should do about the eroticism in this city?"

"You are right, Jonah. When I first arrived in your city I saw openly displayed in the street the kinds of things that are found only in the pagan temple of Diana in my home town. And I have never even been in the temple of Diana myself, so I can only base my understanding of it on what others have told me. However,

---

64. II Timothy 2:22

where we live doesn't make the temptation to sin any less or greater. Remember that our Lord was tempted in the wilderness," I answered. "Our temptations, as the Apostle James makes clear, are from within. As he said: 'Every man is tempted to sin when he is lured in by his own forbidden longing, and then is ensnared.'[65] And as for me, many times I find myself standing in awe of what God mercifully protects me from when my flesh would betray me and fling itself into all manner of unrighteousness. In fact, on this subject of withstanding sexual immorality, when I was very young, just after I became a believer, some friends tempted me to join them in spying on some women in the baths of the temple of Diana. The lust within me was powerful, and I have to say that in my heart I had already given in to it. But our gracious Lord rescued me from carrying out the lust that was in my heart, through no righteousness of my own. He spared me that entrapment to sin. Only Jesus Christ, though tempted in every way that we are, did not sin, because there was no sin in his flesh. He was tempted, but temptation could not latch on to anything in his life from which to mount an assault. The more tolerance we give sin in the secret recesses of our heart, the stronger the pull we will feel from external temptations."

Phillip, a teenager in the group asked, "Are you talking about killing the sin in our flesh?"

"Yes, but it's only the beginning," I replied. I am still learning about this too, but my understanding is that when we attempt it in our power, and it simply doesn't work. It's like holding your breath—at some point you are going to be forced to breathe. Only the power of God's Holy Spirit working in us can deliver us, and this is the basis of grace.

I glanced up at Quintas, who was sitting opposite of me, and noticed that he appeared agitated. When his eyes met mine, I asked what concerned him.

"I thought we were dead to sin," he protested. "I don't understand how I can be dead to sin, while it still seems so very much alive in me. Should I believe God's Word, or what I feel?" That question struck a chord as several in the group chimed in with similar questions.

---

65. James 1:14

"Obviously, God's Word is what we believe first," I said. "That is the basis of our faith, not our experiences. Didn't Solomon exhort us in his Proverbs that our trust in the Lord doesn't need the support of our own understanding?"

"But what if I just can't seem to discover this power you are talking about?" Quintas asked.

"Then we must follow the exhortation given to us in the letter to the Hebrews," I said. 'Look to Jesus the one who established and completes our faith.'[66] In other words, we may struggle in certain areas all our life, but Jesus has dealt with that sin. He became our sin and exchanged it with his righteousness; your sin and my sin for his righteousness. When it seems that our victory over the flesh is difficult and lifelong in its struggle, we look to Jesus who gave us victory over sin and its controlling power and eternal judgment. As John has instructed me many times, our joy is not hinged to our conquering of sin, but rather in the discovery of Jesus Christ. We are never to stop contending with sin but must always be discovering our Lord Jesus Christ. He must be the focal point of our lives."

Peter, a newly married man and one I knew was being over-come by severe sexual passions said, "I guess I've never taken the time to look at it that way, but I think I understand what you are talking about. Instead of working so hard to fight against sin so I can please God, I need to set my heart on growing in godliness knowing he is already pleased."

"That's the point," I replied. "Now this is conducting our lives by faith and not by sight. Do we trust that Jesus was thorough enough on our behalf to please our righteous and holy God? If not, we will attempt, in vain I must add, to please God out of our futile efforts; and when we do, will we find our efforts pleased God?"

"No, of course not," Peter said.

"But how do we deal with the commands?" I asked.

"Obviously you're not telling us that we can disregard and disobey God?" a young man suggested.

"You are right, but what I am saying is that we don't have an inherent strength either to conquer sin or to obey God. The Spirit of God empowers us to overcome sin each day not through

---

66. *Hebrews 11:2*

resistance alone, but more by growing in grace. This is what Paul described in his letter to the Galatian church as walking in the Spirit. The conquering of sin is spiritual, so that means that the proofs or fruit of the Spirit are the essentials we seek in order to resist, fight, or flee temptations. If we ignore God tomorrow, the sin residing in our flesh returns. Until our bodily glorification, sin cannot be eradicated from the flesh. Just because you resisted temptation today doesn't mean it won't be back tomorrow. Our dependency upon the Holy Spirit must be every moment of every day. Thankfully, God's Spirit within us is more constant than our own will to resist sin. But it's not a constant resistance against sin I am describing. It is a constant presence of the Holy Spirit that provides an ever-present resistance through the proofs of his inner work, namely: God's love in us, overflowing gladness, unexplainable peace, endurance in trials or against temptations, desires of kindness towards others, ability to help others, spiritual devotion, integrity and self-control."

"The same principle applies to our obedience too," I continued. "We can't obey without the Spirit's direction and empowerment in us. For this reason, we attend to the Word, whether proclaimed in public services or in our private studies. As a body of believers, we are to build each other up and to confess our faults to one another. As we confess our proneness to sin, we aren't admitting a wrong as much as we are asking for help in a mutual struggle. It's no more shameful to confess our faults than it is for a great athlete in the Roman Circus to hire a coach. The contender who wants to win seeks the best help he can find."

Augustus, one of the older men in the group, said, "I've heard Ignatius say that we can't find happiness in sin because our new nature abhors it, and we can't find happiness in God because we don't know him."

"I have heard that before," I said, nodding in agreement. "The more grace grows in our hearts, the stronger our spiritual desires and strength to withstand the urge of sin to borrow our bodies for unrighteous purposes. I don't find a weakening of sin in me as much as I find a growing sense of God's power in me. I believe it was Peter who said that we are to 'grow in grace and in our understanding of Jesus Christ.'[67] There is no other way to deal with sin."

"You make it sound easy, Polycarp, but it's harder than it seems," Quintas replied.

"I suppose in some ways you may be right, but our new, spiritual nature makes the resistance to sin and the desire for spiritual growth more of a natural response than sin," I replied. "Remember Paul's instructions to the Galatian church when he said that we are to 'crucify our flesh,' namely its ungodly affections and lusts. I believe the struggle or resistance we experience with our bodies is our identifying with the pain of the crucifixion. Moses, as recorded in the Epistle to the Hebrews, is said to have experienced this when he chose to suffer along with his people rather than yield to the fleeting pleasures of sin. But we obviously can't stay focused on the pain and suffering side of killing our sins. I believe that while the flesh experiences the pain of restraint, it is slight as compared to the joy and glory we experience as we live in the reality of a God-empowered obedience. John has told me often that the evidence of divine love is obedience—God's love to us and our growing love for Him in return."

Augustus added, "I recall a message preached by Ignatius when I was visiting in Antioch. He was expounding on Paul's exhortation to the Church at Corinth, I believe it was his first letter to them, where he states, I am not fighting emptiness like one punching the air, but rather I fight the urges of my body and become its slave driver."

"That must have been a good message. I remember that passage too." I said, "Then Paul goes on to put that fight in its rightful context saying that as we encounter temptations, God always provides an escape so that we can endure it.[68] I think the escape he was talking about is the Holy Spirit. We are not lured to sin by outer temptations, but our inner lusts of the flesh. It's like our flesh casts a net into the water, and having caught a sin, pulls it in and the temptation is complete. Growing in grace means our hands are so obediently given to serving God that they reach less and less often for that net of the flesh.

67. II Peter 3:18

68. I Corinthians 10:13

During our discussion, I was happy to see Theocritus enter the room. After listening for a few minutes, he offered an insightful perspective. "All this talk on our sin-struggles brings to mind the story in Numbers where the Children of Israel complained of God's treatment of them, and God sent deadly serpents into their camp. When they repented, God commanded Moses to make a bronze serpent and mount it on a pole, and as the Scriptures say, 'Make a fiery serpent and mount it on a post, and every person who has been bitten, when he looks upon it, will live.'[69] Sins are like those serpents. The people did not live by trying to kill the venomous snakes; they lived by looking at the one lifted up on the pole. I've always assumed that this was a picture of Jesus being lifted up for us. We don't live by killing sin, but by looking at the only one who can and did kill the power of sin. We must look to Jesus as the sin-slayer, and stop trying to defeat sin out of our strength."

Levi replied, "Yes, this makes sense, for by the time you kill one, you turn around, and there are ten more coiled to strike."

"Sadly true, except for me—I can't seem to kill a one; I'm being bitten all over," Quintas said, only half in jest.

Everyone could identify with him and the frustration of dealing with our desire to sin, but as I glanced around the room, I could tell not all of them understood the solution as I had hoped.

"What would you say if I suggested that our greatest time of worship could be in the face of temptation? I am finding that as I learn to trust God in times of temptation, he is always near, and that as I yield my body to him instead of yielding to sin, I experience true worship. As Paul said in his letter to the Romans, placing our bodies at the disposal of the Lord is our true worship."[70]

I could see a small flame flickering in their thinking, but knew God's Spirit would have to fan that flame into full understanding—in my own life as much as in theirs.

After much discussion, and due to the lateness of the hour, I thought it best to conclude with this final thought. "One of my favorite passages is Paul's prayer to the Ephesian saints: "I desire the eyes of your insight be given light to see, and to know what is the future anticipation of his call to you; specifically what is the

---

69. *Numbers 21:8*

70. *Romans 12:1*

glorious inheritance he has saved for you his saints. And to know the magnitude of his greatness that is beyond human measurements to those of us who have received faith, all of which is the result of the outpouring of his limitless energy, that same power that worked in Christ when he was raised from the dead."[71]

<hr />

Later that week, I found Quintas staring off in the distance as he sat on the edge of the city wall. From my observations, I could tell that he was quite discouraged. "Quintas, I am glad I found you. You appear rather disheartened."

"I am more than just disheartened, Polycarp. I honestly feel like leaping off this wall."

I was alarmed. "What has you so upset?" I asked.

He sighed and with anger in his voice he said, "I can't conquer sin. It clearly has conquered me. I wish I were like you. You live in victory."

"Wait a minute," I objected. You obviously misunderstand the victory given to us by Christ. And furthermore, I am not sinless and have hardly attained perfection. Indeed, I never will while I reside in the body of death. Quintas, you focus too much on the defensive posture of your fight, when Christ has given us the advantage. Our battle is an offensive one. Paul edified the Corinthian Christians in his first epistle when he declared, 'Give gratitude to God, who has given us overcoming power through our Lord Jesus Christ. For this reason, we can be, and should be steadfastly focused on what Christ won for us, being unmoved because of such a decisive victory, and always see an opportunity to advance in our joy of that victory. Such an objective is hardly a vain and empty work in light of the Lord's work,'"[72] I exhorted.

"That's fine, Polycarp. But what does that mean to me? What does an offensive weapon mean to me? Where does worship fit in when I feel so unholy?" Quintas begged.

"Tell me, have you ever read the Apostle Matthew's Gospel," I asked.

"Yes, not long ago," Quintas replied.

<hr />

71. *Ephesians 1:18-20*

72. *I Corinthians 15:57-58*

"Do you remember that near the beginning he draws our attention to how Jesus went into the wilderness and was tempted after having fasted forty days and nights?" I inquired.

He nodded and answered, "Yes, I do recall the story."

"During the temptation, we find some guiding insights into how we can resist temptation. However, our resistance is not for the purpose of simply not sinning. Our resistance is based upon positive action. During the devil's final attempt, Jesus revealed the answer when he said, 'Leave at once, Satan. For it has been written that you must adoringly worship the Lord your God, and he alone is the one whom you worshipfully obey.'"[73]

Now Quintas was no longer looking down over the wall but was looking at me.

"Let me explain it in another way," I said. "The fruit of the Spirit highlights the weapons of our warfare. As we walk in the Spirit, we have the fruit of the Spirit actively engaged on our behalf. As we discover God's love for us, it produces a resisting love against our spiritual enemy and opens our eyes to opportunities to busy ourselves loving others as we discover we are loved by God. We pursue peace, embrace joy, and persevere in the development of godliness even if it means that our suffering is long. We go out of our way to express kindness to others; that is gentleness, and seek to do the best and wholesome things in our activities. We commit ourselves to discover God's work in us which is faith; intercede on behalf of others in need when no one expects it, which is meekness, and of course, we practice self-control. I look on self-control more as training my body rather than restraining it. Paul declared that he disciplines or trains his body and forces it away from what is wrong. He told Timothy to flee the lustful desires but follow after what is godly and right. Self-control is more about training our body to follow the Lord than simply refusing to sin. That's part of it, but following or pursuing what is right is the strength-wielding discipline we need. Do you understand what I'm saying?"

"Yes, it's clearer, I think," Quintas remarked.

I decided to sum it up this way. "It's like this, Quintas; Jesus has dealt with our sins. But you already know this to be true. And while he has destroyed the power of bondage sin once had over

---

73. Matthew 4:10

you, there remains the residual effect of that sin in our flesh. We conquer these things out of spiritual growth, not merely resisting them. We mature into obedience, so that when one sin is subdued, we are grown to take on the next one as it were. God's purpose in this is to give us a deeper understanding of his power and glory in us, which in turn makes our worship of him that much deeper. I do not struggle with fewer sins than you, but what I have learned has perhaps given me the strength to struggle less with my sins, and grow in grace and in the knowledge of the Lord Jesus Christ. If I spend my days trying to conquer what Christ has conquered, what have I gained?" However, if I spend my days discovering the joyous victory of the Lord, then I discover him conforming my desires to his desires, and therefore, my actions lead me into obedience, which in turn changes the struggle. I'm not struggling against sin, but struggling to advance in godly obedience."

My time in Hierapolis was drawing to a close. I had spent seven weeks ministering through teaching and preaching, and the new pastor was to arrive soon. The city seemed to grow in vileness, and the hostilities of Lukuas and his marauders were only intensifying. Roman citizens were either departing the city or confining themselves within the protection of the city walls. We soon received word that a list of Romans living in the city had been compiled by the rebels and that my name was on it. They were watching for me outside of the city, and like many unfortunate Romans, they were awaiting the opportunity to kill me too. I didn't mind dying for my faith, but I had no desire to die because I was a Roman citizen. Lucius Quietus, the Roman defender, was not to arrive for a few weeks as he waited for all of his army to join him in Antioch.

Alarmed at the danger I was in, the kind folks of the congregation gathered to plan how they would get me out of the city. I tried not to display my anxiety, but I was quite apprehensive regarding the circumstances, and found it easy to doubt God in the secrecy of my heart. So I battled self-condemnation on two fronts: my weak faith and my hypocrisy of strong faith. "O wretched man that I am," I thought to myself.

As ideas were tossed about the room, one was suggesting I be smuggled out through the gates buried under a wagon of merchandise being taken out of the city. But most of the folk believed Lukuas' men would be watching for this. A few suggested that I should simply wait it out. I rather liked that idea. There were a couple of men, daring and brave-hearted, that suggested that I should be escorted out of the city by armed men in the congregation. I quickly spoke up in opposition to that; first, I didn't want these people whom I love dying because I was a Roman, nor was I confident that any would survive the fight.

After the ideas went quiet, and everyone sat there wondering what to do, Mathias, a godly, elderly man spoke up in a raspy but calm voice. "As you all know, I was brought to Christ at Pentecost, and remained in Jerusalem those many weeks afterward, until my own younger brother, Stephen was cruelly stoned to death for his love and devotion to our Lord and Savior. Like many others, I felt the necessity to leave Jerusalem and finally ended up in Damascus where a new congregation had been formed. I still remember the fear we experienced when we received news that the zealot, Saul, was coming to arrest and kill us. But as you know, he was miraculously born again and became a champion for his Savior. After some time in the city, he became a point of exasperation and torment to the Jews, for he daily, in their synagogues, proved from the Holy Scriptures that Jesus was the Messiah."

"They hated him for that, and like young Polycarp here, plotted to kill him, and they had guards watching the gates day and night. We came up with a plan however, that got him safely out of the city, and I think it's possible to try it again. You may remember that Luke, in his book of the Acts of the Apostles, describes in some detail how they carefully, under the cover of darkness, lowered Paul safely to the ground in a basket.[74] Let's send our young preacher over the wall with an escort. Send him north for a few miles and then westward toward the Orontes River. From there, he can take a boat south into the safety of Antioch."

That seemed to be the most popular idea. Still, I secretly reserved in my heart the desire to avoid any danger at all, but nevertheless, I consented. The next night everything was set. On the walkway at the top of the wall, Mathias put his hand on my shoulder and whispered close to my ear, "Do not fret, Polycarp. It's at times like this when our faith seems most shaken that God,

---

74. Acts 9:23-25

through the power of His Spirit, reveals how vast and strong his gift of faith is in us. You could not be safer. Indeed, if God were to lead you so, you could walk right through Lukuas' tent, and he would never take notice." He kissed me on the forehead and prayed for me. "Take now my dear brother in Christ, God of our salvation, and bear him safely through the entrenchments of those who would seek him harm both in this realm and the spiritual realm. Bring him with the fullness of joy into the company of his brethren in Antioch, and bless his labor in your flock. He has blessed me, and I trust will be your well-used vessel for years to come. Thank you for Jesus Christ, and for the wonder of bearing his name. Amen."

He smiled at me holding me by the shoulders said, "The gods of men tremble at the devotion of men of God," and as tears welled up in his eyes, he added; "You remind me of Stephen."

A couple of the men helped me into the basket that was already dangling over the wall, and I was let down to where Ezra, my guide was waiting. It was a cloudy night, and our movements went unnoticed as we ran quietly into the nearby woods away from the glow of the bonfires near the gates. Besides that momentary thrill, we made it safely to the river where I booked passage for my short journey down to Antioch.

10
THOUGH HE GRIEVES, HE WILL HAVE COMPASSION

The Lord will not cast off his people forever, but though
he permits grief, he will have compassion out of the
abundance of his mercy. (Lamentations 3:31-32)

MY ministry training, as far as John's direct input, was complete. Timothy and John assigned me many responsibilities throughout the congregations. It seemed strange, knowing myself as I do, that God would gift me to help others advance in their spiritual walk and Christ-like character. How many times have I felt like the one needing the help? Herein lies the secret to the gift of being an overseer; my needs are the classrooms where God equips me for future effectiveness in the lives of others assigned to my care. My days were spent in study, seeing to the needs of the spiritual flock and planting and watering of the Gospel in the lives of believers or any lost soul who would listen. However, with all the joy that was flooding my soul, I was about to enter a season of grief and deep trials.

A deadly plague once again ravaged our city; very similar to the one that took my parents' lives twenty-five years ago, and like that dreadful time, it also struck close to my heart when both Decimus and Beatrice died, being called by the Lord to their heavenly home. Just before my uncle died, I walked into his bed chamber, and though he had a fever and was physically weak, and was mourning the loss of his wife who had preceded him by just a week, he talked about the joy of seeing his Savior. I was deeply struck by how prepared he was as he shared what were to be his final thoughts.

"Polycarp, I doubted your mother as she pursued her desire to purchase a little slave boy. I thought that foolishness had misguided her, but I was wrong," he uttered. "You are the greatest joy

God has ever brought into our family. You weren't just Callisto's, for Beatrice and I claimed you as our own too, you know."

I grabbed his hand as he spoke, but was unable to utter a word due to the grief that was tearing my soul apart.

"I want you to know something," he said, I long to see my precious wife again, and my family and friends, but my dear boy, heaven would not be heaven without the glorious presence of Christ. I go to Heaven to be with him forever." He smiled and gasped for his next breath as he said, "I truly doubt my family will be waiting for me at the gates of that celestial city, for they will be before the Lord waiting for me to take my place at their side with him in the splendor of his majesty."

He struggled to breathe, and both my mother and I knew that his departure would be soon.

"I can't wait for my sister, and for you, who have been the glory of my old age, to join me in the presence of Jesus. Don't mourn for me, long for our Lord." Then in nothing more than a whisper he breathed out his last words; "Be faithful to our Lord, even in the face of death," and then he was gone.

I stared at his lifeless body in the same way I would look memorably at a home in which someone I knew once lived. Both Callisto and I wept, for the loss of Decimus and Beatrice was great. I was very concerned for my mother's well-being, for weeks she had cared for them day and night, but while she too became seriously ill to the point of death, she survived to the praise of God, and my great relief. We comforted each other and sought comfort from the Lord. God's Spirit took my thoughts to the psalm; "This has been my comfort in my sorrow, that I am revived by your word."[75] As I was comforted by my God, so I comforted others. The grace of comfort was a vital part of my ministry, for in those weeks that followed I was called upon to minister and reassure grieving families.

A couple days after the burial of my uncle, Timothy asked me, "Were you able to comfort the family of Tobias?"

I sighed, more out of frustration than anything. "Yes, but I feel feeble; inferior to the strength demanded by the sorrow. Truly, I felt helpless in assuaging their grief, for I still feel a great emptiness in my soul," I lamented.

---

75. Psalm 119:50

"Comforting the grief-stricken is one of the hardest ministries we face, especially when it is compounded by our own sorrow," Timothy responded. "You must remember if you are to bear up under the pressure of this work that we are channels of God's grace. The ministry of comforting the sorrowful and afflicted is as great a work of faith as moving a mountain. Grace comes from God to the afflicted much like a wave rolling up on the shore. The first waves don't take away the grief, but rather sustain the grieving. The next waves of grace, which takes place days or weeks later, help the sorrowing in talking and remembering with joy their loved ones. The final waves of God's grace, which continue for a lifetime I might add, give an understanding of the perfect will of God. This grace brings the peace of God that sustains all of us to our own death. Be a faithful servant of our Lord to comfort and cry with his people, as our Lord did at the tomb of Lazarus. Comfort them as Jesus comforts you."

The ministry of comforting others went on for weeks, and though the grief I felt clung to my soul, my desire to serve, help and comfort others only increased. The plague disappeared from within the city walls as fast and as silently as it had entered, sparing no household. Even the Proconsul of Rome, a man sympathetic to Christians, had died. John and others within the Church had shared the gospel with him on many occasions, but he reluctantly refused to consider the claims of Christ as true. I often wondered if at some point before his death he remembered the message of the Gospel.

John was no longer actively ministering. He was frail and didn't have the stamina to keep up with the demands of the ministry. Be assured though, he prayed like no one I had ever seen. Daily I stopped by his home to visit and talk. He was no longer living alone but had moved into the home of another one of his past students, Onesimus.

---◇◇---

"Greetings John," I said.

"Ah, there is my son, Polycarp," he affectionately replied. "These have been trying times, have they not?"

"Yes. I've never been so overwhelmed and helpless," I responded. "I've come to understand in some sense what Jeremiah was saying in his Lamentations, 'The Lord will not cast off his people forever, but though he permits grief, he will have compassion out of the abundance of his mercy,'"[76] I said.

"Yes, this is true. Jesus Christ is the wellspring of compassion, but I also joy in the fact that he uses his people and his servants to apply that compassion. You have done well, and I am pleased with you, as I know our Father in Heaven is likewise. You have experienced that grief first-hand with the death of dear Decimus and Beatrice," John said. "Is your mother well?" he asked.

"Yes, but still weak."

<hr />

In seasons of grief and distress, God sends the refreshing showers of hope and blessing, often through new ideas or direction. I was meeting each week with a few families as we studied together the Epistle to the Galatians in the home of a Jewish convert, Jesher, who was introduced to Jesus under the ministry of Peter in Cæsarea. After moving to Ephesus to minister alongside John, he was an effective witness to many Jews and Gentiles alike. One particular evening as I was teaching, I found myself distracted; not an irritating distraction, but one I found enjoyable. I was fumbling over my words and losing track of my thoughts. I suppose the only way to describe it is that I felt like someone being stirred out of a deep slumber.

My distraction was over in the corner. It was Jesher's oldest daughter, Anna. Obviously, I was struck by her beauty, for she was radiant. Her character was rare, like a treasure chest filled with the finest of qualities, and I already knew of her reputation as a virtuous and godly woman. I had known her for years; we had been childhood friends, but I saw her differently on this evening. Yesterday, she was a friend among many, but today, my eyes were opened in a way I can't explain. Someplace deep in my soul, I knew that she was to be my wife.

My worry, of course, was that what seemed a dream to me could turn out to be a nightmare to her. "Could she see me more than just a friend?" I thought to myself. At first, she didn't seem at all that interested in a deeper relationship with me, but like a team of horses driven by a determined charioteer, I felt like I had to win this race.

---

76. *Lamentations 3:32*

Callisto was amused by how senseless I had become, and encouraged me to be patient. "If she is the helpmeet God has prepared for you, she will come to you when he has finished preparing her for you," she admonished. "In the meantime, set your heart on the Lord and let him give you the desires of your heart."

The days and weeks seemed long and drawn out until she began to show me attention; then I lost all track of time. My waiting and pleading with God paid off, after several months of getting to know each other, and falling in love, we got married. It seemed that all of the sorrow of the past had been washed away by one person—Anna, my wife. I loved her name and cherished her, for she lived in the full expression of it: favored one, grace. Her words and her presence ministered to me. The power she had over me was wonderful, and for the first time, I felt the burden of ministry become lighter. God used her to give me a new sense of responsibility; indeed, I felt an entirely new motivation and strength to move ahead in ministry work. I had a partner, a helpmeet created by God for me and me for her. What a great, creative, and powerful God we serve!

Our newlywed life together wasn't going to be easy. Trouble was on the horizon, but I felt with her at my side we could endure it together. A new Proconsul had been appointed to Ephesus by Emperor Domitian. While the previous Proconsul was tolerant of Christianity, this new one demonstrated excessive ambition to make his name famous. He seemed eager to carry out Domitian's edict that required that we all worship Caesar as a god.

Shortly after the edict was signed into law, hundreds of Christians were being killed daily for their faith in Christ, for they would not worship any other gods but the One True God. The law was initially confined to Rome, but it soon spread outward through the empire, depending on the leanings of the governors or proconsuls. There was also talk coming out of Rome that John was of special interest since he was the last living Apostle of Christ, and was considered the leader of this sect. As one could expect, John was hardly alarmed and never once felt he would escape martyrdom, even at such an old age. While his strength was almost gone, his courage remained steadfast.

◇◇

Gaius Plinius Cæcilius Secundus, or commonly referred to as Pliny the Younger, was an imperial magistrate appointed by the Emperor in the year 84 to carry out the execution of his laws, especially as they related to Christians, whom he held in great suspicion for their obstinacy in their form of worship. He was a young man who had inherited his uncle's wealth, titles, and friends in high places. His uncle was killed while trying to help some friends to his ship in order to escape the eruption of Mt. Vesuvius and the subsequent destruction of Pompeii. He was able to get his friends and crew to safety, but not before the poison gases from the volcano suffocated him. He died on the ship as they fled to the sea.

Pliny the Younger had been sent by Domitian to Bithynia to arrest several prominent Christians charged with treason. Because of the size and popularity of Ephesus, he chose to sail here first and then journey overland to the north. He arrived in the city with great pageantry but said he could only stay for a short time since he was on the Emperor's mission. He informed the town leaders that his first order of business was to arrest the Christian sect leader called John, the Apostle. Without any delay, he was brought to the home of Onesimus, an Elder in the Church, who was to succeed the aging Timothy as Overseer of the Ephesian congregation.

As Pliny entered the courtyard, he saw a venerable man sitting near the fountain, wrapped in a shawl and resting in a chair padded with pillows. He was so engulfed in his reading that he failed to notice that the group had entered the gate. Onesimus got his attention, and introduced them; "John, this is Gaius Plinius Cæcilius Secundus, the magistrate to the Imperial Emperor."

"Forgive me for not standing, sir," replied John in a frail and raspy voice; "How may I be of service to you?"

Having a reputation for being civil, Pliny replied; "You do not need to stand on my account, sir. However, I come with news that will not bring you any comfort I dare say. My Lord, the Emperor has issued a warrant for your arrest, and I am here to carry out his wishes."

"My arrest," John expressed with a smirk of amusement. "What is my crime that would draw the attention of the Emperor?"

"You are charged with subversive behavior and teaching treasonous practices," Pliny said.

John found the charges amusing and replied, "Do I look like a man that could overthrow any government, much less Rome? Has any follower of Christ taken up arms against the Emperor?"

"No, not that I'm aware of," Pliny quickly acknowledged. "However, you do teach loyalty to a King Jesus do you not? And that his followers must obey him over the laws of the Emperor?"

John replied, "You misunderstand our teaching, Proconsul. It is true that Jesus is our King; indeed we believe him to be the King of kings, but his kingdom is not of this world as of yet. His Kingdom is a spiritual kingdom and future kingdom. He is not plotting to overthrow the governments of the world through his subjects. He will bring judgment upon the earth with the army of heaven. Our King teaches us to respect the ruling governments in the land, and that He alone has set them up in power, and likewise removes them accordingly. Truly, even you can see by the testimonies of Christians throughout the empire that we have honored the Caesars since Jesus himself was alive."

"Your king is dead! I have read the accounts of his crucifixion," countered Pliny.

John nodded slowly but affirmatively and replied, "Yes, I was there! He did die. I stood at the foot of his cross and heard him whisper his final words: 'It is finished.' I saw him take his final breath." But now with a serious look, and a voice invigorated with confidence he continued. "I also was an eyewitness to his physical resurrection from the dead three days later. There are additional historical accounts of thousands seeing him, not to mention the Roman guards tasked with guarding the tomb. I trust you have read those reports too. Many who saw him are still living this very day. Have you spoken with them?"

"I have researched the myth of your resurrected savior, but where is he now?" quizzed Pliny.

"Oh, I will tell you," John said eagerly. "'I saw heaven itself open, and there was a white horse at the opening. The one sitting on the horse is named Faithful and True, and in his righteousness he judges and wages war. He is no ordinary King, for his eyes are like flames of fire, and on his head are multiple crowns, and his name is a secret known only by himself. His robe is dipped in blood, and he is called the Word of God. And behind him are the armies of heaven, all wearing fine linen that is pure white, and they are following him on white horses. From his mouth protrudes a sharp sword with which he will tear down the nations, and he will rule them with a rod of iron. He will stomp the winepress of the fury of the wrath of God the Almighty. On his majestic robe is his title: King of Kings and Lord of Lords.'[77] He stands waiting until the purpose of his Heavenly Father is complete, and he declares it to be the end of time," replied John, as if still overwhelmed at the reality of seeing such a sight.

Struck by the awesomeness of this description, and seeking further clarification, Pliny asked; "So it is correct to say that when he returns, he will overthrow Rome?"

"All kingdoms!" stated John as a matter of fact. "A day will come in which all will bow the knee and declare without any degree of hesitation that Jesus Christ is Lord to the glory of God his Father."

"Then there you have it," gloated Pliny as if he had trapped the aged man in his web of cross-examination. "It sounds like subversive and treasonous talk to me! It is out of respect for your age that I don't have you thrown into a cell tonight. But from this day until I return from Bithynia, you are under house arrest. Roman soldiers will guard the house to insure that your loyal followers don't try to remove you secretly since I don't think you are in any condition to run away on your own. Do you understand my instructions? You are not permitted to leave this house. When I return, you will be escorted to Rome to stand trial for your life."

Appearing unconcerned, John requested, "May I have visitors?"

"For now, I don't see that as a problem," answered Pliny. As he departed, he left several soldiers to guard John in his temporary prison. The full weight of this situation fell heavily upon the Church that day. However, John urged all the saints of the Lord to continue with their routine as if nothing had changed.

I still recall him stating with the vigor of a young man, "God is enthroned in his righteousness and directs the hearts of kings and nations like he turns the course of rivers. We will not fear; we will marvel as we see his great plan unveiled before us." In a communication spread to all the churches, John urged the people to remember that 'all things are working out for the best to those

---

77. *Revelation 19:11-16*

who love God',[78] and that love was obedience to the Lord's commands which included trusting the direction he was taking the church, even if it meant through suffering and sorrow.

It would be a few weeks before Pliny's return, so John felt he had much to accomplish before his journey to Rome to stand trial. One of his first tasks was to call for me. When I arrived, I was escorted by Timothy into John's study chamber. "Polycarp, we need to discuss an important matter," instructed Timothy with John sitting next to him.

"Yes sir, what is it?" I inquired.

Timothy continued, "As you are aware, Apelles, the Overseer of the Church of Smyrna died a few months ago, and there is a great need for a pastor for the congregation."

Then John interjected, "Apelles personally requested you before he went to be with Jesus, and while I can't bear the thought of you leaving, you are the best man for the job."

Not fully absorbing the request, this news shocked me.

"On the next Lord's Day, the church will send you to go and preach, teach, and make disciples of the Lord Jesus Christ," explained Timothy.

"Do not be intimidated by men or their gods on this great endeavor," John added. "You are a strong, young man," he stated with his fist in the air, "and the word of God lives at home in you, and you have already overcome the evil one."[79]

They shared many other thoughts and ideas, which caused me to walk out of the room with the confidence of a racer taking his position on the starting line. I ran home to tell Anna and my mother of the wonderful blessing from God.

That Sunday was as splendid a day as a man could ever wish. Everyone loved my Anna and expressed a mixture of sorrow and joy at seeing us off on this new ministry. No one doubted this move, in fact, all affirmed my calling to the work of the pastoral ministry. As a final farewell, the Apostle John addressed the Ephesian congregation, under the watchful eyes of his Roman

---

78. *Romans 8:28*

79. *1 John 2:14*

guards, and provided the official commissioning and blessing of the church upon us.

"My dear son in the faith, permit me to admonish you with a word from the Lord, and a passage you have become familiar with over the years. 'Little children, you have come from God and he has made you overcomers, for he who is in you is greater than the one who is in the world.'[80] And as our Lord challenged the church of Smyrna, so I charge you; 'Be faithful even if it means your death, and I will reward you with the crown of life.'[81] Now go our dear brother and bring glory to your master's name and edify his Church."

At this point, the church rose, and the church elders, led by Timothy, gathered around me and placing their hands upon me prayed for God's blessing on my life and ministry.

Before leaving that afternoon, Timothy came up to me with one final piece of advice: "Polycarp, you are heading into an opportunity that will require more strength than you possess in yourself. Take it from me, you will make mistakes, and some less godly will blame you for those mistakes, and will accuse you in other ways because of your youth. I know from experience the trouble that awaits you." He reached into his cloak and delicately took out a rolled up scroll.

"Is that what I think it is?" I anxiously questioned as my eyes widened at the possibility.

Smiling with satisfaction at my suspicion, Timothy said, "Yes, it is the actual first letter Paul sent to me. Let me show you in his own handwriting how he encouraged me." Unrolling it carefully, Timothy found the section and placed his finger on the words. "Do not let anyone reject you because you are young, instead, be the example of how a believer should live in what you say, in how you behave, in how you love, in your exercise of faith and practice of purity."[82]

I was in awe of being admonished in such a fashion. I'll never forget these words and the privilege of seeing it in Paul's handwriting. "As I have seen you live in godly obedience, by God's grace I'll follow your example, Timothy," I said. I hugged my

---

80. I John 4:4

81. Revelation 2:10-11

82. I Timothy 4:12

old pastor, wept with my faithful teacher, John; kissed my dear mother on the cheek, and being unable to speak over the sorrow of leaving my closest friends, I climbed up in the wagon with Anna and departed for Smyrna to begin the next great adventure of our life. While there was great rejoicing in the hearts of all the people, there was also a lingering heaviness due to John's arrest. Christians were being persecuted in other parts of the empire, and it would appear that persecution would soon tear into the churches of West Asia. Little did I know what a great impact this would have on the Ephesian Church, indeed the entire Church.

◇◇

Two weeks later, I heard alarming reports pouring out of Ephesus. It wasn't until I received a letter from Onesimus that the tragic truth became clear.

"To the Overseer of the Church of Smyrna, Polycarp, and the saints of our Lord and Savior, Jesus Christ, greetings in the name of our Lord. I write with a heart consumed with grief and can scarcely write a word without my tears staining the page. Many of our Lord's choice servants have died and are in the glorious presence of our faithful God, including our beloved Apostle, John, and our under-shepherd, Timothy." My heart sank at the searing words.

I forced myself to continue reading. "As you recall, Pliny departed Ephesus a few weeks ago, and left soldiers whose prejudice against the Christians gave them boldness to stir up the people. They convinced the citizens that there lived among them suspicious people that alarmed the Emperor causing him to question the loyalty of the Ephesians. They began by spreading fear that if he looked negatively upon the city, it could result in his withholding favor and all the privileges and financial benefits that accompany being one of the cities that hold his delight. The people began to murmur and to fear the wrath of Caesar if the Christians were to bring a blot on the town's reputation."

"A rumor was being spread throughout the town that Caesar was to march against Ephesus to destroy it because of the Christians. Anyone searching the facts would know this was not Caesar's intentions, but superstitious people will believe anything. They determined to kill John, which would please Caesar, and once again make Ephesus an adorning gem in his crown."

"As panic spread, angry mobs formed, and they went in force to my home. I was powerless to stop them as they beat me and ransacked my home, driving my family out. As I lay on the ground, dazed but alive, I saw the mob enter John's room. But as they entered, they were stunned by what they saw. John was on his knees, leaning on a bench as if he had been in prayer, but God took him before the mob could harm him. While he may have suffered at the hands of man, he was not given over to them in death."

"Drunk on the desire for blood, John's natural death seemed to enrage the people more, for they were driven to kill. The next person they sought out was Timothy. They did not have to look hard, for as they surged out of my house, there he stood. He was on his way to check on John and me. Just as the mob would have shown no mercy on John, they would show no quarter for him either. They declared that he was responsible for Caesar's displeasure on the city. Timothy attempted to reason with them, but they would not hear. They all knew him, and were fully aware that he would have helped any person in that mob with whatever need they encountered. Finally, Timothy asked what their intentions were. And without answering him, they charged in on him and began kicking him, beating his head and body with rods and trampling on him. They were savages. The civilized world forgot itself, and all the hatred it had stored up against Jesus Christ was directed at this aged servant and friend. I staggered over to the window and saw his lifeless body soaked in a pool of blood. My dear Polycarp, I did not know what to do but run and protect my family. I had no weapons, and you know my weak frame. I was powerless to provide any aid. Though wounded, I fled with others in the church to the outskirts of town."

"The violence of sin is beyond description. They would have butchered us all and eaten our flesh as a celebration of their satanic gods. It is a grievous day for the church. Do not come here! We are safe for now, and God will heal and sustain us. Stay where you are, and do not fear for your mother's safety. She is here with me as I write to you. I shall inform you regarding our situation when the Proconsul returns. Perhaps he will restore order. God be with you and our grieving brethren at Smyrna, Onesimus."

The parchment dropped from my fingers onto the floor as I buried my face in my hands and wept like I have never wept before. Anna placed her arm around me and laid her head on my shoulder, sharing in my grief. God's grace was at work in my heart, and it is good, for I fear that hatred and bitterness would have devoured me. John, Timothy, and many other Christians who died in the panic were buried secretly in places outside the town. Onesimus had his letter dispatched throughout the empire to churches abroad informing them of the tragic sorrow we would bear together. My grief knew no limits as I mourned sorely over the death of my beloved mentor, and over the brutality experienced by my most faithful pastor, Timothy, not to mention my many friends in the congregation. God poured out great grace upon all those who mourned the death of John and Timothy, so that we could endure the trial with an inexpressible joy and unexplainable peace while still bearing the weight of personal loss.

Another dispatch arrived shortly after this, the contents of which would have normally made me angry, but instead, it grieved me due the gross deception of our spiritual enemy. I broke the ornately sealed parchment and when opened, read the few written words it contained. "The gods and our glorious Caesar have spoken out of their displeasure. Where was your God, Polycarp? Cæso Erebus Drusilla."

Anna read it, and said, "How heartless and cold. Has he no compassion?"

I was disappointed too, but the Lord brought to my mind the Scripture, "Great disappointment and shame will be the experience of those who worship and boast of their worthless gods, for all false gods must fall before the True God."[83]

For the next several months, the church met in secret, and Christians were careful as they interacted with the public. While their witness did not diminish, they were more careful to gather secretly, and since Ephesus was such a large city, it was easy to move about without drawing attention to one's activities.

---

83. Psalm 97:7

11

PREPARE YOUR
MINDS FOR ACTION

*Refocus and prepare your mind for action, being controlled
in your thinking by setting your expectation entirely on
the grace of God's favor that will be brought to you
at the revelation of Jesus Christ.*
(I Peter 1:13)

IT was the tenth year of Domitian's reign, and the word coming out of Rome was that he was insane. The persecution continued, but was confined to pockets and localities throughout the empire, but if the rumors were true, it was about to become empire-wide.

I had been ministering in Smyrna for seven years and loved the work. It was a wonderful town, and in every way like Ephesus, just not as crowded. No matter from what direction you entered the city, the view was varied and wonderful. However, my favorite prospect was from the harbor with the dark blue waters contrasted against the white buildings, red clay rooftops, and the lush green trees of Mt. Pagus rising above it all. The temperature was mild year round, with an occasional snow shower in the winter, which was usually a pleasant surprise, especially for the children. The summer months could get rather hot, but the breeze of the Aegean Sea made the heat bearable.

Our little home was starting to get crowded, for we now had two children, and were preparing for the arrival of our third. I loved being a husband and father; indeed, next to loving the Lord, my family was my greatest joy and delight. I invested a great deal of time in my family, for the Scripture is clear, "If a man can't properly direct his house, how can he possibly provide direction for God's church?"[84]

---

84. *I Timothy 3:5*

One evening, as I sat in the small courtyard of our home, a man stepped out of the shadows and introduced himself. "I am Antonius. My companions and I represent some of the churches in Rome. As you may recall, Ignatius of Antioch recommended we seek your counsel." Several other people stepped out of the shadows.

I stood up to welcome them and said, "My friends, I wasn't expecting you for a few more days. Surely you must be weary by your travels."

"Weary, yes; but filled with new energy and joy to finally meet you, Polycarp. God gave us good winds to fill our sails, and we arrived here much quicker than anticipated," Antonius replied.

By this time, Anna had been awakened by the voices, and joined us in the courtyard, and immediately saw to the practical needs of our guests with food and drink. We ushered them into our home where we reclined at the table and fellowshipped together. I was anxious to hear the news from the Christians in and around Rome. To begin with, I asked Antonius, "Who are all these people with you?"

Pointing to his right, he said, "This is my wife, Pheobe." She nodded politely. Next to her is Marius the pastor of the church that meets near Pinciun Hill, within Rome's walls, and next to him is Marcion, his disciple. Marcion's father owns a fleet of ships and not only donated a ship for this trip, but underwrote the expense himself. Next to him is Paul, an elder in my congregation. The other two you see at the end of the table are Mark, pastor of the church in Ostia, which is about thirty miles to the west of Rome on the coast, and with him is his son, Felix, and finally Silicus, a devoted servant of our Lord, and an escaped slave from Caesar's own palace, and the reason we have journeyed so far to see you."

I must admit that I was momentarily startled at the realization that a fugitive slave was in our home. I smiled and looked at Silicus and said; "You are welcome at my table. It does me good to see all of you sitting here with me. You are welcome in this home, and anything you need or desire will become my honor to fulfill for you."

There was great fellowship around the table, and testimonies of God's faithfulness were pouring out of the numerous reports.

As the meal ended, troubling news was addressed. "Polycarp," Antonius said, with obvious signs that he was reluctant to continue. "I realize that the hour is late, and perhaps this should wait until the morning, but I feel inclined to inform you of some distressing news. Our Emperor, Domitian, has developed a rather warped view of himself and has begun to insist that the people of Rome refer to him as master and god. This is why we brought Silicus. First, because as a follower of Christ, he refused to recognize the deity of Domitian and had to flee for his life, and the other reason is that he was an eyewitness to this turn of events in the imperial palace."

I studied the face of Antonius and then glancing downward asked, "Have the faithful in Rome suffered from this?"

"No, not yet," answered Antonius. "For the moment it is contained within the palace and court. Those closest to him and the Imperial Senate are the only ones included. Silicus is precious to the Church. When we were just stepping foot on the boat to embark on this trip he came running up under the cloak of darkness. He told us that the emperor had ordered his arrest and torture, and pled with us for direction. Without hesitation, we felt it prudent to bring him along. He assured us that no one saw him leave and that no one would likely suspect he had the means to seek passage on a ship. We all agreed with him, and Marcion said we could send him northward to Pontus, where he would find refuge with his family. We knew we were all in danger, but when you hear the details of his story, you will understand that the real danger has yet to arrive."

They had my full attention, and I was eager to gain the full picture of the situation. "Silicus, what do have to say? What insight has God given to you that we must hear this evening?" I said.

As we went well into the early hours of the morning, my blood turned cold as Silicus revealed a sinister and ungodly plot that was not only against the Christians, but against all civilization.

Being privy to the actual conversations of the Emperor, Silicus shared what he had heard and observed. "Emperor Domitian has lived under the shadow of his deceased brother, my former master, the great Emperor, Titus. The week before I was forced to flee for my life, I overheard a diabolical plan birthed between Domitian and his advisor, Parthenius."

He then shared his observations in detail.

"How will my name ever be great by being known only as the brother of Titus Flavius Caesar Vespasian?" Domitian cried in sarcastic anguish.

"The answer is not as complex as you might think," answered Parthenius.

"Speak plain man. Your riddles irritate me," exclaimed the Emperor.

"Of course, my Lord," Parthenius replied, then with pompous flair and flowing hand gestures went on to explain; "Worship the gods. Build great temples and shrines in their honor. Even make Titus and your father Vespasian gods. Honor them in front of the people. Instead of requiring great military feats to define you, build great basilicas and splendid architectural wonders here and abroad to define your legacy. Lead the empire; lead the empire in worship of our gods. Even you, my Lord, will be a god among gods."

Domitian stared at Parthenius for a moment, but could not hide the growing smile of delight that had awakened within him. The thought pleased him greatly; especially the thought of hearing the people shout with joy that he was a god living among mortal men. "How do I begin, Parthenius," Domitian anxiously inquired.

"First, my Lord, we must deal with the Christians," he said in a rather anxious tone.

Domitian interrupted as if to tease his adviser, "You have never cared very much for that sect."

"No, to be quite honest," Parthenius said haughtily. "They are parasites; fools and weak people that have a natural appeal to those who are poor. Did you know that they have stated publicly that the root of all evil is the love of money?" Parthenius said with a look of sheer horror on his face.

With a broad smile as if to tantalize his advisor the Emperor said, "Well that explains everything. For you do love your money, don't you?"

"Indeed, my Lord, more than the air I breathe," responded Parthenius as he took in a big breath of air.

To inaugurate his new strategy, Domitian planned a grand, week-long celebration at his lakefront palace, where he desired to stage the new religion to honor the Roman gods. As the crowds gathered that first evening, the Emperor entered in full splendor from the western steps. He desired the blazing sun to be behind him so that the people would have difficulty looking at him.

"Hail, glorious Jupiter, the god of sky and thunder," jovially declared Caesar before the festivities began at the Imperial Palace.

"Hail Jupiter" was the unison reply of his honored guests.

The first to greet him on the main floor was Rabirius. "Rabirius, you are my most preferred architect. You have brought fame to my name, splendor to Rome and glory to her gods. Your talent is beyond human, and if I didn't know better, I would say you are a demigod; a half son of Jupiter."

Leaning in to whisper in his ear he said, "Never forget that it was I who discovered you," gloated Domitian; "and if you are a demigod, what does that make me?"

"You flatter me, my Lord," replied Rabirius, trying to mask his pride behind a false humility; "I have grown accustomed to living in my proper place; in the greatness of your shadow."

"Ah, great Rabirius, you may be right!" Domitian boasted.

As the Emperor walked away to draw attention from other guests, Arrecinus Clemens, the commanding General of Rome's forces walked up to Rabirius and said, "How can you keep a straight face when he says things like that?"

"Ah, my great General, when the Emperor is gone and forgotten, what I build will endure for a thousand years."

"Rabirius, you seem to have more vanity than the Emperor," responded the General."

Laughing as if in disbelief, Rabirius replied, "I don't know General, I see no one in this room who is not fully intoxicated with self-glorification."

However, the General, being irritated by this frivolity responded, "That may be the case for some, but I am out for the glory of Rome."

Not to be outdone, Rabirius patted the General on the back and said; "Of course you are General, just like all the other past Generals who became Emperor. I know your desires; you reek with the odor of ambition. You cannot hide it."

Soon, Domitia, the Empress, was at Domitian's side. "Stand just behind me my Queen. It would not be proper for you to attempt to eclipse my glory with yours," he said.

Used to her husband's conceit, she complied, for she too reveled in the attention of the jewels, costly apparel, and gorgeous palaces he provided for her.

However, not everyone was so willing to acquiesce to the Emperor's unbridled vanity. Across the room fumed Lucius Aelius Lamia, as he watched the Emperor slithering around his guests. Next to him was his friend, a wealthy aristocrat, Titus Flavius Sabinus. "How can you possibly maintain your composure watching this abominable emperor just steal your wife, and then flaunt her here in front of you and everyone else?" he asked Lucius.

With glaring eyes, and seething, jealous anger he replied, "Domitia was my wife, but the Emperor desired her over Vespasian's choice for him. But who eventually won? That man we call Emperor, Savior of Rome. Of course, he could only claim her with the threat of taking my life. He made me divorce her so that he could legally marry her."

"How noble of him," Titus said glibly.

"As part of his treachery, he forces me in this prison of madness as I have to watch him pillage what once belonged to me. I hate the man, and my only purpose to live is to see him die," Lucius said through pressed lips.

"Careful my friend," cautioned Titus. "Such talk, though in the minds of just about everyone here, will get you in trouble. The Emperor may not be a god, but for now he has the power of one."

Meanwhile, as Domitian approached his richly adorned golden throne, surrounded by beautifully carved marble and laden with brilliant gems, Parthenius, his most trusted steward stood near the top. He was a conniving, evil man whose corrupt ambition made him the perfect channel through which Domitian could unleash his most heinous schemes without question or exposure. Nothing was off limits if the Emperor desired it.

"My Emperor," said Parthenius as he bowed in humble adoration; "I observed with great delight how you brought glory to the gods. It is good for your subjects to see you worshipping Jupiter, the greatest of gods. However, it is you and the previous Emperors who deserve worship. This empire is too great to be governed by a mere mortal."

"I have been thinking the same, wise Parthenius. It is remarkable that we should realize the truth at the same time," replied Domitian.

"It is a sign from Jupiter," Parthenius said. "If you wish it, My Lord, I will draw up the law, and tomorrow it can become official that you are to be worshiped as god of Rome."

"This is why I love you," shouted the Emperor so that all could hear, "for not many of my subjects have a mind that can keep up with mine. See to the details."

"Your whispered wish is my full command," bleated Parthenius as he, with great pomp, descended the steps of the throne, bowing as he went. When at last he reached the main floor, he turned to the crowd and with his high-pitched voice, and with an air of self-importance declared; "Hail Caesar, god of gods." The crowd was shocked and fearful not to reply, as they hailed Caesar as god. There were a few who merely mouthed the words, refusing to audibly say them because of their great contempt for Domitian.

Rising from his throne and oozing with self-glory, he reached out for the hand of Domitia and said to her, "My dear, look at this; you are married to a god." All of this being said to the cheers and applause of the guests.

The next day, Domitian, being led astray by his own vanity, signed into law an edict that demanded that all people throughout the Roman Empire restore their worship practices of Roman gods. All people were to offer worship to Caesar—god in man's form and Savior of Rome.

Obviously, these changes did not endear him to the aristocracy, but stirred up a great hatred for him in their hearts, which soon translated into action. However, even this was playing into the strategy of Parthenius. What Rome needed was a fresh infusion of money since Domitian was planning on restoring it to her former glory from ages long past. He also knew that the aristocracy could be easily bought for the right price. In addition to this, unlike many of his predecessors, Domitian's military position was more defensive than offensive. He was not conquering new territories; money was being spent supporting the armies defending the old ones.

"Parthenius," Caesar shouted. "We need money. Where can I get money to pay for all these buildings, glorious celebrations of me, and the needs of my generals?" worried Domitian.

That question was precisely what Parthenius had hoped to be asked. All this talk of emperor worship was just his way to get closer to controlling the money for the Emperor.

"There is a simple solution, besides increasing taxes. There is an old method used by kings and emperors throughout history, and that is to confiscate personal property. And of course, the only way that could ever happen is if property owners were breaking the law, and the only laws that a large number of people would break would be the Christians and the Jews who refuse to worship Roman gods, especially you," extolled Parthenius.

"Oh, you are clever. Your greed and lust for power make you seductively cunning," Domitian replied. "Here is what we must do; I will appoint new proconsuls and governors, and dispatch them throughout the empire to enforce the new law and to confiscate the personal property of those unwilling to comply."

"The Christians, you mean," Parthenius interjected.

"Yes, yes the Christians," Domitian added.

Parthenius suggested an addition. "Let my Emperor declare that Christianity is now a forbidden religion in the Empire due to their intolerance in refusing to offer worship to Roman deities, for we already know they will refuse. Furthermore, add that such actions fracture the delicate unity needed to keep the empire strong. Proclaim your plan to exalt the Roman gods, and restore the worship of Caesar. Publicly commission the immediate construction of temples to the gods, even Vespasian and Titus, and then have another magnificent palace built for yourself."

Domitian was elated as he embraced Parthenius, kissed him on the forehead and then acknowledged, "The gods favor you my Parthenius; now I know why you are my favorite. Come; let's build an empire that will bring glory to me."

———◇◇———

Silicus sighed heavily at the weight of his report, and the severity of the situation burdened our hearts. I felt as if I had been in the palace and heard these things for myself. I was stunned and observed that everyone around the table was looking down.

The first action that came to my mind was to pray. "What else can we do but seek wisdom from above," I suggested. With confidence in the sovereignty of God, I looked upward to heaven and prayed; "God of all Creation, the controller of kings and nations, we do humbly submit ourselves to your sovereign control. Impress upon our Emperor the error of his ways. If need be, humble him as you humbled Nebuchadnezzar when he took glory that belonged to you. Nevertheless, your will be done, for the glory is all yours no matter what man may do to try to snatch it away. To the glory of our risen Savior, Jesus Christ, we intercede before your throne for the flock in Rome and throughout the world. Amen."

All around the table said, "Amen," in solidarity with me.

There was no sleep for me that night. I felt helpless and was unsure why Ignatius suggested they come to Smyrna and seek my counsel. It seems he would have been the wiser choice. What can a group of well-meaning people do against such power and self-aggrandizement? In my mind, I could see the wolves beginning to scatter the flock. But wait a moment, what was I thinking? Whom did I serve? Fear is not becoming of a saint of God. That didn't comfort very much, but it did give me something to fight for in my heart.

12

I DO NOT COUNT MY LIFE PRECIOUS TO ME

Matters such as this do not cause me great concern,
nor do I hold my life valuable as if I
was worthy of some esteem
for I wish nothing more than to complete my race
with great joy and fulfill the ministry laid out
before me by the Lord Jesus, and give testimony
to the great news of the grace of God.
(Acts 20:24)

I RENAEUS was a remarkable young man. He had requested a meeting to share a matter that was causing a great unrest in his soul. I admired his virtue, and confess that I could barely contain my hopes that God would gift him to preach and teach the glories of Jesus Christ. I dared not voice my hopes for fear that I would invite a man to pursue, to his disillusionment, a calling that demands Divine grace over personal talent. But I prayed all the same, knowing the marks that God places on a man whom he has called into the sacred office of an overseer.

God had brought peace to the church over the past several years. There seemed to be a great boiling point of persecution when Emperor Domitian ruled. His successor, Nerva, was not Caesar long enough to stir up any trouble, and died having reigned for a little more than a year. His adopted son, Trajan, had ruled now for the last fifteen years. While practical and considered a man of the people, he was a man of war, and rumor has it, a perverse lover of boys. In spite of these things, he restored the rule of law, and paid little attention to the church, with one exception; he had my friend and fellow pastor, Ignatius, arrested for treason, who is even now being transported to Rome to face trial. The great question is why? No clear answer has been given as of yet, though I suspect he became too much of a challenge to the local authorities.

Ignatius was a godly man and a great help to the church, but his zeal often attracted trouble. His desire to influence the Roman government had led him into many run-ins with both local magistrates and officials in the Imperial Senate. There are many who would take up arms to defend him, and I had warned him of this; he had assured me, however, that he would never let it escalate to that level. God forbid they should die for what is clearly in the hands of our Almighty God. I will find out the truth soon enough, for he is being transported over land through Smyrna.

My current disciple, Zanzar, an Ethiopian, had just completed the doctrinal parts of his training and had assisted me in every aspect of the work of the ministry these last several years. He anticipates returning to his native land within the year. It was my hope that after being commissioned, the Lord would send me Irenaeus as a disciple.

"The things you have heard from me in the presence of others, those same things set before faithful men, who will teach other faithful men."[85] That passage from Paul to Timothy keeps resonating in my mind. I doubt there is a greater honor than taking what you have learned about the glory of God, and teaching others to pass it on. Our Lord called John and trained him, who then trained me, and now I must be committing the Word of God I learned to other faithful men; it is my obligation and my joy!

<hr>

As I stared out the second story window of my study chamber, I noticed the very man himself, Irenaeus, running as fast as he could to my home. I thought it was odd seeing that he wasn't late for our appointment. I heard him bound up the wooden stairs of the courtyard and like a courier with news of the utmost importance, he barged into my room and stopped in front of me, and through heavy breathing was at last able to say, "You must come at once! Leonius has gathered a large group of our brethren to take up arms and attack the Roman guard that is escorting Ignatius to Rome for his trial. The soldiers will most certainly kill them all."

---

85. *II Timothy 2:2*

All I could do at the moment was to sigh out of deep exasperation. Leonius, whose intentions always appeared noble, had an intense hatred for Rome. His brand of politics was the sword, and while he had never drawn blood that I know of, his tongue was always stirring up poisonous unrest. Wherever dissension was found in the Church, somewhere in the mix Leonius was fanning the flames. I love the man, though my love is proven mostly through grace wielding patience and forbearance I must add, and I always have strived to direct the intensity of his zeal to our daily spiritual warfare, but this was a different matter. I had heard rumors of a carefully laid plan to rescue Ignatius and to use this event as a way to build a Christian army to take on and conquer the pagan world in the name of Christ, but I never imagined it would be my own congregation that would be plotting this strategy. Of course, Leonius visualized himself as a great strategist and conquering general, a hero in the church.

"Where are they currently meeting?" I asked Irenaeus.

"You don't understand," he responded. "They're not meeting anymore; they have been training and preparing out at Euclid's farm."

"Are they still at the farm," I inquired.

"No, but there's more," he continued.

I began to feel a great weight sink in my soul as I declared, "Now what?"

I could see the anxiousness in his eyes as he replied, "Someone in the group has betrayed their intentions and has turned their names and plans over to the Roman soldiers at the garrison."

My alarm turned to grief and then to anger as the repercussions paraded through my mind. "The centurion and his soldiers will bring the simple-minded rebellion to a quick close, but it will be the church that pays the price for this lack of discretion," I said. "Can it get any worse?" I blurted out in my frustration.

"I'm afraid so," Irenaeus said.

"What else could there be?" I exclaimed.

"The group, a hundred or so are currently gathering at the agora to drum up more support. "The Judas moment," I whispered.

"What did you say?" Irenaeus asked.

"They will be betrayed," I said.

It is times like this I could easily picture myself working in my uncle's old parchment shop far away from heart-breaking pressures.

"I need to go directly to the Roman garrison," I said.

"What do you want me to do?" he inquired.

"I want you to stay right here. I don't want you mixed up in this any more than you already are. You understand my desires, don't you?" I ordered.

"Well, yes, of course, I'll do as you wish," he replied, feeling a bit defensive as if we both were somehow part of the accused.

As I reached the door, I stopped; I realized that the situation was handling me when I should be handling it like a man filled with faith in the Lord. I turned and smiled at the young man standing in my study chamber, and walked back over to him and placed my hand on his shoulder. "Irenaeus, I am grateful for you. Don't stay here. Come with me and let us pray that God gives us wisdom and patience beyond our natural ability."

As we walked swiftly toward the garrison, we passed the street that would have taken us to it.

"Polycarp," Irenaeus said, "didn't we want to take that road?"

"I've changed my mind. Let's go the agora and find the group. Perhaps we can persuade them to lay aside their plans. I have a letter from Ignatius that may be just the information they need to hear," I said as I tried to keep my breath. Obviously, my hope was that the Roman Centurion would see that I could subdue the threat and that he would see the peaceful demeanor of the men and not feel the need to intervene. It was a mission of faith, and regardless of the outcome; I was going to follow the bidding of my God and King by being an example of his graciousness before the willful power of man. As we walked, the only thought pouring into my mind was; "Some men trust in man-made tools of war and some on the power of their steed, but I will trust in the name of the Lord my God!"[86]

We finally found the group in a field adjacent to the Agora. Euclid was the first to observe our approach and walked towards us and said, "I was wondering when you would show up."

"I'm afraid I should have been here sooner, but I just found out about your plan," I responded.

---

86. *Psalm 20:7*

"Where is Leonius?"

"Leo," Euclid called out toward the group. The preacher is here to see you."

The group separated to create an opening through which Leonius emerged brandishing his sword like a victor who had just returned from vanquishing his enemy.

"O Leonius, what are you doing? Sheath that sword!" I ordered. "Your pride will be your undoing and all these men with you."

"Preacher, let me be clear; it will be your unwillingness to fight for Ignatius, which some would call fear, that will be the cause of bloodshed," Leonius bellowed.

"This is madness and folly. You are condemning yourself to death and your brethren to swift and unbridled punishment by Rome if you continue in your present course," I replied in a firm but patient manner.

"I don't expect you to understand," he quipped. "We have been called by God to rescue Ignatius. The Lord spoke to me personally and told me to do this. And I will do it with or without your blessing."

"You may have received a word or even a sign, but it was not from God, I can assure you," I told him. "God speaks through his Word. You are being deceived into a devilish plot of self-destruction, and I implore you to stop at once. Leonius, I obviously cannot force you, but I hope to appeal to your better judgment," I pled.

"There is nothing you can say or do, Polycarp. We are resolved to see this through," he replied.

Then Euclid added, "Join us preacher. Make this a righteous war against the corruption of Rome. With you behind us, we could raise a real army. People respect you."

"They respect me?" I asked. "If that is so, it is because I trust the Lord and his might over the plotting and stratagems of men. My friends, I plead with you; we are soldiers of the cross, and our enemy is a spiritual enemy; for it is Satan, the forces of hell and the residual desires of sin that exist in our flesh, that demand our warfare. Our struggle is not with flesh and blood, but with the spiritual forces of evil. You simpletons! You are siding with the forces of evil. You are deceived in thinking that you are pursuing a righteous cause," I declared.

I could see that their hearts were hardened by their corrupt plan, so I reached into my satchel and pulled out a letter. "Men, this letter I hold in my hand is from Ignatius. Permit me to read part of it."

I stood up on a boulder and projected my voice so that they all could hear me. "I am writing to all the churches, and exhorting all men to know that of my free will I have given myself to die for God, unless, of course, you hinder me. I bid you, do not show me this kindness. Permit me, if God wills it to be, to be given over to the wild beasts, for through those beasts I will enter the presence of God. I am a grain in God's harvest, and I am willing to be ground to powder by their teeth that I may be pure bread for my Lord Jesus Christ. Indeed, rile up the beasts, that their stomachs may become my sepulcher. May no part of my body be left behind, for I do not wish it to be a burden to anyone upon my death. I believe that this is a worthy cause of a disciple of Jesus Christ, and when the world can no longer view the remains of my body, then my prayer shall always be that through suffering I was found to be a sacrifice to God."[87] There was more, but I felt this was sufficient to communicate my concerns.

"My beloved friends, I love my brother in the Lord. Ignatius and I have been friends for years and had fellowship and corresponded over many issues. No one here would desire to save Ignatius more than I. But does this sound like a man that desires you to kill Roman soldiers to free him? Did our Lord himself desire Peter to unsheathe his sword to defend him from arrest in the garden of Gethsemane? Every man standing before me is no better a swordsman than Peter, whose most accurate blow could only severe a defenseless servant's ear. Who here is a seasoned soldier? Who has ever drawn the blood of another man? You use your blade to butcher defenseless cows, Euclid. Cephas, I've seen you skillfully take down a deer in the field, but it was just standing there grazing, and you Leonius, you can handle a knife when gutting fish, but what happens when you thrust it against a fully armored veteran soldier of the Fifth Legion. Surely you know that they just returned from Germania where they daily fought against ruthless barbarians. What are you to them? You may imagine yourself as determined, but none of you are ruthless," I said.

---

87. *Ignatius to the Romans, 4:1-2*

"The Romans don't know our plan," Leonius gloated.

"They don't know?" I asked with exasperation. "They know I tell you. You have a Judas in your group, and the garrison is aware of your plans. For all I know, they are marching to this very spot to quell the potential of this rebellion. Just the threat alone is enough to justify a deadly response from Rome. And don't think that you alone will bear the weight of your actions. First, your families will be arrested. They will likely ravage your wives and daughters, and then along with your sons, they will be sold into slavery in order to pay for the expense of having to suppress your misguided ambitions. Believe me when I say that I know something about the abuse of that lifestyle. You don't want your children to suffer in this manner."

My warning got their attention as they looked nervously at one another and discussed their situation among themselves.

I raised my hands to draw their attention to my words once again. "Please, my friends. Listen to my words," I begged. "In a message from our Lord Jesus Christ, the Apostle John challenged the Smyrnaean Church, our congregation, many years ago, not to be seized with fear regarding future suffering."[88] The Apostle Peter admonished the church in his first letter that if we suffer for what is right in the eyes of God, this is a blessing. I realize that this does not make sense to our fleshly reasoning, but by the power of God's Spirit in us, he imparts the faith necessary not only to accept it, but live in the blessing of it. 'For this reason we are not to be seized by fear, nor even be troubled by the threat of suffering, but in the secret places of our heart where fear grows we are to honor Christ our Lord. Our preparation for times of suffering and even facing death is to make our defense regarding the reason Jesus is our mainstay, and even this defense is out of gentleness and respect.'[89] He teaches us that it is better to suffer for doing what is good, if that is God's will for us, rather than suffering for doing evil,[90] which is what you are plotting. He further exhorts us that 'when we suffer, it must never be because we are lawbreakers like a murderer, a thief, a doer of evil deeds or as one who seeks to suppress others. When we suffer, it must be because we are

---

88. *Revelation 2:10*

89. *I Peter 3:14-15*

90. *I Peter 3:17*

growing to be like Christ; we are Christians and in this there is no shame. When we suffer, our duty and privilege is to bring great honor to the name of God by our responses. Our defense is Christ our hope. 'Those who suffer while obeying the will of God can do so because they have entrusted their souls to a faithful Creator through following him.'"[91]

Nothing more was said as they stood silently as the reality of their situation began to materialize in their minds. For the most part, they seemed to have listened. A couple, including Leonius attempted to mask their anger as if biding their time. Had we averted disaster? I don't know. I asked that we go to our knees and humble ourselves in body and heart before the all-seeing eyes of God. Before I could even drop to my knees, out of the shadows emerged a Roman centurion and a few of his soldiers. Shock filled my soul, mainly from the standpoint of whether or not I was to be the first one arrested.

He slowly walked through the band of men; eyeing them carefully as his hand grasped the handle of his gladius. He paused for a moment and glared into the eyes of Leonius as if he could see into the soul of the man. Leonius gulped, and I observed beads of perspiration forming on his forehead. Under normal circumstances, I would have had to suppress my laughter at seeing a man who a moment ago was ready to defeat the Roman army, now appearing rather decrepit. However, whatever amusement I may have found was about to fly away as he stepped away and began walking toward me to scrutinize my place in this group.

His presence was intimidating. He was taller than most of us, muscular, and his breastplate displayed the marks of past battles, and adorned with several insignias that commemorated past campaigns. He spoke in a monotone fashion, but with commanding authority. "Are you Polycarp?" he asked. "Are you the one whom the Christians in this town call their overseer?"

Now I gulped, but I calmly answered, "Yes, I am that man."

"Are these malcontents your people?" he inquired.

"They are some of my people," I said.

"Are your speeches subversive?" he continued.

"If you have been listening to what I just said for any length of time you know that my words are quite the opposite," I replied.

---

91. I Peter 4:14-16, 19

"Yes, so it would seem," he said in a rather suspicious manner.

"How far would you go before attacking Rome? I'm curious to know," he continued.

Such questions worried me, and I answered, "I cannot fully tell you. We teach that we are subject to the laws of man until those laws transgress the greater laws of God. We strive to live peaceably with all men."

"The greater laws of God?" he questioned. "Are there any laws greater than the law of Rome?"

"There are," I answered.

"If I told you to kill one of these malcontents, would you?" he prodded.

"No!" I said.

"What if I gave you an ultimatum that if you didn't kill one of these men, I would kill the young man next to you," he said as he drew his Gladius and laid it gently against the neck of Irenaeus. Had it not been for the grace of God at that moment, I fear what would have happened next, but as one could predict, the Spirit of God calmed me down.

"I am still bound to the Word of God, Centurion, and joyfully bound I might add. I trust God to keep this young man safe until his numbered days are up. On that day he will die, whether it is in his sleep or by the point of your gladius," was my reply.

"You speak with authority for a man who cannot see his God," he declared.

"It is true; I cannot see him, but everywhere I look in all the Creation, and all changes within my heart, is powerful evidence of his Almighty hand working and controlling all things. Even you, noble Centurion, are a tool in the hands of God," I said.

"Me?" he jested; "I am a tool in the hands of a god alright, but that god is Trajan; Caesar."

"Tell me Centurion, how faithful, how committed is your god Caesar to you? Would he declare laws that are impossible to obey, and then condescend to live out the very laws on your behalf by his perfection, and then credit it to your life? Would he die for you? Would he die for you as a substitute for your crimes? Would your god adopt you as his child and prepare for you a lavished and an indescribable eternal inheritance? Would he prepare a place for you in his palace, a place you could call your home forever? Truly, sir, does your god even know your name; does he even consider you a friend?" He stood there not uttering a word.

"All those questions that you obviously cannot not answer; I can answer," I said. "My God declared laws that demanded righteous perfection. While man has attempted to obey them, only God himself could obey them. Not long ago in fact, he condescended as a man; God in the flesh, my Savior, the Lord Jesus Christ. He lived as the representative of man, the second Adam we call him, and lived on behalf of his elect; the ones he called out of the lifeless world; this is the church of which I am an overseer. But it was not enough to live a perfect life as man's representative. Since mankind has willfully, since the Creation of the world, given himself to every kind of sin and transgression, a death sentence from God was placed upon mankind.

"He lived a perfect life and was given over to be tried and executed as a criminal even though he had never committed a single act of sin. God used his people of Israel; the might of Rome and the Gentile world to crucify him. However, because he is God, death could not keep him; the grave could not hold him. On the third day following his death, he miraculously rose from the grave by the might of the Holy Spirit of God, and conquered the foes of man; death, sin and hell. He took mankind, his enemy, and united us to not only being at peace with him, but also being filled with his peace. He no longer calls us his servants, but calls us friends; indeed, he has adopted his church as his children. He has reserved an eternal inheritance for each of those in his family and has prepared a place in his presence that will be ours, so that together forever; we can enjoy the glory of his merciful kindness and love. Centurion, I ask you, which God would you rather serve? To me, the answer is obvious, yet it is only obvious because of the grace of God that gives me faith to believe it. Without that grace, and the confidence that God is who is says he is, then like the rest of the world, I would not believe it and would remain God's enemy, and have only exalted men and man-made gods to be my gods."

I noticed that he was no longer looking into my eyes, but was now looking at the ground. He turned again to look at the men standing before him, and after clearing his throat said, "I order you all to return to your homes at once. Any loitering will result in your immediate arrest. I want all of your names as well. If any of you attack Roman soldiers, its citizens or property, I'll see to it that you receive the harshest punishment. I should arrest you all now, but I trust your overseer for the moment."

He looked back at me and then walked away with a couple of soldiers leaving with him. The rest stayed to collect the names of this group and to see that the crowd was dispersed without incident. Of course, Irenaeus and I were both required to provide our names as well. I think most of the men felt embarrassed that I was being implicated in their plot. Nevertheless, I set an example and encouraged the men to head back to their homes, though I did inform Leonius that the church elders were going to discuss this matter with him.

As I arrived back at my home, I found it difficult to hide my anger over the behavior of these men. What were they thinking? And what of the Centurion; for while I'm not a man-pleaser, I couldn't help but to think how soiled the glory of Christ and his church had been in his eyes, but how could I judge them seeing that my heart had been filled with resentment towards them? My dear Anna sensed the welling up of anger in my soul immediately.

"My beloved, I'm afraid I dealt harshly with those men," I said to her.

"Polycarp, you're the most gracious man I know," she replied as she reached out and pulled me close to her. "In these many years of marriage, I have never seen you lose your temper once."

"Well, it's because I try not to show it when you're around," I clarified with a smile.

"Yes, of course," she replied. "Were some of those men unruly?" she asked.

"Yes," I answered.

"Did you warn them?"

"I suppose I did," I said.

"Did you bring comfort to those who were weak minded? Did you strengthen the confused ones?"

I looked at her and just smiled. "You're bound and determined to encourage me, aren't you?" I ask. "Yes, my most favorite husband. You are easy to encourage, and I see it as part of my calling from God to you."

"Most favorite?" I inquired. "Do you have more than one?"

"No, but if I did, you would still be my favorite."

How glorious it was for me to have such a precious wife.

The arrival of Ignatius created quite a stir. I was a bit apprehensive until he arrived, though we did keep a close watch on Leonius. In any regard, there were no incidents on their journey into Smyrna, though rumors were abounding that his entrance into Rome would be a different matter. I went to the garrison on the day of his arrival, and the same centurion that talked with me in the agora took me personally to see Ignatius. I thought it was a thoughtful gesture.

After a tearful greeting, I asked Ignatius, "My friend don't you think you are pressing this issue of martyrdom too aggressively."

"Perhaps brother, but I want Rome to see the virtue and inner strength of the follower of Christ. I want them to see that death for us is nothing more than an entrance into eternal glory," he answered.

"Why? You're certainly not afraid to die for Christ are you?" he inquired of me.

"No, of course not, for my heart echoes the resolve of the Apostle Paul: 'Matters such as this do not cause me great concern, nor do I hold my life valuable for I wish nothing more than to complete my race with great joy,'"[92] I said.

"Amen!" exclaimed Ignatius.

"However, I could find myself a little distracted by how I finish that course," I added with a smile.

He laughed and said, "All of us struggle with that, but it is not a strong deterrent. Rome thinks they are the conquerors when they kill us, but death is the final victory for the followers of Jesus Christ. As a Roman citizen, Paul pled his case before Caesar, and as a Roman citizen, I am determined to do the same. I want the chance before I die to stand before the Emperor, Trajan, and share the glories of Christ. Who else will do this, Polycarp? Tell me, who can do this? This opportunity to plant the seed of the Word in Caesar's heart is more important than my life. My blood will be the water for the seed in the ground of his heart. I will have it no other way."

I loved his resolve but questioned his methods.

After a couple days of rest, the patrol left with Ignatius. It would be the last time I would see him on Earth. His courage

---

92. Acts 20:24

stirred me, and though I must confess that I questioned his plan, I must admire his motivation. He is bold, and he will face death as a champion of the cross.

It was several months before I received the news of Ignatius' death. If the Romans in that Coliseum knew the quality of a true champion, they would have never permitted him to be put to death. As the letter to the Hebrews so eloquently describes it, he was one 'of whom the world was not worthy.'[93] My heart ached for the loss of my friend. People do not often understand the bond between preachers of the Gospel. We are stewards of the Gospel of Jesus Christ, laborers among the sheep of our Lord's pasture. We seek nothing for ourselves, but only the good of the flock and the glory of the Great Shepherd.

93. *Hebrews 11:38*

13

IT GREW AND
BECAME A TREE

*It is like a grain of mustard seed that a man took
and sowed in his garden, and it grew and became a tree,
and the birds of the air made nests in its branches.
(Luke 13:19)*

I WALKED along the shoreline bearing a heavy heart. It had now been just over three months since Ignatius had visited, but now he was dead to this life, but alive in the presence of Almighty God. His death created a vacuum as congregations searched for leaders to help guide them. Ignatius left word that the churches should seek me out; however, he failed to inform me of this. Delegations from all over the empire came daily to seek my help in settling disputes and provide direction and counsel. It was not a responsibility I sought, but one that sought me out and would not permit me to escape. While I loved helping others and edifying the church, the time demands were great, and I felt I needed a break or some encouragement to breathe strength back into me.

As I walked alone trying to collect my thoughts, I heard someone walking behind me. It was Irenaeus. To my joy, he was my new disciple, but the busyness of my present circumstances was making this difficult. I was sad over my neglect, for he was an extraordinary man; virtuous, godly and talented. Perhaps God sent him to me not just for the opportunity to help prepare him for the work, but maybe for the assistance he could provide me. He was to become what I had been to John. For the moment, however, he was a welcome break, for I was weary and fatigued by the duties placed on me.

"Polycarp, there is a delegation from the church in Athens waiting at your home," Irenaeus informed me.

I sighed and smiled, but was yielded to the Lord in whatever way he would choose to use me.

"Irenaeus, I must exhort these dear people to examine the Word of God for answers and solutions. They come asking what our Lord would do, or what instructions the Apostles would give them? And I simply tell them that the Lord and the Apostles already have given clear and wonderful instructions found in the Gospels and letters they left for our edification. I fear that if I continue in this fashion, I shall be lifted up into a position as head of the church, which is not as the Lord intended. However, for the moment I will see what I can do for them," I replied.

"How do you bear up under this weight and pressure of all the demands for your time?" he asked. "I heard some urging you to refuse to meet with these groups for it infringes on your role as pastor. Others have begged you to get away and rest for a time. Perhaps go and recuperate at the hot springs of Hierapolis. Honestly, most don't know what to say to you or how to be helpful; myself included."

What could I say, but; "My dear friend, to be honest, I don't know what would help me. I live each day more dependent on the grace of God than I did the previous day. If the Lord wasn't constantly restoring my soul, I fear I would quit. Come, sit with me, and let's fellowship and pray before we return to the town."

While the few minutes we shared were sweet, we were both men serving the Lord and were always to be in the frame of mind to serve and help wherever there was a need we could meet. At the moment I uttered my first words in prayer, we heard a voice behind us; "Pardon my interruption."

As we looked up and turned, Irenaeus stood up, and I was equally alarmed by the presence of the centurion who had confronted us and others in my congregation just a few months ago. I stood up too and wondered if Leonius was up to his old tricks. "You are welcome here. What do you seek?" I asked.

"Peace; I want peace with God," he blurted out. "Ever since we conversed in the agora, your words continue to ring in my ears stronger than the cries of men on the battlefield. They torment me."

"I cannot give you what you ask," I replied. "Only the True God can give you that. However, you wouldn't be here seeking the truth if He hadn't put the desire for it in your heart. It's the evidence of His grace at work in your heart."

"What do you mean by grace?" he asked.

"Grace is His Divine favor upon a soul whereby he provides what is necessary to grow in the wisdom and understanding of His ways. Grace blends our wills with the will of God so that they appear as one will," I replied. "Why don't you sit with us, and perhaps I can help explain what is happening in your soul."

He sat on an adjacent log while he took a few moments and prepared a small fire for which I was grateful, for the sea breeze was starting to make me cold. As the fire crackled, he looked up over the flames and said, "My name is Justin. I am a Centurion Hastatus Posterior.[94] I have just in the last few months been reassigned to this district. I have already served several years in Britannia and other outposts."

"Do you have a wife and children," I asked.

"None; and no living relatives," he answered. "I sold my family home in the south of Italy, so I have no place to call home either."

I observed the hardness of warfare in his countenance that perhaps had seen one battle too many. "What do you think of Smyrna?" I asked.

"I don't like it. It's small; I would rather be in Ephesus," he said.

"Ephesus is a fine city. I was born and lived there many years," I told him.

"Justin, you say you seek peace with God. Why do you desire it?" I inquired.

"You placed before me a God unlike any god I have ever heard. He lays out demands like a God, but fulfills His demands out of, well I suppose, genuine love. He doesn't need appeasement, but it would appear that he has fulfilled his righteous demands. I don't understand this. I could maybe think he is passive, but he seems strong and caring. My struggle intensifies when I lay my wretched life before such kindness; my vileness appears greater than his compassion."

"What you are experiencing in your soul is one of the remarkable attributes of God's grace, for as a man approaches the righteous God, he sees more of the emptiness of his soul. Grace is

94. *Equivalent to a junior officer*

185

God filling that soul with his virtues that produce the ability to repent of sin, and to believe that God has sent His only Son as the redeemer. You are given a new birth from above in a spiritual sense. His grace does not stop there either, for it gives his children the capacity and the opportunity to live in daily, holy obedience, and ultimately to live forever with Him. Grace is the glorious inner working of God in us," I explained. "It's like a monstrous wave that crashes over the greatest acts of sin. It washes away the stain of guilt with the fresh newness of forgiveness."

"I secured some parchments from a fellow officer. It was a lengthy transcript from a disciple of Jesus Christ, whose name was John. Have you heard of him," Justin asked.

"Heard of him," I said with delight, "he was my mentor, and one of my closest friends. Did you understand what you were reading?" I replied.

"In some ways, perhaps," he responded. "I see the concept of being born again and that the power to believe comes from God, though I find it confusing. I can see the significance of the cross and the importance of the resurrection in light of the sacrifice necessary to atone for sin."

"Then you understand a great deal," I replied. "The ability to believe is one of God's greatest works in us, for it dismantles our human reasoning and replaces it with the ability to see God working in us, and responding in obedience to him. Faith does not need human reasoning to guide it; only the will of God to obey. I believe you are here today not simply because I planted a seed of God's Word in your heart a few months ago, but also because of the time you have spent reading the Gospel according to the Apostle John. This type of belief is grown out of the Word into our hearts and minds and then is fully expressed in our actions in obedience to God's will."

As we continued to discuss the power of the Gospel, the Spirit of God opened up the heart of Justin, and he was spiritually birthed by grace through faith in Jesus Christ. "I stand amazed and humbled before God," he exclaimed. "Just yesterday, I was his enemy and resisted any contemplation of his existence, and now at this moment I stand before him a changed man. He changed me! He took me from being a hater of his name to be a lover of his name."

"Let's talk to him, and thank him for this great gift of redemption," I suggested. Then falling to his knees like a loyal subject before his Sovereign, he looked up toward the heavens and with childlike faith talked with God for the first time.

"My King, I am not skilled or knowledgeable about how to approach you as you sit in might upon your Holy Throne. You have changed me by faith, and therefore by faith, I bow my knee and declare you as my God, my King, my Lord and my Savior. You have seen fit to save me from my sins and give me peace—more than I could imagine. Truly, you are great, and there is none like you. I am yours; do with me as you please."

I then joined Justin on my knees, and placing my arm around his broad shoulders brought praise to my God. "My gracious Father, I am again amazed by your grace in bringing Justin into your family, and making him one of your sons and one of my brothers. I shall never tire of beholding your great works of redemption in the lives of vile men as we would be without your saving grace. Use Justin as a standard bearer for the truth in an Empire ruled by godlessness and paganism. Grow us in the grace and knowledge of Jesus Christ our Lord as we come before you in his name, covered in his robes of righteousness. For the glory of the cross of Christ, we lift our souls in praise to you. Amen, and may it ever be so."

By this time, all three of us were weeping, but Justin even more, for though he had strived to be a virtuous Roman, he had been a rejecter of the most gracious God, and the weight of God's loving-kindness and forgiveness simply broke his heart. As we walked back to town together, Justin was a different man. He was free, and at last he had peace with God, and even more, the peace of God. I was refreshed by this miraculous encounter. On the way, we introduced him to several others in his new Christian family, who rejoiced with him and praised God for the saving of souls. Even Leonius, whom we met along the way, was stirred to repentance by the goodness of God.

Later that day as Irenaeus and I walked into my study chamber though my spirit was lifted up to the heights, my body was still feeling the full weight of the demands being laid against me. But even under great pressure, I was able to realize that peace is a proof of God's Spirit at work in me. It is the proof of God's control over all things.

A few weeks later, I received news that Clement, a pastor in one of Rome's churches had invited me to come and spend some time with him and his congregation. He desired it both as a time for me to have a change in venue and rest, and if the Lord would so lead, to preach and teach. The Elders in my congregation agreed, and strongly suggested I take Clement up on his offer. After careful consideration and prayer, it was decided that my family and I would travel to Rome. The day before we were to depart, I received another surprise; Justin was being sent to Rome on official business, and would be one of our traveling companions. His presence rejoiced my heart all the more.

Rome was immense! From the moment we disembarked at the docks on the Tiber River, I was overwhelmed, maybe even intimidated by the size of this famous city. My good friend, Clement, greeted us, and with the exception of Justin, we rode in a cart to the east side of the city. He took us by the Circus Maximus, then the newly built Coliseum that was a spectacle to many deadly and bloody sports, including the death of my friend, Ignatius and other Christian brethren. A chill penetrated deep in my soul at how the spilling of another man's blood could be found so entertaining. From here we rode past one of the Emperor's palaces and then the Senate. I prayed for the Emperor and the leaders of our government, and was resolved from that day forward never to cease in that practice as Peter had strongly admonished the Church to do. Seeing the ostentatious display of power in the buildings, art, and the memorial of military conquests made me ill. I felt my faith shrinking at the display of such might. However, I quickly came to my senses when I reminded myself that even the most powerful emperor of all time still received his power from God. Now that's my King!

After a few days of rest and fellowship, my mind was restless. I wished to help, to minister to the needs of the flock anywhere in the world, including Rome. "Clement, what are the needs you see within the Church here in Rome," I asked.

"There is what you would expect," he replied. "Gnosticism is an ongoing battle, the glorification of the mother of Jesus surfaces for a while then disappears. Persecution is on the increase. Christians are banned from the Royal Palace. Domitian established the law, and while Trajan seems unconcerned with the Church, he hasn't changed the law. I suppose that the greatest challenge we face is the rise of the false teacher Marcion. I believe you may know him for he has dropped your name on several occasions."

"I have heard of him, and met him once, I believe," I replied. "Wasn't he part of that group you sent several years ago to warn us of the Emperor's edict? I believe it was his father's ship that transported the group."

"That is that man," Clement said. "Unfortunately, his father died, and Marcion inherited his family's fortune. The lust for what money can accomplish has consumed any godly wisdom he may have formerly claimed. He is full of error and is building a large gathering of apostates. He's even trying to buy a pastoral position. That's one of the reasons I requested your presence. The churches respect you, and when Ignatius was brought to Rome, he told us that you were the man to seek out for matters that affected the church as a whole."

"I have only been able to gather small amounts of information on his doctrine. What exactly is he teaching? What alarms you?" I asked.

"First, I'm sure you've heard of this: he teaches that the God of the Old Testament could not have been the Father of Jesus Christ. He refuses to consider that the One True God could possess the attributes of wrath and justice," explained Clement.

I laughed at how ludicrous his teachings were as I tried to figure out how he could derive his principles from the Scriptures. "How does he handle the passages that obviously contradict him?" I asked.

"It's not complicated," replied Clement, "and it will make you angry; I'm sure of it. He has rewritten the Scriptures to suit his beliefs. He has totally thrown out the Old Testament as no longer relevant, and most of the new writings of the Apostles. What he has kept is a carefully scripted document that includes a grossly edited Gospel of Luke and a few of Paul's works. Anything that contradicts his opinion, he simply has removed from the compilation of what he calls scripture."

"It must be a mighty small document," I said. "What could be his objective?"

"He appears to have developed a lust for a large following, and the fame and authority that accompanies it. To this end he has developed a teaching on the goodness of God and nothing else.

He only shares on the love of God but never on the holiness of God and his hatred of sin," Clement said.

"Then He has taken away any need for a Savior," I interjected.

"This is true," Clement continued, "But the source of his error begins with his view of God. The God of the Old Testament is not the God in the Gospels. He views the God of Abraham as vindictive and compassionless. He sees Jesus as one sent from another more loving and merciful God. He and his followers deny that Jesus came in bodily form, but was a spirit that manifested itself as a man. The Marcionites despise rules, commands, and calls for obedience, and they abhor the thought of God's wrath, hell, or anything to do with eternal punishment. They want the Garden of Eden without the fall of man."

"Are you telling me that he sees two different Gods?" I asked.

"Yes, and I'm afraid it gets worse. He believes that the God of Israel and the Old Covenant was inferior to the God who sent Jesus as Savior," Clement explained.

"So he has no concept of the Trinity, either?" I asked.

"No. You can see it's a blend of many philosophies and false religions. He feels he can reach more people if he can perhaps soften the image of God," Clement added.

"So what you are telling me is that by his actions he is positioning himself to appear more merciful than God, if that were possible, of course," I suggested.

"Not consciously, I'm sure, but he dilutes the severity of sin, the fall of man and eternal judgment. Many will be condemned to eternal hell over his doctrine," Clement added.

---◇◇---

I had the joy of preaching to congregations all over Rome, and I saw their famous faith as Paul had noted in his letter to them. As I talked with many of the various pastors and elders, it became apparent that we needed to confront the Marcion error. It's not that the pastors were being misled, but many of the simpletons and weak Christians were being led astray leaving their faith shipwrecked. Clement called for a gathering of the pastors of each congregation, including myself, in order to correct Marcion, or if necessary, rebuke him for preaching another Gospel contrary to the Scriptures.

One hundred pastors were present, and I was the spokesman. Marcion shared his beliefs, which were in direct contradiction to much of the Scriptures. We replied to him using the Scriptures, but he countered every objection with his reasoning and his misinterpretations of the Word of God. Realizing that we seemed to be going in circles, I decided to draw this debate to a conclusion, for it was obvious that Marcion was determined to pursue his errors.

"The point of the gospel begins first with the wrath of God, and the focus of his love to deliver us from it. His wrath is always directed towards evil and unrighteous actions. Those godless actions smother the truth of the gospel in the hearts of those dead in trespasses and sins; those whose minds have are blinded by the devil, the god of this world. Satan's goal, since his expulsion from the courts of God, has been 'to keep people from beholding the light of the gospel, which is Jesus Christ; the very image of God.'[95] We are made in the image of God, Marcion—the God you say is not God. Just as he loves and hates, so we reflect the attributes of our Creator in both our love and hate. Hatred is not a sin unless directed at anything other than that which is evil. No man, woman or child is without excuse, for God has called all people to repent," I said.

Marcion had listened with an impatient scowl on his face and at last spoke up, "Your own argument both betrays you and strengthens my case. You say you are created in your God's image and yet you confuse the God you say you serve with the inferior God of the Hebrew scriptures. My teachings present God as one of love, not wrath and fear," he replied.

But I responded; "The fear of the Lord is not the dread we experience with God's attention on us, but rather his focus on sin. Our fear is the wrath of his hatred against sin. This same God is pure, holy and without any contamination of sin whatsoever. Out of his perfect love he has provided a way through his only son to escape his wrath and live in the eternal bliss of his immeasurable love. As the writer to the Hebrews has so effectively articulated; 'Your throne, O God, is eternal, the scepter of perfect sinlessness is the scepter of your kingdom. You have loved righteousness, and you have hated the willful violation of your law.'[96] We are

---

95. II Corinthians 4:4

96. Hebrews 1:8-9

not to apologize for the wrath of God as if we were embarrassed by him. We are to preach it; bring it out into the open for all to see, for it is real, and the unbeliever will experience that intense hatred with the devil and his demons forever. It is not a pleasant thought, but that is no reason to stop declaring it as the first step in understanding the eternal love of God. Marcion, you are like the children of Israel at Mt. Sinai, who saw the presence of the Lord descending upon the mountain with smoke and fire. The mountain quaked, and the sounds proceeding out of it grew as trumpets playing louder and louder. The presence of God caused panic and fear, and what did they do, Marcion? They built what seemed to them to be a harmless god in the form of a golden calf. They built something they could admire; something they didn't need to fear; that which could never show wrath, but only garner admiration. That is what you are doing. You have built a figurative golden calf, and have called it the love of god; for there is nothing to fear with that god."

"I can't believe you are using that story to argue against me," he said, breaking into my discourse again. "You know that I reject those Jewish teachings. Maybe they are interesting, but certainly not relevant to a correct understanding of God. The God I preach is a God of love and forgiveness not a God of superstitious fear."

Clement interjected his thoughts and said, "The great divide between your corrupted theology and the truth of Scripture is your resistance in seeking to understand the holiness of God. No one can ever come into a true and living experience of God's love until they begin to grow in their understanding of his holiness. You have thrown away the Old Testament of God as if it were refuse for the dunghill, not realizing that it provides the very contrast you are missing to discover the glory of the gospel. The Old Testament explains why we need the New Testament of Jesus Christ. You have parsed the Holy Scriptures to suit your beliefs instead of having the Holy Scriptures shape them."

Marcion just sat and stared at us, appearing annoyed that we were consuming his time.

I then resumed my final thoughts by saying; "Paul, whom you admire, warned Timothy of people just like you, and times like this. 'The time is coming when people will refuse to hold up sound doctrine, but having ears that itch, will bring together teachers to teach what they wrongly long to hear, and as a result, they will abandon the truth and turn away following fiction as if it were truth.'[97] Or, is that one of the passages you have blotted out? We realize you don't recognize the writing of the Old Covenant, but you should, for in the second psalm, the writer has included you."

"I'm not familiar with that psalm," Marcion replied.

"Let me stir up your memory," I said. "Why are the godless tumultuous, and the people set their thinking on what has no intrinsic value? The Kings of the earth gather, and all the rulers conspire together against God Almighty and his Anointed, and say, Let us tear away his yoke upon us, and throw off of us his tethers. But God will shatter them with a rod of iron and scatter the useless pieces like pottery. O kings of the earth be wise. You who lead people, you have been warned. Labor before the Lord with fear, and shudder at the shallowness of what causes you to rejoice. Recognize the authority of the Son and be affectionate, remove his anger, or you will perish for you will discover that the withholding of his wrath is for a short time. Oh, how blessed and happy are those who find their safe hiding place in him.[98]

"Paul himself taught that the Old Testament was providing a narrative of the kingdom of God with its culmination in the Lord Jesus Christ. Luke records this in his Acts of the Apostles. 'When the day had been set aside for Paul, they came in large numbers, and from morning until evening he explained to them the kingdom of God by convincing them of Jesus from the Law of Moses and from the prophets.'"[99]

Again, Marcion countered, "But of course Paul used the Old Testament. He was talking to Jewish people and had to talk to them in ways they could understand—even if it was a limited understanding. And besides, Paul too was a Jew, unlike you and me, Polycarp. Since we are not Jews, why should we give credence to their scriptures?"

"'Why,' you ask? In part because both Jesus and Paul clearly gave great reverence to the Word of God as they had it. But you miss the whole idea of the very mission laid out before Jesus—a mission that was rooted in the Hebrew scriptures—for he was the

97. II Timothy 4:3-4

98. Psalm 2:1-2 & 9-12

99. Acts 28:23

mediator between God and man. Man was the enemy of God due to sin, but it was God's foreordained plan that through the work of Jesus Christ, the two would be made one. You are throwing out the initial part of the equation. You have made your Creator, the grace-giving God your enemy. Notice the harmony of the two in Paul's second letter to the Corinthian church: "Our declaration is not about ourselves, but Jesus Christ as Lord and we as your slaves for the sake of Jesus. For it is God who said, 'Let light shine forth from the darkness,' and he has shown that light in our hearts to reveal the true light of the glory of God as seen in the face of Jesus Christ. We possess this priceless treasure in us who are like mere clay jars, in order that he may demonstrate that this overwhelming power belongs to God and not to us. It's the presence of this power that explains why we are being afflicted in every way possible, but never distressed; we may have no idea what to do, but we don't experience utter loss. We experience persecution, but that doesn't mean we will be forsaken; strike us down, but we cannot be destroyed; the truth is that we will always carry in our bodies the death of Jesus, in order that the life of Jesus can evidence itself in us.'"[100]

When I had finished, and Marcion for once seemed to have nothing to say, Clement added an important perspective. "When Paul exhorted the Thessalonian Church with his second letter, he was careful to address the doctrinal teaching like that which you have concocted when he said: "God considers it equitable to pay back with tribulation those who afflict his people, and to provide help in those afflictions, for when our Lord Jesus is revealed from heaven with his mighty host of angels who will come with flaming fire. They will have revenge on those who did not know God, and on those who refused to heed the Gospel of our Lord Jesus. They will pay the price with eternal destruction, alienated from the presence of the Lord, and from experiencing the gloriousness of his mighty power."[101]

"I have heard enough," Marcion shouted as he slammed his hand on the table in front of him. "I am fully persuaded regarding my beliefs, and respect your differing opinions, but you will not

100. *II Corinthians 4:4-10*

101. *II Thessalonians 1:6-9*

force your beliefs on me. I have given to this assembly a great sum of money; surely you can see my intentions are noble."

"You have indeed, but you are deceived by your intentions. In that chest over by the door is every gold piece you gave. Not one coin is missing. We cannot accept this money," Clement said.

"The truth is not for sale," I added. "Marcion, you leave us no option. The Apostle Paul does not mince his words when he tells us how to respond to preachers like you when he says in his letter to the Church of Galatia; 'If anyone preaches a gospel contrary to the Word of God, let that preacher be banned from the church.'[102] It pierces my heart, but you have left us with only one alternative, and as reluctant as my flesh may be to move on this issue, Scripture is, and must remain our guide. It is time for judgment to begin in the household of God, and it must begin with us, right here, for if we fail in this, brethren, what will be the results that flow from those who refuse to obey the gospel?"

"You cannot do this," Marcion declared. "I have as much right to preach as you do; perhaps even more for my eyes have been opened to the truth."

"We obviously cannot stifle your public speaking. We do not possess that power nor would we wish it for that matter, but as far as serving as part of the presbytery of the Church, we are and will continue to exercise the authority yielded to us by the Word of God, the very God you deny," I replied.

"Do as you please then, but I assure you, I'm not going away. I feel what I am doing is right. That money in the chest over there, I'll just use it to start my own churches," Marcion said.

"Beware, Marcion, you are not resisting us; you are flaunting your puny power in the face of Almighty God," I declared.

Marcion got up, and calling over two of his servants, ordered them to pick up the chest and carry it out. He even stopped at the door and removing his sandals shook the dust off them before leaving the room. The next hour we spent on our knees seeking the grace of God to repair our troubled hearts, and to seek the protection of God over his church from such errors as Marcionism.

A week later as we were preparing to make our way back to Smyrna, I came across Marcion on the street but was determined not to speak with him.

---

102. Galations 1:9

He did not like this, and when I walked by, not even looking at him, he stopped and said, "Don't you recognize me anymore?"

To which I responded, "Yes, I know who you are. You are the first-born of Satan." And then I continued walking away. And so we should act toward any, whom in denying the existence of God, molest the church and fabricate the Scriptures to fit their view of the world.

———◇———

Over the next several years, as God grew my faith, he grew it to be spent on the lives of others through preaching, growing followers of Christ, encouraging churches, writing, and challenging teachings contrary to Scripture. They were peaceful years, at least for the churches in Asia, though I experienced the heartache of my mother's death. As I looked down on her lifeless body, I was struck with a profound but grateful thought and how significantly God has used her to shape my life in godliness. She left this world surrounded by her family and friends.

Wherever persecution afflicted the church, we prayed and mobilized what help could be assembled to meet the needs and strengthen the endurance of those affected. Don't misunderstand me, for when I say that I was blessed, I'm not implying they there were no trials during that time. Quite the contrary, for trials are the great heaven-sent purifiers of our faith. But that's my point, these trials did not tear us down, they built us up. When we discover that our trials are sanctified by the Lord, and are given to reveal our spiritual growth, we live in the constant discovery that they are like steps being built over a wall called life. Because of this we are lifted to see beyond this life and to discover the glories of God shining into it, and leading us toward that perfect day of being united forever with Him.

14

BLESSED IS THE NAME
OF THE LORD

*Now after you have endured great
hardship, the grace giving God,
who has called you to his eternal glory in
Christ, will himself repair you,
make you stable, make you strong, and be your foundation.
(I Peter 5:10)*

I HAD labored in the spiritual field of Smyrna for several years, and continued to see the faithfulness of God in every aspect of the work. I had a home, food on the table, a lovely wife to grace both my house and my life and three children. John was my eldest, named after my mentor, the Apostle John. His interests seemed to lie in the work of the ministry. Our second son was named Timothy after our first pastor, and to my happiness, he seemed not only interested, but had a natural talent in the work of a parchmenter like my uncle, Decimus. My youngest was our daughter, named after my mother, Callisto. Truly, she was the apple of her father's eye.

While there had been memorable years of blessing, this year had been a strain on me. Marcion's following was growing, and his doctrinal error was dooming thousands of deceived souls. They called themselves Christians, but were bound by all forms of licentiousness. It would appear that they were making up the rules as they went. And there is always a battle against spiritual shallowness or lukewarmness in the hearts of the saints. Such growth of carnality is due, largely in part, to the neglect of the Word of God, which is the essential part of being equipped for obedience, growth, and the enjoyment of the fruit of God's Spirit in our lives.

A lot of the error I saw was in the form of spiritual superstition, added with other pharisaical practices that create a form or appearance of godliness, but is void of power. Many believers live in a false sense of security, as if by fulfilling certain rites or practices they are acceptable to God. Of course, once these entrapments are engaged, godly obedience and its fruit of love dry up, and hypocrisy becomes the new spiritual norm. It would seem that people cannot trust the effectual work of Christ Jesus our Lord. They declare they have faith, but rely more on their efforts and not of our Lord. Such teaching is not new in the church, of course. It just appears to me to be a greater stress at this moment in my life than in the past. Nevertheless, what does God require of me as one of his stewards but to be faithful? So I daily saturate my thinking in the Word of God to learn by the example of His faithfulness.

I find my heart stirred by the grace of God evident in the life of Job as he faced the greatest trial of his life. What a precious submission he displayed before God, and what defiance towards the enemy of God, the devil, when in deepest sorrow he valiantly declared, "The Lord gave, and the Lord has seen fit to take away." That in itself is splendor-filled submission, but what he said next, won the day: "Blessed is the name of the Lord."[103] An admission like that is not the response of a natural man, but the glorious work of God in that man. Such circumstances are not something for us to fear, but to anticipate. Truly this is what the Psalmist was expressing when he so eloquently stated: "Whom do I have in heaven but you? And there is no one on earth I take pleasure in than you my God."[104]

What a weapon when facing the spiritual battlefield of discouragement and despair! What a scourge for the Lord's servant, but it has recently become a constant battlefield in my heart. I've never been one to be overly discouraged, but I feel I'm growing weary with the fickleness of many weaker Christians. Daily I am confronted by people, who don't like the way I declare the Word, or they compare our congregation to larger congregations in Ephesus. I ache as I see young people rejecting their upbringing because of the hypocrisy they see lived out in their homes instead of genuine godliness. I even have people in my congregation determined to overthrow Rome. If it's not one fire I have to put out, then it's another one. Anna consistently has to calm me down, and remind to be patient with them all. "Oh yes, be patient

---

103. *Job 1:21*

104. *Psalm 73:25*

with those who desire to make me a captain of their army and attack Rome," I often jest. And she would continue the joke by telling me how handsome I would look in armor. What's a weary pastor to do?

As I have examined my heart over this past year, I suppose my discouragement ultimately flows from a fleshly discontentment, on the one hand, and perhaps some fatigue on the other. I haven't been getting much rest, and when I'm not studying and discipling, I'm correcting and rebuking; not to mention that my first ministry begins with my family. They're proof that I am capable of ministering to others.

Still, discouragement can be a threshold for sin, and grave danger for any who tolerate its nagging presence. I have concluded that I have allowed the care of the ministry to usurp my affection for my Lord. When I am joyful in him, discouragement evaporates, but take away that joy, and I feel I cannot bear the load.

On occasion I complained to my wife at how difficult the work was here in Smyrna. The Lord did say that the synagogue of Satan was in the town, and I could easily believe it. If it wasn't immoral paganism or the worship of Caesar that blinded the hearts of the lost, then it was legalism that blocked the light of the Gospel of Jesus Christ. I had to be careful, but sometimes I wondered if my ministry life would have been easier if I had stayed in Ephesus, but I know that such a thought is nonsense.

The solution to my condition was found in Paul's exhortation to Timothy: "Godliness with a contented heart is truly a great gain."[105] "What a great remedy for the subtlety of self-centeredness," I often thought to myself.

⋄

Being edified by others is a wonderful way to embrace the encouragement sent from the Lord. One day I recall with great delight seeing the impact of this truth on the young people in our congregation. I had the sublime delight of listening to Irenaeus challenging a group of parents and their young people.

He began by stating; "We live in a pagan culture that worships every god the imagination can make up, but ultimately we must come to understand that regardless of the false gods, it all goes

---

105. I Timothy 6:6

back to just one god man seeks to exalt. It was out of the lurid deception of the devil in the Garden of Eden that the gods of men were birthed when the tempter said; 'God is aware that the day you eat of this forbidden fruit you will be enlightened, and you will become like him, becoming a god; being your own god and deciding for yourself what is good and what is evil.'"[106]

"This is where sin begins, and this is the target of God's hatred for sin and his harsh judgment on it. Perhaps you can see how it has ruined mankind, for even to this day, we like to reserve the right to decide what we believe to be right or wrong. To acknowledge that there is a Supreme Being; a Creator of all things is to expose man's wickedness in exalting himself into the place of being a god. Pride is man's downfall, and your ruin hinges on whether or not you live in the reality of the Almighty God, and whether or not your desires are for him. Otherwise, you position yourself as his competition; if such a thing could ever exist."

"The difference we make in this world, and the impact we have on this culture is dependent on how much of the True God is our God, and how much of ourselves we set up as a god. This is the heart of Paul's message to the Corinthian Christians when he challenges them regarding their flirtations with the world and the lawless ones; the unsaved to be exact. He says, "You all must not align yourselves with those who do not belong to God, for what true fellowship can light have with darkness? What terms of commonness could Christ have with the wicked one, the devil? Or what do the faithful have in common with the unfaithful? You must see that we are the dwelling place of God; for it is God who said, 'My dwelling place will be among you, and I will accompany you wherever you go, and I will be your God, and you will be my people.' For this reason, stop going in the same direction as the godless. Distance yourself from their direction by going the opposite way, do not embrace their unholy lifestyles; for in doing this you will find my welcoming hand, and discover me as a caring father to you, and you will be my sons and daughters, declares the Lord Almighty."[107]

Irenaeus continued; "Young people and parents, listen to me, the presence of God in you is to crowd out the little gods in your

---

106. *Genesis 3:5*

107. *II Corinthians 6:14-18*

life. Grow in grace and in the knowledge of Jesus Christ. Commit yourself to the discovery of his life-changing, thought-changing grace in you, and he will lead you by desire and wisdom out of the clutches of the world, and will give you the strength to remove yourself from being a little god. Destroy the god of self, and the One True God will use you to tear down the gods of the nations which are idols."

◇◇

Part of my work was discipling and training others for the work of the ministry. Irenaeus was my primary pupil, and my son, John, was expressing interest; though I was careful to make sure it was God's direction in his life and not his attempts to please me. I assured him many times that his love for the Lord was the greatest satisfaction I could ever have, and I loved him deeply for it. His obedience to the Lord had a dynamic influence on the direction of his younger brother and sister.

Many other young men and struggling pastors visited with me; some staying for long periods of time. Such was a young man who was to arrive today. I had heard of him and believed that God was going to use him in powerful ways. He was remarkably courageous, marked with a natural ability and keen mind to put up a strong defense of the faith. He was a philosopher and was developing into quite an apologist. He was to arrive today from Ephesus and spend the next year with me. He was born again a few years ago while visiting in Ephesus. During that time, he was mentored in philosophy from the standpoint of the Scriptures and now he wished to gain experience in the pastoral side of the ministry. His testimony was true, and the change in his life was a blessing to witness by all who knew him. His name was Justin Cantius Priscus; though he recently starting adding the suffix "The Witness" after his name, since he desired to declare to others what he saw, learned, and experienced as a devoted follower of Christ. He later would come to be known simply as Justin Martyr.[108]

As a student of philosophy, originally a Platonist, he was determined to show that the search for true logic and wisdom can only lead to the One True God. He had a delightful personality, and was absorbed in his studies—maybe too absorbed. Some of

---

108. *Martyr comes from the Greek word* martus, *which means a witness*

the great philosophers of Rome were his mentors, and due to his family's wealth, he was able to afford to travel throughout the empire and experience many life's lessons; many good ones, but also damaging and hurtful lessons as well.

When he arrived, we sat down over some food, and I began to get acquainted with him. "What are your plans for the future," I asked.

"I desire to pastor, but perhaps in a less tradition role," Justin remarked.

"Traditional role," I questioned; "Is there a tradition in the pastoral role?" Justin appeared perplexed, not understanding my reaction.

"Perhaps 'traditional' was not the word I was looking for," he replied. "I look at the work you are doing, and while I admire it, it seems too broad and vast for me. I am seeking a more narrow focus of pastoring."

"What do you mean? What is your burden?" I inquired.

Justin leaned in towards me, and with a growing intensity in his voice and his eyes brightened, he explained, "What if I could take a group of young people, ten to twenty, I'm thinking. What if I discipled that group in being able to provide a defense of the faith in the philosophical societies of Rome. We possess the truth in clear, powerful, and life-changing ways, and I want to take courageous and bold young people and harness that enthusiasm. That's what I desire. I want to pastor a small group with a central mission that takes the Word of God into the whorish lair of Roman idolatry: Philosophy!" Then he leaned back and crossed his arms as he awaited my reaction.

I smiled, not out of disbelief or that I considered his view a misdirected enthusiasm. No, on the contrary, the plan intrigued me. After a moment of consideration, I said; "So you want to take a small group, disciple them to, in essence, turn the world upside down." He nodded his head. "Sounds like a familiar method that was used by our Lord with his twelve. Though I must warn you, do not limit yourself. Your intentions are noble, but what if God gives you more than twenty?"

"Well, of course, he may do that if he chooses, and all would be welcome. However, my focus remains steadfast. I want to focus on apologetics,"[109] he said. "Some have criticized me in thinking that I'm simply starting a school. But as I see, Polycarp, since when is the church not to be a school? We are to persuade through the preaching, and instruct through the teaching. Is this not correct?" He asked.

"It is correct, and we must work hard not to permit a separation between the two," I replied. It is the responsibility of every pastor to train his people to be prepared to provide answers regarding the hope that motivates them. If a pastor fails in this, he fails in his calling. We do not merely watch the sheep as a bored, hired hand. No sir, we are called to oversee the work the shepherd is accomplishing amongst the flock. We encourage it; protect it; constantly persuading the congregation to listen and follow the shepherd instead of this world and all its false teachings and snares of life. Truly, I think if pastors focused on what they were training their congregations for, they would be less focused on simply obtaining a greater number of attendees."

"This is what captures my heart. I want to train the congregation to be equipped, active and interacting with all who would be watching, from Caesar, government officials and philosophers, to the commoner in the market place," he said. "Will you help, Polycarp? Will you help me refine this vision? It nags me day and night, and demands I give it legs to move."

"Of course, Justin; it would be a privilege to assist you any way I can," I answered. We finished our meal as he told me of the many philosophers he had met in his travels.

◇◇

The next day Justin joined Irenaeus and me as we made several calls on the congregation. I have always enjoyed meeting up with the men in my congregation at their place of employment. We agree on an appropriate time, and they show me their work and introduce me to fellow workers as we discuss how to worship the Lord in the workplace. It's this kind of practical theology that aids me in my study and the declaration of the Word.

Justin desired a view of Smyrna, so we ventured up to the top of Mt. Pagus, and made our way around the ruins of the ancient Greek fortress built by one of Alexander the Great's gen-

---

109. *Defense of the Christian faith*

erals, Lysimachus. Parts of the old fortress are currently used as a Roman Garrison, but most of it lies in ruin. However, from the edge of the walls that were still standing, we were able to find a beautiful prospect of the city and harbor below.

As we walked along and stopped at various sites around Smyrna, I took the opportunity to challenge Justin and to ascertain where he was in his spiritual understanding. "To be an effective pastor; to successfully lead others in their discovery of life-changing, indeed life-saving truth, you must be graced by God with endurance," I said. "I know this sounds remarkably odd, but I have discovered that it is the quintessential principle necessary for leadership, and when I say leadership, I am referring to our ministry to the people. Administrating the various works of the ministry is easy by comparison; in fact, it can be a distracting enjoyment. Projects don't talk back," I jested.

"Nor do they get discouraged, and they don't get offended, either," Irenaeus added.

"True, very true," I said. "However, people, on the other hand, are troubled and perplexed by the problems they encounter in their spiritual growth, as well as being troubled by life in general. But that's why God has given overseers to his church as gifts. I know it's hard to visualize ourselves as spiritual gifts to God's people, but a godly and growing pastor can be a remarkable help and guide to those looking to advance in their spiritual maturity."

"Polycarp, what would you say are three of the most important principles you want to see strengthened in my life while I am here," Justin asked.

"Well, you seem to have a grasp on how to study. That, of course, is paramount. Obviously, a deep and devoted love for the Lord is the greatest quality a pastor must possess, and while I have no doubt of your love for the Lord, that is where I think I will focus my attention. If a Christian underestimates the importance of loving the Lord with all their heart, that person will miss everything. Overseers are particularly vulnerable here I must confess. We can become enamored with the influence we possess, or the wisdom we seem to have, or the glory we feel at the sound of our voice echoing over a crowd, to such a degree that we lose the love of our calling. We love the Lord Jesus Christ, and our calling centers around being an example of that love, and making the love of God and its multiple demonstrations the theme of our preaching.

And I must add; the love of God is not only contrasted by his wrath, but also by his holiness."

As we sat on the edge of the wall and looked over the city below, I quickly consolidated the principles of love that I felt would be best for Justin at this time in his life and preparation.

"Justin, to answer your question, the first principle would be faithfulness," I answered. "You have been appointed to a position of leadership, but don't mistake leadership for headship. As you should be fully aware, that is our Lord's position; the church is his, never ours! We are at the highest level only servant-leaders who are entrusted with major responsibility but no true authority over the people. Our authority is the Word of God, and in that we faithfully study and proclaim the truth of the Gospel."

"Truly, if faithfully serving the Lord to his people is not your heart desire, the office of overseer can be quite miserable. Working with people involves more work, greater responsibility, longer hours and most of all, a thicker skin. Remember the illustration of our Lord and the responsibility of the talents given to the stewards. Two invested properly and were rewarded with greater responsibility while the third did nothing and lost the opportunity. Do you remember the key word in that parable? Faithfulness! That's the word—faithfulness. Remember that word, and it will be a reliable guide through the most difficult and challenging of times. You may even be facing your death; be faithful to what you have been called to do, and it will keep you loyal when you may be inclined to betray your loyalty. It will stabilize you when everything around you gives way, and when you feel alone, which is an often under-estimated emotion that can bring down the strongest of men. It will be your closest companion that sweetly reminds you your purpose in being born, and why God has granted you life."

"How did our Lord communicate this message to the messenger of our church in John's apocalypse? 'Be faithful in the face of death, and I will give you the crown of life.'[110] 'Be faithful.' he exhorts and the reward will be a crown. That crown is not a trophy for the shelf, but a promotion to greater responsibility. But first, we must be faithful in the little things, and the most important area our faithfulness is required, is in our relationship

---

110. *Revelation 2:10*

with people. We must love people, especially those in our own Christian family, the church. But let me clarify that this love is not out of our emotions; I'm not speaking of brotherly love, but rather, divine love. This love of God for us, in us, and through us comes only through obedience to his Holy Word. In other words, being faithful to God's Word produces in us a stronger devotion to him and others that give us the ability to exercise greater faithfulness."

"I see clearly what you are saying," Justin replied. I believe one of my greatest weaknesses is a focus on intellect without love. I love philosophy and debate, and at times I fear I love them more than my Lord. I suppose it's easy to be faithful to a cause while being unfaithful to the head of that cause."

"Let's walk a little," I suggested. "There's a cluster of trees just beyond those rocks; let's find a place in the shade." As we made our way over to the clump of trees, I introduced the second principle necessary for all Christians, but leaders especially as it relates to the example they set.

"Justin, I believe the calling of every believer is to discover genuine worship, and devote your life to it. I am astonished by the confusion in this area, and I tremble at the scores of people who clumsily attempt to worship God out of a Cain-style of worship."

"Cain-style; what do you mean?" Justin questioned.

"Simply put, it means that we bring before the Lord what we think he wants, having never put out thoughts to what he truly desires," I said. "We were born to worship God. Truly, there can be no greater honor than for a person to be fully absorbed in the adoration of God. True worship is conformity to God's plan and purpose. It should never reflect us, but only his perfect work in us. Worship is the harnessing of our emotions to our actions. It is loving the Lord with more than our words, but rather our obedience. Worship results when we obey. Obedience is adherence to the will of God, as expressed exclusively in His holy Word. The Word of God equips us for everything good, and what is good prepares and guides our heart in worship."

"It is an often overlooked fact, but worship requires the fear of the Lord. On the one hand we tremble at his might and power, and are moved to show great respect regarding him. It is also being awed by his qualities and attributes," I exhorted.

"What you are saying is that worship is connected with being in the presence of God," Justin said.

"Yes, worship is more a result of being in God's presence more than it is being ushered into His presence," I clarified.

"The third principle, and least desirable to our flesh I might add, is to endure affliction as a determined soldier of the cross. I saved this one for last because it is the one that will grate against you the most. Faithfulness holds us to a steady cause; and worship is where we find our fulfillment; but affliction makes us feel alone, adrift, maybe even abandoned by God. It's one of the most effective tools our spiritual enemy will use to spit out his lies into our thinking. Enduring affliction is vital to our calling as ministers and all the followers of Christ," I said.

"Like jars of clay, we are filled with a vast wealth in order to show that the exceeding power of that treasure belongs to God and not to us. For this reason, we expect tribulation from every side, but we'll never be crushed by it; we may feel trapped, but never despondent; persecuted, but never abandoned; thrown down by our opponent, but not defeated.'"[111]

"A pastor can minister from a position of godly strength as he helps others through the calamities of life, but what happens when he also is among the suffering?" I added. Little did I know how crucial this one quality would become as a catastrophe would strike my life and home the very next day.

———◇◇———

The next day began like any mid-July day. It was hotter than the average summer days which compelled people to work in the mornings and late afternoons in order to avoid the intensity of the mid-day sun. Justin joined Irenaeus on some church-related errands, and I made my way down from my home which was situated above the base of Mt. Pagus, down through the agora where I greeted friends and church family as I passed through the crowded market place. Just south of the town, on the shoreline of the harbor was a shady oasis where I could often find seclusion in order to pray and ponder the Scriptures for the various duties that demanded my attention.

---

111. II Corinthians 4:7-9

I focused my thoughts for the day on the passage for the next Lord's Day. It was never a challenge to wonder what I would preach on, for I found a delightful satisfaction in preaching word-by-word through the Scripture and expounding upon the thoughts of the writers. Since "all scripture is breathed out by God and is beneficial for teaching, rebuking, correction and providing instruction in righteousness, and to perfectly equip us,"[112] then it should be preached as such. Preach it all in sequence for this forces the pastor to study and understand the more difficult texts and doctrines. It's too easy to sweeten a sermon, or scratch itching ears with glossy topics. Uncover the truths the Holy Spirit was conveying through the talents and style of the writers. Home in on that message. In this way God makes his servants think and link thoughts together to truly equip God's people.

I had been there for what seemed a few minutes, but actually had been four hours. The refreshing breeze was replaced with a hot blast off the warm waters of the Aegean. I was now feeling uncomfortable, and realized that I would need to retreat to the coolness of my home in order to continue my study. As I stood up, I was confronted with a strange sensation. The ground beneath my feet began to tremble. I have experienced the quaking of the earth many times, for this area is subject to frequent movement, but this one was more than a tremor, and was increasing in strength as each moment passed. Trees began to fall, and dislodged boulders from the hill behind me began to tumble down towards me. Then a sight I had never witnessed before; the sea rolled back exposing the bed of the harbor, and with tremendous ferocity, it slammed back onto the shoreline and surged beyond its natural boundaries into the low-lying areas of Smyrna.

I was on the coastline, but on a ridge overlooking the sea. Water splashed up around me, but did not reach me, which was good for I was still dodging the rocks being hurled down the hill behind me. As I ran off the ridge, trying to keep my balance as the earth shook beneath my feet, my heart collapsed as I saw buildings fall around the town. Parts of the wall on the great fortress atop Mt. Pagus crumbled, as did segments of the arena and the palatial mansions on top of the hill. My eyes quickly focused on the location of my home, but the billowing dust blocked my view.

---

112. II Timothy 3:16

Sudden fright, compounded by the awe of such a catastrophe unfolding right before my eyes was quickly subdued by the tragedy of injured people and the death that would undoubtedly be discovered when the dust settled. With haste I ran back towards the town as I leapt over debris and stopped many times to answer the cries for help.

I ran by the church meeting hall where I found Justin and my three children. I called out for them and waved my arms hoping they could see me through the dust. "John, Timothy, Callisto!" I yelled. They heard my voice and looked in my direction.

Callisto was the first to see me, and shouted, "Look! It's father."

"Where? I don't see him," John replied before he was able to make out my image as I stumbled across some fallen columns.

I hugged them all tightly, and considered myself a blessed man to be able to do so, but I stopped suddenly, alarmed that someone was missing. Being moved by alarm, I asked, "Children, where is your mother?" They became alarmed as no one could account for her whereabouts.

"Where did you see her last?" I asked.

"We were on our way here before the quaking, but she forgot something and returned home and sent us ahead of her," Timothy answered. "She said she would meet us here."

"Stay here with Justin," I demanded. "I'll make my way home and find her. Don't worry children." With that, I made my way through the rubble, stopping briefly to help some in distress. I finally arrived at what had been my home. Not one wall was left standing. It was a giant heap of stones.

"Anna!" I cried out, hoping that perhaps she was nearby helping our neighbors, but I did not hear her voice. I shouted several more times as I made my way around the rubble resisting the thought that she may be under it.

As I began my frantic search, I heard the voice of a woman from behind me. I turned to see an injured neighbor. She said, "Polycarp, I saw Anna enter back into the house when the tremors began. I did not see her come back out," she said.

Now my heart sank as I once again inspected the heap of stone that once was a haven of rest and protection for my family, and that may now entomb my wife. I began to turn stones with what strength I could muster, but I felt on the verge of fainting. I was ill at the thought she may be under the debris. Several neighbors came to assist me. Some were part of my church family, and others had rejected the gospel, but all were friends, and I was grateful for their help.

It didn't take long until someone shouted, "I found her. She's here." I bounded over the rubble to the location, but to my horror and grief, her body lay there lifeless. I could not begin to assimilate the emotions that were flooding in and out my soul. It seemed impossible, though the proof of her death was right in front of my eyes. "What of the children?" I thought. "How will I break this tragedy to them?"

At this point, my spiritual nature kicked in, and God's grace was clearly at work, for my thoughts were nothing more than ceaseless prayers lifted up to God. When we cleared away the rubble, I was finally able to reach down and hold her against my breast. I could not hold back the tears as the weight of my loss confronted me.

My first thoughts went immediately back to my meditations from the other day regarding Job, as he faced horrendous losses. How did this faithful man respond? As I thought it, I began to speak it; "The Lord is the one who gives, and the Lord is the one who can take away what he gives. Blessed is the name of my Lord." These are not the thoughts of a fleshly man but are the marks of God's masterful grace. I could not deny the sorrow, nor would it have been normal to try, but I felt protected from the bondage of bitterness so normal in people who don't understand the ways of God.

The staggering part to sorrow is that I was not the only one affected. Many of those in the congregation were also suffering loss. Many will look to me not only for comfort, but more than ever, as an example of godly faithfulness. I decided in those unforgettable moments that my course of action would be to comfort others as God comforts me, and weep with those who weep.

Some close friends to Anna and me volunteered to prepare her for burial so that I could be with my children, and while I longed to feel the embrace of their hugs, I dreaded the grief I would be forced to place upon them. I made my way back to the meeting hall. Though in a daze, I was able to provide assistance to others; some who joyfully reunited with loved ones, and some who had to endure the agony of loss.

When I saw my children ministering and helping those in need, I had to hide from them as a wave of agony overtook me again. Those tender children. How could I tell them? As I came around the corner, Irenaeus had made his way to the hall and was the first to see me. He could tell that something was wrong. Justin observed this too and moved my children away from the crowd over near a garden where I could talk to them privately.

"Polycarp," Irenaeus said, "What has happened?"

"My dear friend, for the glory of the Lord, he has seen fit to take Anna from this life, and has ushered her into eternal life with him," I forced myself to say not knowing if I should answer as a pastor or as a husband or if there was a difference.

Irenaeus hugged me, and did what he could to console me as other church elders who began to flock around me and comfort me. There was much weeping and people praying together, and I felt strengthened by their concern. However, I realized that I needed to be with my children.

As I approached them, I could tell that John was already discerning what had taken place. Callisto asked, "Father, where is mother? Did you find her?"

I smiled and held her close to me. I embraced Timothy and then John, who was already trying to restrain his tears. I let out a long sigh as the tears began to flow down my cheeks. "I found your mother," as I ran my fingers through my daughter's hair. "I am very sad to tell you that she is dead. Our heavenly Father has taken her home to heaven." I felt terrible in the way I said this, but I was ignorant of performing such a difficult task in a more gracious way.

Callisto buried her face in her hands, and Timothy just stared downward. John hugged me and asked through a broken voice, "Are you alright, Father?"

I looked into his eyes as they filled with tears and answered, "Yes, yes; God is faithful, and he will see us through this."

I got the attention of all three of them and said, "I cannot describe to you the immense happiness I have in seeing you, and to behold your diligent ministry of encouragement you have been demonstrating to others today. Your strength, courage and kindness have given me great strength and courage and kindness."

The children and I, along with many from the church, gathered at the home of a friend to grieve and to bury Anna. Many shared personal experiences of Anna's kindness and godly life and I gave public glory to the perfect will of God. I stood in the middle of a great crowd, with my children sitting at my feet, and declared, through choked words, the virtues of God's working in the tragedies we encounter in life.

"We grieve because we do not fully understand the heavenly dwelling place of God. If we did, we could with fullness of heart rejoice that our loved ones have arrived safely at their eternal home. But our Heavenly Father has permitted, for the time being, that such understanding still remain as a mystery, and desires that we conduct ourselves by confidence in him and not in what our eyes tell us alone. Trials, adversity and times of sorrow will flood into our souls, but God permits them for a season for the sole purpose of revealing an authentic faith in Him. Just as gold is purified in the furnace, so the afflictions of life purify us. I believe that God permits times of agony to squeeze out of us his godly virtue whereby we see a welling up of spiritual desire, namely love for God, joy, peace and a greater dependency on him. But I am also convinced that the trials of life leave us with a deeper understanding that this life is temporary, and therefore should not be the focus of our desires."

As I looked around the room at the mourners, many of whom had lost loved ones in this catastrophe—though fighting to keep my grief under control—I knew our gracious God would see us through this calamity, and reveal more of his power and might through it. We prayed and wept together, and then buried our dead, and comforted one another as God instructed us through his comfort of us. It is a truth of life that God's best work often takes place in what are our worst times.

◇

In every trial, just as God reveals his will and guides us by his grace, so our spiritual enemy, the devil makes an appearance seeking to thwart God's will, and hide it from our eyes. He seeks to plant seeds of bitterness where God is growing joy. He chokes out peace with doubt and anger, and digs up love for God and replaces it with self-pity. However, it is when we seem to be most vulnerable that we discover God guarding us even closer.

Over the next couple of weeks, my days were spent comforting my children and the scores of others who lost loved ones in the disaster. Rubble was being cleared, and homes and buildings were being rebuilt. I remember one day in particular as I was removing the rubble from my home that an old nemesis of mine, Erebus, was sitting across the lane observing me, with a young boy, presumably his son, standing by his side.

"Hello Erebus," I said as I removed my gloves and walked towards him. "I'm surprised to see you here in Smyrna. Last I heard, you were living in Rome."

"Indeed, you are well-informed," he replied with a hint of condescension. "I am here in Smyrna at the behest of Caesar, and figured while in town I would purchase some property."

"I trust you suffered no injury in the tremor?" I asked.

"No, as you can see I am quite well, and as you may already be aware, not every sector of the town was devastated. That makes me wonder, Polycarp; why did your God permit this to happen to you, one of his ministers? Why does your God permit his people to suffer?" He said.

"I can understand why someone like you might ask that question." I responded. "But I can assure you that it is not for the same reasons your so-called gods would unleash such havoc on their people. Already I have heard disdain for Zeus and Diana. I have heard exasperation as to why Caesar could not intervene. What do you tell them, seeing you are such a loyal servant to the gods?"

Erebus stood up and walked around the rubble, and seemed rather amused at my question. "Perhaps they are impatient at our tolerance of you Christians. Perhaps you are the scourge of our glorious empire, and they are expressing their displeasure," He suggested.

"Well, I would say they were a little off target seeing that they destroyed homes of Christians and their temples as well. The Temple of Diana near the agora lies in ruin. Perhaps she wants a new temple?" I quipped.

"I hear your wife died in that rubble over there," as he pointed to the ruins of my home.

I hesitated for a moment, not wishing to discuss such a hurtful issue with one who was not here to show sympathy. I let out a heavy sigh and replied, "Yes, my dear Anna died in the quake, and we buried her several days ago."

"It's a pity your God didn't see fit to grant her a longer life," he said. He then looked beyond me and asked, "Who is that young man standing over there," as he pointed to my home.

I turned and noticed that my oldest son was watching and listening in on our conversation. "That, Erebus, is my firstborn son, John," I replied.

He smiled and said, "John, of course, you would choose that name. That was the name of your mentor, was it not?"

"Yes," I answered. By this time, John had made his way over to my side.

"Young man," Erebus said to John, "Your father and I were childhood acquaintances. I even recall that he was once a slave to the old man, Crixus. Let me guess, you are one of those Christians too?"

"I am," John said confidently. I was rather proud that he didn't seem at all intimidated by Erebus.

"Well, I am not," Erebus replied sharply. "Quite honestly, I don't have time for the gods until it's convenient or profitable for me," he said softly. "I am as devoted to them as I find them devoted to me."

"Erebus," I said, "Let me give you some perspective. Life is harsh, and sin is cruel. But I am standing before you with full understanding that the One True God has never, nor ever will do me wrong. Even in the destruction of my property, and the grief of my wife's death, God is working out of it all a greater and more glorious plan that produces a deeper joy, a longer lasting peace, and a greater love for him and others. Such a thought doesn't diminish my sorrow, but it does bring a profound and remarkable comfort to my sorrow. It is for this reason that I can't lose heart. Though my flesh is wasting away, my spiritual man, my inner-self experiences a daily renewal. This comparably, light affliction is being used by God to prepare me for a heavier, weightier and more substantial glory, the like of which the splendor of this world could never compare.[113] So you see, Erebus, my God is not motivated out of maliciousness, as your gods have proven to be by historic proportions. The followers of Christ emerge from the afflictions of this life better than when we entered. The death of my wife is not the end, but is only the portal as it were, to a

---

113. II Corinthians 4:16-17

greater, eternal life. As I see it, her death is simply one less link in the chain that holds me to this world."

"Yes, of course, you say that. I would have been disappointed at anything less. Follow your God then, Polycarp. Be the fool," he replied. Erebus reached over and pulled the boy standing next to him over to his side. "This is my only son." He then looked down at the boy and said, "Take a good look at these two. They are the enemies to a pure Rome. You will never want to be like them, do you understand what I am saying?" To which the boy nodded his head. "Come lad, let's not defile you another moment with these rogues."

As they walked away, John said to me, "He doesn't seem like a very friendly person."

"No, I suppose not. Ever since I refused to follow him into his sinful excursions, he has despised me, and in some ways seemed to delight in being a thorn in my side. I do not hate him or strangely enough, even dislike him. I feel sorry for him, and would wish that he was more receptive to the Gospel," I replied.

"Father, may I ask you a question?" John asked.

I looked down into his face and put my arm around his shoulders, and said, "Of course, you may ask me anything," and then I squeezed him tight.

"How is this trial, you know, our ruined home and mother's death; how can good possibly come out of this?" He inquired.

I could hear the pain in his question and the stirring of doubt in his soul. I suppose it was the same thing I sensed deep within my soul in some ways. "That is an insightful question, and it is appropriate you should ask it. I am glad you did," I replied. "First, let me say that the answer is not an intellectual one, but is a spiritually discerned answer, and must be seen and understood out of spiritual perception. Do you comprehend what I am saying?"

He nodded in agreement, so I continued.

"We live to the glory of God, to be supremely impressed and satisfied in him and with him. It is crucial you grasp what I am saying for it will be the difference between a frustrated life filled with disabling temptations and a joyful and fulfilled life. I'm not saying one has less trials then the other, but rather a life that is content with God's working will be a stronger life. The one who is discontent, on the other hand, and fails to see the glory of God in life's events will be frail, weak and easy prey for the devil."

I looked at John, and while I sensed he was following me, I felt I needed to illustrate it. "John, we enjoy archery, don't we?" I asked.

"Yes, it is an activity we have enjoyed for a long time," He answered. "I still have the first bow you gave to me."

"I like to think of myself as an arrow positioned in the bow that is being firmly held by the hands of a mighty man. God is that mighty man, John. He crafts me into a straight arrow with a sharp tip and prepares to launch me towards the enemy, using me to wound, overpower, and kill the threat of that enemy. But here is where the illustration applies to us right now. Before an archer can launch his arrow, he must apply great pressure." With hand gestures and intensity in my voice, I continued. "How many times I have felt I was going backwards and was crumbling under the pressure, when all the time I was simply feeling the tension of the bow, and the backward motion as preparation for battle. And at the right moment, under the strain of the pressure, the arrow is shot into the air as it accelerates towards its target."

"My son, the arrow lives for the tension. The greater the pressure, the more power it possesses when launched at the target." He nodded his head as he contemplated the illustration.

"Let me be clear, for on the other hand, when we permit sin to have its way with us; when we refuse to wrestle, fight and run, the devil prowls around us like a roaring lion, and seeks to devour those made weak by sin and the ravaging effects of is consequences. The seed planted and cultivated by sin is bitterness, and while it may not appear as bitterness against God, our spiritual enemy's plan is to make sure that's where it ends up. Let me speak plainly, if we are not prepared and aimed by God to speak against our spiritual enemy, then that same enemy will be taking aim at you."

"So while we are sorrowing," John interjected, "we are being made better by God's grace?"

"That is my point," I responded, "Godless people experience the horror of separation when it comes to death, and they struggle with the bitterness of life. I have observed many times how the godless find it convenient to blame God when life is hard. They refuse to hate life or whatever it is they worship, but will shift the blame to the One True God as if he owed them a trial-free life."

15

FILLED WITH THE FRUIT
OF RIGHTEOUSNESS

*For the present, all difficult training seems painful
and not pleasant, but afterwards, it yields the peace-giving
fruit of righteousness to those who are being trained.*
(Hebrews 12:11)

FIVE years had elapsed since my Anna died. I think of her
every day, but God is faithful and fills the empty void that
could enslave me in grief. My son, John, was training under
me for the ministry and was a constant source of joy to my heart.
I had the pleasure of apprenticing my other son, Timothy, in the
craft of being a parchmenter. He caught on quickly and was far
more skilled than I had ever been. Decimus would have been very
proud of the lad. My precious daughter, Callisto, was growing
up too fast and insisted on taking care of the home. I loved her
dearly. With her smile, sweetness, and quick wit she was a constant encouraging reminder to me of her beloved mother. I see my
children and my happiness as a banner of God's faithfulness, and
I adored him all the more for it.

Many congregations grew out of the Smyrnaean Church,
and with meeting places all around the city. While I had trained
most of the pastors and teachers, I desired that each congregation
maintain their autonomy, and I served as a help and an encourager
in their work. The congregation was also active in sending out
servants of the Lord throughout the world as far north as the isle
of Britannia. As for my congregation, I had hoped that Irenaeus
would someday replace me as the overseer of this flock, but he
came to visit me recently and shared that the Lord had other plans
for him.

"Irenaeus, come in, for the demands on our time have limited
our fellowship," I said.

"I too have missed them. Times with you are like drawing fresh, cool water from a deep well," he replied.

"You mentioned in passing a week or two ago that our Lord was drawing your heart to a needy congregation. I had so very much hoped that you would replace me here in Smyrna," I said.

He paused for a moment, perhaps wanting to be careful not to hurt my feelings. "Polycarp, I can't think of a greater honor than to assume the pastoral responsibilities here. However, I would fail in replacing you. To be completely open with you, however, God has been turning my heart in an amazing way; in fact, I would never have conceived such a move."

"My heart has filled with longing for the Christians of Lugundum, in Gaul,"[114] he said. "I have friends there, and they have shared the plight of the believers, and I desire to aid them.

"Are you aware that the church has endured persecution from both the Roman authorities and the barbarians in the region?" I inquired.

"I have discussed this at length with my wife and family, and I desire to go to that vast frontier, and bring the Gospel. Will you support me in this?" He asked.

I was exuberant, and with joy replied; "My dearest friend, you know that I would never withhold you from sharing the Gospel and strengthening the church of our Lord anywhere on earth. You were born for a time such as this. I cannot be selfish for my faithful God has blessed me with twenty years of fellowship with you. Your friendship alone is more than I deserve. You do not need my blessing, but you have it in abundance all the same. I'll set to work on the plans for your commissioning when you have established a departure date."

As he walked out of my study chamber, the emotions were bitter and sweet to me. We train servants of the Lord to send out; not to hoard them for our personal delight, but to send them out into the fray. In many ways I feel like every time I have sent a young man into the work of the ministry, I am launching a great Roman ship of war. I first pray they float, and then I hope they fight, and that they prove deadly against the forces of evil. Irenaeus will do this and more I believe. Truly, I see him more as a fleet than a single ship! Most men would not be able to handle the stress he'll

114. Lyon, France

face in Lugundum, but he will, by the grace of God, and so will his wife for that matter. What a perfect helpmeet God has given to him; soldiers of the cross in every way.

The next day I was meeting with the elders of my congregation and many others from surrounding churches as we fellowshipped and discussed various church issues and our response to them. I began by exhorting them not to be over zealous in increasing their numbers for the sake of numbers.

"We must not be motivated to fill our ranks in order to draw attention to our vast numbers. I'm not implying that we should not be aggressive in sharing the gospel and discipling the saints, but not for building attendance. Some congregations are becoming so large that they have become too much for a man to oversee, and this concerns me. The Lord is to build His church; we labor in vain if that is not our focus. We are not to peddle the truth, but to live it. We plant the Gospel in the hearts of the lost by the followers of Christ being just that; a follower, a disciple of our Lord and Savior. Build the church, not the numbers. The measurement of success is in the growth of spiritual maturity, not the size of the crowd."

We also discussed rumors that were coming out of Philippi of the corruption of one of the overseers in the congregation. One must always be cautious with rumors, for the devil delights in intercepting such communication as it leaves the lips of the observers, and twists and corrupts it before it reaches the ears of the recipients. I needed the facts, for if the news was even partially true; I needed to take immediate action, and I began thinking of whom I could send to ascertain the facts.

To my surprise, that very day I had a visitor from Philippi. "Father," my son, John said as I looked up from my reading, "Crescens from Philippi has come to see you." Crescens was an elder in the Philippian Church, and a former disciple of mine.

He walked in, and I embraced and welcomed him. "My friend, it fulfills me to see you well, and your presence delights me, for I have been hearing troubling news and was to send someone to glean the facts, but you are here, and I will be able to discover firsthand of the happenings in that great congregation.

"My dear pastor," Crescens said, "I do not come with good news. I come with a grieved heart with urgency to return with direction and advice from you. The Church in Philippi is greatly pained."

"Pained!" I exclaimed, "Dear soul, what disturbs the precious saints?"

"May I sit down," he asked.

"Oh, yes. I apologize for my lack of hospitality," I said. "I was just taken in by the heaviness I sensed on your heart." He sat in a nearby chair and leaned up against my table. "Now, tell me please, what trial have you been called upon to endure?"

"It regards our overseer, Valens," he replied. "He has been pierced through with the consuming pain of the love of money. It has come to the attention of the entire congregation that he has been stealing from the church funds. His theft has become infamous throughout the entire area and has filled us with shock and shame. We are not a wealthy congregation and don't have a lot stored up, but enough to support the pastors, and provide aid to the widows and the poor. Over the past several months, we were always coming up short in our ability to meet our regular obligations. The original counts were in contradiction to the amounts distributed. Valens said that he would look into it, and that's where his theft was discovered. He was caught falsifying the records. Upon further investigation, we found he had been taking the funds and gambling on the Roman Games. What adds to this tragedy is that it would appear his gambling paid off. He has left the city with the money, and from what we have heard he has fled to his native Spain."

I began to pace the floor as I contemplated what our next move should be, as Crescens continued. "The congregation is deeply hurt, and our reputation around the town questioned. We need help, Polycarp. We need your advice."

"Who now serves as the pastor?" I asked.

"No one man provides oversight, but we take turns preaching and teaching. We need a leader, and for the present, the elders have chosen me, but are also asking for your blessing regarding me," he answered.

"First, my friend, you do not need my blessing or permission, however, the elders have my full support in their decision. You will make a wonderful pastor to the flock. As far as advice, I believe the church must move on, being aware that their actions, words, and attitudes are being weighed in an unbalanced scale. For this reason, the church must make a concerted effort to restore their godly reputation. I'm not speaking of a form of godliness that lacks power, but a return to the basics of godly, obedient living. If it pleases you, I will write a letter with specific instructions that you can take back with you, and use as a guide in repairing the people and reestablishing a godly reputation. If you need me to do more, I will be glad to supply it. In addition to this, please let John know what funds are needed to restore your financial ministry, and the Smyrnaean churches will be joyed to provide assistance, I'm sure. Is this direction what you had hoped?" I said.

"More than I would have hoped," he responded.

"Return to me tomorrow, and I'll have the letter ready for you, as well as paid passage back to Philippi," I instructed.

"John, please see that our brother is well-cared for during his short visit," I requested.

"Yes father, I'll see to everything," he replied.

A letter to the Christians in Philippi was not on my list of tasks for the day, but the urgency of the need meant that I must clear the day in order to inscribe the right thoughts, challenges and encouragements to help our hurting brethren in this troubling time. I sat down at my table, selected a few sheets of freshly made parchments that Timothy had provided for me, and peered out the window as I pondered my approach.

After a greeting, I began with the enduring and powerful heritage that had been passed down to them since the Apostle Paul established the congregation.[115]

Polycarp and the pastors, teachers and elders that minister with me, to the Church of God, which labors at Philippi. Mercy and peace to you all from our Almighty God and Savior Jesus Christ be multiplied to you.

My joy overflows in the Lord Jesus Christ because of you. You have always welcomed the bearers of true love as one would

---

115. *The contents of the letter are Polycarp's actual thoughts to the Philippian church*

expect from you, and those who were escorted in chains, as has been the condition of many saints. The very ones who saw their affliction as a crown reserved for those who were chosen to suffer by God and our Lord. Also, because of your firmly rooted faith that has been acclaimed throughout the years, and to this day still perseveres. It is bearing fruit to the glory of our Lord Jesus Christ. He endured to face death for our sins, the one whom God raised up, having loosened the travailing pain of death's power. Though you have not seen him, you have unwavering faith in him with an indescribable and glory-filled joy. Which, I must add, many others desire to experience, and we know that it is by grace we are saved, and not out of our works, but by the will of God through Jesus Christ.

For this reason, prepare your minds for action. Do not allow yourself to become disoriented, rather serve God out of true reverence and truth, forsaking vain and empty talk, and the error of others. Instead, believe on him who raised our Lord Jesus Christ from the dead and gave him glory, as well as a throne at his right hand. He is the one in whom all things in heaven and on earth were made subject, to whom every living creature serves. He comes as the Judge of those living and dead; whose blood God will require of all those that are disobedient to him.

The One who raised him from the dead will also raise us, if we do his will and walk according to his commandments, and love what he loves; abstaining from all unrighteousness, covetousness, love of money, lying and being a false witness. That also implies that we are not to repay evil for evil, or to insult when insulted, or strike a blow when struck, or curse when cursed. Instead, you must remember what the Lord said, "Do not judge from your self-righteousness, or the same will be rendered against you."[116] Forgive, and you receive forgiveness; show mercy and mercy will be shown to you equivalent to the portion you yield. And also, "Glorious joy describes the poor in spirit, as well as those who are under persecution because of righteousness, for to these belong the kingdom of God."[117]

---

116. Matthew 7:1

117. Matthew 5:3, 10

I felt a sense of urgency to warn them that while I was being led by the Spirit in the writing of this letter, it was about the Scriptures and not to be confused as Scripture. My hope was that these thoughts would direct them back to the sanctifying Word of God.

I am writing regarding righteousness, brethren, not out of my initiative, but because you requested my assistance. No one, not even I am able to bestow upon you the wisdom of our blessed and glorious Paul, who, when he came among you, taught the men of that day regarding the word of truth. After his absence, he wrote a letter to you, and by diligent study of the inspired writings, the faith given to you will be built up, which like a devoted mother guides all of us. Hope will follow, while love for God and Christ, and for our neighbors leads the way. If this work is your occupation, the righteousness of which I am writing will be fulfilled. One who has God's love is far away from sin.

But the love of money is the beginning of all troubles. We know, therefore that we brought nothing into the world; neither can we take anything out. With this mind, let us arm ourselves with the armor of righteousness, and let us be taught first to walk in the commandment of the Lord; our wives also, to walk in the faith out of love and purity. They must cherish their husbands in all truth, and loving others equally with chastity, and to train their children in the teaching of the fear of God. Our widows must be clear-minded as touching faith in the Lord, and should be making intercessory prayers without ceasing for all men, and to abstain from all slanderous gossip, speaking evil of others, giving false reports, loving money and every evil thing. They must remember that they are God's altar and that he carefully inspects each sacrifice. Nothing escapes his vision, not even their thoughts, intentions or any secret in their hearts.

Upon further thought, I desired to exhort the church leaders as they strived to live as examples to the flock and not lords over it. If we do not follow the guidance provided in the Scriptures when called upon by its author to endure trials, our decisions will be led by carnal traits and not character formed by the power of grace in our lives. Grace forms character much like a rushing stream carves and shapes the stones.

*Knowing then that God will not be mocked, we must live in
a manner that is worthy of the commands of his will and his
glory. For this reason, the deacons should be blameless in the
presence of his righteousness. They are servants of God and
Christ and not of men; they are not to be liars, or hypocrites,
nor lovers of money; rather they should be patient in all things,
men of compassion, diligent in their service, conducting their
lives according to the truth of the Lord who served as a deacon
of all his people. If our lives please him in this present world,
then we will receive the world to come also, and this comes from
the promise that he will raise us from the dead. If we conduct
ourselves in a manner worthy of him, we will reign with him,
but all this is the work and result of faith.*

*In addition to this, I desire to address the younger men also
to be blameless in all things, expressing concern for purity in
thoughts and actions, and avoiding every evil. It is a good thing
to flee from the lusts of the world. Every lust wages war against
the Spirit, so that fornicators, male prostitutes and homosexuals
(those who act on their immoral passions) will not be able to
inherit the kingdom of God. This goes for all who surrender
to any form of perversity. You are doing well if you abstain
from such behavior and follow the godly lead of your pastors,
elders and deacons as you would God and Christ. It is vital for
all virgins to walk in a blameless manner out of a pure and
undefiled conscience.*

*Pastors and elders, you must be compassionate and merciful
towards all men, find the straying sheep and return them to the
fold. Visit the infirm, and do not neglect the widows, orphans
or those who are truly poor. Meet the needs of others in a way
that is honorable in the sight of God and of those who may be
watching. Stay clear of anger, favoritism, hasty or thoughtless
judgment, knowing that we are all debtors to the Lord when
it comes to sin. Remember that if we seek God's forgiveness, we
must also forgive; for since we cannot hide before the eyes of our
Lord and God, we realize that we all must eventually stand at
the Judgment Seat of Christ, where every man will be required
to give an account of his life. With this in mind, serve God with
fear and with all reverence, as he himself commanded; as the
Apostles preached in the Gospel, and as the prophets proclaimed*

long ago before our Lord's birth. We are to be zealous regarding what is good, and naturally avoiding offences and the scourge of hypocrisy. It is the neglect of this that leads foolish people astray.

I felt that I needed to take a break and perhaps take a walk in the garden. I needed to seek the Lord on where to go from here. What else needed to be said regarding the trials they were facing and what had created such challenges. My walk was cut short due to the cool breeze that made the weather unseasonably cooler than normal, but it was refreshing enough to gather my next thoughts. It is during trials that we are prone to get lost, and I felt the need to give clear warning regarding this fact.

Anyone who appears religious, but is unwilling to admit the truth that Jesus Christ came in the flesh, is an antichrist. Anyone who will not admit the true accomplishments of the cross of Christ is of the devil. Anyone who perverts the teachings of our Lord to fit his lusts, even to go as far as to say that there was no resurrection nor future judgment, that man is the first-born of Satan. Forsake these vain people and their false teachings, and turn your focus to the Word. Don't allow yourselves to be disoriented by the world; instead, pray and fast, and seek the all-seeing God with supplications that he would deliver you from such temptations. Remember what the Lord said, The spirit is willing, but the flesh is weak.[118]

Let us therefore, without ever giving up, steadfastly set our hope and our deep desires of righteousness upon Jesus Christ who took our sins upon himself on the tree. As you know, he never sinned, nor did any deceitful words come out of his mouth, but for our sakes, he endured all suffering in order that we should live in him. If you understand this, be imitators of his endurance, and if you should find yourself suffering for his name's sake, then glorify him. Never forget that he set this example to us all, and this is what we believe.

This principle is undoubtedly one of the more difficult concepts for Christians to grasp. It's easy to read of endurance in the face of trials, but when we encounter them, we often fall into

---

118. *Matthew 26:41*

the fleshly traps of despair and complaining. I believed the Lord would have me press the issue a little more.

> *I urge you all to be obedient to the word of righteousness, and learn and practice the fruit of endurance. Remember the examples you have observed with your own eyes from the blessed life of Ignatius, Zosimus and Rufus, as well as many others from among your congregation; not to mention Paul and the rest of the Apostles. They were all convinced that they did not run in vain, but rather ran the race by faith and in righteousness, and now they are experiencing their eternal reward in the presence of our Lord, who suffered with them. The difference is that they did not love this present world, but loved him who died for our sake and was raised by God for us.*

> *Stand fast, therefore, in these things and follow the example of the Lord, being firmly established in faith and immovable in love. Regarding your brethren, cherish one another as partners with the truth. Forbear one another with the gentleness of the Lord, and despise no man. When you can do good, don't neglect the opportunity. Your pity for others could be used to deliver them from eternal death. Submit to one another, and have a lifestyle that is unblameable among the worldly, so that your good works would serve as praise to the Lord, and he not be blasphemed because of you. Woe to the one whose actions cause others to blaspheme the Lord's name. For this reason, teach all men not to lose focus by the world in which we must all live.*

My thoughts shifted from the people to the cause of their deep trial. Their pastor, Valens, had brought reproach to the name of Christ, and his actions blasphemed that sacred name. It would appear that his love of money also opened up sensual pursuits as well; such is the scandalous nature of sin. Oh, how my heart grieves not only for him, but for the depression he has brought into the hearts of believers, and the scorn that he has birthed in the lives of the lost. He has failed to realize that sin births more sin. When we permit a sin to run unchecked in our lives, it creeps about like an escaped convict within a prison, where it finds the key to other cells holding worse sins, and opens the doors permitting sin to run amok in our lives. In the end, those sins quickly bring us into ruinous transgressions we never imagined we could commit.

I was exceedingly grieved for Valens, who served as a pastor among you. He is so ignorant of the trust demanded by his office as an overseer. Let his life be a warning to you all to refrain from covetousness, and to live a life governed by truth and purity. Stay clear of evil! How can a pastor who is unable to control himself, possibly be effective in teaching self-control to others? If one does not refrain from the lusts of covetousness, he becomes an idolater, and will be judged as the godless that have no concept of the judgment of the Lord. Do we not know that the saints will judge the world, as Paul has taught?

However, when I hear of you all, I don't find such pursuits, neither have I heard any report to that effect among those whom the blessed Paul labored, and to whom he wrote years ago. Indeed, he boasted about you throughout the churches that knew God. All this grieves me all the more for Valens and his wife. I pray that God may grant them the ability to repent. But as for you all, don't be distracted by these events, nor declare them to be your enemies, but as much as you can seek to restore any frail or erring members so that your whole body (the church) is helped. In doing this, you build up one another.

These thoughts seemed complete to me. Now I desired to reassure the church family in Christ of the sanctifying work of the Spirit in their lives and the whole congregation. I desired that they would be challenged, and yet refreshed at the same time.

I am thoroughly convinced that you all are well-trained in the Scriptures and that nothing is hidden from you. Follow what the Scriptures say; "Be angry and don't sin in that anger. Don't let the sun set on your wrath."[119] Glorious joy awaits those who remember this, and I trust that this truth is in you.

Now may the God and Father of our Lord Jesus Christ, who is our eternal High-priest, the Son of God, build you up in faith and truth, and in all gentleness, and in all avoidance of wrath, in forbearance, long-suffering, in patient endurance, and in purity. I pray that he grants unto you a share and portion among His saints and to us with you, and to all that are under heaven, who shall believe on our Lord and God, Jesus Christ,

---

119. Ephesians 4:26

*and on His Father that raised him from the dead. Pray for all
the saints. Also pray for kings, powers and princes, and even
for them that persecute and hate you, as well as the enemies of
the cross, that your fruit may be obvious to all men finding you
perfect in Him.*

*The letters of Ignatius and others I am also sending to you,
which I believe you will find helpful. These additional letters
comprise faith, endurance and every kind of edification, which
pertains to our Lord. As you know, I write these things to you
by Crescens, whom I sent to you a few years ago, and now
commend unto you again for leadership. I know him to be a
man who has walked blamelessly with us, and I believe also
with you in like manner. Farewell in the Lord Jesus Christ and
his grace, you and all yours. Amen.*[120]

I was relieved to have written instructions to the saints in
Philippi, but I could not deny how deeply my heart ached for
them. To have your trust betrayed by the one you believe is guiding
you into the truth creates quite an opportunity for the devil to
intrude, and like a wolf among the sheep, to scatter the flock, and
devour the weak and sickly that have lost their way.

———————◇◇———————

The next morning, Crescens was punctual, as was his way.
"You are faithful as always," I remarked. "I trust you are well
rested."

"I am well, and feel a sense of urgency to depart immediately
for Philippi," he stressed.

"I am sure of it, and I do not wish to detain you a moment
longer," I replied. I handed him a leather-bound folder and in it
several letters including my instructions. "My friend, I am recommending
the church make you the overseer of the congregation.
My letter provides clear direction for you and all who read it.
They are not simple instructions and will take effort on the part
of the people and attentiveness from you to cultivate the growth.
God will enable you to do the work of a vine-dresser, I am sure.
I send you back to your flock as one entrusted with the ministry
of spiritual healing. Warn, comfort, and support those who need

---

120. *Actual letter from Polycarp to the Philippians*

it, and I trust the gracious, loving-kindness of our Lord to direct and protect you."

We embraced and prayed, and then like a soldier with special orders; he was off to war. He did not depart as one frightened of his mission, but as a fearless soldier fully aware that he had already won. The grace God gave him wore off on me, and I was invigorated and overflowing with joy.

16

BLESSED ARE THOSE WHO ARE PERSECUTED FOR THE SAKE OF RIGHTEOUSNESS

Gloriously joyful are those who suffer
for the sake of righteousness,
for the kingdom of heaven belongs to them.
(Matthew 5:10)

QUITE a stir was being made over the Prince's new published work, The Meditations. Marcus Aurelius, the adopted son of Emperor Antonius Pius, was recently appointed as Consul of Rome, and also declared to be the Pontifex Maximus,[121] which made him the head of the Roman state religion, and he wished to make a name for himself.

He assumed the role of a philosopher, a stoic; I believe. However, I observed such a mixture of ideologies in his writings that it made me wonder if he actually believed in anything other than himself. In some ways, it would appear that he desired to create a new Roman religion built on philosophy in an attempt to emulate the Greeks.

At eighty-six years of age, I felt as if I had lived beyond a normal life span. While my body moved slower, my mind was alert and active, and I realized that my time on this earth was short, which meant I had much to do to encourage and prepare the church for my eternal departure. I lived with Callisto and her

---

121. *The High Priest in the college of the Pontiffs in ancient Rome who was responsible for administration of state religious laws*

husband. Timothy lived nearby, and John was working in a congregation in nearby Pergamos.

While I had experienced persecution in various forms, I survived to be one of the oldest pastors in the entire church, and knew that the work of the ministry was being passed on to more capable, younger pastors. I had one more student to train, and that was Germanicus.

He was an orphan, who had been adopted and raised by another family until abandoned. He ended up in Smyrna and eventually with me, where he lived with Irenaeus and his family. He was more than a student, for he served as my legs running errands for me, and eyes since mine were growing dim—and often my hands as well, as he served as my scribe. He was a tender young man, with a zeal for the Lord that was rare among his peers.

As I observed him working at a nearby table in my study chamber, I saw that he appeared disturbed over something. Such a conclusion is unnatural, for he was almost always joyful. Today, though, he struck me as distracted, even discouraged.

"Germanicus," I said, "What is troubling you? Have I placed too much on your young shoulders?"

"No, you haven't," he replied. "It's something else. I apologize if I have worried you."

"If you don't feel free to share with me, I understand. But if it's something that I can help you with, then fulfill my joy and let me be of some encouragement to you," I replied.

"It's nothing serious; it's just that I've been rather frustrated with my studies lately," he said.

"I'm satisfied with what I am seeing come out of your studies. What seems to be the hardship," I asked.

"You may find this frivolous, but I can't find a suitable place to study. My normal study chamber at home feels confined and seems to stifle the illumination I seek, and other places seem too noisy, trampling my thoughts with interruptions," he said.

I mused at his dilemma and replied, "Perhaps your focus is off, and it's not the location at all. I understand the drive to glean useful insights, but there is a step in this study process you are missing. Germanicus, you are the study chamber of the Holy Spirit, and he desires for you to serve as his scribe as he reveals the glory of God to you. His voice, though it appears inaudible in your heart can be heard over any clamor no matter how loud or distracting. We're distracted when we aren't listening to him and are trying to track our thoughts. What is he telling you regarding God's work in you? What Scriptures does he shed light on when you are reading? Whether you are eighteen or eighty-six, the joy of studious insight is developed from the inside out, and not what we try to cram into our heads. Never forget Paul's exhortation to the Philippians; 'It is God who is at work in you, fulfilling what he determined to do, and what brings Him delight to do.'[122] Our happiness and fulfillment in life and ministry is discovering what God is doing in us, and upon that discovery, delighting in him as he is delighting in us. I know of no greater joy in this life than that fact."

I could tell that I had stirred his thoughts, and that he would ponder it until he discovered its value. "While you are thinking about what I said, would you please go and fetch Irenaeus? I need to speak with him on an important matter."

◇◇

Being alone in my study chamber, I walked over toward the window to think. It was the winter of February in the year 144, and I was troubled by recent events. The Churches were prospering all over the world in places I had never heard of. There were pockets of confrontation, but most of it was due to Christians being confused with dissenters or other localized rebellions.

Once again, Rome was drunk on her glory. If history were any indication of future events, the Church would once again find itself in a precarious conflict with the demands of Rome. Though the conflict wasn't necessarily aimed at Christianity, the pagan laws dedicated to their man-made gods would make us natural enemies of the government. I hoped that my discernment was misguided, but I have lived too long not to take notice of the times.

As I gazed out of my window, I heard the voice of a familiar friend and a member of my congregation, Drusus Servius, a brother and local politician who always seemed light-hearted and jovial; a true encourager.

"Excuse me, Polycarp," he said, "I hope I'm not disturbing you, for it appears you have hold of a deep thought."

---

122. Phillipians 2:13

I laughed as I turned, and greeted him; "No Drusus, a stream-like thought that has quickly moved on. I'm very happy to see that you have returned to us safely. I prayed for your protection."

Before he could reply, Irenaeus walked into the chamber. "Irenaeus, come in, I was hoping that you would drop by today," I replied. "I trust the details of your departure are in place."

"Yes, we have sold most of our belongings and have been making final preparations to depart next week," he said as he greeted Drusus and took a seat next to him.

"Have you heard the news of Pothinus?" Drusus asked Irenaeus.

"I received a letter from him a few months ago. He said everything was in place for me to come and assume the pastoral responsibilities in his stead. Have you heard more?" Irenaeus asked.

With a hint of panic in his eyes, Drusus glanced at me and then looked at Irenaeus. "Pothinus is dead!" He informed us.

"Dead," Irenaeus replied in disbelief. "I was aware that he was in poor health, but he never let on that his condition was serious."

"He did not die of natural causes," Drusus said. "He and forty-seven others were killed for their faith in the town's arena. As you know, Lugundum is famous for the worship of Rome's emperors, and they have a great temple dedicated just to them. From what I gathered during my recent trip to Rome, they were murdered for not participating in the deification of our late Emperor, Hadrian, as ordered by Caesar."

Both Irenaeus and I sat silently, stunned by the news. Drusus had just returned from Rome as part of the Smyrnaean contingency sent to confer with Caesar regarding local issues. "How did Rome react to the news," I inquired.

"Oh, I am sure you can imagine. They made a great deal of it going as far as to declare them as sacrifices to the new god, but I found many who secretly felt such bloodshed was pointless."

"And what of our Emperor; what was his reaction?" I inquired.

"What else would you expect? He was flattered over the devotion of the man that carried out his edict."

"Surely the people of Rome see that the emperors are just men?" Irenaeus declared.

"True, they all know. It doesn't take long for even a dullard to grasp the vanity in it all, but if people want Imperial favor, they will say and do just about anything to obtain it," Drusus said.

"Do you believe that this persecution will head eastward?" I asked.

"I believe so," Drusus cautiously responded. "History reveals that the zeal of the Roman religion tends to intensify at the death of the Emperor or the ascension of a new one. You can probably testify to this more than most, Polycarp, for you have lived through seven or is it eight Caesars?"

"No, eleven if you are counting," I mused, "and what you say is true."

Drusus nodded in agreement and pressed us to listen to what else he had learned in Rome. "I must tell you that I also met our new Proconsul, Quadrates is his name, and he seems quite zealous to make a name for himself. He is a close friend of Marcus Aurelius and seems all too eager to impress his exalted friend. He too considers himself to be a philosopher. He invited our little contingency to a banquet at his palatial home, and the Emperor was present as his guest of honor, as well as both the princes. Listening to the Proconsul's conversation, I believe he intends to 'educate,' I believe the word he used, the wayward Christians, and enlighten us to the wisdom of submitting to Roman laws regarding the worship of Roman gods. He went as far as to threaten the use of force if compelled, and Caesar didn't appear bothered by his words. It could have been the wine talking, or maybe he simply wished to impress Caesar, but regardless, he's out to make a name for himself."

"You saw this coming," Irenaeus said, looking over at me.

"I may have had the misfortune of seeing this coming, but how to prepare for its arrival is a different matter," I said. "Nevertheless, God has been preparing the church for the evil day; however, this is not the time to seek the counsel of our fears. No, my friends, more than ever we must walk by faith, by spiritual guidance and not by our limited physical perception. Our eyes cannot see the invisible works of God until they have transpired."

"Drusus," I inquired, "Do you realize the awkwardness of your position? Irenaeus and I are shepherds of God's flock, and everyone expects that we must stand for our faith, but you are a magistrate. You'll be expected to set an example for the community. Are you prepared to stand alone? I fear that you'll be the first to feel the blunt pressure of these new laws if they come to pass."

Drusus laughed nervously and said, "A little blunt pressure will do me good; I must confess. In my profession, compromise is the aphorism of Roman politics, and standing for principle is, shall I say, incongruous. Who knows, maybe it will shock them enough to reconsider their plans." His jitteriness gave away the fact that he was quite frightened by the prospects of suffering for his faith.

But I comforted myself with the thought that fear is good soil out of which great courage can be grown. Something we all would learn soon enough. "My hope for you, Drusus, and for all the faithful followers of Christ, is that in the hour of temptation we all will stand for Christ as an example to the community. Let us be about the business of praying for one another, for like our Lord's disciples, our spirit is willing, but our flesh is weak."[123]

After praying together and edifying one another, Drusus left, but Irenaeus lingered a moment to say; "My head was spinning with the threat rising up against the church, not only where I live, but to the town where I am going. It's one thing to face this trial as a man, but what about my wife and children. Polycarp, can I bear the load of seeing them suffer for the cause of Christ? I know the truth of Scripture that when we are persecuted for the sake of righteousness, we are blessed, but now I feel as if I am trying to balance myself while standing on the edge of Rome's gladius."

"My dear friend, I understand your fear, and could easily find myself paralyzed by it if it weren't for the truth in John's first epistle. 'In love no fear can be found but love being worked into our hearts drives human fear out.'[124] Fear cannot dwell in the heart that is abounding in the love of God. Discover his love, and fear will flee, leaving you with a loyal courage that only his love can produce."

"That is true, I know it. How easy it is to submit to the flesh," he responded.

"Irenaeus, before you go out, I have one small request for you. Would you take that crate over on the table there, and bind up my parchments?" I asked.

"Your parchments?" he replied.

"Yes, they are the chronicles of my life and thoughts. I hoped that perhaps they could be of some help and encouragement to

---

123. Matthew 26:41

124. I John 4:18

the church after I am gone. In fact, if you are willing, could you continue to serve as my scribe and record the events of the day and your observations? The pain in my hands is making it very difficult to form my fingers properly to the quill; would you help me with this?" I requested.

"You know that you don't even have to ask. I see myself as your servant and would be honored to aid you in any way. However, you do remember that I will be departing for Lugundum soon?" He said.

"Yes, yes, I remember. How could I forget? It is a joyful thought seasoned with sorrow. But if you can bind them, then I'll have you pass them on to Germanicus," I said.

"I'll see the details," he replied.

Irenaeus walked over to the crate, took out some of the parchments from the top and looked through them, and then looked up at me and smiled warmly. I walked over to him and handed him my quill, whereupon he took the top parchment out and began to write below my last notes.

"What are you writing?" I asked.

He then spoke as he wrote with bold strokes, and underlined each word, "**These are the thoughts, acts, sermons and life of Polycarp; Pastor of the Church of Smyrna. From this point on, the words you read will tell of his life-example as observed by his son in the faith, Irenaeus**".[125]

Polycarp, smiling with satisfaction, patted me on the shoulder and said he was going to lie down for a while, and he left the room. It seemed strange to me to be writing in the journal of this godly man. The crate was full of parchments that needed organization, yet I can't help but think of the volumes that people could write who have watched him and been blessed by his life.

⎯⎯⎯⎯⎯◇◇⎯⎯⎯⎯⎯

I hoisted the crate up on my shoulder and began my walk home. I made my way through the market, greeting friends and bidding farewell to all the people I knew and the places I had grown accustomed. But as I fellowshipped with my friends, I realized that very soon life could become complicated and danger-

---

125. *Here ends Polycarp's account in his own hand, as his friend and protégé Irenaeus continues the story.*

ous for them. Behind every word I spoke was a prayer for God's abounding grace for us all.

As I continued towards my home, I heard a familiar young voice calling out my name from behind me. It was Amatus. "Irenaeus, Irenaeus," he shouted over the ruckus of the crowd. I waited for him to catch up with me. "Have you heard? The new Proconsul is arriving any moment here in town," he informed.

"He is arriving earlier than predicted," I thought to myself. "I thought he was to arrive in Ephesus first," I replied.

"No, for some reason he had chosen to come here first. He'll be making a public address in the forum by the upper agora. Everyone is making their way to hear him," he said. And with that, he quickly ran off to find a spot that would afford him an advantageous place to see and hear the address.

Smyrna was a Roman port city, and therefore a major thoroughfare for travelers to the east. It wasn't as popular as Ephesus to the south, but for those desiring a less crowded city; ours was the favorable alternative. While not as wealthy as other Roman cities, we were famous for our ferocious loyalty. The city was profoundly patriotic to Rome, to its commerce, and to its citizens. In fact, emperor worship was practiced in Smyrna even before it became a law. The same ingrained loyalty, moreover, was transferred over to the Christians and their devotedness to Christ.

After a brief stop at my home to drop off the crate, I made my way back towards the upper agora near the fortress on Mount Pagus. As I approached the crowded forum, I saw Polycarp and ran to catch up with him. "Polycarp, what are you doing here?" I asked.

"I received news that all leaders from the community, business, city officials and religious representatives must be present. I sent Germanicus to find you, but it would appear that we will now have to find him," he replied.

As we walked together, Polycarp was greeting and being greeted by those in the crowd. He was loved by the brotherhood and respected throughout the entire community. I could see Quadratus, the new Proconsul, standing to be noticed on the stage talking with other Roman officials. Although appointed by the Imperial Senate, everyone knew that he was one of the favorites of the Emperor and was considered a rising star within political circles. As Proconsul, he was determined to impress Caesar, and hopefully earn himself a future place in the real seat of power, the Roman Senate.

When we finally arrived near the entrance of the forum, I saw Amatus waving his arms at us and pointed to the places he had saved for us. As we took a seat next to him, he asked my opinion on the political situation.

"It appears to me that the Prince, Marcus Aurelius is setting the new social norms. His study in Stoic philosophy has revived people's interest in it, and is influencing their views on what I would describe as opposing points of view. The Prince seems indifferent towards other religious beliefs, but it is common knowledge that he is suspicious of Christianity and our inflexibility towards participating in the worship of other gods; he finds our ways disrespectful to the beliefs of others. The friction is intensified by the fact that we worship another King named Jesus Christ. Any pagan king, Rome or otherwise would view such devotion as a potential threat to their reign. From what I can gather from the Christians in Rome, his suspicions are inflamed all the more by his previous teachers and counselors, many of whom are hostile to Christianity and who take great pains to keep the Emperor's Court on edge regarding them. The Prince's tutor and the Emperor's closest adviser is Rasticus, who was also recently appointed as the Imperial Prosecutor. He has been responsible for the prosecution of many cases against the Christians back in Rome." I stopped speaking for a moment to observe the Proconsul as he studied the crowd of citizens before him.

"Rasticus," Polycarp stated. "I have an old friend in Rome who has been a strong apologist in his debates with the prosecutor."

"Are you talking about Justin Martyr?" I asked.

"Yes. He is one of our champions in Rome," Polycarp replied.

"I have heard from credible witnesses that in order to display his great, philosophical wisdom, you could find the Prince often engaged in debate and deep discussions with other famous philosophers in the Great Forum outside the Senate Hall. He has also written extensively, both poetry and philosophical works. In fact, it was just a few months ago that he published what is considered to be his greatest work so far, *The Meditations*. It is a twelve volume work written to himself, if you could imagine that, and he claims it is for the purpose of personal guidance and self-improvement," I explained.

"Have you read his works?" Amatus asked.

"Yes, and as I read it, I was especially troubled by the heart of what he was saying like: 'Everything harmonizes with me, which is harmonious to thee, O Universe. Nothing for me is too early nor too late, which is in due time for thee. Everything is fruit to me which thy seasons bring; O Nature: from thee are all things, in thee are all things, to thee all things return.' You must understand that Stoicism teaches the development of self-control and fortitude as a means of overcoming destructive emotions."

"There is more to it than that," Polycarp added. "You will find that his book is mandatory reading for any seeking societal respect. In his writings, all will read about his goals and how he wishes to improve the lifestyle of all Roman citizens, and to extend the borders of the great Roman Empire into Germania in the North when he is Caesar. His plans are to conquer the barbaric tribes on the outskirts of the Empire, and from within the Empire he plans to remove those who are not dedicated to building a united, utopian society which he feels is part of his responsibility to educate and produce."

As we awaited the grand introduction of the Proconsul, Germanicus finally found us. He was a vibrant eighteen-year-old, and showed great promise. He was a handsome youth, olive complexion, dark hair and eyes, and had a friendly disposition that made him welcome in any group of people. His love for the Lord and others and his desire to know and live the Word of God was a delight. His reputation in the church and the community was stellar: honest, humble, loving and always trying to serve those around him. His life had not been an easy one either. His father was a Roman government official sent to manage operations in a remote outpost near Germania. Tragically, both of his parents were killed in a raid by barbaric tribesmen from the north. Somehow the infant was left unnoticed and unharmed in the rubble. As the Roman soldiers arrived later that day, a Roman tradesman, who had lost everything in the raid but his life, found the infant in the ruins, and took pity upon him and claimed him as his own. Since he didn't know his name or his family name, he simply gave the child the name, Germanicus, which means "out of Germania."

Pondering what could transpire, Germanicus, with a touch of alarm, asked me; "I have heard that Christians are being killed for their faith in Jesus Christ in the city of Rome. Do you suppose the Proconsul will bring it here?"

"It's hard to say," I replied. "Previous proconsuls have passed through our town, but none that I can recall have ever stopped to speak or enact new policies. It would seem, however that a wave of persecution may be heading our way. The climate in Rome itself is growing rather intolerant of Christianity."

"It has been over fifty years since this area received a violent proconsul, and that was primarily in Ephesus. John died that day, as well as Timothy and hundreds more," Polycarp added.

We all stopped talking, and sat there looking over the crowd, still deep in thought as to what to expect. It seemed apparent that persecution had finally made its way to our little town. The voice of Drusus broke the silence. He is a wonderful brother: humorous, the life of any gathering, and one whose wide girth proved that he obviously enjoyed food too much. What we find most entertaining is watching him laugh hysterically at his own jokes.

"Well, I see you fellows have picked an advantageous perch," he said, trying to be jovial, but being burdened in heart as well.

"Drusus, your countenance appears perplexed; is everything alright," I inquired.

"No, I'm tied up in knots with worry, and I will tell you right now that you will not be pleased with this address," he replied with his eyes opened wider than normal. "I have been informed that as part of his effort to impress the Emperor, Proconsul Quadratus is passionate about giving special honor to the Emperor. To commemorate his victories in the East and to encourage him in future conquests, the Proconsul is to declare a week of worship to the Emperor as a deity. As Seneca has said, 'Religion is regarded by the common people as true, by the wise as false, and by the rulers as useful.'"

Polycarp interrupted him and said; "Well, this, of course, will be nothing new to the average citizen. Emperor-worship has been quite common throughout the empire for centuries."

"True," Drusus replied, "but as we know, people today are very superstitious and worship many gods in order to entreat their favor for productive crops, military triumphs, fair weather, good fortune, or anything else that is important to them. In fact, before I became a Christian I would even pray to my ancestors for help and assistance in times of need though I can't recall a time any of them ever came through for me," as he let out a big laugh and slapped Germanicus on his back. "I don't know why that even surprises me, for we never got along when they were alive. I think

I could be justified in blaming my hardships on them more than their help," he joked.

"This is certainly going to be a challenge for new Christians," Germanicus added. "Several of my friends are young believers and bring many of their superstitions with them."

"Superstition is a vice which births all kinds of strange beliefs," Polycarp said. "Faith in God alone is the only power that can break it."

The commotion of the crowd settled when a Centurion cried out; "Citizens of Smyrna give heed. By the order of the Imperial Senate, and the will of our beloved Caesar, welcome your new Proconsul, Lucius Statius Quadratus," as a roar from the crowd went up to welcome him.

Making his way up the forum steps in order to properly address the people, he knew he must act quickly to endear the hearts of all, not to mention his need to establish his authority in the process. As he faced the audience and reveled in their adulations, he raised his arms to signal that he was ready to speak. A hush grew over the crowd as he spoke with an eloquent confidence driven by a commanding voice, saying;

"My people, I come to you in the name and authority of Caesar, the divine Antonius Pius, and with the blessings of our illustrious Imperial Princes, Lucius Versus, and my close friend, Marcus Aurelius. They love you and desire your happiness and prosperity. They are wise and powerful and have subdued rebellions in far off lands. Their writings, public lectures, and poetry are inspired by the gods. Truly, they are blessed among the gods, and we are blessed to worship them."

Again, the crowds cheered, though you could see pockets in the throng not cheering, including our section, and I should note, this did not go unnoticed from the podium.

The Proconsul continued: "Our noble prince, Marcus Aurelius himself, shared with me these words before I embarked on my journey to Asia. 'Observe constantly that all things take place by change, and accustom yourself to consider that the nature of the Universe loves nothing so much as to change the things which are, and to make new things like them.' I am here to bring about the changes in Smyrna that reflect the great kindness and wisdom of our Emperor. For this reason, I hereby command Smyrna and all the cities throughout the Province of Asia that beginning today, and for the next seven days, every citizen, every slave, and every visitor within our borders be given the privilege and duty to offer worship and sacrifices of incense at the shrines to Caesar. To fail in this sublime celebration is punishable even if it means a cruel death."

He milked the momentary silence of the crowd, and then with his stretched out arms and an air of euphoria, declared; "Who doesn't wish our Emperor well, and to nobly seek his sublime blessing for the prosperity of our town and neighbors. Only the perfidious would desire otherwise. Most noble citizens of Smyrna, glistening gems in Rome's crown, your patriotism is in the love and loyalty you express to your Sovereign. Hail Caesar! Hail Marcus Aurelius! Hail Lucius Versus!" Shouts hailing our Emperor and the princes erupted from the crowds, as the Christians were forced to endure the awkwardness of being silent in a sea of shouting people. The Proconsul's prosperity rested in Caesar's satisfaction, so the people knew that their prosperity rested in satisfying the Proconsul.

After marching down the steps, he was greeted by Herod, the town magistrate and other community leaders eager to make a positive impression, though I had observed a few who stood away, including Drusus Servius. As the Proconsul worked his way among them, I was close enough to hear him inquire regarding the Christians. "Will they submit to my edict, or can I expect trouble?"

Herod replied; "Polycarp, the overseer of the Christians is an old but wise man and has endeared himself to the community for his good works. Furthermore, he is considered a great leader among the Christians abroad for his mentor was a man named John, a disciple of the man referred to as Jesus, the Christ; the head of the subversive movement. As I understand it, Jesus is their king."

"Yes, I am aware of this," the Proconsul answered. "But will they submit?"

Herod was hesitant to answer, but finally stated; "I would expect some resistance from them, Your Excellency. Perhaps you should address your question to a few here who are part of that movement," as he pointed towards Drusus and a few other Christian leaders.

The Proconsul turned to look at them and berated them by asking, "Are you a sheep? Are you part of the flock?" As could be expected, some of the other politicians imitated the bleating of sheep that produced a lot of laughter at the expense of the Christian leaders. Amused, Quadratus silenced the group and asked them, "Will the Christians comply or resist? You are one of them; what will you do? Or are you too timid to answer me?"

Sensing the awkwardness, Drusus nervously stepped forward and with great respect in his voice said, "Proconsul, Caesar will find no group of people more loyal to him and his reign than the Christians. You can expect the church to honor our Emperor as we honor you, but we will not, nor can we worship Caesar as a god, for it is forbidden. You will see our response in the life of the best example we have here in town, my Pastor, Polycarp. While you will find in him the best of men, he greatly loves the One True God. He will be unshakable in his resolve."

After realizing what he said, and to whom he said it, he swallowed hard and sheepishly bowed and took a few steps back as if in shock that he would take such a strong stance on anything. Antony, a fellow politician and believer, leaned over and whispered in Drusus' ear; "Could you have been a little more subtle," he said with a smirk. Drusus tried to smile, but his heart was pounding, his palms sweaty and his face beet red. I thought he would collapse out of exhaustion. Not wanting to appear weak before the town leaders, the Proconsul arrogantly responded to Drusus; "Perhaps the threat of seeing his congregation, maybe even you, tortured or killed will weaken his resolve."

I felt a cold chill go up my spine at hearing those words. I glanced over at Germanicus and Amatus, and they both were pale with disbelief. Polycarp, who had slowly made his way down to where we were standing, heard the threats, but appeared calm, but I could see he was contemplating his next steps of action. I leaned closer to Polycarp and whispered; "This is no small matter for the church. It's going to be a long week."

He just shook his head in agreement and said, "And then another week will come. God still reigns, and all the Caesars will one day have to bow the knee and confess before the One True God what we already know, that Jesus Christ is Lord of all. We cannot permit the worries of this week to be our guide. Come; let's make sure the church family is comforted and prepared."

―――――――◇◇――――――――

The Smyrnaean Christians were being sustained by the grace of God as word spread regarding the Proconsul's edict. Some left the city for places in the country, hoping to hide, but for the most part, everyone stayed in their homes and trusted God to direct and protect them, or if necessary, to give them grace to face death for the sake of the Lord Jesus Christ. The pagan boasts in the superhuman feats of their gods, but none of them can compete against the grace of God being firmly entrenched in the hearts of his people. God was making his people fearless in the face of what would normally be disabling fear.

As I returned home that evening, having called upon a few brothers and sisters in Christ who were being overly troubled with fear, I noticed that Germanicus had already arrived before me. When he started his ministry training under Polycarp, he moved into the spare room in our home. In fact, he was to stay under Polycarp's tutelage a few more years, and then come and join me in the west. I loved the example of godly desires and obedience he set for my children. He was the perfect older brother to my children, and my wife and I loved him like a son. My eight-year-old daughter, Livia, was especially observant of him. As I walked past his room, I paused as I heard him share with her a powerful testimony to God's greatness.

"Germanicus, what is in that wooden box on the table?" she asked as she pointed to the study desk positioned in front of the window.

"That is the only possession I have from my mother and father," he replied with a sense of reverent pride. "Would you like to see what is in it?" he said, fully knowledgeable of what her answer would be.

"Yes, please," was her grateful response.

To be honest, I wasn't even aware of the contents of the box, so he piqued my curiosity as well. He carefully opened the box as if the contents were extremely fragile, and then he slowly pulled out what appeared to be a dried, twisted twig, shaped in the form of a ring with only a few brown and brittle leaves loosely hanging on to it. Then it suddenly dawned on me that it was an old laurel wreath—a victor's crown. "What was he doing with one of those?" I wondered.

As my daughter stood there staring at what was now a worn and useless twig, she got a puzzled look on her face and asked him what it was. "Livia, this is a victor's crown that was given to my father by Caesar. The only reason I know this is due to the inscription on the inside of the lid. It says; 'For persevering with endurance, strength and virtue; and for refusing to quit in the face of impossible odds. To the victor belongs the crown.' And beneath the inscription was inscribed, *The Divine Emperor, Hadrian.* You can see his official seal next to his name," as he handed her the lid for further inspection.

"I don't even know what is was for; or what great feat he performed, but I do know that it was important enough to be brought to the attention of the Emperor, and that while others would have quit, he refused to be defeated and instead persevered to win. His reward was this crown, and even today, it is a great honor to receive one of these."

Germanicus then took the crown and placed it on his head, and then smiling, placed it on Livia's head. "Do you want one of these?" asked Livia.

"Sure, who wouldn't? But I am after a greater crown that will never become old or as unattractive as this. The great Apostle Peter said that I will receive the unfading crown of glory, and Paul called it a crown of righteousness. Whether or not I die next week or live to be as old as Polycarp, I want to run the race God has placed before me with endurance, being led by His joy."

"You sound like my dad," Livia replied with a grin. That made me chuckle for it was true. I was glad that she was observing me. What she asked next truly astonished me.

"Germanicus," Livia asked followed by a short pause, "Are you afraid to die?"

Puzzled, but nevertheless undeterred, he replied, "No, not really. I may be concerned about how I am to die, but God has promised his followers courage in the face of death. For me, the joy of living is serving Christ. To die is better than that, for I will be with him."

"God, the One True God, may this be the grace you pour out upon your people this week as we are forced to walk beneath the shadow in this valley of death," I whispered as I marveled over what I had just heard.

17

RUN AWAY FROM
IDOLATRY

My little children, stay far away from idols.
(I John 5:21)

I T was a perfect morning as the sun rose over Smyrna, and
Quadratus desired to take a morning stroll, and he requested
that Herod and his security detail join him on a walk through
the agora, and on to the newly erected shrine. He thought it would
be wise to mingle with the commoners and to view firsthand the
people's compliance with his first edict. As they walked, he questioned Herod regarding his knowledge of the local Christians for
they were a growing aggravation to him.

"What do you know of the local sect called the Christians? I
asked you before, and you evaded the answer. What are they like?
How are they responding to my edict?"

Herod answered; "From what I observe, they are apprehensive."

"That's good. They should be," Quadratus replied. "That
means they are considering their options."

"I wouldn't put it that way," Herod said. "They are a very
peculiar people, you know. They live their lives by writings they
hold sacred, some of which are the ancient texts of the Jews and
other more recent writings, that command them to obey the laws
of the land, and to honor the Emperor. To be quite honest, in my
humble opinion, there are no people more loyal toward the good
of the empire and its leaders than the Christians. I have found
their message and demeanor, well, quite inviting."

"You sound like a convert," Quadratus scoffed.

"No, not at all, Your Excellency. In fact, I believe a man limits
his potential in serving only one God," he anxiously replied.

"Well said," agreed the Proconsul.

"My father has pounded such beliefs into my thinking," Herod said.

"Your father is a Senator, is he not?" Quadratus asked.

"Yes; he has always been an ambitious man and lives by the rule that a man worships the gods as personal benefit requires," Herod answered.

"A concept too high for the Christian it would seem," the Proconsul remarked.

Herod went on to say, "That may be true, but I tell you; they are impressive people. For right here in this city and throughout the Empire they have established homes for orphans, provided medical care to the afflicted, even to the point of endangering their lives to see that those overcome with the plague and leprosy receive proper care. They are self-sacrificing towards those whose lives have been shattered by our wars. They minister to anyone in need whether they are a slave or an aristocrat. I think what amazes me the most is that they have their own form of discipline for erring members. It is rare to see Christians in court for illegal activities or for wronging another person. What I find so ironic is that in every respect, Christians are the model citizen, with one exception."

"And what is that exception?" Quadratus asked.

"They will only worship what they describe as the One True God. I have witnessed throughout the Empire that they will not offer worship to anyone or anything other than their God, even under the threat and pain of death," Herod replied.

"Impressive people, but such loyalty should be directed to the worthiness of Caesar, don't you think?" Quadratus countered. "They may serve or worship whomever they wish, but they must not be permitted to be disloyal to our nation and Emperor. You seem like a logical man, Herod. Let me ask you; who will protect them from the barbarians in the North, their God or almighty Caesar? Who will care for their city in times of famine, their God or Caesar?"

Herod did not reply, for he knew there was only one correct answer in the mind of the Proconsul. As they walked, they both observed a commotion down the road toward the shrine. "I must find a way to break their commitment, and I think I have figured out a way to do it," boasted the Proconsul with an air of secret, newly-found confidence. For as they walked closer to the shrine dedicated to Caesar, they observed a Christian caught in a very difficult situation and in what would appear, a moment of weakness.

"I will use that lad right over there," as he pointed towards the shrine. I believe I can use him to turn the Christians into submission to my will." Standing nearby in front of the shrine was Germanicus, who appeared stunned and uncertain.

You see, Germanicus was also walking through the market on his way to meet with Polycarp, having just delivered food to some of the widows. As he made his way through the crowd and passed the shrine, he saw his friend, Florian, walking along with his parents. As he made eye contact, they waved to him and asked him to walk along with them. Germanicus had shared the good news of Jesus Christ with his friend on many occasions and felt that Florian's heart was softening toward the message of Christ. However, as they walked along and conversed, Germanicus, oblivious to his surroundings suddenly discovered the awkward situation he had walked into, for there, right in front of him was the shrine to Caesar. And to add to his uncomfortable surprise, Florian's father paid the fee and registered his family by name, and then each one took their place in the shrine, bowed the knee, confessed Caesar as Lord, offered incense to his glory, and got up to leave. To make matters worse, he even generously paid the fee that would be required of Germanicus too.

At this point, a rude silence rushed over those who were standing in or near the shrine as everyone was looking at Germanicus waiting for him to follow their example. Poor Germanicus just froze. The pressure was intense and was about to get greater, but he knew he could not worship Caesar.

Florian, with nervousness in his voice, said, "Germanicus, why are you waiting? Everyone is watching."

"I can't do this, Florian. It's wrong!"

Florian's father became impatient and irritatingly said; "For the love of the gods Germanicus, you are humiliating me. I paid your fee; fulfill your duty to the community and to the Emperor. Stop delaying, you ungrateful, fainted-hearted boy."

It didn't take long for the crowd and the guards to become increasingly impatient with Germanicus, especially seeing that the Proconsul was in the audience. Not only was he refusing to obey the edict, but he was holding up the line as well. The guards threatened him and yelled at him to move along, and the people thought him to be insensitive for not wanting to bless the community by worshiping Caesar. Florian's mother appealed to him like a son, thinking that perhaps a softer approach would help.

"Germanicus, you are one of the finest young men I know. I love you like a son. I know that this must be awkward for you, but as you have told Florian, your God is a forgiving God. If this action troubles you so greatly, surely he will forgive you for this if what you say is true."

Germanicus could not move or speak, and felt nauseated. His mouth became dry, and his thoughts seemed so scrambled he could not think what to do. It was all surreal to him.

Finally, Florian's father spoke again, feeling that he needed to separate himself from Germanicus; "Young man, you are unfit to be my son's friend, and I am ashamed to have had you as a guest in my home. You are a disgrace to this town and to our divine Caesar; you atheist!" He shouted. "How dare you reject our gods!" Others too joined in with accusations and insults leaving the frightened young man feeling alone and rejected.

Germanicus could take no more; he could not stay, and he could not defend himself, and with great terror welling up in his soul, he bolted through the crowd as quickly as he could run, hearing only the fading insults and laughter of those behind him. With both fear and deep grief gripping his heart and tears spilling down his face, he ran towards the only comfort and protection he knew, his faithful teacher and friend, Polycarp. As he arrived at his study chamber, he threw himself down next to Polycarp and wept bitterly.

The concerned and fatherly pastor reached down and placed his hand on Germanicus' head and pleaded with him to explain why his heart was so grieved. "My dear boy, what troubles you so greatly? Tell me so that I can comfort you. Do not be afraid to share with me what is on your heart."

With broken speech and through great tears Germanicus blurted out, "I have betrayed my Lord and fled like a coward. I hate myself!"

"No, no, no my child, this doesn't seem like you, you're one of the most courageous Christians I know," replied Polycarp.

Germanicus wept even harder at hearing this lofty opinion of him, and after what seemed an eternity of deep sorrow, he finally related the incident to Polycarp.

"I was with my friend and his family in the market, but what I didn't know was that they were going to worship at Caesar's shrine. I froze and didn't know what to do. The guards became angry with me and the crowds began to pressure and accuse me, and mock me."

Waves of remorse stifled his speech until he was able to squeak out with an air of shame, "I failed."

Alarmed, Polycarp began to feel the pressure of disappointment welling in his own heart as he asked; "Did you too bow the knee and offer worship to Caesar?"

Germanicus looked up as if shocked at such a question. "No! Never! How can I possibly do that? No, I didn't bow the knee, I ran like a coward driven by fear and as one ashamed to take a stand for my Lord."

Polycarp sighed and could not refrain from smiling, and even let out a chuckle. He got up from his chair and knelt next to his grieving pupil. With affection, like a tender grandfather, he placed his arm around him, and through tears of joy, praised God for the courage of Germanicus. "Thank you, my faithful God for the strength you have given your servant, Germanicus, on this day. Praise be to your great name now and forever!"

Germanicus seemed shocked by such an unpredictable reaction.

"You are hardly a coward my dear boy, your courage to stand strong in the face of great pressure inspires me to do the same. You know, you're not the first to flee in the face of hardship and persecution," Polycarp explained. "Remember what we talked about a couple weeks ago from John's first epistle? 'I am addressing you, young men, because you are powerful, because the Word of God is alive and active in you, and you have overcome the evil one.'[126] Didn't King David flee his rebellious son, Absalom? Did he not exhort us in his Psalm to fly away like a bird to the mountain when the wicked seem to advance against us? Elijah fled Jezebel after he had courageously slain six hundred of her pagan prophets. He too felt like he betrayed God, and what did

---

126. I John 2:14

God do? He fed him and gave him rest. That doesn't sound like a disappointed God to me. Elijah discovered as you will too; he was not condemned by God but loved and cared for instead. When the Apostle Paul was in danger of being killed in Damascus, he escaped by being dropped down in a basket over the city wall, as did I in Hierapolis. And speaking of Paul, notice how he exhorted the Corinthian Christians in his first letter: 'My brethren, run away from idolatry.'[127] From my perspective, dear boy, it looks to me as if you obeyed to the glory of God. Well done!"

"I remember when I was your age and my mentor, the Apostle John, was guiding me through the Gospel he had just recently written. He related to me the time when the great Apostle Peter ran at the arrest of Jesus in the garden of Gethsemane. Of course, he didn't run until after he cut off the ear of a servant named Malchus. He fled in fear. But what he did next left all who knew him in disbelief. You see; he lingered at a safe distance behind the mob, and observed the trial from the High Priest's courtyard, and while he warmed himself by the fire, he did far more than just run. On three separate occasions, he denied even knowing Jesus Christ. And in the end, he did it with such profanity that no one would have believed he was Christ's disciple. You want to see grief; you should have seen Peter."

"My dear child, you did not betray your Savior. You ran because you did not have the experience to defend what you believe. But, everyone standing there knows where your loyalty lies because you would not betray Jesus, though under great duress and danger. I could not be happier with what God has revealed in you today. I truly believe my dear son that history will record you to be a truly courageous man of God that I already know you to be."

"What do you think may happen next?" inquired Germanicus.

"That is what we must prepare our hearts for," replied Polycarp. "The Proconsul seems very determined to make a name for himself before Caesar, and his ascension will be on the heaps of bodies he will have slain. Prepare your heart, young man. I don't believe the episode at the shrine was your trial, I believe it is only an introduction for us all."

---

127. I Corinthians 10:14

After finishing up some time with his mentor, Germanicus went for a walk along the coastline and used it as a time to reflect on the scriptures that Polycarp had given to him. After feeling renewed by the faithful kindness of God, he decided to make his way back into town. That afternoon, a group of young people were to meet for study and fellowship. As he made his way through the town for the study, another teenager from the church, Sisera, joined him, and they walked together. As they conversed, Sisera asked, "Do you think the Proconsul is going to arrest all the Christians in Smyrna?"

Germanicus replied, "I don't think they have enough prison space for us all."

They continued making their way through the crowd, but were unaware of the terrible events about to unfold. Earlier that day, when Germanicus refused to worship Caesar at the shrine, the Proconsul and Herod, the magistrate, were observing him from a distance. Quadratus was incensed by his arrogance and obvious refusal to obey such an easy edict. He was determined to make an example of this teenager and dispatched soldiers to find and arrest him.

"What is all that commotion about up there?" Sisera griped as he pointed towards the noise several yards in front of them? People were running and getting out of the way as something was rapidly approaching the location where the two boys were standing. In no time, ten fully armed Roman soldiers pressed into the crowd towards Germanicus. Having no idea of what was taking place, they too moved out of the way.

Immediately the commander shouted, "Stop that criminal! Do not let him escape!"

Frightened out of his wits Sisera shouted, "He's pointing at you, Germanicus."

Germanicus froze in fear at the sight of these monstrous guards, each with a drawn gladius as they plowed through the crowd, and finally pushing both boys down to the ground as if they were some great threat. Without any explanation, the soldiers bound them and at spear point took them both to the Judgment Hall of the Proconsul.

As they were hurried away and forcibly conveyed into the Hall, many others who witnessed the arrest hurried off to inform

Polycarp. The news was spreading through the city like wild fire. Prayer was being offered up to God at the Church meeting house. Polycarp was comforting his people, and dispatched me to go to the Judgment Hall in order find out what was happening, and to try to give the boys much-needed support and encouragement. I also wanted to see if Drusus Servius could be of assistance.

In the Judgment Hall, the Proconsul peeked around the curtain to see how many had gathered to watch, and then he turned around towards the town leaders waiting with him and asked them, "How serious are these Christians? Will they force me to shed blood?"

The nervous leaders didn't even know how to answer the question, and looked over to Drusus Servius and the other Christian leaders. Out of fear, no man said a word, for the Proconsul seemed unreasonably agitated.

On the other side of the curtain, Herod shouted authoritatively out to the crowd, "Silence! I demand your silence! All stand in reverence for his Excellency, Quadratus the Emperor's Proconsul in Asia." With great pomp, Quadratus walked into the chamber and sat on a very ornate chair on top of a small platform.

As silence ruled the moment, the Proconsul surveyed the crowd. With a smug smile, and like a predator homing in on its weaker prey, he decided to begin the interrogation himself, with the most vulnerable looking youth, Sisera. "You seem awfully young to be a criminal young man. What are your parents going to say when they hear of the trouble you are in?"

Nervously and with a quivering voice, Sisera squeaked out, "Your Excellency, I don't even know what trouble I'm in."

"Ah, the innocence of youth," quipped the Proconsul. "You can't imagine the number of times I've heard other criminals say that very thing," as muffled laughter rippled throughout the hall.

The proconsul raised his hand in an effort to silence the crowd, and then smiled at Sisera and said; "My naïve lad, you have committed a capital offense against the Roman Empire that's all. However, you do not need to be afraid of me, for I am committed to your protection and happiness. It is Herod over there that will prosecute you. I'm here to save you. Our divine Caesar has ordered me to protect everyone here on his behalf if I can." Then cautiously as if speaking down to the teenager he said, "You are here because of your friend, Germanicus." With a shocked expression and beads of sweat forming on his forehead, Sisera looked over to Germanicus.

The Proconsul continued: "Yes indeed, your friend here. You see, today I observed his refusal to offer worship to our divine Caesar. Upon further investigation, I found that you had not offered worship either, and so not wanting you to be a fugitive of the law, I'm going to give you a chance to do that right now, right over there."

Both Sisera and Germanicus turned their heads to the right of the Proconsul, where they saw a beautifully adorned marble statue of the Emperor. "I worship at the statue myself. In fact, I haven't worshiped at it just once; I worship at it every day. How's that for devotion?" The crowd rallied in support of the Proconsul with cheers and applauds.

With all the noise, Germanicus turned around to scan the crowd. To his great encouragement, his eyes met mine. While we were too far apart to speak, but I believe the sight of a friend and brother gave Germanicus courage. With this new found confidence, Germanicus leaned over and told Sisera, "Be courageous; God will give us grace. Truly, with God guiding us, we have nothing to fear."

"Germanicus, are you crazy? I've never been more frightened," lamented Sisera.

Finally, after order was restored to the Hall once again, the lofty Proconsul looked squarely into the eyes of fearful Sisera and ordered him to step forward and before all these witnesses offer worship to Caesar.

Sisera hesitated at first and feeling rather embarrassed said, "Your Excellency, I am a Christian, and Christians are forbidden to worship any other gods."

Irritated, the Proconsul growled; "Where in this Judgment Hall is your God? Here is my God," pointing towards the statue of Caesar. "There is no one on earth more powerful than he is, and no one more thoughtful, forgiving and generous to those who show him proper allegiance. You have far more to gain by submitting to me than to lose. In fact young man, you will lose your life if you reject me one more time. Right here; right now; only Caesar can save your life. Stop playing the role of a fool you ignoramus."

Recovering momentarily from his anger, the Proconsul again tried a softer approach. "You see, even in the face of defiant disobedience, I too reflect the everlasting forgiveness of our most magnanimous deity." Sisera began to take small steps toward the altar, and then hesitated.

"Bow down you worthless idiot," shouted the Proconsul. "Are you so stupid that you cannot see it is the difference between life and death?" To add pressure to the situation, Sisera's parents were suddenly ushered in before the Proconsul. They were wealthy merchants in the town, and while not Christians, they had no objections to their son experimenting with this new religion; at least until now.

"Sisera, Jesus is not worth your life," gently, but with fear, implored his mother.

"This is true," declared his father. "Your potential is great in this world, and we must learn to flex and adjust according to the times and the situation at hand. I didn't get to where I am in society by holding to such narrow views. I am successful today because I believe in myself, and am wise enough to align myself to the powers that be."

Here the Proconsul interrupted; "You have wise parents, Sisera, and I'm prepared to reward them handsomely if you submit to me. When you honor the Emperor, he honors in return. Declare Caesar is Lord; bow down before him, and offer the sweet aroma of incense into this fire. This is your final chance."

To the horror of every Christian in the Hall, Sisera stepped up to the statue of Antonius Pius, and bending to his knees, declared in a suppressed and rather shameful voice, "Caesar is Lord!"

But at this the Proconsul stood up and being filled with rage yelled, "Louder! Convince us you mean it. Is Caesar your god?"

Feeling all was lost, Sisera cleared his throat, and as if he had never believed in Jesus Christ shouted out; "Caesar is Lord, and there is no other!" As he got up off his knee, he looked back at Germanicus with an air of defiance as he threw a fistful of incense into the fire. The momentary silence shattered as the crowd erupted into cheers, and praise to Caesar and for his faithful Proconsul. Sisera's parents ran up to their son and hugged him for obeying them.

I was stunned as I watched how easily he dismantled Sisera's beliefs. Truly, a picture of the seed planted in the rocky soil that grew only to be offended at the trials of life. Would Germanicus fold as easily, I wondered? How can a man, much less a boy stand against such intimidation? "Almighty God, in this hour of temptation, grant your servant, Germanicus, courage beyond his understanding," I whispered.

The Proconsul was rather pleased with himself to say the least. He not only showed great strength and power, but endeared the people to him by showing great mercy. Everything was going according to his plan. He looked over to Herod and boasted; "I rather enjoy being the messenger of god; I like wielding his power!"

As the crowd was told to be silent once again, all eyes turned to Germanicus. "What will it be young man? Will you be wise like your friend, or will I need to feed you to my hungry wolves, lions and bears? You can't run like a coward as you did yesterday."

To my surprise, there seemed to be a wave of comfort combined with great courage in the heart of Germanicus. He did take a step forward, but not toward the idol, but rather toward the Proconsul. Then with resolve only the grace of God wields, he made his address.

"Kind sir, you are a powerful man, and you do possess the authority of Caesar in this place. Let it be known that I honor Caesar, and am grateful for the life that has been provided for me in Rome from my infancy in being delivered from the burning rubble of my village in Germania, to the life I enjoy here in Smyrna today. But the credit does not belong to Rome, but to the Almighty God, who gave Rome its splendor, and Caesar his power."

While his defense filled me with loving pride for my friend, it did not sit well with the Proconsul or the crowd, but was met with disdain and harsh condemnation. Quadratus managed to control his rage and employed another tactic to motivate Germanicus.

"Let the boy speak," commanded Quadratus. "I find his notions rather entertaining."

"Your Excellency, even my Lord Jesus Christ, Son of the Living God, when being interrogated in a similar fashion as I am, replied to the Roman Governor of Judæa when he flaunted his authority by saying; 'Are you aware that I have authority to release you and authority to crucify you? Jesus answered him; you have no authority over me at all unless it has been given you from above."[128] Confidently, but with respect, Germanicus concluded: "Jesus Christ is my Lord, and there is no other!"

Gasps of anger echoed throughout the Judgment Hall. However, as I looked around the room at the Christians I knew were present, I saw courage growing. It seemed so strange to me, but at that moment we all felt humbled and honored to be followers of Christ. Fear fled our souls, and love filled its place.

With an air of superior confidence, the Proconsul leaned forward and gave the youth a belittling smile; "Fellow Roman, I, more than any here, can appreciate the zealousness of youth. In many ways, you remind me of myself. But perhaps you need a little more educating in order to arrive at a better conclusion. If memory serves me, Pontus Pilate exercised his considerable power and killed your Lord. My friend, you can expect the same if you continue in your stubborn course."

With loving resolve Germanicus countered; "It is true that the Roman Governor did have my Lord crucified. However, he gave up his life. And furthermore, unlike the tombs of the Caesars in mighty Rome, my master's tomb is empty. He is my Lord, and the only Lord, not just because he died bearing my sins upon himself, but he arose three days later, according to the indisputable facts from eye witnesses and documented facts, and he now rules at the right hand of his Father, the Almighty God. He is my advocate and eternal security. He desires that you too would discover his glory and declare him as your Lord." The Hall went silent as if a great death had befallen them.

"Wrong answer!" shouted the Proconsul as he slammed his fists upon the arms of his chair. "You will pay for your folly, and the citizens of the town will be the wiser for it for they will have observed great mercy from my god to your friend, on the one hand, and his great wrath towards you on the other. We'll see if other Christians find Jesus Christ more loving than the divine Caesar as they are torn apart by wild animals or better, burned alive in the fire. Away with this atheist; away with him! Remove him from my presence."

---

128. John 19:10-11

As the formal charges were about to be read, the only thing that came to my mind was; 'Don't fear those who can kill the body, but cannot kill the soul.'[129]

129. Matthew 10:28

18

DO NOT BE SURPRISED AT THE FIERY TRIAL

Dearly loved ones, do not be surprised at the fiery trials
when they intrude upon your life to test you, as though
something out of the ordinary was happening to you.
But rather rejoice, for we are partakers
with Christ in his suffering...
(I Peter 4:12-13)

"MAGISTRATE, read the charges," Quadratus ordered.

"Germanicus, you are hereby charged with high treason against Rome and her most gracious Sovereign, Caesar Antonius Pius, in that you have failed to comply with the edict of our most illustrious Proconsul of the Province of Asia, His Excellency, Lucius Statius Quadratus. Furthermore, you have acted out of perverted self-love in exalting your good over the good of this community, the success of the Empire and the favor of the gods by your refusal to demonstrate proper and legal approbation to the deity of our Emperors. You have blasphemed their kindness towards you and have embraced atheism. Moreover, you did willfully attempt to mislead others into following your errant ways. It is the judgment of the Tribunal that you be taken to the public arena and be put to death by the savagery of the lions."

Herod, who read the judgment, appeared pale and remorseful as if he pitied the boy, but nevertheless, he gave the order for Germanicus to be taken to his cell and held until evening.

I could hardly believe my ears. I had never witnessed such ridiculous injustice. I fear if I had possessed a sword, I might have attempted a foolish rescue. I was angry and disheartened. Blood was to be shed, and it was the blood of an outstanding citizen, and an extraordinary Christian. I made my way through the Hall and when I was free from the crowd ran as fast as I could to the

Church meeting house where I was certain to find Polycarp and the church family interceding before the Lord.

As I rushed into a large open room, it was filled with Christians from all over the area. Polycarp saw me enter, and stood up to address me. "Irenaeus, what is the word on our dear brother, Germanicus?"

"My dear pastor and my brethren, Germanicus has been charged with treason and has been sentenced to death this evening," I exclaimed. A gasp echoed throughout the room.

"Dear ones do not be too hasty in giving way to fear," Polycarp exhorted. "Irenaeus," he continued, "you must take me directly to the Proconsul. I will speak with him. Perhaps I can appeal to his better judgment. He must see that we mean no disrespect to Caesar, nor do we intend to bring any harm to Rome."

As he made his way swiftly through the congregation, he met me outside, but we were not alone. Other pastors and elders met us on the steps, and it became obvious that they were there to stop Polycarp.

The first to talk was Leo, a man who was to replace Polycarp eventually as the overseer. "I'm sorry my friend, but we will not let you pass. If you go, we will lose you too."

"He is right about this, Polycarp," said Justin, the former Centurion. "You will play right into the Proconsul's plan. I suspect that you are the goal, and by the end of this week, there will likely be a price on your head."

"Justin, you are familiar with these things. Is Quadratus bluffing, or will he kill Germanicus?" Polycarp asked.

"Sir, he is not bluffing. The political fallout would be catastrophic for him if he reversed the charges," Justin replied.

"Well," Polycarp said with exasperation, "If I am the prize, then I shall not keep the Proconsul waiting. He shall have his worthless prize. I do not fear the lions, and I know we all would stand boldly with Germanicus in his final moment. What is death to the servants of Christ? It is our faint and final breath yelling 'Victory!'" he shouted with his arms raised toward heaven.

"Polycarp, you are correct," Justin replied. "I am familiar with these proceedings. Permit me to go in your place. Perhaps the Proconsul will see my credentials and be willing to hear me out. I will intercede on behalf of Germanicus. But if I am to do this, you must not stay here. As long as they don't have you in custody, perhaps it will give us more time to persuade him."

Everyone agreed with this, but Polycarp, of course. I recommend that he go to Columba's farm and that another Church elder, Cato, accompany him. "As soon as we have some word, I'll send it to Columba's home," I said to our preacher.

"For the well-being of your church family, let me handle this, my friend," Justin said.

"Do as you must, but please convey my utmost joy to the noblest of God's servants, my precious Germanicus. Tell him that I would have no greater joy than to stand in his place. Tell him that, Justin. Also, I am a bargaining chip. If my arrest frees Germanicus, you must not hesitate to make an exchange," Polycarp insisted.

As Justin approached the arena, crowds were already assembling at the gates. The people were thirsty for bloody entertainment, and he was bewildered at how easily a friendly town could turn so quickly upon itself. He made his way to a private entrance reserved for gladiators and soldiers. Being well known in military circles, he entered into the gates without being questioned. He made his way first into the holding cells, where he hoped he would be permitted to visit with Germanicus. Again, he was given complete access.

As he walked down the corridor of cells, he found the man he was looking for peering out the small window into the arena. "Germanicus," Justin said, "how are you holding up?"

He turned from the window and said; "Justin, much better seeing you standing there. How did you get in here?"

"Let's just say I was owed a favor or two and leave it at that," he replied. Justin reached through the bars and placed his hand firmly on the lad's shoulder. "I can make you no promises, but I hope to make an appeal to the Proconsul for leniency, maybe even a pardon. But I'll be honest with you, unless God moves in his heart, I don't have much hope."

"I would be surprised if he gave in to your request," Germanicus stated.

Justin sighed and nodded his head in agreement. "Aren't you concerned that you may be placing your life in jeopardy by being here?" Germanicus added.

"That is possible, but I want you to know that I have taken greater risks in my life for people not nearly as worthy of it as you are," Justin stated. "What is my life, but a vapor?" Justin proceeded to share with Germanicus the prayers and desires from Polycarp and others, and then made his way up to the private chamber behind the mezzanine reserved for visiting dignitaries.

When he was brought in before the Proconsul, Quadratus greeted him warmly and gave recognition to Justin's years of faithful service to the Empire. "Hail, noble centurion! The Empire salutes you, and I welcome you." Justin stepped forward and bowed on one knee as a show of respect. As he stood back up, Quadratus took a seat and asked, "To what do I owe the honor of this visit, noble Justin?"

Without hesitancy, and with the force of a man who knew how to command, he stated, "Your Excellency, I humble myself before you to plead for the life of the young boy, Germanicus. I know him personally, My Lord, and you will not find a more exceptional young man in this province."

"Ha! A centurion humbling himself before me on behalf of a treasonous criminal; I don't know what to say," Quadratus replied. "First, let me declare that I am troubled you would know him, and knowing our laws, would possess the audacity to plead for his release. Tell me Centurion, have you killed any traitors in the past?"

"Yes, of course; but those traitors took up arms against Rome. The words of that boy are not deadly like rebels taking up their weapons against the citizens of Rome," he stressed.

"You're a soldier, and it is natural you would see him in that light, but I am a different kind of protector. I protect the people from wrong or harmful ideas. And Germanicus and the Christians are seditious; well-meaning perhaps, but dangerous all the same to the religious structure that the Roman Empire requires for its stability," Quadratus explained.

"Proconsul, there has been more seditious talk toward past Caesars in the Senate," Justin said.

"Careful, Justin, you are here before me because of your gallant reputation. Don't squander it on dangerous assertions.

Furthermore, I can't keep myself from wondering why you are even here appealing my sentence," he warned with an air of suspicion. "Tell me, are you a Christian?"

Like a soldier on orders to charge without hesitation into a deadly fray, Justin quickly replied, "I am not just a Christian, my Lord, I am a devoted follower of Jesus Christ.

"What a waste," Quadratus said.

"A waste?" Justin questioned. "My life before Christ was a miserable shame. I was heartless, cruel, angry, and I must confess quite sarcastic, even to the gods of Rome. On the battlefield, I found only one god—my general. I didn't know the emperors. I didn't know the gods. Who was Jupiter to me? I knew my general; I was willing to follow him into the Kingdom Hades if he ordered me to do so. He was my god, and bloodshed was our worship. That's what amazed me about Jesus Christ. I discovered that he knew me, and I could know him better than a human commander. He didn't order me around; he changed me. He made me a new man, a better soldier and citizen, not to mention a better husband and father."

"I have heard enough, Centurion! You are embarrassing me and shaming your legion, your legacy and your nation. Christianity has made you feeble, and it is making me sick," the Proconsul complained. "However, you prove my point, for look at how powerful a little idea can be, for a crucified criminal has conquered the mighty conqueror, Justin. That is why I must suppress Christianity. Tell me, Justin, have you obeyed my decree and offered worship to Caesar?"

"No, sir! Nor will I ever if I value my life," Justin replied.

"We will see about that," the Proconsul gloated.

"If you think I fear for my life or am afraid to suffer under the pain of death, you will be disappointed," Justin said.

"Oh, I'm certain of that, but I have something far more interesting in mind," Quadratus replied as Justin looked skeptically at him trying to figure out to what he was referring. "You have already admitted to killing traitors, and you obviously have ordered soldiers into battle knowing they would die. Are you prepared to send Germanicus to his death, brave Centurion?"

Justin appeared alarmed and asked; "Are you suggesting I go into the arena and kill him?"

"No, though that would be fascinating to watch I must admit. No, my friend, I will give you a chance to save the young boy's life, or send him to his death. The choice will now be yours. I relinquish any part of it. As Governor Pilate washed his hands regarding Jesus, so I wash my hands of Germanicus."

"I don't understand what you mean by this," Justin said.

"No, of course you don't. Let me explain it to you. In gratefulness for your extraordinary military service to Rome, I will guarantee the immediate release of Germanicus if you, right here, right now offer worship to Caesar as god." The Proconsul stared into Justin's eyes hoping to become the conqueror of this mighty soldier.

Justin stared back with equal intensity. He knew what he was going to do, though he was distracted by the momentary temptation to assassinate the Proconsul. "What a satanic notion," he thought to himself. With unyielding resolve, yet sobered by the tragedy of his decision, he stated; "Proconsul, while common sense may say this is an offer worthy of consideration, Jesus Christ is my Lord; he alone reigns as King of Kings and Lord of Lords. He is my Savior and the One True God. Sir, there is no other to whom I can declare my allegiance. God help me! My public confession to my final breath is that Jesus Christ is Lord; there is no other!"

The Proconsul's face turned red, and his face was distorted with fierce anger as he shouted, "You ungrateful coward. I and all Rome turn our backs on you in shame. You have sentenced Germanicus to a terrible and torturous death. Shame shrouds you and your glorious past. As part of my judgment, you will join me on the portico and watch as your sentence on the boy is carried out," as he pressed his finger into the chest of the old soldier. "I want to see the look on your face as he is clawed and ripped to shreds. I want to see you grimace at his blood-curdling screams. And when there is nothing left but the blood-soaked ground, I will have you marched into the arena as added entertainment." Quadrates took a step back to take in the full picture of Justin's reaction, but he saw none. The grace of God was a greater force in Justin than all the fear and dread the Proconsul could muster.

"Have you nothing to say," he blurted out with exasperation.

"Only this; God's will be done on earth as it is in heaven," Justin replied.

"Tell me centurion, are you sixty, maybe sixty-five years old?" Quadratus asked.

"I am sixty-three," he answered.

"And how old were you that last time you drew your gladius in battle?"

"I was forty-eight."

"Fifteen years is a long time, especially for a man that will be forced to draw his gladius one more time, but this time it will not be for the glory of Rome, but for the satisfaction of Rome. The soldier is about to become the entertainer," the Proconsul boasted. "Tonight, following the death of Germanicus, you will be ceremonially marched out, where you will meet three deadly gladiators, who love Rome and are eager to inflict pain and death on her traitors."

"Guards," the Proconsul shouted. "This man is under arrest for treason. Take him to his cell, and return him to me before the young man's execution." Then gritting his teeth, he muttered, "Away with this atheist."

That evening, as I sat outside the hall where the church had gathered, I was receiving sparse reports of what was taking place in town and at the arena. Polycarp was moved discreetly out of town and was unaware of Justin's arrest. I felt the need to go to the arena in order to witness the martyrdom of Germanicus, and now it would appear, Justin as well. I desired to communicate to the Church abroad the valiant testimony of these two men of God. The question was how could I go about it undetected? I found a hooded cloak and went out under the cover of darkness to the arena. I found a secluded place from which to watch, still struggling with whether or not I should be there.

The trumpets blared as the Proconsul, and his guests entered the portico and took their cushioned seats, surrounded with the finest food and wine. After they had taken their places, a stool was set next to Quadratus, and I observed Justin bound and being escorted in, and forced to sit. As the Proconsul reclined and sampled the delicacies placed before him, he laughed with the crowd at the pre-show follies making fun of the Christians. After a short time, he became bored and gave the signal for the activities to begin. To the front of the portico came Philip, the Asiarch.[130] With a deep and booming voice he hushed the crowd to announce the beginning of the games.

"Citizens of Rome, this evening we have for your entertainment savage animals and gladiators." The crowds erupted in celebration. "Could this be Smyrna," I thought? "I do not know my own townsmen."

Once again, he had to silence the crowd. "First, under sentence of death for high treason, I offer to you Germanicus, the atheist. We will see if his God will deliver him from the mouths of lions like he did the fabled prophet, Daniel. Before you give way to sympathy, remember that Caesar would have shown mercy and delivered him, but Caesar is not a god, he says. Let us see if his God can spare him. Away with the atheist," he shouted. As he repeated it, the crowd joined the chant, "Away with the atheist!"

My heart sank as I saw that virtuous young man standing alone in the center of the arena, enduring the mockery and insults of the crowd. He was a David before Goliath. He didn't shake or cry, though I was. His face glowed with the joy of the Lord as if he had won the race and was now taking his rightful place on the victor's platform waiting the crown of victory. "Oh, if the saints of the Lord could see the power of God that dwells in them as I am beholding it in this man, how dramatically changed our lives would be," I groaned to myself. I wept as I saw his joy as he faced such vile and heartless brutality. Truly, if the death of His saints weren't precious to him, God would consume this place with the fire of his wrath.

All of the sudden, the cheers of the crowd crescendoed as out of the dark passageway sprung three adult lions, harassed and abused to make them more fierce. They eyed their prey, and the only question they would be considering is who would be the first to bite and tear?

I could watch no longer. My heart grieved at what was inevitable. As I turned and drew back into the shadows, for I was weeping almost beyond control, the roar of the crowd surged in both elation and revulsion.

---

130. *A Roman official appointed to serve as the emcee of government sponsored events*

What startled me were the words of a spectator near me; "I cannot believe my eyes; he is running towards the lions."

Another person next to him replied, "Is that courage or stupidity?" The crowd groaned with shock as the lions tore into the young man and ripped his body apart. I never heard him scream, nor did he try to evade death.

Another woman in the crowd complained that it had happened too fast and that she felt she didn't get her money's worth.

Observing from the portico was Justin. The seasoned veteran cried as he watched a champion of Christ murdered. He turned to Quadratus and said, "In all my years of fighting and the brutality that I have ordered or inflicted upon my enemies, I have never seen such a display of courage in the face of death. He ran to his death like a man who had already defeated it."

"It's a wasted life," Quadratus snapped. "I shall look forward to your gallantry, foolish Christian."

The sight was gory, and not a common thing to see in Smyrna. I believe the blood that stained that patch of sand in the center of the stadium began to have a sobering effect on the crowd. Many of these people knew Germanicus; some of them were the recipients of his kindness. It had been a long time since this town witnessed an execution of this kind. The Proconsul seemed alarmed that the crowd was regretting his decision, and he had to move decisively to keep his plans on track. He immediately stepped up to the front of his portico and nudged the Asiarch out of his way.

His voice echoed powerfully through the arena as he declared, "Who is responsible for this outrage? Who refuses the favor of Caesar's blessings on this city?" The place fell into silence as the citizens pondered the stirring questions of the Proconsul.

"This was a young man who had been misled by erroneous teaching, and it was what condemned him to death. Tell me citizens of Rome, has this young man interacted with your children? Has he planted seeds of corruption in their minds? Has he attempted to convert them into betraying the gracious gods of Rome, gods that have made this nation great? Look at that blood on the ground," He demanded. "Look at it! That could be your child's blood. Christianity is a bloody religion. They claimed to be washed in the blood of a lamb. How pathetic is that I ask you?" He pointed to the bloodstained ground and asked, "Is this stained ground the future you desire for your children?"

That whipped the feeble-minded crowd back into a frenzy as they shifted from sympathy back to fear and anger. The Proconsul, seeing this as his opportunity ordered, "Away with the atheists," and again, even louder, "Away with the atheists!"

Within in moments the delirious crowd sought only one thing, the order from Quadratus. "Who is responsible for this young man, and for the beliefs that condemned him to die?" He inquired from the crowd. The response was quick and spread like fire from person to person when at last in terrifying unison the people shouted over and over, "Polycarp! Polycarp! Polycarp!"

Finally, the Proconsul was able to get in one more word before the crowd was out of his control, "Find Polycarp, and bring him to me!"

<hr>

Chaos wreaked havoc in the streets of Smyrna. What was once a respectful crowd of Roman citizens in the thriving metropolis of Smyrna had quickly turned into an uncontrollable mob looking to blame every problem and tragedy upon the Christians. As I saw the crowds pour out of the arena, my heart sank even deeper as I heard that there was now a bounty on Polycarp's head. I also became increasingly aware that no Christian was safe tonight, for word was spreading that any Christian could be detained and questioned, and even arrested. It would appear that each citizen in that arena had been in some form, deputized to search out and apprehend Christians.

As I began to feel the pressure of my circumstances, while still hidden in the shadows of the arena, my fear was heightened as I heard the voice of a soldier behind me. It was Flavius Arius, the Centurion in command of the Roman Garrison here in Smyrna. While not a professing believer, we had talked about spiritual matters on several occasions. He was born and raised in Gaul, near the city I was to depart for this week.

"Irenaeus, are you mad? Do you realize the danger you are in being here in this arena?" He asked.

"Yes," I hesitatingly replied. "Should I be even more concerned right now?"

"If it were one of my guards, yes, you would be in grave danger. They've been dispatched to detain Drusus Servius and the other Christians on the town council. While there are no particular warrants out for Christians in general, when they capture Polycarp, indictments may be handed down. The Proconsul is determined to establish his reputation in this province."

"So, you are not going to arrest me?" I asked.

"No. I don't understand your faith, but I do admire your courage, and I have found our conversations to be interesting and even helpful. Follow me; I'll lead you to safety," He instructed.

What a tragic time when family members turned on each other, and friends turned against their Christians friends. Even loyal customers and those engaging in business together were betrayed by former associates wishing to garner favor from the Proconsul. It suddenly became profitable to hand over the Christians to the authorities. Again, the people did not understand why the Christians couldn't offer any worship to Caesar, even if they didn't mean it. The prisons swelled beyond capacity with Christians under arrest.

There was a mad search for all the followers of Christ and Polycarp especially. Among the more aggressive was a man named Icarus, a sculptor and seller of pagan idols. For a long time, he had resented Polycarp's work for the negative effect it tended to have on his business. He claimed the Polycarp's sermons were bad for business, and that only intensified when his business partner was born-again. Out of bitter resentment, he led the search for Polycarp.

"In the name of the gods, tear this town apart," Icarus clamored. With the promise of free drink and a share in the bounty, he drew all manner of lowlifes and criminals. "He has ruined our businesses; split our families; forsaken our traditions. The troubles that surround you are the god's frowning in displeasure for the tolerance we have shown to these diseased minds.

Icarus continued fanning the flame of hatred as he bitterly preached; "Find the atheist and let's see how powerful his God is to deliver him from us. I say; Hail Zeus; give us power over these atheist parasites; Diana, grant us success; Neptune, stop them from escaping by sea, and Hades, swallow them up in your dreadful flames. Hail Caesar, in whose name we search out these worthless beasts."

Some ran off with torches and crude weapons, pitchforks, butcher knives, large fish hooks and the like, towards the church house and others towards Polycarp's home where they found Callisto and her husband and took them captive. When they found his study chamber, they ransacked the place and torched all the parchments, including the library he had inherited from Decimus, some of which contained original letters from the Apostles. However, Icarus knew that Polycarp frequently visited a farm outside of Smyrna, which his former business partner, Columba owned. With other trusted and base fellows, they secretly made their way to the outskirts of town.

At that very farm, Columba and his wife Gratia ministered to their concerned pastoral shepherd.

———◇◇———

"While I am truly blessed by your care of me this evening, I cannot help but think that I am forsaking my responsibility," Polycarp spoke in a rather discouraged manner.

"But pastor, what could you possibly do back in town," inquired Gratia? "How can you help anyone if you are being beaten, tortured, or killed?"

Cato added, "It is true, we all must ascertain what exactly is taking place. We have not heard anything yet. Perhaps Justin was effective."

"But if I could just talk with the Proconsul, surely he would see that we are sincere in our support of this community and the reign of the Emperor," bemoaned the old preacher.

"That is possible, but surely we must wait and see what Justin was able to accomplish, and of course, there is also Drusus Servius. Perhaps he can address the Proconsul," Cato replied.

"I fear it will not be as easy as it sounds," Polycarp replied as he looked anxiously at Cato, "Have we heard anything from Justin? And what of poor Drusus, he is a weaker brother. I fear he is not ready for this hour of temptation." He dropped his head and sighed while staring at the floor.

Just then, Columba and Gratia's youngest son suggested, "Maybe we should pray."

Feeling the humbling of childlike faith, Polycarp smiled, looked up, and patting the head of the child said; "Now that's what a man who trusts God would do." Upon this Polycarp looked upwards and said, "My gracious God; Almighty in all things. Ruler of nations, we face hardship that is beyond our understanding, but not beyond your control. We intercede for our brother Justin and Germanicus. If they are still alive, grant them favor before the Proconsul. Oh, dear Father, for tender Drusus I plead that you will give him courage at the right time, for just as you warned your servant Peter that Satan desired to sift him as wheat, so he would delight in sifting my dear brother. Almighty God, how could we face this trial without the same resolve as our Savior did in his hour of trial; so with him we say, remove this cup from us. Nevertheless, not our will, but your will be done. To the praise of your precious Son, Jesus Christ, to him be glory forever and ever. Amen."

When Polycarp finished praying, he looked around at those in the room with him and reminded them of Peter's admonition; "Dearly loved ones, do not be surprised at the fiery trials when they intrude upon your life to test you, as though something out of the ordinary was happening to you. But rather rejoice, for we are partakers with Christ in his suffering. Trials are our opportunity to share in and identify with the sufferings of Christ for us. In this fact, we can rejoice and be truly happy when he reveals his glory at last. If we are publicly humiliated and defamed because of Christ's name, then God calls us blessed, and that blessing he is describing is the Spirit of glory and God being refreshed in us and upon us. However, it is not the same if we suffer because we have committed true crimes like murder, stealing or other evil deeds against man. If we suffer for nothing more than simply being a Christian; do not be ashamed, but rather give great glory to God for it.'"[131]

<hr />

Back in town, chaos still ruled. The local jail was overflowing to the point where they would just simply ask the Christians not to run away. They were good to their word, of course. The garrison likewise could not handle the new surge of prisoners. The soldiers beat up a few, but for the most part they were being gathered together and held until further direction had been given.

<hr />

131. I Peter 4:12-16

While they tried to encourage one another, they also realized that they too may face death like Germanicus.

In the arena, Drusus Servius had been detained by Quadratus. "Your Excellency, I was instructed to appear before you," Drusus said.

"You are Drusus Servius?" asked the Proconsul.

"Yes, my Lord, I am an elected elder of this city," he answered.

"I have heard a disturbing rumor that you too are also a Christian, who refuses to offer worship to Caesar. I pray that this is not true," the Proconsul said, "For it makes Rome queasy to arrest and prosecute its elected officials."

Hesitantly, Drusus cautiously stated, "I am a Christian. A new one and obviously a terrified one at the moment," he admitted with a nervous laugh.

"You should be terrified. You are obviously a respected man in the community, and I believe it is in your best interest to reevaluate your understanding of worship. I could use someone like you to serve as my liaison in this district. That would be an admirable promotion for someone like you. Wouldn't you agree?" The Proconsul offered.

"It would be very beneficial to me, sir," acknowledged Drusus. "What are you proposing?"

"My request is hardly complicated?" explained Quadratus. "I need a respected leader like you in both the community and the churches, if that's what you call them, to set an example of compromise. You're a politician like me. We both understand the meaning and benefits of compromise do we not?"

"Compromise? Is it ever safe to compromise one's values?" Drusus inquired.

"That depends on whether or not your life is more valuable than your principles," expressed the Proconsul. "Please, come with me, let me show you something." Together they walked down the steps into the arena toward the bloodstained sand in the center.

Then stopping and looking down at the blood soaked ground littered with bone fragments and the torn flesh of Germanicus, Quadratus looked over at the pale face of Drusus and asked; "What are your principles now councilman? Look around you at all these empty seats. In a few hours, they will be filled again with a bloodthirsty mob; now picture lions, bears, and wolves released from their cages, and lunging out after you to tear away your flesh from your bones. And look at you; you are no small meal either. They will feast on you." He paused as he walked around the blood-stained ground, and inquired again, "So, Drusus Servius, shall we continue debating values?"

Trembling at the sight, smell and thoughts of what is happening around him; Drusus was overcome with nausea and vomited. He began trembling and struggled to hold back his tears.

"Now, now councilman, there is no need to lose your composure. I am a reasonable man. No one will ever need to hear of this embarrassment. Come, let's go together and worship Caesar, and thank the gods for your protection this night," suggested Quadratus.

"Proconsul," Drusus blurted out, "Comparing what little I bring to His holy name to the mountain of sins I have committed before knowing him, I would rather trust my eternal life to him than my temporary life to Caesar. I am truly the least in the kingdom of my God."

"You are a fat, bumbling fool, Drusus. How could you be so stupid? What is it that makes you Christians so willing to die for an invisible God?" Then shouting out of exasperation the Proconsul said, "See that bloodstained ground? That is a reality; your reality if you continue following a fable."

To his great surprise, Drusus suddenly discovered an inner strength he had never experienced before, and finding that inner resolve that comes with Spirit-given faith, he calmly said; "Proconsul, I do not expect you to understand what I am about to say, but it is nevertheless the truth. The corrupting power of evil ruined my life. I reveled in lewdness and debauchery. I was cruel and a cheater; even a murderer. Then one day I heard the preacher you seek, Polycarp, declaring the truth of a Savior named Jesus Christ, Son of the living God. His words confused me greatly, but they pierced me like daggers and I felt they would kill me as overwhelming guilt erupted in my heart. However, those same words miraculously became sweet, tender, and—may I say—life changing. I cannot explain it. One day I was a hater of God, and would have been the first in line to see the benefits of worshipping Caesar. The next day, to my surprise, I loved Jesus as my Savior because he loved me first. Why would he do that, Proconsul? Jesus Christ claimed me as his possession. It's like I was born anew. Everything about who I was fell off me like broken pieces of pottery, and I was made new from the inside out. How does a man deny this? I beg for your answer."

With regained composure and confidence, Drusus stated; "Quadratus, I could no more deny Jesus Christ than I could deny that I had been born a Roman citizen. A barbarian could torture me to deny my birth, but my birth-origin would remain the truth regardless. So it is with my spiritual birth. I am a follower of Christ by second birth. There is no power in me to choose not to be, nor even in the face of painful death can I even find a desire to try. Foolish as it may appear to you, I cannot, and by God's grace, I will not deny the truth of what he has done for me and in me."

The Proconsul was silent for a moment, whether moved by what he heard or incredulous at the foolishness of Drusus, but he finally spoke quite calmly, "Then you will join the other atheists in the holding cell, and no doubt will provide some amazing entertainment for us all later. Even your God will get a laugh out of seeing your fat, worthless body strewn across this arena."

A few moments later, Drusus joined Justin in the cell, and together they found courageous joy and peace, and worshipped God together.

"Drusus, I remember Polycarp sharing with us his belief that he would die for his faith," Justin said. "He didn't seem alarmed or even the slightest bit worried. When I questioned him on this, he shared a powerful illustration from the life of Peter. After our Lord's resurrection, he sat with Peter by the seaside and gave him a glimpse into how he would die. He told Peter that 'another would dress him and carry him where he did not desire to go. He said this to show what kind of death he was to glorify God.' Did you catch that, my friend?"

"Indeed, I see it clearly," Drusus replied softly, "a death that would glorify God." That builds up my confidence, Justin. That makes me strong in the Lord that here in my final and most humbling hour; God will be exalted in the highest." He laughed and humored himself; "Well, finally, God will be glorified in me."

"Drusus, God has glorified himself through you and me in more ways than we can imagine," Justin added.

"I know," Drusus replied. It just strikes me as odd, that at the hour appointed for my death, the radiance of God's glory will shine. It makes me want to see him and puts eternity with him in perspective. I'm ready to go, Justin. I am ready!"

"As am I," declared the old Centurion. "Never have I been more ready or prepared to face death."

19

GOD IS OUR PROTECTION AND DEFENSE

You are my place of protection, and my defense
because my expectation is in your word.
(Psalm 119:114)

"THE hardest part about waiting on the Lord is the battle of uncertainty and doubt that creeps up in your soul as you anticipate the revealing of his plan," Polycarp remarked to those sitting around the table. "Praise God for his indwelling Spirit that keeps such faithlessness at bay."

Hours later, long after the sun set, Columba rushed into the house, "Be prepared to move quickly," he said to Polycarp. "A lone rider is heading this way, and I cannot see if he is a friend or foe." Moments later, everyone in the room could hear the galloping of a horse as it approached the gated courtyard.

To everyone's surprise, Leo entered the house disguised as a Roman soldier. "You gave us quite a fright," exclaimed Columba. "I thought they found us."

"I apologize. Justin suggested I wear this before he left to see the Proconsul. He felt it would allow me greater freedom to move about the city and make my way out here to you all without stirring up suspicion," he explained.

He then looked over at Polycarp, who could tell by Leo's countenance that he was not the bearer of good news. "I am grieved to share some heart-wrenching news. Germanicus is dead, and Justin is under arrest, as is Drusus, as well as many in the congregation." Polycarp sat down hard in the chair as his mind attempted to absorb the horrific news.

"And what of Irenaeus?" he asked.

"The reports I have received came first hand from him. He had been in the arena where he witnessed the death of Germanicus, then he was smuggled out, and he and his family are being hidden, though I am not aware of their location. That is not all, however," continued Leo, "for as I made my way here, I saw Icarus and a threatening mob coming up the road from the valley. They're heading this way. It's obvious that he suspects you are here."

"What a treacherous man," grumbled Columba. "He has sought revenge ever since I became a follower of Christ and abandoned our business. His hatred for us both is intense. He blames it on you," He said as he looked over at Polycarp.

"Columba, please take me to town; this must end," implored Polycarp.

But Columba wouldn't consider it. "Pastor, I fear we could not make it into town without great harm coming to you before we arrived. Icarus will kill you and then drag your body back into town with some lie about how you tried to escape. Let's wait a little longer and see if we receive any hopeful news. There is a hideaway beneath this house where you will be safe. I know how to deal with Icarus. But you must trust me."

"What if we smuggled you to Ephesus? It would be safer for you," Cato suggested.

"No! I will not ever consider it. I will not abandon my congregation. They will never see me flee!" Polycarp firmly stated.

As they continued to discuss various options, they heard another rider quickly approaching the house. Polycarp was the first to get up and head for the door much to the dismay of everyone in the room. As they gathered in the courtyard, a man rode so hard toward them, that he was almost thrown from the horse as he attempted to stop. It was Zeno, a slave of Primas and his wife Jana. Like his master, he was a devoted follower of Christ, and part of Polycarp's congregation.

"My precious Zeno, your presence is always an encouragement to me," Polycarp warmly greeted.

"Pastor, my master Primas dispatched me with great urgency to find you. He instructs me that you are to leave at once. Icarus is very close with a mob of people and seeks to bring harm to you and kill you before taking you to town."

Upon hearing this Columba turned and ran toward the barn to fetch a wagon and horse. Moments later, he drove the wagon to the front of the house.

"Polycarp, get up into the rear of the wagon, for this is no time for debate, sir. Cover yourself with that quilt. It is imperative we move you to a safer location," Columba demanded.

Polycarp felt helpless and weak, but conceded, and with great reluctance, and without being given a chance to speak, found himself being quickly ushered from the courtyard and into the cart that sped him away to a safer place.

As they reach the top of the hill, Cato sounded alarmed; "Look back at the farm. Icarus has just arrived. "We could not have left a moment later."

"Columba, what of your wife and children, will they be safe?" asked Polycarp.

"Yes, they are using the hiding place I had reserved for you."

"Pastor, you must prepare for a very uncomfortable ride. In order to avoid other people, we have to stay off the roads and maneuver through the fields," Columba said.

<hr />

As they made their way in the darkness, being guided only by the brightness of the moon, Polycarp sat up and saw in the distance the torches being carried by the mobs searching for him. As they rode along, he wrestled with the thought that he should turn himself in to the Proconsul. The notion was weighing heavy on his heart until he came within sight of the farm belonging to Primas and his wife Jana. Both were faithful believers, not to mention that they are also wealthy, respected Roman citizens with many powerful connections in Rome. Their farm was vast, and there are many places to hide someone. It was even close to the sea, so they anticipated smuggling Polycarp out of the Province by boat. As Polycarp climbed down from the cart, he was immediately met by Primas and his family.

"Polycarp, we grieve for all you must endure right now, and ache over those who suffer for the sake of righteousness," Primas said. "However, my friend, you are safe in our home for the time being. I hope it will be a time for you to rest and regain your strength."

"Thank you my dear brother; your servant Zeno had perfect timing in rescuing me. A moment later and I am afraid I would be in the hands of that idolatrous brute, Icarus."

Jana stepped forward to greet her pastor; "We have an upper chamber ready for you with fresh water, fruit, parchments for your reading from our library, and of course a comfortable bed."

Being deeply touched by their tender love Polycarp said; "Thank you faithful ones, your kindness is overwhelming to me." He adjourned to his room to enjoy some fruit and spiritual refreshment in the Word and much-needed rest. He noticed that Primas had set aside for him the Gospel of Jesus Christ by his old mentor, the Apostle John. That night, he saturated his heart and mind with the equipping and restorative power that comes only from the Word of God. He went to sleep full of faith.

The next morning he awoke to the roosters crowing, and breathing in the fresh sea air of a new morning, his soul filled with refreshing hope. "It is because of the Lord's unending mercies I am not destroyed by him. Every day I find them renewed before me, great is your faithfulness, my God,"[132] he prayed as he sat up. However, the night had not been without any trouble, for he remembered a disturbing dream that seemed as if God was giving him a glimpse into what he must suffer for his Lord. He refused to yield to fear and again, gained assurance as he meditated on the next thoughts in Lamentations: "The Lord is all I need, for this reason I will patiently endure."[133]

As he made his way downstairs, his thoughts pressed on the possibility that maybe the Proconsul had seen enough blood. Perhaps Justin was able to make an appeal and reason once again with the town leaders. Then speaking out loud to himself, he said, "Regardless, God has made this day, and for that reason I will rejoice in it[134] whether by my life or by my death."

As he joined the family for breakfast, they asked him to share a portion of Scripture and offer thanks for the food. He quoted for them a familiar text, a Psalm of David:

> *God is our hiding place and strength-giver,*
> *always present to help in times of trouble.*
> *For this reason, we will not be afraid even if the*
> *earth falls apart, though the mountains are hurled*

---

132. *Lamentations 3:21-23*

133. *Lamentations 3:24*

134. *Psalm 118:24*

into the depths of the sea, though its waves roar and
foam, though the mountains shake at its tides.

There is a river whose streams cause the city of God
to rejoice, the holy place of the Most High.
God lives there; she shall not be moved; God
will help her when morning dawns.

The nations are out of control; the kingdoms reel
to and fro; he speaks and the earth melts.
The Lord of hosts is with us; the God
of Jacob is our fortification.

Come, look closely at the works of the Lord, how
he has brought destruction upon the earth.
He stops wars from one end of the earth to
the other; he breaks the bow and destroys the
spear; he burns the chariots with fire.

Be silent and still, and know that I am God.
I will be exalted among the nations of the world;
I will be exalted in the earth! The LORD of hosts is
with us; the God of Jacob is our fortification.[135]

Polycarp paused for a moment to reflect on the passage, and then bowed his head to offer thanks to God. "Holy Father, our One True God, our hearts are beyond the reach of fear when we believe your promises. You are forever a faithful and loving God to your people. My heart is greatly comforted by the fact that my dearest friend, Germanicus, stands in your glorious presence right now. I love you for saving his soul. You gloriously take the troubled heart and create peace. You take mirth and replace it with joy. You overcome hatred by perfect love. Even here on this table before us lie wonderful and delicious reminders of your faithfulness. Thank you for not only providing for us this food, but giving us also the ability to enjoy it. Bless it for your glory, and strengthen us for the tasks you will assign us today. Be glorified now and forever our Great God. Amen!"

---

135. Psalm 46

"Pastor, did you rest well last night?" Jana asked.

"Yes, I rested well for a portion of the night. However, I was awakened after a dream where God told me I would die very soon. It wasn't to fill me with fear, but rather for me to submit myself to God's will as our great Savior Jesus Christ submitted his will on the night he was betrayed in the Garden of Gethsemane," explained Polycarp.

"Well, that is distressing. Did you receive insight as to how you would die?" asked Primas.

"As remarkable as it sounds, I died in the flames. At least that's how it appeared in my dream," he carefully responded with a slight smile as he looked around the table at the shocked faces.

"How dreadful and frightening; how can you possibly endure such a thought," inquired Jana?

Polycarp, desiring to assure all at the table said, "First, by the Scripture I just shared, and by God's grace that puts Job's words in my heart: 'Though he put me to death, I will put unwavering trust in him.'[136] When God takes away our fears by his love, we are left only with courage. I truly believe that how we face death is what defines how we lived in our heart. The Apostle Paul described it quite succinctly when in his letter to the Philippian Church, he said, "For me to live is Christ, to die is to have the advantage."[137]

"I don't understand what you mean by 'advantage,'" inquired Primas.

"It's very simple actually. Look at it this way, to the unbeliever, death is their greatest fear. It is a great and dreaded unknown. But to those of us who do believe, death is miraculously converted into a doorway. You leave this life only to enter a better, more perfect one," he explained.

"I believe that. I just wish there was a more pleasant way to get through that doorway," Primas jested.

"Well, there is some truth to that, my friend," Polycarp mused, "but nevertheless, that is where we discover the power of God's grace. Look at this way, Paul preached this concept powerfully when he said, 'When the perishable puts on the imperishable and the mortal puts on immortality, then shall come to pass the saying, Death is swallowed up in victory. O death, where is your sting?

---

136. Job 13:15

137. Philippians 1:21

And O hell, where is your victory? The poisonous sting of death is sin, and its power to rule is in the law. But this victorious grace is from God through the victory of our Lord Jesus Christ.'"[138]

"Have you ever given thought that the truth of this passage is one of the last but greatest insights a Christian will have regarding life before taking their last breath and entering into the presence of God? What better way for this life to end than by exclaiming, 'Death, where is your sting and victory?' And you will discover, death cannot provide an answer," Polycarp said as he lightly patted the table. "The insight is not the thought; it's in living it, even in death. God initiates and establishes his work in us here, in a corrupted world, and completes it to perfection in Heaven with Him. That, my friends, is the doorway we fear. This type of confidence in facing death is not an inherent human trait but is totally the work of grace."

Back in Smyrna, the search had not ceased; in fact, it was becoming more focused and organized. Icarus received new intelligence that Polycarp may very well be at the Primas farm, but realizing that this was a powerful family, he needed more proof before soldiers could move within their gates. He felt the gods were favoring him when the news came that a slave of Primas was in the marketplace. After offering a good bribe, he was able to persuade some soldiers to join him, and there in the market they found Zeno, the young and faithful servant to Primas. Seeing him place supplies in his cart, Icarus nonchalantly approached Zeno and cornered him.

"I hear rumors that your master is harboring a criminal," he said with a touch of provocation.

"You must not believe everything you hear, sir," responded Zeno.

"You are a Christian, aren't you?" asked Icarus.

"Yes, I am," responded Zeno unabashedly. "Are you going to have me arrested," he asked.

"No! Of course not, for you are a slave, and belong to Primas," Icarus answered. He continued as if setting a trap for the boy. "I figured that since your master was a believer, you have to be too."

---

138. I Corinthians 15:54-57

"That is not accurate. I am a Christian by Jesus Christ saving me just as he saved my master. In God's eyes there is no difference between us," Zeno boldly responded.

"Slave equal with his master you say," he scorned. "This is treasonous talk."

Leaning in close to Zeno's face, Icarus bitterly spewed out, "This is stupidity. Tell me now, boy, is Polycarp being protected by your master? I demand you answer me, or I will make you curse the day you were born."

"Sir, I am a slave. My master is not required to tell me his business. You must believe me. You must speak with my master," urged Zeno.

"No, you miserable slave, I don't believe you. Take him to the garrison," ordered Icarus as if he was the commanding general. He laughed as he looked into Zeno's eyes and said, "Very soon, you will be squealing like a pig, and you will tell me everything I want to know. That is a promise."

Zeno was taken to the garrison where he was severely interrogated and soon tortured in order to see if he knew the location of Polycarp. After being whipped and burned with hot pincers, Icarus gave him one more chance to answer. "Is Polycarp being protected by your master, Primas?"

Under great suffering, Zeno could take no more and blurted out, "Yes." Then Icarus, filled with rage, took a dagger and plunged into Zeno, and watched the boy die. Then turning to the calloused guards, he smiled and sarcastically said, "Don't worry, he's in a better place now."

With this morsel of information and an air of self-importance, Icarus found the Proconsul and being invited in to share the intelligence he had gathered, he declared; "Your glorious Excellency, I have indisputable proof of Polycarp's whereabouts."

"Where is he?" Quadratus asked.

"Well, first, do I get my reward?" quipped Icarus.

"You will undoubtedly get what you deserve," responded Quadratus with growing impatience.

"My Lord, he is being harbored in the home of Primas," he replied.

"And how did you acquire this information? For even you know that I can't just march out to his farm and search it. He's an influential man in Rome; indeed, he is a distant cousin to the

Emperor. One wrong step and I could dampen my prospects of a bright future," Quadratus declared.

"His slave, a boy named Zeno was willing to divulge this intelligence," Icarus said.

As he spoke, the Proconsul grew suspicious regarding the story and asked; "Bring me the slave boy. I want to hear it from his lips," he ordered.

"That may be a bit difficult," Icarus sheepishly replied.

"Why?" asked the Proconsul.

"Um, well, I am sorry to say, Your Excellency, that he is dead," Icarus answered.

The Proconsul looked at one of the soldiers with Icarus and ordered him to answer truthfully; "How did the slave die? Did you do it?"

"No, Your Excellency, Icarus ran the boy through with a dagger after he revealed what he knew," the guard quickly answered.

"Was he tortured in any way for this information?" continued the Proconsul.

"Of course he was. He was flogged and worse," answered the guard.

Turning to Icarus the Proconsul said, "Tell me, did I authorize you to torture or kill anyone?"

Sensing the danger in that question Icarus cautiously said, "Well, no; of course not, but he was just a slave."

"Just a slave," shouted Quadratus. "A slave to one of the wealthiest, most powerful men in this Province. You filth; is it not enough that I have to contend with unruly Christians, now I have to endure the thoughtless missteps of a bumbling fool like you." Quadratus was obviously distressed by this botched interrogation. He stood up and in silence began to pace the floor considering how to save face with Primas, on the one hand, and yet invade his home on the other.

He finally turned with a look of agitation on his face and said to Icarus, "You have troubled me today almost more than Polycarp. You are reckless and may very well have placed me in a horribly awkward situation with a powerful family. The only thing I can think of that will appease Primas is for you to receive equal punishment. I told you I would give you what you deserve." He looked over at the soldier and ordered; "Kill this parasite." Within moments, Icarus slumped to the floor dead.

"Enough of this," said Quadratus. "Send Herod with armed soldiers to the home of Primas, and if he resists in any way, instruct him to address his complaint to me. Deal with him shrewdly. Arrest Polycarp, and then bring him to me. Are your orders clear," demanded the Proconsul.

"Yes, they could not be clearer," responded the guard.

"Make sure they are conveyed precisely to Herod, and if Polycarp should arrive dead, you'll take his place in the arena tonight," commanded the Proconsul.

———————⬦⬦———————

With this evidence, the Proconsul ordered the arrest of Polycarp but left strict instructions not to harm Primus or his family. He would deal with them at another time. Armed with clear orders, the Roman soldiers overran the farm, where Primas confronted them before they even entered the courtyard.

"By whose authority do you illegally intrude on my property," yelled Primas.

"By the authority of the Proconsul," said Herod in an overly confident manner. "Do you see the affixed seal?" as he held it out in front of Primas, "it is the Proconsul's seal affixed to this page. Any argument you have may be taken up with him. I must obey my orders. Besides, you are harboring a fugitive of the law; a man named Polycarp. Hand him over to us, or we'll have to arrest you too," ordered Herod.

"Permit them to enter Primas," Polycarp said from inside the doorway.

As the soldiers poured into the entrance of the stately mansion, they were stunned to find Polycarp standing right in front of them. He further added to their astonishment when he turned to his hostess, Jana and said, "My gracious lady, my request is unusual, but would you be so kind as to feed these soldiers. It is time for the noon meal, and I would hate to think that they came all this way for me and left hungry. Please, dear sister, accommodate me. Feed them well."

"Whatever you wish, pastor;" she replied as she hesitatingly turned to the servants to give them their instructions. Then looking back to the soldiers she said; "Please, find your place around the table."

Polycarp looked over at Herod, who was obviously enjoying this royal treatment, and asked; "While you eat, may I adjourn to this adjacent room to pray until you have finished?"

"You aren't going to try to escape are you?" asked Herod.

"No, you have my word," assured Polycarp. "I only wish to pray." While they ate, he prayed aloud for his congregation, the Lord's Church throughout the world and his persecutors; some even by name like Herod. His prayer was so powerful that several of those that came to arrest him regretted their orders to seize him. After being well fed, they were confounded that Polycarp was still praying as if enjoying a long conversation with a most-cherished friend.

With some awkward reluctance, Herod interrupted his prayer-time and ordered Polycarp to accompany them back to Smyrna. Primas provided a donkey for him to ride on, and no one put up any resistance to this gesture.

As they made their journey back toward the town, they were met by an ornate, covered carriage. Herod instructed Polycarp to join him in the carriage, and added, "My father is in the carriage, and wishes to converse with you during your journey back into Smyrna."

"Your father desires to speak with me?" Polycarp inquired.

"Yes, he says he is an old friend of yours," Herod replied.

Polycarp dismounted the donkey, and stepped up into the carriage, and as soon as he looked up to see its occupant, and only one word escaped his mouth, "Erebus!"

They rode in silence for a few minutes, when Erebus finally said; "It is strange that we find ourselves at this crossroad, Polycarp. It would appear that your God has failed you and that the gods of Rome have won."

"That all depends upon how you define winning," replied Polycarp.

"After all these years, you still have not changed," Erebus said. "From one old man to another, what harm is there in declaring Caesar as god, or even sacrificing to him in order to escape death? A little compliance would spare you and your congregation a great deal of grief and pain."

Polycarp made no reply, but both Herod and his father persisted. Feeling exhausted by their ceaseless appeals, Polycarp said, "I shall never betray my God, the One True God."

"What is it with you Christians that you flaunt your stubbornness?" Erebus impatiently declared. "We have known each other for decades, and you have done surprisingly well in this community. Stop being an old fool." Polycarp just shook his head no. "I, however, have served as Proconsul and still serve Rome as a Senator. The gods have been kind to me, Polycarp," Erebus bragged.

"I'm surprised you have changed your position," Polycarp responded.

"Changed positions? You aren't making any sense," he replied.

"Years ago, you stated that you did not believe in any gods except yourself. I am surprised you have room for any other gods in your little universe," Polycarp chided.

"Oh yes, I remember. I have not changed; it's just that belief in the gods can be expedient, especially if that god is Caesar, and he is the one that can promote you. Anything my heart has desired I have sought with all diligence to get. With every breath I take, I worship the ground upon which I walk. All men are the same, Polycarp. You of all men should have observed that as you have devoted your life to forcing men into worshipping only one God. To me, gods are like a vast array of food on a banquet table. I partake what fulfills my immediate appetites. Did you notice how I said that? I enjoy the gods that fulfill me. So here we are; you are to die a tortured old man; forgotten by his God, and forced to die alone. A sad end, but one I never doubted you would experience," Erebus heralded.

"Will you come to your senses?" he asked.

Polycarp just smiled and said; "Eternal life with God begins where human life ends, and that's what I am looking forward to."

Being fed up with his refusal to listen to reason, Erebus ordered the carriage to halt, and then had soldiers throw Polycarp out and down onto the ground with such force that he injured his leg in the fall. They did not stop either, nor was anyone permitted to aid him. Nevertheless, he was a strong and courageous soldier of the cross. He got up, though in great pain, and cheerfully walked the next several miles into town where he was met with jeering, disrespectful crowds gathering to gawk and celebrate as if a vile criminal had been captured and was being brought to justice.

20

BE FAITHFUL
UNTO DEATH

Do not be afraid for what you are about to suffer.
It is true; the devil is about to throw some of you
into prison, this is a test, for soon you will experience
tribulation. Be faithful, even if it means your death,
and in so doing, I will give you the crown of life.
(Revelation 2:10)

CURIOUS people crowded into the Judgment Hall wondering if Polycarp would save his life and offer worship to Caesar. The guards escorted him into the crowded hall. As he entered, he looked up toward the nearby gallery, and saw the radiant countenance of a new brother in Christ, Rasmus, who shouted down to his beloved pastor; "Polycarp don't quit like weak men. Be strong!" It was too noisy for him to respond audibly, but he nodded his head in agreement.

They led him through throngs of people to a holding room. While he was waiting, Flavius Arius led me into the room where he was being held.

"Irenaeus, what are you doing here? If something were to happen to you, I fear I could not endure the grief," expressed Polycarp.

"I'm sorry to alarm you, dear friend, but we may never speak again, and with the help of my friend here, I had to see you," explained Irenaeus with an embrace.

"Did you know that your friend is the centurion for the garrison here in town?" Polycarp asked with a degree of exasperation.

"Indeed, and he said he was very desirous of meeting you too," Irenaeus said teasingly, "and I don't mean to arrest you either."

"You have nothing to fear from me, sir," stressed the centurion. "I greatly admire your faithfulness and dedication to God. I do not understand your faith, but I believe someday I will."

"Then please receive my wholehearted thanks for allowing me this farewell with my son in the faith," Polycarp acknowledged.

I grasped both of his forearms as I spoke. "We don't have much time. I saw Germanicus die, and he did so with the strength and glory of our Savior." Tears overflowed his eyes as I conveyed the details. "He did not flinch in the face of death, but rather victoriously crossed the finish line of faith."

"I truly loved that boy," Polycarp mournfully expressed.

"I'm afraid it doesn't end there. Justin is also under arrest and is to die this evening, as well as Drusus Servius."

"Drusus? He did not yield?" Polycarp asked with pleasant surprise. "God gave the lamb a lion's heart. I would have never foreseen this from him. Once again, I am thrilled by the grace of God."

Then looking over at Flavius Arius, he said, "Centurion, some-day I believe you will discover that the Lord's followers move from one surprising expression of God's grace to another. Even here, today, each step I take is accompanied by new discoveries in God's all-sufficient grace."

"Irenaeus, we cannot tarry. We will be discovered if we don't leave at once," Arius warned.

I looked at Polycarp and tried to paint in my mind his image, for this would likely be the last time we would talk on this side of heaven. I could not hold back my sorrow. "My dear pastor, I must leave you now. May our great and kind God sustain you and keep you in your hour of this fiery trial. I will be watching from a secluded place in the Hall. I'll be praying for you."

Polycarp hugged me firmly and said, "And the Lord bless you my son. Be strong in the Lord, my deeply loved brother." He stepped back, still holding my shoulders, and his final words to me were: "Comfort the people; give them hope. Feed the flock by preaching the Word as one changed by it, and if necessary, face death as a faithful champion of Jesus Christ."

As Arius and I headed for the doorway, I stopped and turned to look at him one more time. He smiled and said, "Pray I give a good defense for the glory of Christ as I face this crowning moment of God's glory."

Moments later, the guards entered the room and escorted their prisoner into the Judgment Hall where Quadratus was waiting. "Silence in the Hall!" shouted a guard. The commotion died down as everyone was wondering what would happen next.

"This court has been graced by the presence of one of Rome's illustrious Senators, Cæso Erebus Drusilla.

"Smyrna salutes you noble Drusilla, as do I, your humble servant," the Proconsul declared.

The Proconsul stepped forward and walked up to the old preacher and said; "You are an old man, highly respected in this town, and in many other places throughout the empire. Do yourself and those who love you a favor, and end this madness, and make a public proclamation that Caesar is Lord, and add to it, 'away with the atheists' so that all other Christians will know to follow your wise example."

Polycarp looked squarely into the eyes of Quadratus and then after a few moments turned towards the anxious crowd and said with great vigor, "You wish to hear a statement. So be it. Away with the wicked, for they need the Savior, the Lord Jesus Christ." Hisses and boos with a hellish disdain erupted from the crowd.

"Silence in the Hall!" commanded the guard to the angry crowd.

Once again, the Proconsul impatiently repeated, "Proclaim that Caesar is Lord, and I will let you go."

With deep conviction and strength of voice to match, Polycarp replied; "I have served my God for eighty-six years, and he never did me any harm, but rather much good, and how can I blaspheme my King and my Savior? If you require of me to proclaim that Caesar is Lord, as you call it, then hear my free confession: I am a Christian, but if you desire to learn the Christian religion, appoint a time, and hear me out." Throughout the crowd, you could hear some people expressing disgust for him while others desired to see the conflict intensify between the two leaders.

The proconsul abruptly said, "Persuade the people."

But Polycarp countered, "My discourse is expressed toward you, for we are taught to give due honor to princes as far as is consistent with religion. But this crowd is an incompetent judge and is not qualified to judge me."

The crowd roared in protest.

The Proconsul assumed a more threatening tone and said; "I have wild beasts, and I will feed you to them."

"Call for them," replied the pastor, "for I am unalterably resolved not to change from good to evil. For one is right when he passes from evil to good."

Not to be outdone, the agitated Proconsul further added; "If you are not afraid of the wild animals, I will cause you to be burnt to ashes."

Polycarp again answered resolutely, "You threaten me with a fire which burns for a short time and then goes out, but are yourself ignorant of the judgment to come, and of the everlasting fiery torment which is prepared for the wicked. Why do you delay? Let us discuss the Lord Jesus Christ, or bring against me what you please. There is only one Lord, Jesus Christ my Savior, and only to him alone will I offer worship!"

I watched from a secret vantage point; my heart was overwhelmed by what I saw. For while he said this and many other things, my old teacher and beloved friend appeared refreshed in a spirit of joy and confidence. His countenance glowed with a certain divine grace and pleasant cheerfulness, in such a way that even the Proconsul himself was struck with a moment of admiration. Still determined to break this old man, he ordered a crier to make a public proclamation three times in the Judgment Hall for all to hear: "Polycarp has confessed himself a Christian. Polycarp has confessed himself a Christian. Polycarp has confessed himself a Christian."

At this proclamation, the whole multitude gave a great shout for his death. Herod stood up to face the audience for the purpose of reading a public statement made against Polycarp. When he was able to restore order, the chamber echoed with the words of his indictment.

"This is the great teacher of Asia; a father of the Christians; the destroyer of our gods, who preaches to men not to sacrifice to or adore our deities." Herod unexplainably hesitated, alarming both his father and the Proconsul. In a moment, he regained his courage and declared; "Away with the atheist!"

All of a sudden the mob, as if moved by some force of hell, demanded that Polycarp should be burned alive. The Proconsul looked at Polycarp and shrugged his shoulders as if helpless in altering the situation, and no sooner was the request granted; then everyone ran with haste to gather wood scraps and converge upon the arena to see the old man die.

Escorted by a band of soldiers for fear the Christians might attempt to free the beloved pastor, the Proconsul took the opportunity to walk Polycarp through the dungeon. He showed him the scores of Christian brethren, many of whom were part of his congregation, who were facing execution that night. He walked past the cell holding noble Justin, who saluted the old pastor. In the adjacent cell was the gentle Cato, and next to him stood Drusus Servius; not the weak, but the strong. Cell by cell were men and women Polycarp loved, and children born under his ministry, and many of whom he introduced to Christ and baptized under his care.

"There is one more cell you need to peer into that I believe will shatter your faith," Quadratus claimed. They moved on to the next cell where Polycarp gasped as he saw his beloved daughter and her faithful husband.

Callisto rushed to her father, and they embraced through the bars. They could not contain their tears, but to the Proconsul's amazement, Callisto said, "Do not fear for me, Father. I am ready to suffer for Christ. You must not allow them to coerce you in betraying Christ. Tonight, we shall be gathered together with mother before the glorious majesty of our Lord."

"My dearest child, it has never been my intention to place us in a harmful situation. But here we are, truly discovering the power of grace to sustain us in the most heart-wrenching of times. God be with you my dearest," Polycarp said.

"And with you, my father," she replied.

"You're a fool, Polycarp," expressed Quadratus. "I would never permit my daughter to suffer in this way."

"Then you would doom her to an eternal hell," Polycarp stated. "This cruelty my daughter will be called upon to endure is not from God but is the result of vile sin working through its defiled agents. You are the cruelty, Quadratus. I shall pray that God has pity upon you and saves your soul. But if he doesn't, he will have my revenge. Never forget that, Proconsul. All the armies of Rome will not protect you from his wrath."

As they reached Polycarp's cell, Quadratus turned to the old preacher and taunted him; "One word from you could save all their lives, old man."

"My faithful God has taught me not fear those who kill the body, but cannot kill the soul. Rather fear him who can destroy both soul and body in hell."[139] These children of God do not fear you or death. Look at them Proconsul. They are victors awaiting a crown of righteousness. I have seen some of them grow stronger in this day than in their whole lifetime. I am sad for what they will suffer; I would gladly endure it all for them." Then turning to face the Proconsul he said, "Young man, the world is unworthy to have these creations of God living among them."

The next hour, Polycarp wept like he had never wept before. First, there was the valiant Roman Centurion, Justin. Though there was not a cowardly bone in his body, he refused to bring harm to any of the gladiators put up against him though he had the skill to defend himself. Before Justin died, he dropped his gladius and shouted at the top of his lungs for all to hear: "I have fought the good fight; I have finished the race; I have kept the faith."[140] After this declaration, he was rushed upon by the gladiators, and ushered into the glorious presence of God. All of this displeased Quadratus, who had hoped for a longer, more torturous battle to the death.

Even the timid, Drusus Servius stood fearless with the rest of the men, women and children who were rushed out into the arena to face all kinds of vicious and tormented animals. The wild creatures tore mercilessly into the huddled masses. The crowd moaned with a sick delight at the bloody spectacle.

At last it was Polycarp's time. As the pyre was being prepared, he was marched out into the arena to the disgraceful taunts of the mob. He did not look at the bodies of his beloved friends and family, but looked straight toward the cross he would be called upon to bear. I couldn't help but think back to the day Callisto rescued him from slavery and her desire to protect him from death in the arena. Here he was, a champion, who, whether by life or death, was the overcomer. As he approached the ladder, he removed his outer coat, and without any aid climbed up onto the wood pile. The executioners would have nailed him to the stake to keep him from running away when he was burning, but he said to them;

---

139. Matthew 10:28

140. I Timothy 4:7

"Permit me to be as I am. He who gives me grace to undergo this fire will enable me to stand still without that precaution."

They contented themselves with tying his hands behind his back, and in this posture, looking up towards heaven, he prayed: "O Almighty Lord God, Father of your beloved and blessed Son Jesus Christ, through whom we have received the knowledge of you. God of angels, powers, and every creature, and of all the just that live in your presence! I bless you for out of your goodness you have been pleased to bring me to this hour that I may receive a portion in the number of your martyrs and partake of the cup of Christ for the resurrection to eternal life, in the incorruptibleness of your Holy Spirit. Grant me to be received this day as a pleasing sacrifice, such a one as you yourself have prepared, that you may accomplish, O True and Faithful God, what you have foreseen. Wherefore, for all things I praise, bless, and glorify you, through the eternal High Priest, Jesus Christ, your beloved Son, and the Holy Spirit be glory now and forever. Amen."[141]

As he finished his prayer, the great pile of wood was set on fire, which soon increased to an intense, mighty flame. All who were watching could not believe their own eyes as the wind that blew into the arena caused the flames to form into an arch that gently encircled the body of Polycarp, but did not burn him. This only exasperated the blood thirsty crowd all the more, and they ordered a spearman to pierce him through, which he did at the nod of the Proconsul. He had to be pleased with the results, for Polycarp's blood gushed out of the wound and started to subdue the flame, which made his death longer and more painful.

Death came; the doorway into the glorious presence of Christ was opened wide for the Lord's servant, Polycarp. He lived to the fulfillment the words of Christ given through the Apostle John to the Church of Smyrna, "Be faithful in the face of death, and I will give you the crown of life."[142]

---

141. *Polycarp's actual prayer as he faced execution*

142. *Revelation 2:10*

EPILOGUE

Death is devoured in victory. O death, where is
your triumph? O death, where is your pain?
The pain of death is sin, and the
enabling power of sin is the law.
But take great pleasure in God who has given us
complete victory through our Lord Jesus Christ.
For this reason, my dearly loved brothers, be firm,
unshakable, and always excelling in the Lord's work, fully
understanding that your labor in the Lord is never in vain.
(I Corinthians 15:54b-58)

WHEN Polycarp died, I felt as if thieves had stolen part of my soul and that the world had extinguished one of its guiding lights of truth. Erebus seemed untouched by the scene, but the Proconsul appeared distressed. Polycarp had won. The church was not afraid of death, though he had dealt it out as cruelly as he knew how.

After he died, they left his body lying on the heap for several days, forbidding us to bury our dear pastor. Finally, as one last spurt of bitter disdain, the Proconsul ordered his remains to be burned to ashes. Only fragments remained, which we collected and reverently buried in Smyrna.

———◇◇———

Quadrates was to face his humiliation, for news reached Rome regarding his actions, and while the Emperor didn't take notice of the massacre of Christians, he was angered at how some of those who were Roman citizens had not been beheaded as was their right. He left Smyrna defeated since he could not break the spirit of the Christians. He fled in disgrace and never held public office again. Rumor has it that he went insane and eventually took his own life.

Erebus left the arena feeling as if he could carve another notch in his belt of accomplishments, but that evening, his soul would be required of him. That same night he died and discovered that

Polycarp was right. There is only One True God, and he was under his wrath along with all the other gods of men.

On the day we entombed Polycarp, as the crowd dispersed I was startled as I observed Herod standing far off. I was uncertain if he was present to arrest me, but seeing that no guards had accompanied him, I approached him. "Of all the people that would have been here at this place today, you would be one of the last I would expect," I said.

He struggled to hold back his tears, and expressed, "I have watched Polycarp for many years since moving to Smyrna; in fact, I have been watching all the Christians, and am moved by my observations. Of course, I could never share my admiration with my father and tried, perhaps in a weak and indirect way, to shed a softer light on the Christians to the Proconsul. But I cowered under his rebuke. I am tormented by my actions toward you all, and to God. I could've helped Polycarp escape, or at least attempted to sabotage the Proconsul's plans. The blood of your people is on my hands."

"Sir, you did nothing that wasn't according to the specific will of God," I assured him. "You do not have to bear this weight of guilt. Are you here because some man has placed pressure on you, or has the Spirit of God been working to lead you into repentance?"

"It must be repentance," he answered. "I can't describe it, but it's like I have been awakened to the reality that there is only One True God, and he has become my God. The evening of Polycarp's death, as I sat by the bedside of my dying father, I couldn't help but be moved by how they both left this life. We tortured Polycarp, but he died like a man leaning into the finish line. My father fought bitterly for every last breath and went out of this life like a man trying to grasp the edge of a great precipice. He left hating everything, in the comfort of his room surrounded by family and friends. Later that night, I became a follower of Jesus Christ. It is beyond my comprehension to explain, but I was changed, much like a corpse being brought back from the dead. How I look at life was totally different than the previous day. I was blind and in utter darkness the day before, and that new morning I could see. And not only me, but my wife and son too. Does this sound normal to you," he inquired.

I smiled and answered, "Yes, quite normal." I could not help but imagine how cheered Polycarp would have been to have witnessed what his death and final bout with Erebus had accomplished. And I suppose he did, for if the angels of heaven rejoice when a sinner repents,[143] how much more the redeemed in heaven must rejoice.

"I have a request," Herod continued. "I understand that you are to depart for Lugundum very soon."

"That's true," I said. "I was to depart next week, but I have postponed it for a couple of months."

"There is nothing here in Smyrna for me. I have resigned my post. I have my father's inheritance, and I wish for my family and me to join you in your work. I would like it if you would train my son, Hippolytus[144] if God so wills, to be discipled by you as Polycarp taught you to be a herald of the truth," Herod requested.

"The work will not be an easy one, and it would appear that the level of persecution is more severe in Lugundum than here. But if your wife is supportive of you in this, and God has impressed this burden on you, then your presence is welcomed and appreciated," I replied.

As I stood before the congregation on my last day with them, it seemed like a lifetime since we were last together just a week ago. Not wanting to draw attention to our congregation, we decided that after today, this large body would break up into several smaller groups with the pastors that had been trained by Polycarp, and various elders overseeing the individual congregations in private and safer locations. For today, however, we decided not to meet in our normal place, but rather met in a large building in the deserted area of the port.

Leo had requested that I address the congregation. My heart was exalting the Lord, for while I grieved over our losses, God had lovingly turned my weeping into joy. "What a great and faithful God I serve. Is there no end to his loving kindness?" I thought to myself.

---

143. Luke 15:10

144. *Hippolytus did go on to become the disciple of Irenaeus, and was a great champion for the truth of Christ.*

As I walked toward the front of the room, I turned to address the Lord's Church in Smyrna one last time.

"Two months have elapsed since our deeply beloved pastor, Polycarp; our beloved elder, Cato; young Germanicus, noble Justin and several more of our closest and devoted brothers and sisters died for their faith in Christ. As you may have heard, the Proconsul had to call off the search for the Christians due to the additional riots and chaos it produced. While some praised his zealousness for Caesar, his handling of the arrests and the pandemonium it produced has also brought him heavy criticism. For the sake of the peace, he has been recalled to Rome. Don't be deceived, my dear family, for we knew that this is not the end, but perhaps a reprieve to give us time to prepare for future conflicts. Be of good courage, for as you grow in godliness, so you will grow in steadfast and unconquerable, overcoming faith."

"My precious brethren in Christ, truly my dearest friends in the entire world, all here who are deeply loved by our Savior, the Lord Jesus Christ, take heart and be of good courage. Nothing has happened over this past week that revealed for even a moment that God was not in control. As our loving pastor told us just last week, 'those who live a life of godliness in Christ Jesus will suffer persecution.'[145] We have suffered; that is true, but not as a punishment for ungodliness as if we were trying to stir up His church out of its slumber, but quite the opposite. We are alive, active, alert and advancing daily upon this earthly evil kingdom of God's enemy, the devil. Like Job of old, Satan was permitted to touch the Church in Smyrna. Some have died gloriously for their faith, most still remain and are here, but we all grieve."

"Your godly response is being used by our Heavenly Father to plant and water the seed of his Gospel in the hearts of the lost, even in the hearts of our persecutors. Right now, right here in our assembly is the Garrison Commander, Arius. He helped me escape the arena, and God's grace used me to help him escape the eternal torment of God's wrath. Last week, he was lost a lost lamb, but today, like the rest of us, he has been found!" Such a report produced shouts of joy, and praises were lifted up to God for his power to save. "But his salvation is not the only one, look at all the new faces around you."

---

145. II Timothy 3:12

"What was the design of the devil to eradicate the followers of Christ, God has used to bring more children to himself. Near the back is the Roman Prosecutor, Herod and his family. God used Polycarp's testimony to bring about a spiritual birth in their lives. God used our beloved pastor, whose name, Polycarp, means much fruit, to produce a harvest of souls and changed lives. We cannot help but grieve over the ones we have lost, but we also rejoice with those who have been born-again into God's family as a result of this persecution. They have seen your faith, and God has awakened within them a desire for the same; 'Oh, the depth of the wealth and both wisdom and deep understanding of God! How unsearchable are his decrees and how incomprehensible his ways!'"[146]

"I bid you farewell, my dear ones. Today, just a few blocks from this location, I will be leaving for Lugundum,[147] in Gaul, and will begin ministering to the suffering Christians for the glory of the Lord. As you know, I'm not going alone, but am to be accompanied by my dear wife, and precious children, with Herod and his family who will follow me very soon. You are not being left shepherdless, for overseeing all the congregation is Leo, a man of God Polycarp was preparing to take his place. He is ready to serve you, minister to you, lead you, and if necessary, die for you."

"Farewell beloved ones. God be with you now and forever, Amen!"

---

146. Romans 11:33

147. Irenaeus died for his faith in Jesus Christ in the year 202 under the reign of Emperor Septimius Severus